Boo
Walt

Cookery Books:

A Slice of the Pyrenees.

The Snail Cookbook.

Fiction:

Billy Ruffian's Courier.
Part one - Rites of Passage

Billy Ruffian's Courier.
Part two - Hawkshaw.

Billy Ruffian's Courier.
Part three - Baltic Exchange.

www.gunncomms.co.uk

Walter Gunn

Billy Ruffian's Courier

Part 3 - Baltic Exchange.

This book is dedicated to
four inspirational uncles and one good friend:

Walter - journalist, posthumous author (Letters from a Soldier), idealist and all round good guy.

Ben - Italian POW escapee - artist and another good guy.

Jack - ornithologist - his legacy, a passion for birds butterflies and all things natural: things that became my family's love.

Bill - encyclopedic knowledge and from whom I get my love of all things engineering.

Eddie Jelonek - the long-term mate and critic: so helpful in writing this trilogy.

Wherever politics is involved, truth will be jeopardized. Whenever politics and intelligence are in the mix, intelligence will be compromised.

Admiral John Jessop. (Deceased)

Billy Ruffian's Courier　　　Part 3 - Baltic Exchange.

Contents.

Chapter One
Blood-letting not an Option.

January 1965 Tunworth House Hampshire.
'You are not to kill any of them, Sims.' Admiral Billy
Ruffian Jessop handed over the list of names. 'Blood-
letting is strictly forbidden... that includes persuading
them to commit suicide. The term is not dead or alive,
just alive. Do you understand?'

He, Sims, glanced at the hand-written list, 'Not even
in self defence?'

'That is unlikely to be necessary.'

'But it *is* possible?'

'In theory, I suppose so. Stick to your brief - we need
to know what they know, who they know and who else
is involved. That's the task, lad. Nothing else. No blood.
And where you're concerned I should, for safety's sake,
add no garrotting, guillotining, disembowelling or
poisoning.'

'Still... I'll carry my Browning just in case. And, as a
matter of interest, what makes you think I persuaded
him to commit suicide?'

Billy hrumphed and leaned towards him. 'Sims, lad...
I'm not a nozzer and I'm not bloody stupid. Do you
honestly expect me to believe it was a coincidence that

you met Lord Aston-Heyford at Bosham Castle and you then both went to Chichester cathedral where he just happened to take his own life. Good grief... of course you persuaded him! It's damn near common knowledge in NID. What you said to him is what we'd all like to know.'

Sims sniffed, he didn't consider this a question and changed the subject, 'Who compiled the list?'

Billy knew by now this was as much as he was getting from him. 'I did... most of them left with the late Lord Aston-Heyford after the Defence Committee reception you and Anne attended. On the list, there are a few other suspects... *suspects*, not condemned criminals. Please bear that in mind.'

He folded the paper and slid it into his inside pocket. 'All poofs?'

'Not all. Some just ratlin climbers... career barnacles clinging to a hulk they thought was going somewhere.'

'I'll keep an eye on who they attach themselves to next... might help chart out the enemy.' He got up to leave, 'As a matter of interest, disembowelling's gone out of fashion and poisoning the method of choice for outraged wives. I'll let you know about the other two.'

'Get on with you, lad, and remember, *blood letting's not an option.*'

*

Hell Head House Hampshire.

The heavy door to the library stood half open, even so, Anne had not heard him arrive. Sims padded into the quiet room. He didn't feel or look confident of the outcome of the next few minutes. The impression given;

one of impending defeat.

She had been engrossed. Anne, getting up from her work, smiling, and giving him a kiss, said, 'Hello, darling, I didn't hear you come in. Now, how did it go with Billy? You must have lots to tell me.'

'Oh fine... fine. Of course, he was disappointed you weren't with me. Yes... it went well really. Okay... nothing much.'

She read the runes, stopped smiling, planted her feet defensively and frowned.

'Just a little job... piece of cake.' Sims had rushed it; far, far too quick off the mark, 'Nothing I can't handle on my own... it's not much, not much at all,' he said, shrugging.

She stood back, glared at him, '*No!*'

'Oh, for Christ's sake... listen, babe, you cannot risk yourself in your condition... please see sense, you've got to take it easy for all our sakes.'

'*No!* You listen to me, Sims Sherwood-Reeves, I'm pregnant... not disabled.'

He had floundered, shuffled and fluffed his argument. His flaky line of logic didn't improve - she did this to him, 'Have you any idea what Dad, Jean and I felt like knowing you'd been shot?'

'As a matter of fact I have... good *God!* What sort of question is that?' She was frowning one of her specials. 'Cast your mind back, dear...'

Oh, Christ. *Fuck it*; not *dear* again, he thought.

'...I was on The Island with you, remember? Forget it, Sims, that argument won't wear with me... and... and what was it you said? "What didn't happen mustn't dictate how we spend the rest of our lives".

3

What happened to that impeccable piece of reasoning, Commander Sims Sherwood-Reeves, eh?'

'Hell fire, sod and bollocks, I just knew it... I just knew you'd get flappy... why is it you always have to dig your heels in and get all awkward? Look, love, see reason; Dad and Jean will go ballistic if they know you're in the firing line again. How are we going to explain that one away? Go on, answer that.'

Ignoring his question, Anne stood with her hands on her hips, head to one side, eyes narrowed. 'What firing line, Sims? You said it was just a little job, a piece of cake... nothing much... ...listen, I'm coming, *Sims*.'

'Jesus Christ,' he muttered, and caved in. 'Okay, just this one time you can come... but only to Pompey... just this once, though, and then that's it.'

The skirmish won and the way cleared for victory in the bigger battle to come, she smiled and said, brightly, 'What are we going to do, darling?' And, as though her daily routine offered little but dawn to dusk mundaneness, 'Something interesting?'

'No, dead boring.'

*

Milton Cemetery Portsmouth.

A thin biting wind from the east scythed its way round hard edged headstones, sharpening its blade as it did so. It cut and bit into them. Hunched forward they crunched along the rimy gravelled pathway.

Anne huffed frosty breath, 'Why are we here?'

'Disinterment.'

He stopped.

Leaning on him, 'Are we exhuming someone? We'll

need a spade, won't we? Don't tell me you forgot it?'

He smiled, 'No, just digging for a lead or two. Are you warm enough, love?'

'Let me get inside your coat with you and I will be.'

She helped him unbuttoned his greatcoat. With her back to him, he folded the flaps around her, held them closed and her tight, 'How's that?'

'You're always so warm.'

He nuzzled her neck, 'And you always smell so nice... wish we were back home.'

'We will be later... Keep your mind on the job. Now, answer me, why are we here?'

He pointed, 'Look at the name on the headstone in front of you.'

'*Commander Crabb!* So this is where Buster's buried. Not very grand for a British spy and hero.'

'Only part of him... headstone's hardly appropriate... gravestone better... head missing, remember?'

'Didn't James say his hands and feet were also missing.'

'He got that wrong, that wasn't entirely the case... hands yes, his feet were still in his flippers.'

Always impatient for answers, 'Sims, you still haven't answered my question... why are we here?'

'When you were at Whale Island taming your Beretta with Cedric and Les, I came and paid a couple of visits.'

'Why? What... just out of the blue you decided to have a look round this cemetery? Come on, what else?'

'More or less as you say, out of the blue. At first, just nosing around. Buster's a problem. There's plenty about his disappearance that doesn't tie up. And, honey, we're standing near one piece that particularly niggles me.'

5

'What?'

'Pardon's more polite.'

She nudged him, 'Why?'

'I don't know why... social nicety I guess. Well bred people say, pardon.'

'*God*, I shall bash you in a minute.'

With later on his mind: time to move on, 'Look at his headstone, love... take it all in and tell me what you see and feel.'

IN EVER LOVING MEMORY
OF MY SON
COMMANDER CRABB.
AT REST AT LAST.

Wrapped tightly, she gave a greatcoat modified shrug, 'You've had longer to think about this.' Inference clear: *tell me quick*..

'Okay then, let's put it this way, if that was my headstone and you'd composed the sentiment on it, how...'

'Don't... please don't.' The memory of his broken, bloody body savaged her. She scrabbled round and held him as close as she was able.

'Steady, Babe, let me get to the point then. His father was dead, so a reasonable supposition would be his mum wrote it. Now, don't you think if she *had* written it, she might have used his christian name somewhere? Don't you think she might have been proud of his George Medal and OBE? Anne, my love, it doesn't even mention the Royal Navy for Christ's sake. It's an epitaph that could have only been written by a bureaucrat, and probably a sociopathic one at that.'

Anne, calmer now, looked up at him, 'Is this what Billy's asked you to do?'

'No. Not in as many words.'

'But you're going to do it anyway?'

'We can't not... can we?'

She pinched him, 'You said, *we*,' she said, laughing, victory plastered all over her face.

'*Fuck!*' he said.

***

Chapter Two.
Two Headings to Steer By.

'So, what do you think, Stinton?'

'It's a soft job, it will test his diplomacy skills.'

'Do you think he has any?'

'Submerged... lying deep... they're there, though. They'll surface at the right times... that, I'm sure of. It will be a good task to smooth some of his rough edges.'

'I think Anne is already doing that quite handsomely... she has the measure of him.'

'Yes, she has at that.'

'He didn't baulk at being given a relatively easy assignment.' Billy stood looking out of the window; pondered, scratching his large, jutting jaw. 'And, I suppose the question is, why? I'm concerned he'll go off on one of his tangents.'

'His tangents have been useful, and you know him as well as I do, perhaps he has other business on his mind.'

'Anything in particular?'

'He has an element of the terrier in him... doesn't let go... unfinished business. Buster Crabb and my son Miles... but I think you know that. You didn't set a time-scale for completion of his job.'

'Hmmm, NID is going to miss you, Stinton, and I'll miss your counsel.'

'Don't concern yourself, he'll be an excellent replacement... an old head on young shoulders; just what's needed. And, I'll be living just a few miles from Hell Head... a stone's throw down the road near Netley. Where, I might add, he's doing a fine piece of work lecturing new recruits. He fits the niche nicely; experienced agents talk highly of him and newcomers follow his every word. Our over tangential commander has been on the receiving end... they respect that.'

*

He drove up to the main gate of Netley Royal Naval Hospital and showed the guard the first of two passes he possessed. The guard saluted and waved him through. He drove most of the way down the long avenue - almost to Southampton Water's shore. He turned left down a narrow lane and one hundred yards later pulled up at a second security gate hidden amongst the trees and bushes lining the water's edge.

'Commander Sherwood-Reeves, good morning, sir,' the guard said, smiling, saluting and ignoring Sims' second, and much higher security, pass.

'Morning... nice day, Dusty. How did you get on at Whale Island with Lieutenant Hennerbury?'

'He's hard work, sir. Doesn't let up.'

'Yes... yes... we know *that!* But how did you get *on?*'

'Difficult to say, fine, I think, sir.'

'He didn't tell you otherwise?'

'No, sir.'

'That means you did okay... well done. You'll know when he's not happy, he has a way of making this known.'

'I had noticed, sir. Sir? Has he actually ever shot anyone for not being up to scratch?'

Sims laughed. 'Always on the cards... not for sometime, though,' he said, getting back into the Land Rover.

His story had travelled rapidly by word of mouth; practically instantly. Certainly by the end of their first lunch break everyone knew who he was. Their new lecturer was someone who'd been at the sharp and gory end of the intelligence business. He held their attention and high opinion.

A month earlier Captain Miles Stinton introduced him to Unit 3, the centre for Naval Intelligence Division Induction and Instruction. The acronym NIDii served two masters: the first known and understood as Induction and Instruction. The second not for general consumption and known only to a few who occupied the adjacent building, Unit 4, the Special Psychiatric Disorder Section. Here the second NIDii acronym had a profoundly sinister meaning: Naval Intelligence Division Internment and Interrogation. A covert operation also responsible for debriefing refugees and defectors.

His duties were straightforward. He was to lecture and instruct recruits two mornings a week. The lessons extra curricula - a little field experience from an operative who had been shot in a little field. They left it to Sims to decide how the lectures would be structured. He needed to find his feet, he decided to open the floor up for questions straightaway. This, he reasoned, would give him an insight to what experience and operational knowledge his students lacked. Most had doubts about their

skill with side arms. They pummelled him with questions from every angle. This approach was a success and
led to his instigating all new recruits having to prove
themselves on the pistol range at Whale Island. Within a
week, he had this extended to ordinary ratings inducted
for surveillance support duties: guard, Leading Seaman
Dusty Miller being one of them.

'I have learned the importance of being able to use a
side-arm...' He paused; they waited. '...accurately. There
is little strategic advantage... hang on, let me rephrase
that; there is *no* strategic advantage to be had from
being unable to shoot your way out of a tight spot. By
the end of this course, you are all going to be able to
do this. Also,' he stressed, 'it is essential you have total
confidence in your partner to do the same. Teamwork
and excellence are the only ways forward. You should
understand this: if you cannot make the grade with Lieutenant Cedric Hennerbury there will be no place for you
within NID. So, listen to him and work hard. He is the
best there is. It is likely I would not be alive today but
for his dedication and rigorous approach to detail. If you
survive the course with him you won't be better shots,
you'll be excellent.'

Two mornings a week lecturing gave him ample time to
get on with his own agenda. Billy's task could wait... he
hadn't been given a deadline.

*

Black Sea coast - Ukraine.

It was not Mika at the door. These people were not
civilians: that much was clear. NKVD agents have a

cast about them; an unpleasant grey faced expressionless aura. A characteristic of their occupation gradually absorbed into their pores from day one of their induction. After five years in service they stand out like an alien species.

Radleigh stood to one side and let the two men into his beach-side apartment. There was little point in doing otherwise; he could see that.

He closed the door. 'And?' he said, shrugging. 'What do you want?'

One of them stepped forward - the more slab faced of the two, 'You are familiar with a young man called Mika Kozlov... is this him?' he said, shoving a photograph close to his face.

Gerald Radleigh took a pace backwards. Over the years he had signed execution warrants by proxy. He had been partly responsible for sending many men to their deaths. From these acts he had been remote - they meant nothing. Even the loss of his compatriots from les Grands Amis did not greatly upset him... they were simply a part of his past, nothing to grieve over. Mika, was different though, he was current and close. Radleigh sat down, 'What happened? What has happened to his tongue?'

'It isn't his tongue.'

'Oh, God.'

'His body was washed up this morning not far from here. He did not drown, he had bled to death before being dumped in the water.'

'Why would anyone do this to him?' Radleigh whispered.

'Who knows? The Mafia, gypsies, bandits, any of them. They all have their own rules of conduct. His way of life would have transgressed the moral codes of all of them. We will probably never know. Anyway, it is not our business. Today, you are our business.'

Only Radleigh's fingers moved. The rest of him sat still and pale.

'It is thought that this is a good time for you to move on. There are two reasons for this: we think your safety could be at risk, that is number one, and you are needed in Riga, number two.'

'But I am retired, I have a state pension. Why on earth am I wanted in Riga?'

'You are also a hero of the Union of Soviet Socialist Republics, and heroes, like all good citizens of the USSR, have a duty to the mother state: they must do as they are told.'

'But, why am I wanted in Riga?' he asked again.

'We do not know... orders from on high... Moscow... Moscow insists, and when they do so, we obey.'

*

Anne hurried down the corridor to his study, 'Darling, you need to come. Remember the Latvian interpreter, Beatrise Podnieks? she's just arrived!... she's talking to Jean in the kitchen.'

'Come again?' He put down his pen, pushed his chair away from the desk and stood up, 'Did she say what she wanted?'

'No, she wouldn't say... perhaps because of Jean.'

'Does she look okay?'

'Yes... fine.'

Sims glanced towards the polished wooden box that held his Browning 9mm Hi-Power. It was the briefest of glances. Anne noticed.

'You won't need that,' she said.

'You're sure there's nobody with her? Nobody in the car?'

'Definitely, I checked... and she's fine, just looks a little tired.'

He closed the door behind him, took her hand, 'Okay, let's see what she wants.'

Jean, with her dog Harry assisting, herded them into the library, 'Coffee's brewing, I'll bring it in when it's ready.'

Sims shook hands with Mrs Podnieks, 'How are you?... bit of a surprise... nothing wrong I hope?' he said, playing for time while trying to weigh both her and the situation up.

In her curious mixture of academically correct and *Tap Room* English, she apologised, 'Forgive me for not informing you of my intentions of popping in on you... one never knows who's listening... eavesdroppers all over... my husband thinks there may be people monitoring our calls... it's possible, is it not?'

Jean came in, 'Coffee and biscuits... chocolate digestives for you Beatrise... your favourite.'

'Thank you, Jean, you're very kind, duck.' She'd picked English up from varied sources; *duck*, she'd learned somewhere up north.

Surrogate mother, housekeeper, she checked the correctness of things: and those all in order, Jean Calver said, 'I'll leave you to it, then.'

'Commander, I have a message from Dāvis Lŭž. He insisted it must only be delivered to you and that only you should know about it... I think his auntie has advised him on this.' Uncertain, Beatrise looked at Anne: did Dāvis mean both of them? 'She doesn't trust intelligence forces.'

'Anything you have to say to me can be said in front of Anne... anything. If you remember, she was with us on the *Viktor Abakumov.*'

She, nodded, relieved, continued, 'He says the British defector, Gerald Radleigh has been seen in Riga. Of course he is going by his Soviet name of Anisim Polzin. I know this is true, I have had all this confirmed by other sources. This man was one of those that helped expose twenty-five intelligence agents - all of them died. One of them was his aunt's fiancé. The Forest Brothers would like revenge.'

'Is that all he had to say?' asked Sims.

'No, he says Radleigh has been given an apartment and a maid. So it is possible he will be there for some time. They would not bother to do this for a short stay.' Beatrise Podnieks paused while she sipped her coffee, dipped in a digestive and then ate it. She finished and wiped her lips. She looked around at them, 'I love dunking biscuits in coffee and tea, I have put on pounds and pounds since living in England... shall I go on... continue?'

'Yes, yes, please carry on,' said Anne, smiling. 'The extra weight suits you. You were very thin when we met you on the *Viktor Abakumov.*'

She smiled, 'Thank you, my husband likes it too. He

15

says I am more cuddly. That's a nice word isn't it?' Without pausing she added, 'Dāvis says he can kidnap him for you if you want.'

Sims, post biscuit bite crunching and coffee mid-sip, choked, 'Is he serious?'

'Oh yes, they have it all planned... they know just how to do it... they need to know if you're interested. They don't want to kill him themselves... it would bring reprisals. Dāvis, or someone else... possibly his auntie again, thinks if he just disappeared and then was seen again in England Moscow would think Radleigh had betrayed them. That would be nice wouldn't it?'

'How long have we got before we answer him?' Sims asked.

'I think he'll want to move fast... but, I don't really know.'

'Have they any idea why he's in Riga?' asked Anne.

'Not yet.'

'How can we contact you.'

'I'll contact you. We live in Southampton now. It doesn't take long to drive here. One other reason for my visit is to tell you I now work at the Netley Royal Naval Hospital too. I think Admiral Jessop and Captain Stinton must have arranged this.'

'I've been lecturing there for some time,' said Sims.

'I know I've seen you.'

'Are you with NIDii?'

'Yes, myself and my husband.'

'What section?'

'Unit 4 - Internment and Interrogation.'

'That's probably why I haven't seen you.'

'Yes, possibly... I don't think we ought to talk there.

If you need to talk to me hang this from your rear view mirror.' She handed him a small Union Jack with a looped gold cord, 'It is my symbol of freedom,' she said, simply.

'What if you want to contact us?'

'I will call you, if that's okay.'

'Of course it is,' said Anne. 'You'll call from a telephone kiosk I suppose.'

Beatrise nodded.

Sims; curious, 'Why don't you want to talk at Netley?'

'We've learned it's best not to trust too many people.'

'Wise move.'

'And it's nice to know you trust us,' said Anne.

'Yes of course I do,' she said standing up. 'I must leave now, I have other work to do.'

In the hall she diverted: Beatrise looked into the kitchen, 'Bye-bye, Jean, thank you for the lovely coffee and biscuits. I hope to see you again.'

Jean came into the hall and gave her a goodbye kiss, 'Take care of yourself. Now look, listen to me, don't worry, there are some very nice people in England. You'll see. I hope you settle down soon.'

'I'm sure I will.'

Beatrise Podnieks drove away eating a digestive biscuit she'd taken with her.

'Poor lamb,' said Jean.

Anne looked puzzled, 'Jean, did you know she was coming?'

'No, love.'

'How on earth did you know chocolate digestives were her favourite?'

'Oh, quite easy really, I asked her.'

'That simple?' said Sims.

'Of course,' she tutted, as she left the room.

*

She had her family all together again. *Alice Alacrity* sounded happy; her rigging hummed a snappy tune in the brisk wind. Each time she dug into the rolling, heaving swell, her bow wave curled over splashing creamy ringlets that ran down her sides and into her wake. She felt alive, her years stripped away, her timbers tight, rigging taut once more: this is how old ketches are meant to feel.

Rear Admiral Bob Sherwood at the helm. Fresh sea air, face tingling spray, sunshine, the Celedon Sea. Responsibilities shelved for a short while, just sailing *Alice* with his family in The Solent. Here, he was happy too. When I retire, he dreamed, I'll sail all day, every day on her. *Alice Alacrity* was where he and his new wife Alice spent their honeymoon and Anne had been conceived.

Sims hadn't had much to say, he'd busied himself making a Turk's head knot on the end of a heaving line. Finished, he stowed it away, sat down with Anne and looked over at Dad. He had reached a conclusion, a decision had been made. Straight to the point he asked, 'Do you have any subs operating permanently in the Baltic?' He backed off the inner jib a little and tensioned the main.

'Which part?'

'The Russian part... Gulf of Riga.'

'No, not officially. We sneak that way occasionally.'

'So, yes, then.'

Hello, this is new, what's on his mind? This is why he's not said much, thought Anne.

Not often the case in dealings with his son-in-law, he was reserved: a bit cagey. He was beginning to read him well, 'The answer was not yes but maybe. Why do you ask?... what are you up to, son?'

Sims rearranged his coat around Anne's shoulders, 'Are you warm enough, love?'

'Yes.' Intrigued and impatient, she nudged him, 'Answer Dad.'

'I need to pick someone up.'

'Need officially or want unofficially?'

'Second option I guess... depends how we play it.'

'*We?*' Bob Sherwood laughed. 'I see I'm already committed. To answer your main question, I have,' he said.

Overt operations and manoeuvres in the Baltic came under the command of, and controlled by, NATO. The Admiralty, though, still regarded British covert dealings as their business. To them, they were submarines of the Home Fleet and following Bob Sherwood's advancement to Rear Admiral, covert and tactical ownership of those Royal Naval submarines were his and his alone.

'Come on, Sims, perhaps a bit more detail... why?'

'We've had a break... it's been dropped in our laps. There's a chance we can drag Gerald Radleigh back to Britain. He's in Riga at the moment... our source says he might be there for some time. I'm worried he might not be. He is the last of Les Grands Amis and possibly the only person left alive who knows the truth about Buster Crabb and Lieutenant Miles Stinton. I want to get him back without too many people knowing how.'

'I will need more detail... much more detail.'

'I'm not asking for the go-ahead, all I'm asking at this moment is if there is a possibility he could be picked up and brought home in a sub. That's all I'm asking for the moment.'

'It is possible we could pick him up... bringing him home, is not. Now, this is classified... I have three *Oberon* class subs on permanent patrol in the area. Covert operations like the one you ask for was one of their main design specifications. Although where we patrol is more or less up to us, my subs are on permanent call there with NATO. So, as you can see, bringing him home is a different matter. Added to this restriction, access to and from The Baltic is controlled by three passages between Denmark and Sweden: The Little Belt in the west. The Great Belt in the middle and Øresund in the north east. Theoretically the eastern side of the Great Belt is an international waterway. In practise, they are all choke points and we have the capability of closing them to non-friendly traffic. No shipping passes through these straits, either on the surface or below, without us or others knowing. Strategically, we have an agreement with Denmark that certain movements of our underwater shipping are not logged officially... we sneak in and out using the western side of the Great Belt... we do not like to abuse this arrangement.'

'I can understand that, I'll do some more thinking and

keep you in the loop.'

*

At Whale Island pistol range Sims headed straight for the armourer's workshop. A redundant question, 'Hi, Les, got the kettle on?'

'Always... how's things, lad?'

'Interesting and getting more so.'

'Your recruits are keeping us busy,' said Les, swilling boiling water around and warming the tea-pot.

'Any idea how Leading Seaman Miller's getting on?'

'Glenn?... he seems okay... better ask the boss.'

'*Glenn!*... not with two n's?'

'Yeah... his mum and dad were war-time big-band fans.'

'Poor bugger... what an upbringing! The Glenn Miller sound.'

'Some people had it really rough in the war, lad.'

Sims watched the small group through the workshop door window.

'God give me strength,' He ranted. 'It's so bleedin' simple,' Lieutenant Cedric Hennerbury was hammering them. 'If I say you need to place your feet further apart, it's because you need to place your fuckin' feet further apart... that can't be hard to grasp, can it?... not even for a soddin' electrician... don't wait until I have to tell you... think and act for yourself, lad,' he thundered. 'Stop acting like a bleedin' virgin... open your legs up and brace yourself... God give me strength. What did I do to deserve a bunch like you?'

'He looks pleased enough with this lot,' Sims

commented.

'You sure? How can you tell?' Les asked, pouring out two cups.

'Still his normal pulsating puce colour... hasn't turned purple yet... volume still muted to bellow.'

Les laughed.

'Better pour another cup... looks like he's had enough... he's on his way here.'

'He smelt it.'

'How they doing, Cedric?'

'Not bad... not bad at all. Pretty good bunch.' Contradiction all in a day's work for a gunnery officer.

'Hmmm... thought you looked happy. How's Leading Seaman Miller doing?'

'He'll pass no problem... good shot... very good in fact. Competition material, that one.'

'Great,' said Sims. 'Do me a favour and push him hard: harder than the rest. Push him just like you pushed me. Get him on the .303 range as well, and, God forbid we have to resort to one, get him sorted with a Lanchester as well. They all on Brownings?'

'Standard procedure for your men now... got a job for him? He's a good lad.'

'Well, I may need a top-end partner shortly... don't say anything to him yet.'

'Mum's the word. Things sound interesting... something other than Les's tea's brewing, then?' Lieutenant Hennerbury asked, panning for a snippet or two.

'Don't panic, I'll keep you posted... as and when.'

***

Chapter Three

Ackers for an Apostate.

Sims hung her little symbol of freedom on the Land Rover's rear view mirror for two days before Beatrise Podnieks came. This time she was not alone.

'This is my husband Artis. He is a member of the Forest Brothers too. We are sorry we could not come straightaway.'

Introductions over; tea served with a slice of freshly baked boiled fruit cake, Beatrise took a bite,'Ohh, I like coming to your home... how can I help you?'

'I want...' he quickly corrected, '...we want Radleigh. How to get him to England is the problem... when you escaped, do you mind telling me how you got here?' he asked, gauging their reaction closely. There was no hesitation, no holding back, nothing to indicate reticence.

'We were smuggled into Estonia from Latvia and then crossed to the Swedish island of Gotland by a small boat,' replied Artis, his English first class, hardly a trace of accent.

Beatrise chipped in, 'We chose very rough weather in winter for the journey... there was a lot of ice... we hoped the Russians would think that nobody would travel in a storm and in such cold... it was a terrible crossing... many times I didn't think we would make it. The noise when our little boat hit the ice: all the time I thought it would tear us to pieces. I'm glad we are here eating cake.'

Bad memories and leaving home, Beatrise hugged herself. Artis took her hand, squeezed it, and said, 'The Forest Brothers have contacts all over the Baltic. From Gotland they took us to the Danish mainland and there we made contact with NATO and the British navy, and that's how we first came to know Admiral Jessop and Captain Stinton.'

'Was it The Forest Brothers who helped you get from Latvia to Estonia?'

'Yes... the Brothers are very strong there,' said Beatrise.

'Do you think they could get Radleigh to Gotland for us?'

'I think it is possible.'

'Will you ask them as soon as you can?'

'Yes, I will get a message on its way to them tomorrow. I cannot do it sooner. It will take several days to reach them,' replied Artis.

'Will you also ask them what they will need from us.'

'They will do it for nothing... but money is always useful... American Dollars.'

'Cash, I can see that. I actually meant if we could help in any other way...'

'I will ask.'

*

In the afternoon after one of his lectures Sims went down to Hell Head Harbour: a little messing around in boats was called for, it helped him think. Anne had worked that morning, and then a little longer than usual at Spice Island Spices. Business was growing and she was concerned that Mo and Pearl might start to feel stretched for cash. They were now close friends, she was not going to let this happen. Later back at Hell Head House she sat with Jean in the kitchen, 'Where's Sims?'

'I think he's got something on his mind,' said Jean.

'So, he's down working on *Alice*... doing something with ropes no doubt.'

'Yes... better take him a sarnie or two... he didn't stop for lunch.' In normal chat between the two women they would have been called sandwiches. As they were for Sims, sarnies; the preferred term.

'Hmm,' said Anne. 'I had a feeling something was brewing.'

Harry saw her coming down the quayside. His tail a blur of wags he ran to greet her.

'Where's that husband of mine?' she said, stopping and stooping to pat him. She ruffled his ears, 'Shall we go and find him?'

Harry turned and headed for *Alice.*

Sims spotted them, 'Hi, Babe,' he called.

Long used to being called Babe, Anne smiled and waved.

'Jean's made a couple of bacon sarnies for Harry... he says he'll share them with you... I can give them all to him if you don't fancy them.'

'I'm peckish, he can have what I leave.'

'So, the poor dog gets nothing, then... I'll make some coffee while you finish what you're doing.'

While you finish what you're doing, he thought.

Sounds like we're in for a grilling session.

From the main cabin she called, 'Coffee's ready... *now, Sims...* before it gets cold.'

Hatch closed - warm saloon, 'God, I need this... nippy up there.'

They sat side by side. Just a few minutes quiet except for the rhythmic slap of wavelets against *Alice's* hull. She shifted her position on the cushioned seat, 'Sims, my love, I'm waiting.' There was no need to explain what she was waiting for.

He shrugged, 'I need to get myself squared on a few things.'

'We know.'

'*We?*'

'Jean and myself... what do you need to square?'

'As I said, a couple of things. Honey, I don't feel too good about working behind Billy's back... if I take over from Captain Stinton, I suppose he has every right to be kept informed. Otherwise, although he might back what I do when I've finished whatever I'm doing, he might not trust what I say beforehand...' He tailed off, still not entirely clear of his own logic and whether what he'd said made sense.

'Listen, *if* doesn't come into it... you *have* taken over from Miles... it may not be written down on vellum, but trust me, it's understood by us all and possibly many others we know not of. So, not *if*, Sims, please. And, what is more, you're doing absolutely the right thing in telling him what you're thinking, darling.' She sat looking at him, sipped her coffee, and then said, 'There *is* another point of course: you may well need all the assistance he has at his disposal in getting Radleigh back. What we're planning has all the makings of a political nightmare for someone. You'll need things in place in case it doesn't go to schedule.'

'Any chance of you coming with me to see Billy?'

She leaned over and kissed him, 'Of course!... as though I'd say no!' she said, rubbing her hands together. 'Will I need the Beretta?'

'Hope not... not at Billy's anyway. Might need the Browning, though.'

'What, at Billy's?'

'Just a little signal to make sure he keeps his hands off you.'

Too good to miss, she needled, 'You're jealous, Commander Sherwood- Reeves.'

'*Rubbish!*'

He sat eating... feeding bits to Harry... drinking... silent.

Anne took hold of his hand, lightly bit a knuckle and then kissed it, 'That's not all, is it?... what else?'

His face drawn solemn, he said, 'Hmm, well, got to face it sometime. Look, in a few months you are not going to be able to partner me... I need to train somebody else... you must understand, whoever it is will never be as good as you. I don't want this to happen, love, but unless you don't mind me working on my own, it's inevitable.'

'I don't want you ever to work solo again. I know you will need a partner, I've known this for sometime... but just promise me not until it's absolutely necessary.'

'So, you're happy with that, then?'

'*God no.* No I am not. How could I be? If there is any consolation at all, it's knowing this was so hard for you to broach. But as you say, and I have known, it's inevitable... and that's what we have to deal with, isn't it?'

'Sure. You'll have to help me make the selection. You know, what colour hair?.. what size bra?'

'Sims, get one thing clear, it will *not* be female.'

'Bugger.'

He went quiet again. Harry nudged his hand for more attention and a piece more bacon.

'Can you tell me what you're thinking... where we're going with this?'

'I have a few ideas. Before we go and see Billy I need to have them shaped into some sort of plan... it's going to be a bit of a selling job.'

'Come on, we can do this better at home.'

Harry got home ahead of them - one never knows what's going on in the kitchen. Jean met them in the hall, 'I thought you wouldn't be far behind. Sims, you're going to have a proper lunch... you can't think on an empty stomach. And... and, you haven't given me a kiss today,' she said, a parody, hands on hips, hugely amplifying her best indignant look.

He quickly remedied his unforgivable shortcoming in diplomacy and threw in an extra one for luck. Jean seemed satisfied and huffed off into the kitchen.

'Ten out of ten for a good recovery,' Anne said.

He carefully placed his knife and fork down, 'If Dad could have got Radleigh back in a sub, I know he would have said so.'

'It still may be he could, but only when one was officially recalled.'

'That might not be soon enough for The Brothers.'

'Okay, what if he was able to pick him up and dump him somewhere on the Baltic coast, where, and when we can get at him?'

'Yes... that's good... we'll sound him out. That would leave just two headaches for us to sort out: getting him back quickly ourselves to ensure there are no reprisals in Riga and then hanging on to him once he's home and dry.'

'Keep using "*we*" and "*us*", darling.'

In thought, he finished his lunch, sat back in his chair and said, 'It's Running Fox time, we need to see Mike Mason. Then we'll go and see Billy.'

*

The sun had been set over an hour when they were called into Admiral Sherwood's study.

'Come in and sit down,' he said, looking out of the window towards the quayside lights of Hell Head Harbour and navigation lights of ships on The Solent: port and starboard, red and green. Turning, he said, 'We are family: you are my family, and it is that which makes it difficult for me to say what I am about to.' He halted, drew the chair out from his desk and sat down. 'However, we have to come to terms with the separation of family loyalties and those towards our country. My naval responsibility is for the submarine home fleet - that, as you know, includes the NATO Baltic fleet. In this matter I answer to the Lords of the Admiralty, not to the intelligence services or even to my family. I have said this so that you both fully understand my position.'

'But, that is understood and never been in doubt,

Father,' said Anne.

'Absolutely... no question about that,' agreed Sims. 'There is something else I have to say in all seriousness: I hope you are both going to inform Admiral Jessop of your rather clandestine intentions.'

Her chair scraped back an inch or two, 'We have already decided that was the right and proper course of action. True, we have yet to tell him. We are to arrange a meeting as soon as possible, but only after our plans have crystalised further.'

'Are you happy about that, Sims?' he asked, looking doubtful. 'You are known to have been flying solo for much of time you've been with NID... perhaps all of the time. You may have got accustomed to working that way.'

Before he could answer, Anne leapt to his defence and interrupted, 'No, no. I won't have that... that is not fair. It was *his* idea, Father. And, when he was a courier he had little option but to work alone... everybody was out to get rid of him... you can't have forgotten *that!* That really was not fair of you.'

'Of course you're perfectly correct.' He sighed, 'I'm relieved to hear you're going to see Billy... and, I have to tell you I've got quite used to being called dad,' he said, smiling. 'Now tell me more about your plans.'

'I have a better grip now on what I would like. Beatrise phoned, the Forest Brothers are reluctant to deliver Radleigh all the way to Gotland... Soviet patrols are on the increase, The Brothers have almost been caught twice recently... they're going to lay off their runs for a while until things quieten down. So, I need to pick Radleigh up at sea... close to the Estonian or Latvian coast and deliver him to the west coast of Gotland... that's it in a nutshell except I want to get in close so that we don't risk the kidnappers' lives,' he said, studying his father-in-law's face for a reaction. 'It's either pick him up or forget the whole thing... and I really don't want that.'

Admiral Sherwood scratched his forehead. 'With anything we undertake, Gotland would be out... Sweden is not, and never has been, a part of NATO. That's a no go area, Sims. Why not take him back to Denmark? We use their naval base at Korsør on the eastern side of The Great Belt. Why not take him there?'

'How far is that from Riga?'

'Depending on the route taken, about five hundred and fifty nautical miles. Look, as long as Admiral Jessop is kept fully informed and with us all the way, I'm sure we can do something. When your plans are finalised and fully detailed, we'll get him to look over them.' Bob Sherwood looked at his daughter, 'Anne, if all goes ahead, I will expect Sims to accompany us on board,' he paused. 'You must understand that it will not be possible for you to do so.'

Chair scraped back a further couple of inches, 'Why not?' she asked, indignantly.

'It is out of the question... superstition... cramped conditions. I will not be questioned further on this matter.'

Sims stepped in, 'If we're to use Korsør we will need someone I can trust to man our operations base there. That's you... it can only be you.'

'Sims, tell me straight, did you know I wouldn't be able to go to sea with you?'

'I thought it might be the case. To tell the truth, I guess

I thought it highly likely. But using a sub is the only way I can see us achieving the plan safely and quickly. If you can think of a better and more secure way, I'll run with it. That's a promise.'

Anne thought it through and reluctantly said, 'You're right, it's probably the best way... Sims, just promise I can come to Denmark and help run things.'

'I promise.'

She was, nevertheless, bitterly disappointed; it showed, 'Father, you said I wouldn't be able to accompany *us*. Does that mean you're going too?'

'Yes. All my skippers are first class tacticians... so are theirs. I'm going to see if the Russian Baltic Fleet Commander, Aleksandr Evstafyevich Orel is as good as he used to be... we've crossed swords before.'

'Father, you have no objection to me being a part of the team in Korsør, I hope?' she said, with more than a hefty touch of huff in her voice.

'None at all.' He turned to Sims, 'We'll probably use HMS *Odin*.'

'Viking territory: appropriate,' he said.

They sat quietly for minutes. Sims thinking of his next move: Bob Sherwood wondering what Sims' next move might be, and Anne trying to come to terms with the disappointment of only playing what she considered to be a bit-part on the periphery of the action.

Sims leaned over to her, 'Honey bunch, this has not been an easy meeting for any of us, I think it's time... perhaps we ought tell him our bit of news.'

She brightened and nodded enthusiastically, 'Yes, yes, let's do that.' She stood up, 'Dad, our home will soon be much more noisy... you're going to have a grandchild.'

The steely tactical commander of Home Fleet submarines, submerged. Her father surfaced, less control, lost for words.

'We waited before we told you until we new everything was ship-shape,' Sims said.

Bob Sherwood stood up and beckoned to Anne, 'Come here, my girl.' He gently hugged her, rocking her backwards and forwards. 'I'm *so* very happy... very, very happy... have you told Jean?'

'No, not yet.'

'We must do so now. She's been muttering hints for months.'

Sims fetched her, Anne gave her the news. Jean Calver sat down: overcome - many weeping minutes to recover. Then, recovered, 'Anne, I've been thinking about the nursery...'

'We know.'

'Shall we go there now? We ought to go and sort out a few things?'

'Jean, I'm just over two and a half months gone... there's plenty of time.'

'Seven and a few months to go... well done, lad,' said Bob Sherwood, shaking Sims' hand. 'Are you allowed to drink, Anne?'

'Only chilled champagne.'

*

Sims dialled.

'Patrick Harvey here,' he said, half mindedly - the other portion on his crossword.

'Pat, it's Sims. Are you awake? Put the crossword

down. Have I got your attention? Everything okay?' he asked. The last question inferred several; have the janitors been in lately? Are the lines clean? How about eavesdroppers?

'Completely... how did you know I was doing the crozzie?' Pat replied, pushing the puzzle to one side.

'You always are, it's what you do... squad still in action?'

'It's been a while... interesting question,'

'Been busy. Stop fucking about, Pat... in action or not?'

'We keep in touch. What's the problem?'

'I might need a hand... how about you rounding them up for a session at The Running Fox?'

'How soon?'

'Asap.'

'I'll get back to you.'

'Okay... make sure Mike Mason comes.'

'Interesting.'

'Thought you might be getting bored.'

'It's been relatively quiet... you about to change all that?'

'If you're lucky.'

*

They arrived at The Running Fox before any of the others turned up, 'Cedric Hennerbury wouldn't tolerate this tardiness,' Sims said. 'He'd tear their ears off.'

'It's us that's early, not them late. It's still only five to seven.'

'Hrumph... The Forest Brothers aren't going to wait forever... I want to get on,' he said, looking out of the window to the car park.

'That, my darling, is pretty evident.'

All but Fiona and Mike were there by seven - they wandered in about two minutes past.

Anne jabbed Sims and whispered, 'It's their own time remember. Don't say anything... no moaning, not a single word.'

'Give me a break, that's what we've come for. I don't know any sign language, I can hardly stand up and stay dumb, can I?'

'You know very well what I mean... I shall bash you in a minute, you sod.'

Sims waited until everyone had a drink and a plate of sandwiches in their hands. He stood up, 'Something you need to know before we go any further... for domestic reasons, Anne will, in the near future, no longer be able to partner me in the field. I have identified another possibility and have started training him. There is no need for him to be aware of the Squad's existence.'

'You going to give us a name?' asked Allan Johnstone.

'No reason why not: Leading Seaman Glenn Miller... he's very good.'

'Glenn with two "*n*"s?' asked Archie Abbot.

'"Fraid so.'

'Poor sod.'

'That's what I said.'

'I hope nothing's wrong, Anne.' Shirley wore a worried *I don't want to pry* look.

'Oh no... nothing wrong... quite the opposite. To use

Sims' quaint little mess-deck expression; I'm up the duff.'

'What a coincidence... it must be catching,' said Fiona, 'so am I.'

Mike, shattered, spluttered, 'You never said anything... you never told *me!*'

'I only found out for sure today... I tried to get through to you on the way over... all you wanted to talk about was bloody football and buggery Cilla Black... anyway, how do you know it's yours,' she said, cackling. 'Are you having morning sickness, Anne.'

'No, I haven't so far.'

'I probably won't notice. I've been waking up next to Mike for years... nuff to make anyone sick.'

Mike sat there looking blank.

'Christ, what is this, a bleedin' mother's meeting?... is this all we've come for?' asked Archie Abbot.

Arms folded under bosom, Shirley said, 'Well I think it's lovely news.'

Sims, in impatient disbelief, had stood there looking from one to the other as they spoke.

Patrick stood up, 'Congratulations both of you... I have a sneaky feeling someone's getting edgy... perhaps back to you, Sims.'

'Thank God for that. I have a quick question for you all. Simple job... a doddle... how do you fancy helping to snatch Radleigh and dragging him back to the United Kingdom?' He waited for that to sink in.

'Are you serious?' Fiona coughed.

'Deadly so.'

'You got the king-pin, you sure Radleigh's worth the

trouble?' Archie said.

'Of course he is... he helped shop our agents in the Baltic to the Soviets and, he may be the only man alive who knows the truth about Buster and poor Miles Stinton junior.' said Anne.

'I'm in,' said Pat. 'How are you going to do it?... what's the plan? What would you need from us?'

'Plan's still being shaped at the moment... we're pretty sure we can get him back, though. Mike, we're going to need a British Passport for Radleigh and another for him under a different name.'

'I'll need an up-to-date photo... any offers?'

Shirley offered. 'I can get that.'

'I also need a Russian and another British Passport with Radleigh's details in it and a Radleigh look-alike's photo inserted... we need him to act as a double.'

Anne piped in, 'We've yet to find this look-alike.'

'Thank Christ, a bit of action again... once more, our own Royal Navy to the rescue,' Fiona said, slapping Mike on the back.

'The fun will start when we get Radleigh home. That's maybe when I'll need help most... I've got big plans for him,' Sims said.

Fiona looked doubtful, 'Who can we trust to act as a double and still sleep at nights?'

'Nobody I know who we can rely that much,' said Archie.

Patrick nodded in agreement, 'We'll do some thinking. There is someone... Billy knows him... don't know if he's still around, though... Alistair Duncan. A strange mixture of sharp, in that he's always got his eyes on a deal, honest as the day is long, experienced, and very,

very good... might be retired or late.'

*

Admiral Robert Sherwood travelled to Tunworth House with them. From the back seat Anne mused, 'I see Billy still hasn't managed to sell Tunworth yet. I'm surprised, it's a lovely place.'

'He doesn't want to,' said Sims.

She, indignant, 'You said, he said he was going to sell it and move to London.'

'I did... and that *is* what he said. What *I* said was he doesn't want to sell it.'

'*Explain!*' She didn't tack on the lurking exasperated '*darling*'.

'Christ! It's simple, why do you struggle so? Listen, if he really did, he would have done so. He's set the price too high and he knows it.'

'Hmm,' she hmmed.

'There's no *hmm* about it. It's commercial nous... something accountants know little of.'

'Okay, smarty, how would you price it?'

'Fifteen thousand less.'

'Why fifteen, smarty?'

'*Why!* Because I checked the going rate with other selling agents, dear. Then I phoned his estate agent and made an offer. They said they'd had similar offers and he had refused them. Corollary, he doesn't want to sell it. My reckoning is he wants to be nearer to his ketch *The Anne Sherwood-Reeves* when its finished. It's so bloody obvious when you think about it. All it takes is a little male intuition.'

After leaning forward and thumping him, she sat

mulling this for a while. Bob Sherwood sat smiling at this interplay - their exchanges better than watching television. *She is Alice. He hasn't heard the last of this.*

*

Sims looked up from his notes. The briefing began. Billy Ruffian stood by the window watching, waiting. 'We have solid information that Gerald Radleigh is in Riga. If it were to be a fleeting visit it would not be of particular interest. However, our intelligence has it he may be there for some time. The Forest Brothers have a plan to kidnap and deliver him to us... for our part, we will have to collect him from somewhere in the Baltic. How we get him back to the UK is our problem... we need to act quickly if we're to go ahead.' Now he, Sims, in his turn, watched and waited for Billy's response.

Billy did not hurry, he stalked around the room several times, eventually, halted and said, 'How long have you known about this?'

'Not long... I needed to get most of my nuts in a row before asking for your go-ahead.'

Billy looked surprised, *'My go-ahead?* Well there's a first time for everything, I suppose,' he said, sarcastically and raising his eyebrows while looking towards Admiral Sherwood. 'Out with it, lad, let's hear your plan.'

'The fine details have to be gone over, but broadly, HMS *Odin* picks Radleigh up at sea off the Latvian or Estonian coast. Myself, and a Leading Seaman Miller will escort Radleigh back to Denmark: Anne heads our team there. As soon as we arrive we get the next available plane from Copenhagen home. From there we travel by car to Netley Unit-4 where we will interrogate him.' He paused, 'Okay, so far?' Billy nodded for him to continue.

'I need three British passports and one Russian. I've spoken to Mike Mason... this is not a problem, we have fairly recent photos of Radleigh.'

'Why so many passports? and why Mike Mason? You could get them officially through NID and MI6.'

'Mike is sound, I don't want anyone to know what we're up to, and MI5 and MI6 are the last bunch I want to get a sniff of what we're doing. When we've got what we want from him and I'm ready, they'll find out quick enough. As for the passports, I want one British one with all Radleigh's details and photo, another one with his photo but an alternative identity... this is the one we'll use to get him back to the UK from Copenhagen. I need a Russian one in the name of Anisim Polzin with a Radleigh look-alike's photo... this is the name he uses when on Russian business... we'll use this one to travel with his double from Copenhagen to Zurich... Radleigh appears to have clearance to travel and regularly visits his bank there. From Zurich to London Heathrow we'll use another British passport - Radleigh's details but the double's photo.'

Billy held his hand up and pointed a gnarled belligerent finger. 'You skipped over the reason for Radleigh's legitimate copy.'

'No deliberate skipping... I was just coming to that. If anything goes wrong, it will be that one I leave on his body. That will make it look as if he'd been trying to return to Britain by his own means.'

'Goes wrong?'

'The Forest Brothers are thick on the ground in Denmark too. There are plenty of them who would like to take a bit of revenge and rid the world of him... that's also why I need Leading Seaman Miller as a back-up... we'll both be Radleigh's guards.'

'And, the double?'

'Yet to find one.'

'I'll talk to Stinton. He keeps in touch with Alistair Duncan... retired MI6... he'd make a good substitute... always itching for a bit of action. And, may I suggest, you may need additional help... perhaps three of you to guard. Lecturing at Netley, you are the best placed to recruit someone young, fit and able. There's something else. I'll get you and your team introduced to NIDii Unit 4. And, while you're there you'd all better do the interrogation course.'

He saw no reason why he should mention he already knew of the name Alistair Duncan.

Billy turned to Admiral Sherwood, 'Robert, no doubt you've all discussed this, how would it fit in with your Baltic sub fleet?'

'It can run alongside normal patrols... there's nothing like real-time action to iron out operational wrinkles... good experience for the crews. Given final and fine detail, I don't have a problem with the exercise... I shall accompany them on *Odin*.'

Billy turned back to Sims, 'Anything else on your mind?'

'Yes, funds... they're short of cash... they prefer US dollars... ackers for an apostate; dollars for a defector.'

Oh, I like that... ackers for an apostate, that's very nice... he gets ten points for that one, thought Anne.

'How much and where and when do you propose the exchange is made?'

'Two thousand dollars... no exchange. We give them the cash upfront.'

A sharp intake of breath, 'Sounds risky... if they have the money, what incentive have they to deliver the goods?'

Sims stood his ground, 'This is big stuff for them... they want him dealt with... preferably not on their patch. This is no small deal, we're not buying stuff off a market stall and The Forest Brothers are not spiv greengrocers. Beatrise and Artis said they're operating on a shoe-string. It's my opinion if we want this mission to be a success, I think it's better we oil the wheels - the upfront cash may just ensure getting the delivery made.'

Anne who had sat taking notes, chipped in, 'I'm sure you've come to know it already, however, in case you haven't, although Sims is not an accountant, neverthe-less, he has not a bad business head... he's a good street trader... a barrow-boy's instinct for a deal.'

Touché, thought Bob Sherwood, smiling, should be a good trip home.

When she thought only Sims could see her, she poked her tongue out at him. Bob Sherwood noticed as well: Alice, he thought.

Less stalking now, Billy ambled round the room. He did his stock routine of pulling out a book from the shelf, opening it, closing it without reading, replacing it and then sitting down once more.

'I want the truth about Commander Crabb possibly more than I want Gerald Radleigh, to get both would be a tremendous bonus for the Naval Intelligence Division. Get your plan fully detailed, Sims, and if it's a good one,

I'll back you to the hilt.'

'Perhaps you should know, when we have Radleigh, I will use any method possible to find out about Lieutenant Miles Stinton as well.'

'I fully understand your reasons... don't overstep the mark, lad. It's too easy to let the job overcome morality.'

Shite, that's not a bad one coming from you, he thought.

A similar thought crossed Anne's mind.

*

A good mix: his men from NIDii, Royal Naval and Marine trainees, number Three Range was busy. Lieutenant Cedric Hennerbury saw Sims arrive. He left two petty officers in charge and came over to talk.

'Okay, Cedric, apart from Dusty who's showing form?... I may need another man.'

'Dusty's definitely the best of the bunch. There's a Sub-Lieutenant Mountford, he comes a close second.'

'Think I can I take a look at him?'

'Sure, we're going to the combat range in five minutes.'

'If it's okay, I'll watch from the side lines.'

Controlled relaxation of the target range recast as barely controlled tension: the combat run commenced. Mountford threw himself into the task. Scored a max and came back looking pleased with himself, sweating, passing a comment to Leading Seaman Miller. Dusty Miller smiled, nodded and rubbed his hands together.

They're keen, thought Sims. The young sub-lieutenant looked familiar. He couldn't place where he'd seen him before.

'*Subby Mountford!*' bellowed Lieutenant Hennerbury, 'The commander wants a word with you.'

Mountford ran over and saluted, 'Sub-Lieutenant Mountford reporting, sir.'

'All yours, Commander.' Cedric returned to his group under instruction.

'At ease... you're not doing badly, Sub-Lieutenant. Your face is vaguely familiar. Why? You're not one of my regular students. So why do I think I know you?'

'We have met before, sir, very briefly, a couple of years ago. You gave a demonstration... ten shots in ten seconds... all bulls. I've never forgotten it. I promised I'd get that good. I was one of the midshipmen under training in this very range.'

'Now I've got you... you said: that's really awfully good shooting, didn't you?'

'Yes, sir, and it was.'

'You've done really well... Lieutenant Hennerbury is impressed with you. Well done.'

'It's difficult to know whether one's doing well or not with the lieutenant. He can give fearful tellings off.'

'Where I come from the word is bollockings, lad.'

Mountford relaxed a little, 'Those as well, sir.'

'What made you join the Naval Intelligence Division?'

Mountford coloured slightly and looked awkward, 'Word gets around, sir... I heard of your exploits.'

'Mostly bull shit.'

'With respect, sir, I don't think so. It was a hell of a story: a leading stoker kills two enemy agents. I knew it must be you right away.'

'Yeah okay, give it a break. I said you've done well. I want you to try and do even better... can you?'

'I can only try, sir. I'll do my very best.'

'How do you get on with Leading Seaman Miller?'

'He's good... very good. We both enjoy trying to outdo each other. He's got the right spirit and very competitive.'

'How do you feel about being transferred to my group at Netley?'

'Thank you, sir. I'd like that very much.'

'Right get yourself back to your training and see if you can't leave Dusty in the dust.'

Sims watched him go. He'll do, he thought.

He poked his head into Les Goodwin's workshop, said goodbye, and left the range. 'It's a small world,' he said, quietly.

***

Chapter Four.
Old Habits Die Hard.

Sub-Lieutenant Mountford drove Dusty down to Hell Head House from Netley. Their instructions clear: they were to use a private vehicle and on no account should they tell anyone where they were headed and on what business.

Harry, always on watch, lying on the top step, barked as they came up the drive to the front door. Anne, now alerted, stepped out to greet them. Dusty's jaw slackened and Mountford, caught for words, stuttered slightly, 'We've... we've an appointment with Commander Sherwood-Reeves, ma'am.'

'Yes, I know,' she said, brightly.

Sims appeared beside Anne, 'You can close your mouth now, Dusty. Lads, meet my wife, Anne. She is also a member of the Naval Intelligence Division. Don't be fooled by her good looks... she's no passenger... could outshoot both of you.'

'Come in... come in. I bet you're both starving,' she said.

Jean Calver entered the hall, 'Hello, lads, lunch will be served in a jiffy. We know how to feed matelots here.'

In full dress uniform, Rear Admiral Robert Sherwood came in from his study, 'Morning, men. Normally, I'd eat with you... have to attend a do in Pompey... going to miss Jean's cooking... tragic.'

Sub-Lieutenant Mountford and Leading Seaman Miller were still at stiff attention. Bob Sherwood looked towards them, 'At ease men... at ease... come on, relax!' and then to Anne and Sims... 'I need to speak to you both, can we have half an hour or so together later... before supper?'

They both nodded, 'Sure,' said Sims.

Anne went to her father and kissed him, 'Don't be too late, Dad, you're looking a bit tired.'

His staff car arrived, Dad saluted the two lads and left.

'Right, let's go into the dining room,' said Anne, shooing them in front of her. 'Go on... go on, or Sims will get there first and there'll be little left for us.'

Sims standing, said, 'Before we eat and get down to business there are a couple of things I want to get clear.' He paused. 'You probably want to know why you're here and why we're not having this chat at Netley. It's a simple issue of security. What we're going to do is highly classified... top secret. Now, this bit is where you two come in. There is a need to form a team for a covert Naval Intelligence assignment.' He studied them for a moment, 'There's no question that you two are the pick of the bunch at Netley, and, apparently, you work well together... is that so?'

Both nodded and said, 'Yes, sir.'

'Then, you will be a part of that team. How do you feel about that?'

'Excellent, sir,' said Mountford.

'Same here, sir,' said Dusty.

'The fourth member of the immediate team is Anne. I shall not brief you at this time on the operation. The point of getting you here is to drill it home that I don't want you to miss a single trick in your training... any part of your training. It ends in a couple of weeks time, isn't that so?'

They nodded.

'When you've completed the course, you will be billeted at HMS *Dolphin* until further notice and you are to use our office in Fort Blockhouse. While there it will be handy for Whale Island and the ranges and, you will also be put through a familiarisation course on *Oberon* class subs... this will take in a couple of days' sea trials. You will have the pleasure of spending much more time with your favourite gunnery officer, Lieutenant Hennerbury. On a lighter side, I'll also introduce you to our nippy launch *Big Sylvie* and her driver Sam Bradley. *Sylvie* is fitted with a radio. So is our ketch *Alice Alacrity*... call sign *Gateau*. There's a radio in the office as well. Now, Sam's a tiffy, and he and his stoker keep her on top form. I don't know what experience you two have with launches... it won't hurt you to learn. Sam may be a tiffy, but don't write him off... don't underestimate his skill and he knows the local waters well. Remember, *Sylvie* is Sam's responsibility... and she's a beast.'

'Sounds fun,' said Dusty.

'She is.'

'The sub course, sir, will that include training in the escape tank, sir,' asked an eager Mountford.

'Yes, tank drill always comes first before being allowed to go to sea on a boat. All of us except Anne will do so. Unfortunately she can't... we're having our first child.'

'Oh, well done, ma'am,' said the sub-lieutenant.

'Hang on, hang on, I played a part in it as well.'

'And well done you too, sir.'

Lucky bugger, thought Dusty. Then he piped in, 'I'm a submariner, I've already done the tank... though I don't mind another bash, sir.'

'Good, good. Now, to touch on the obvious, the difference in our ranks makes it clear I'm in charge. That also makes me ultimately responsible for what we are about to do... so, I want to make it doubly clear that you understand whatever happens, what I say goes.' For a few seconds Sims remained silent while he let that sink in. Then, 'However, jumping up and down saluting and saying, yes sir, every time I speak might slow things down a bit. So... here's how it is: the second time I went sailing with my future father-in-law he introduced a protocol. It went something like this: unless there are other naval personnel around we'll be on first name terms... it will make for a better crew. Although not everybody agreed at the time,' he said, glancing at Anne, who showed just the tip of her tongue to him. 'We became a top rate crew. This was mainly due to his piece of wisdom and my patience with the person who disagreed. We, lads, are going to employ the same logic. Dusty, is it going to be Dusty or Glenn?'

'Please not Glenn,' said Dusty, 'I've tried to keep it quiet for years... and somehow it doesn't seem to fit well with being in NID either.'

'Dusty it is then.'

'David, for me, sir,' said Mountford.

'You know mine's Sims.'

'And mine's Anne,' she said, smiling at them both.

'Another point, at the moment, nobody except ourselves, Anne's father and Vice-Admiral Jessop know anything about this operation - make sure it stays that way. If anyone is to be added to that list, myself or Anne will tell you first. Don't take anybody else's word it's okay to spill the beans. All clear?'

'Yes, sir.'

Jean came in with lunch. 'This, lads, is Mrs Jean Calver... she possesses more wisdom than is decent for anyone to lay claim to, and, on top of that, she makes the world's best bacon sarnie. If you both behave yourselves, one day she may well condescend to make you one... she will need my permission first, of course. Such things as Mrs Jean Calver's sarnies are not a right, they have to be earned.'

'I should think so too,' she said, closing the dining room door behind her.

'We'll carry on with this conversation round the dining table... only try not to pose questions just as I've filled my face with this pie.'

It seemed like a convenient moment, David Mountford raised his hand, 'Sir..'

'Sims,' he correct him.

'Sims, why aren't you going to use agents with more experience than us?'

Considering how best to answer, Sims studied Mountford for some time. The young sub-lieutenant looked uncomfortable under his gaze. He said, 'Well, that was straight to the point, you don't mess about, I like that.'

Mountford looked relieved. 'The direct approach... and a good question too. Now to answer, let's touch on something political. If you don't already know it, you'll soon discover there are allegiances and factions within NID and the other intelligence services, and that these factions have networks that extend and infiltrate into areas far beyond their original scope for national security... they grasp the slimy hand of political ambition and reach into God knows where else... these politics are possibly darker politics than you might imagine. With Anne and myself, you are going to be involved with two jobs, both different in nature but related... it would not be wise for us to work with someone who has an established affiliation to one of these factions. In the future, as you become known, it is likely someone will try and recruit you into their fold... be very careful, they might sound very plausible... always beware of plausible sounding politicians. Remember, they lie for a living.'

Anne sat quietly listening to Sims. Just a very small part of her regretted referring to him as having a barrow-boy's instinct. To him she wouldn't admit regret, but she would make it up to him later.

'Can you tell us anything at all?' asked Dusty, whose mouth constantly engaged in eating had rendered him incapable of decent mannered conversation - his appetite every bit matching that of Sims'.

Worried that Dusty might clear the table, he looked to Anne to take over.

'Your first role will be one of surveillance. I have not been involved myself, however, those who have say it can be extremely boring. As boring as it may be, it can throw up gems. I understand your training has covered this subject thoroughly?' she asked.

The two men nodded.

'Everything you do while you are with Sims and myself will prepare you for working together as a team on your own... you must learn to trust each other... implicitly. Now, the group you are going to watch may be innocent or not... that is why we're watching them. They were connected at sometime or other with a group of known double agents... Sims has a more accurate term, he prefers to call them double traitors. The full brief on this task will be given at a later date. The second task is more complicated. You will be briefed on that when the time is right.'

'Do we carry side arms?' asked Dusty.

'Always, and always made ready,' she said, glancing at Sims. 'Events happen in an unpredictable way.'

He put down his fork, 'Take note of what Anne has just said, "events happen in an unpredictable way", and they do. Once, there was a shooting incident, if Anne had not been ready and made ready, I would be dead. As I just said, take note.'

Mountford looked at Anne. So, she's killed someone, he thought.

Later that afternoon driving back to Netley, Dusty said, 'I wonder what that incident was all about... I think Anne is tougher than she looks... I'm going to enjoy this.'

'I had wondered what his wife would be like... couldn't imagine him being married to a wet.'

'I reckon she killed the other party in that incident.'

'Exactly so. I wonder who it was.'

'Good practice to find out,' said Dusty.

'Exactly so.'

Mountford parked in his slot next to the NIDii Unit 3. training block. He put his hand out to Dusty, 'I guess we're partners,' he said.

Dusty shook his hand and said, 'Looks like it, and as I'm the better shot, it's only right I should be protecting your back.'

'Where did you get this idea you're a better shot?'

'The evidence in front of us. I just looked at the targets. It was obvious, sir.'

'We'll see about that.'

Dusty threw his arms wide, stretched and looked into the sky, 'What a job, a commander with an essence wife; an admiral who calls us "lads"; and a pie with pastry to dream of... taste of things to come I hope.'

'Maybe... I don't see how they can possibly get any better... God, that Anne is gorgeous. You know, when I first saw Sims, I vowed I'd be as good a shot as he was... my list of ambitions has just been updated to include a wife like his.'

*

He called them into the dining room, their half hour meeting with him was due. It would probably extend to an hour, that's the way it had become.

'Social events, and that one in particular, are a complete bore and waste of time,' said Bob Sherwood. 'We would have been better served out on The Solent with *Alice Alacrity...* and, probably achieved a lot more. Too much waffle and not enough work,' he ranted.

'Fancy a beer, Dad?' said Sims.

Anne smiled. Damage control in progress, leadership

shown, situation in hand, she thought.

'Yes, Son... what a good idea.'

Sims poured him one, 'Fancy a chaser?'

'Why not?'

Sims handed him a rum.

'This is all highly illegal, do you mind telling me just where you get this Pusser's from?'

'Sorry... classified information... need to know basis only... and unfortunately, you're not in the loop. Perhaps it's best you sit back and enjoy it.'

Rear Admiral Bob Sherwood did just that, he leaned back in his chair and waited for the Pusser's glow to hit home. 'That is indeed better,' he said. 'Now to business. Previously, I had said we will probably use HMS *Odin*... I can now confirm that this will definitely be so. We will be accompanied by HMS *Ocelot*. Should we be contacted by the Soviet Navy and they show aggression, *Ocelot* will act as a decoy.' He took another pull at his beer. 'There are many tactics we can employ to escape detection. For example, if we are required to go to busy Soviet waters, let us say, deep into the Gulf of Finland, it would need us to pass close to the Soviet Navy's submarine training base at Paldiski. It's now operational, though still under construction. To pass unnoticed we would employ a technique called "under-hulling"...'

This was a term Sims was not familiar with, 'Under-hulling, okay, what precisely is that?'

'Hitching a lift under a merchantman or even under a Soviet sub... I've done that before.'

Anne, listening to this action she would be excluded from, and smarting from not being part of the sub pick-up team, was not going to let this pass. She jumped in. She knew something Sims did not. 'I remember hearing Dad and someone else discussing this,' she said, glaring at him with a "didn't know I was listening, did you?" look on her face. 'Do you know, Sims... *Oh* how silly of me, of course you don't, it was classified. Well, they sneak up underneath ships and follow them just a few feet below their keels. They take photos and film of propeller design and other things. *Oberon* class subs are very quiet.'

'You were not supposed to be listening, my girl,' said Bob Sherwood, wondering what other operational secrets Anne had been party to during her upbringing.

'Well, I was. And very interesting it was too.'

'Hrumph... at least you won't look blank when this term is used in company.'

'Sounds edge of the seat stuff,' said Sims, stifling a grin.

'Yes, yes indeed. Trust me, it is. All my Baltic skippers have to be top notch under-hullers. It's imperative we get around undetected.'

They were not going to get off lightly. 'As I was telling the woman in the paper shop' - she hadn't, 'they also hide under layers of water with different temperatures, and the Baltic's salinity can vary dramatically... they use that to hide under as well,' Anne condescendingly explained, while her father exasperatedly looked on.

'What else did you listen in to?'

'Oh, lots... did you know, Sims, they also call under-hulling "underwater looks" and during these little surveillance exercises they get as close as six feet to the other ship's hull... apparently very dangerous in a good swell... that piece went down really well with the darts team in the pub.'

Smiling, Sims sat with his chin resting in his hand; this woman just gets better and better, he thought.

'Despite the submarine training base at Paldiski, Dad will still probably prefer the Gulf of Finland to a pick-up further south... just below Riga there's a huge Soviet base at Liepaja... he'll want to avoid that,' she said, knowingly. 'He almost got trapped there once. Didn't you, Father?'

Admiral Robert Sherwood mirrored Sims' pose, and with his elbow on the table rested his chin in his hand, 'You are so much like your mother... perhaps you'd like to run the entire operation? *She* would have done.'

'I'd love to... but you won't let me on board a sub, will you, Daddy darling?' she said, frowning at him.

Better and better, Sims thought again.

'If I can take back some measure of control of this conversation...' He looked at Sims, '...one does have to be careful under-hulling... it doesn't do one's career any good hitting the vessel you're tagging.'

Anne stood up. 'Now I've brought you both up-to-date on sub warfare tactics, shall I do something more fitting for a woman and go and see how supper is progressing?' she said, frowning and stalking out of the study.

'I wondered how it would manifest itself,' Sims said.

After another pull at his glass. 'What?'

'Well, she was never going to let her exclusion from our underwater mystery tour pass without some sort of retaliation, was she?'

They sat quietly for a few minutes while Sims helped

himself to a beer and Bob Sherwood took a pull at his and then a swig of rum.

'Sims, Son?'

'Hmm.'

'Now you're married to her, how do you find her?'

'Perfect. I wouldn't change a single thing about her... except perhaps her occasional clouts. If she catches you just right, they can really make your eyes water.'

'You have no idea how much like her mother she is... thumps and all.'

'You were never tempted to marry again?'

'You Sims,' he said, sadly, 'are probably the only person apart from Jean to understand why that is so... some things are simply not repeatable.'

*

He had always feared flying. Perhaps it was the unnecessarily grisly detail carried in every part of the press that sapped his confidence... *poor visibility... downdraught... extreme turbulence... hit mountainside... bad weather... wreckage sighted... swathe cut through forest... no survivors.* Soviet aircraft it can be assumed, if one went by the facts as reported by Pravda, never fall out of the sky. However, Radleigh's trust in Soviet airlines and Soviet built aircraft did not bear public or official scrutiny - he was dedicated to avoiding both whenever possible. His fear of vertical plunging was not eased using American aircraft and only somewhat mollified using British.

The British Civil Aviation Authority airworthiness notices and directives are issued for every incident or fault found in British Aircraft. The Americans issue fewer directives. Not that there were fewer faults: the yanks were simply less forthcoming. So, statistically their aircraft were safer; not actually, just statistically. Radleigh had been assured this was true. He was no engineer, it was knowledge gained elsewhere. A diplomatic mission he had been sent to smooth over: a hiccup with the French. Hiccups with the French are best overcome not by drinking water from the wrong side of a tumbler but by drinking wine at the dining table and by best employing diplomats that speak impeccable French - there is then no claiming at a later date that the conversation had been misunderstood. Antoine Leclerc, senior fonctionnaire in the French Ministry of Transport explained all in detail. None of Leclerc's arm waving explanation allayed Radleigh's horror of the banging and rattling moment before take off, the thud of undercarriage burying itself into the fuselage, and every small atmospheric bump while airborne. A colleague had tried to convince him these inconsequential turbulent bumps were no more damaging to the aircraft than was road unevenness to a car. He had said, 'But, my dear, roads can have deep potholes that wreck one's suspension. I fail to be convinced. And,' he added, 'if an engine fails one can pull over to one side.' Statistics that showed one was more likely to perish from eating truffle pâté failed to convince him.

There was no direct flight from Ukraine to Riga. First, it was to be an eight hundred mile long haul to Moscow. This would have remained a tedious flight if it had not been uncomfortable, served indescribably poor food - the sparsity of which some judged beneficial, and suffered from frisky to moderate turbulence over Kursk. Little relief waited for him in Moscow; he did not get to leave the airfield precincts. Radleigh quickly escorted to a military transport aircraft: noisy, comfort hellish, food unpalatable, more bouncing, teeth rattling turbulence over Pskov. Termination of his journey and relief from the hazards of aviation were the sole benefit he felt from his arrival in Riga, Latvia.

He had spent much time there. He knew his destination well. In one respect, Latvia was little different from other countries and Riga was little different from other cities: money the common denominator. Cash is the true universal language. Without even trying, it achieved all that Esperanto did not. Cash is multilingual. It goes therefore, money talks all the time and everywhere, an incessant finger thumb rubbing babble, Riga no exception.

Liquidity proved only a marginal advantage here in tatty Latvia, scarcity headed the daily menu, rarely plenty and, then, what was available often not worth buying. Radleigh, a king in Parisian café society missed the comfortable, luxurious culture. Idealism, it seemed, was a subject best theorised about in the pampered bosom of a Cambridge university - and left there. He later claimed he had dropped communist ideology shortly after joining the diplomatic service but was in too deep to turn back.

A bright chilly Monday morning. Thick ice in the harbour cracked into ragged plates by early water traffic: at long last Gerald Radleigh had been called to the old Commissariat buildings in Riga. 'And about time too,' he muttered to himself while shaving. He should have known better and kept quiet: his maid was listening - she was without doubt NKVD planted, and speaking out loud had caused him to make a small cut on his chin. He blamed his equipment, 'God, Russian razors are quite pathetic... can it really be so difficult to make a blade with a decent edge?' The expected gloss that would come from living in the Soviet Union had disappeared: he had admitted its absence during the first few weeks of his defection. Radleigh's ego had been spiked: he was not treated as a celebrity. Following this personal affront by the state, disillusionment with his new life set in rapidly: the honeymoon period that had never left the church was over.

Fur flaps of his ushanka pulled down over his ears, collar turned up, breath, freezing, smoking gouts, he strolled to his meeting with the new boss of the Riga Commissariat in Peschanaya Ulitsa - Latvians still called it by the name they had always done: Smilšu Iela. The languages different, the same meaning preserved: Sand Street. Walk slowly he reminded himself. Twin bouts of pneumonia as a child at his prep school had damaged his lungs and heart and left him weakened - it was painful to breathe deeply. He found it almost a contradiction that he should feel more energetic in the cold weather - there is more oxygen in a lung full of cold air he had been told by a Swiss doctor. So, although feeling like a brisk walk, he ambled carefully.

Direktor Nikolai Zima, a model of diplomatic correctness, asked to be excused for the delays in getting down to business, 'Let me apologise, these buildings are but a temporary home for us until the official offices are refurbished... a new boss must sweep clean; they must make their mark,' he said. 'And, sadly, Anisim, this may affect our progress... it may mean it could be some time before we can proceed. There is much to be done. The previous direktor was not a busy man... you knew him I think?'

Radleigh ignored the question, treated it as if it were a statement. And, he was not sure he liked being called by his first name by this man... he's too polite, too friendly, he thought. He asked, 'My dear Direktor, proceed what?'

Zima in his turn ignored this question, 'Matters of state must come first... but, of course, you understand that, don't you, Anisim? You have been loyal to the USSR all your adult life... of course you would understand that.'

'How long am I going to be here?'

'I cannot say for sure... but, some time. We will have important work to do.'

'And what type of work exactly am I to do? I really do think an explanation is called for. Surely, I deserve *that* common decency.'

'Let us leave that to discuss until a later date, Anisim,' Zima smoothed.

'In the meantime, I take it I'm allowed my normal privileges, to travel to Zurich for instance... my bank is there.'

Moscow felt confident that Radleigh was unlikely to trespass anywhere the British Intelligence Agencies could easily get their hands on him - MI6 would be wary of creating diplomatic havoc in Switzerland. Zima knew this. But, Zima would need Radleigh's full cooperation in the future and today's exercise was to begin the process of dominating and controlling him. Curtailing his liberty would make him, Zima, master, 'Of course... of course. Just come and see me first for your travel documents.' Compliance with a barbed sting.

'Why so? That is not normally necessary. I have a Russian passport and been assigned full diplomatic freedom. I have always been allowed to travel more-or-less freely.'

'I think that is exactly the point, Anisim, more-or-less freely,' said Zima, smiling less warmly. 'Now, for the moment, it is just, less. Yes.. yes, let us say, less.' Zima looked at his watch and stood up. 'Excuse me for one second, Anisim... I have a little other annoying business to deal with.' He left the office door slightly ajar.

Radleigh shifted his chair and felt the cut on his chin. He thought, he has made his point clear, I am just another piece of annoying business. Zima shouted down the telephone for a good three minutes. There was no one at the end of the line; he was play-acting, a pantomime of his authority and strength. He returned looking angry; more acting, 'We shall have to call this meeting to a halt.' He opened a drawer took out a sheaf of papers and leafed through them. 'You must be patient, Riga is full of incompetents, they sap my time, energy and patience... in the meantime, until we start, enjoy your wait, there is plenty to do in Riga.'

Is there really? This is news to me... you don't know Riga very well then, do you? Radleigh thought.

Zima gripping Radleigh's elbow escorted him out of the office, he halted, he said, 'On a different matter, Anisim... a word of warning, I advise that you avoid overt displays of affection towards those of your own sex.' Zima let go of his elbow as if concerned Radleigh might be enjoying his proximity. 'I have received a report regarding the disturbing death of your young friend, Mika Kozlov... it does not make good reading... it is as disturbing as the young man's death. You must not do the same thing and put yourself in danger here in Riga, Anisim. Do not go down this road, or you will find your-self without friends, and while you are working with me you will need them.'

Zima knew all about Mika's murder days before he received the report - it would have been surprising if he had been in the least bit shocked. Nikolai Zima had himself organised it. A short phone call to the Black Sea and his Ukrainian mafia contacts was all that was necessary: Mika's empty veined demise merely work in progress.

Though neither officially condoned nor tolerated, homosexuality and pederasty were universally used by the Soviet secret services as persuaders: the blackmail-er's weapon of choice with foreign diplomats. Mika's removal would be documented as a simple assassination of a goluboi: the murder of an homosexual would cause few waves: boats would not rock. Golubie were expend-able. The deed might, however, help persuade Anisim Polzin to accept and make a rapid and safe departure from danger. Nikolai Zima knew of the former drug trade through Riga to Britain and wanted to re-establish it. There was big money at stake. With it, good living and maybe a splendid dacha built, not a peasant one, but one with a steep roof in the woods by a lake. Take in enough money and he might live in a fashionable apartment on the Black Sea too. He needed Radleigh's knowledge of the trade route.

Radleigh quickly bored with the practically nonexistent night life in Riga - military choirs and cossack dancing have their limitations as nightly entertainment. Once in a lifetime is enough, he thought. His daily constitutional began to take in krogs, cafes and restaurants with little variety of food to offer. It was still icy cold, and even in summer one can easily tire of herring and beetroot salad: Siļķe Kažoka. He sought music and once, just the once, he trudged round Richard Wagner's old residence. Eventually, the proverb; "Old habits die hard", came true. He did not heed Zima's advice - some nights he did not return until late.

The waterfront and docklands became his evening haunts. Riga's suburbs dense with sprawls of military bases, it's seedier quarters near the docks heavy with army patrols. Despite this, muggings of the few Soviet military personnel seeking relief were common. Most kept clear of the area. Those unseen shadowy people following Radleigh were not muggers nor were they agents. The route to his favourite haunts mapped and covered by an ever changing network of part-time sleuths. The Forest Brothers had been tagging him since he had been first spotted in town - smouldering memories of past atrocities.

Dāvis Lūž's aunt, Krista Bērzs coordinated the operation and planned Radleigh's kidnapping. She would have preferred to have killed him herself - with her bare hands... but this would cause problems for her people. It would be better to hand him over to the English commander and his wife, they would know what to do with him. They thought like The Forest Brothers.

***

Chapter Five.
Interrogation.

'Come in and see my new arrangement. Sewell, in a shifted allusion to a public house, calls this room my *Smug.*' The long wall hung with paintings: not prints, originals. Spacing perfect, no one interfering with the other; balance and perspective. To do both, a contradiction. Art discreetly dominating the room and furniture threatening little conflict to the display. In this room, smoking prohibited.

The bell sounded. Blunt and the banker finished their dealings. Rate fixed, funds would be loaned for the purchase for the work of a relatively obscure Italian painter. Surveyor of the Queen's Pictures smiled; this purchase was for his own collection. It is a curious but nevertheless interesting piece of trivia, that Blunt, albeit expert and lecturer on the works of Nicolas Poussin had missed a trick. A small framed painting relegated to a place on an adjacent wall - not worthy of the main display, had kept its secret. Catalogued as a Poussin, he, like many others, had considered it too inferior to be so, and bought it first and foremost out of curiosity and secondly because it failed to reach a high price. It was the most valuable in his collection; indeed, it was in fact a genuine Poussin. So, there we have it, the Surveyor of the Queen's Pictures had not recognised it for what it was. Blunt's curiosity a better judge than his obsession with perfection and the painter.

They stood up and shook hands; the deal was closed. 'We'll use the smoking room.' Blunt said.

'What does Sewell call that?'

'The public bar. He says I ought to hang a dartboard.'

The banker did not stay. He excused himself and left. As he went out of the door, he turned, 'Good luck with the "locals",' he said.

Blunt smiled, 'They're useful.'

'Aren't we all?'

'Ahh, but you are very special, you own the world.'

'My family maybe... not me.'

Talking noisily, Peter Scammel, young Brian Sewell and Laurence Heston, entered together. Moments later the bell rang again and in came Jack Passant.

Heston cut a direct path to the drinks cabinet, 'I have word that Radleigh's back in Riga,' he said. There was kudos to be had by throwing the odd bit of diplomatic news into the ring - news he was sure nobody else in the gathering was aware of.

'Why would he want to go there?... always complained bitterly,' Sewell airily questioned.

Thinning Brylcreemed grey hair; receding forehead, veined face and large nose; stooped., Passant, a frequent sufferer from phlebitis, spoke: 'He didn't *want*, he was sent,' he said, acidly.

'Very well, let me rephrase; why was he sent there? I understood he was quite settled on the Black Sea coast...

Ukraine, wasn't it? You said so, didn't you Heston?'

Rather than reply Heston drained his glass and poured himself another. He was annoyed his "exclusive" had been spiked.

Sewell pursued, 'And, how do you know he was sent, Jack? For what purpose?'

Passant responded curtly, 'I don't *know* he was sent, I made an assumption. I am guessing that nobody in their right mind would choose to go to Riga at this time of the year.'

Fresh opportunity: Laurence Heston made a grab for the topic helm, 'I suspect someone is trying to establish old links. Radleigh knew the route and kept much of it to himself and the others of Les Grands Amis. Knowledge is power, wealth and, I suppose, sometimes insurance.'

'My dear, Radleigh is an educated fool,' Sewell heavily aspirated the 'f' and flicked a hint of a 'w' ahead of the 'l'. The effect, one of exasperation with the world and the idiots populating it. 'Radleigh moved in the best of circles, had all the appearance of intellect though possessing little. How little, proven... proven by his determination to defect; a foolish measure, one that predestines his certain disaster.'

Sewell's old tutor, Sir Anthony Blunt, gaunt, broad upper lip, horse faced, predatory, had watched the way the evening's business was heading. 'He was always rash; there was little need to jump,' he said.

Laurence Heston matched Sewell's exasperation, 'All this character assassination is irrelevant. What *is* of concern is the question of him possibly stirring puddles just as the mud is settling nicely.'

Passant spoke, 'That is precisely the point. We know

who he's chanced upon at his Black Sea nest and we know about his dealings in Berne and Zurich. He's now in possession of information ring-fenced by our Cabinet's cordon sanitaire on MI6 funds and in addition he has knowledge of that protected by the fifty year rule on Crabb.'

'Mother's little helper... our shopkeeper frogman,' Sewell said, looking sniffishly at Anthony Blunt for enlightenment about MI6 Swiss deposited money.

Blunt was not forthcoming.

'I do not see why his removal to Riga should cause reverberations here,' said Scammel.

Heston looked doubtful, 'It may not, but when there's a change in the air, it always pays to carry an umbrella.'

'In my opinion, it amounts to no more than a relocation... possibly temporary,' Scammel bit. Like Heston, he seemed forever in need of a drink.

'Not so... he's been given a flat and a maid; he'll be there some time.' Heston turned to Blunt, 'Anthony, you said Radleigh had little need to jump. Perhaps he realises that now,' he said.

'I do indeed think and hope so.'

A successive stream of drinks eased discretion, Heston laughed, 'Interesting times if the old route is opened up. Aston-Heyford and Throagh out of it now, he'll need people at this end... who's it going to be?... any volunteers? Anyone short of cash?'

'Not you, Heston,' cackled Scammel. 'My Lord, aren't we grand, a place on the Beaulieu River... called *Gins* isn't it, Laurence? Most appropriate.'

'That happens to be its historic naming... not my choice,' replied Heston.

'Still, most appropriate wouldn't you agree? And then, there's the luxury launch hitched up to a private jetty. Convenient for Sherwood-Reeves' old partner's boat yard... what was his name? Fox-Eastleigh, that's it, used to be in our line of business. You might get a discount. But, I digress. Gentlemen, Laurence Heston is a rich man. And, tonight, he's going to tell us how he made his money. Isn't that so, Laurence? Oh God, forgive me,' he then said, with mock anguish, 'you're not running short are you? Is that why you brought the subject up?' Scammel cackled his irritating laugh once more.

Heston poured himself another drink and ignored the question.

A brief icy statement: 'Everything will be fine as long as he doesn't return to England,' said Passant.

'If that happens there's going to be much trouble, he could never keep his mouth shut,' Scammel said.

'Don't worry, if he returns, the naval gang that rid us of Aston-Heyford and Through will want to see to him... collect the full set,' said Heston.

The meeting broke up. Brian Sewell called no one; political gossip bored him. He remained behind with his old tutor - the sole reason he had been invited.

At their respective homes, Jack Passant phoned Nicholas Rede Elliot. Both Heston and Peter Scammel phoned James Ross, he then called Charles Greave. Charles Greave immediately called St. John Le Fanu and William Creasey. Minutes of the meeting not taken; put to memory and quickly disseminated.

*

He, the lecturer, now the lectured: the subject: inter-rogation, never one to beckon his interest, now begged study. Radleigh *would* be taken, and if he was to deliver his secrets: under one of these methods he would surely give way.

Lieutenant-Commander Woodruff, Senior Instructor Unit 4 NIDii, lectured with the insistence of a dentist's drill. His voice, metal against enamel, finger nails scrap-ing blackboard. 'There is nothing mysterious about interrogation. It consists of no more than obtaining needed information through responses to questions.' He consulted his notes, 'We no longer use the Judas Chair, the Rack, the Brazen Bull or indeed the Chinese Iron Maiden. In today's civilised world, sound interrogation rests upon a knowledge of subject matter and on certain broad principles. These are chiefly psychological and are not hard to understand. The purpose of this course is not to teach you how to become a good interrogator but rather teach you what you must learn in order to become a good interrogator.' Those notes again. His finger running along a line and making a pencilled initial in the margin. 'The interrogation of a resistant source...'

What the fuck does he mean by source? Sims thought. It became clear.

'... who is staff or agent member of an orbit intelli-gence or security service or of a clandestine communist organisation is one of the most exacting of professional tasks. The odds favour the interrogator, though, those odds can be significantly reduced by the training, expe-rience, patience and toughness of the interrogatee. In such circumstances the interrogator needs all the assist-ance he can muster. If we can bring pertinent, modern knowledge to aid us, we enjoy a huge advantage over a service which conducts its clandestine business in an eighteenth century mode.' He sipped carefully from a glass. His every move one of precision. Woodruff studied his notes: he made an alteration and its apostil. His audience did not exist. He looked up. His audience came into focus, 'Psychologists have conducted inquiries into many subjects closely related to interrogation: the effects of debility and isolation, the polygraph, reactions to pain and fear, hypnosis and heightened suggestibility, narcosis, et cetera, et cetera, et cetera.' For emphasis of this last clause, he chose the legitimate option of separating etcetera's components.

And so Lieutenant-Commander Woodruff continued: 'Moral considerations aside, the imposition of these interrogation techniques for manipulating people, carries with it the grave risk of later lawsuits or adverse publicity.'

Moral considerations aside... that's them neatly shoved under the carpet, thought Sims.

'Interrogations techniques will be discussed in order of increasing severity as the focus on the source resistance also increases. It is vital that these lectures and the coercive techniques discussed should not be miscontrued as constituting authorisation for their use.'

Sims almost choked: In other words, lads. This is your job, and this is how you do it, but, the responsibility for doing so is firmly in your lap. Neatly done... problem dumped.

'All coercive techniques are designed to induce regression. The result of external pressures of sufficient intensity means the loss of those defences most recently acquired by civilised man. Degrees of homeostatic derangement, fatigue, pain, sleep loss or anxiety may impair these functions...'

He uses terms coercion techniques and civilised in the same breath and sentence. Sims wondered how Woodruff would respond to his own methods... probably enjoy them he concluded.

'... As a result, most people who are exposed to coercive procedures *will* talk and *will* reveal some information they might not have revealed otherwise. The response to coercion contains at least three important elements: *The Three D's* - debility, dependency and dread. Remember, gentlemen, the last of the three: *dread*.' Woodruff placed weight on the word and repeated it, 'Dread... you should all understand that fear of pain is a greater weapon than pain itself.'

It had been a crash course. He was glad to be through with it. They had studied application of duress and the relief granted its subject when lifted. How to intensify the subject's desire to cease struggling. They had learned how arrest, detention, deprivation of sensory stimuli through solitary confinement or similar methods, threats and fear, debility and pain all eventually would destroy resistance. All of them *civilised* coercion techniques.

Sims had despised their language couched in terms of reason and reasonableness. The ordinariness; matter of factness; everyday occurrence of that pushed by Woodruff appalled him. The source: not source, the person, he had thought, and what if he's innocent? By the time they find he is, his mind's destroyed and trust in the goodness in humanity possibly lost for eternity. He did not enjoy that which he had listened to. The advice, guiding them with concerned voice against coercive overuse sickened him. Sims sought to justify his possible future actions by concluding he knew his victim and the guilt he carried. *They*, the frequent manhandlers, destroyers of intellect, knew not their victims: guilt was assumed by incarceration. But, they were neither judges nor jury. These, *The Employees*, were unconcerned excavators of the mind. Every day stuff for the security services and now I'm one of them.

He despised them, and yet part of him became one.

***

Chapter Six.
Alistair Duncan

Message and biscuit held in her left hand, cup in her right, Anne sat looking at the paper in front of her.

```
Message to: Commander Sherwood-Reeves.
        Sims, these are the names of those who
        left the Defence Committee meeting with
        Lord Aston-Heyford:
        St. John Le Fanu.
        William Creasey.
        Laurence Heston.
        Charles Greave.
        and these are three associates:
        Peter Scammel.
        James Ross.
        Jack Passant.
From: Vice-Admiral Jessop.
```

'There are only three names other than those who left with Aston-Heyford after the meeting. Why only three? Aston-Heyford must have had many more contacts than three. Why did Billy only include them? Why bother with them at all?' she asked.

'Because of Gerald Radleigh... you know as well as I do he's always been interested in him as well... he wants the full set.'

'Did he tell you that?' she asked, taking a bite.

'Indirectly, yes. We got Throagh and then Aston-Heyford. That only left Radleigh. You were there when he said getting at him in France made it difficult.'

She dabbed a few crumbs from her lips. 'He also said he wanted the truth about Buster more than he wanted Radleigh.' She stared at the message as if new words would write themselves large.

'You can look at that as long as you like... that's all there is, unless he's written something on it in lemon juice... got a candle?'

Her eyes flashed dangerously, 'Watch your step, Commander.'

Looking at Anne, Sims sat with his elbows on the *Bellerophon* table, his chin cupped in his hands. Observing, just looking at her: a favourite pass-time. God, how did I get so lucky? he thought. He said, 'He may not have mentioned Radleigh by name, that doesn't mean he's not interested in him. What it means is Billy's done some filtering. He knows Radleigh may be his only chance of ever getting the truth, and I'll bet you those three extra names are more to do with Radleigh than Aston-Heyford.'

Eyes flashing, no longer dangerous, she smiled, she well knew his reason for watching her. It wouldn't be long before he made his move. 'A bet eh?' she said. You're probably right, but, I'll go for it. What stakes?'

'I'll think of something... against... whatever.'

'Do I get time to think?'

'Take your time... makes no difference, it's in the bag. By the way, he didn't specify who the three were associates of... he just says three associates.'

There was only so much of this he could take. He

walked round to her side of the table, took hold of her hands and gently made her stand up, 'You're absolutely bleedin' gorgeous, you know.' He leaned forward.

'God!...' she said, softly, 'they always... always... get me, Sims... come on, where *did* you learn to kiss like that?'

'I'm just a natural, and I spent many a night practising on a chief stoker... he reckoned I was pretty good too.'

'Do I come up to scratch? Am I as good as him?'

'Hmmm, well... nearly... not quite... plenty of room for improvement.'

Anne clubbed him and then dived in for practice.

*

Deep in thought over his notes, something scrabbled into his inner consciousness and nudged. As soon as the car had turned into the drive, the engine note had been registered somewhere deep. The inner male, now alert, considered it worth rousing him, 'That sounds interesting,' he said, getting up and looking out of the library window and then quickly making his way to the door. 'Christ! Anne, he's only got himself a Jaguar XK120,' he hissed on passing her.

She looked up from her work, 'Jaguar make vans now, do they?'

It was wasted on him, he was already waiting on the bottom step, 'British Racing Green... my favourite colour... oh bloody hell, simply gorgeous.'

Mid-sixties, impeccably dressed, Alistair Duncan, with just a small amount of effort, eased himself out of the driver's seat, 'Young man's car... you must be Commander Sherwood-Reeves,' he said, his accent as immaculate as his dress.

'Yes.' They shook hands. 'This is more than beautiful. If it gets too much for you to handle we can do a deal.' he said, taking in every detail of the machine in front of him, gently running his hand along one of the wings.

Anne appeared on the top step, 'Perhaps we'd better go inside. That way we might get some of his attention. Don't be surprised if the conversation frequently drifts back to the car.'

'I say, isn't this Billy's table?... prize piece, how on earth did you get it? Must be worth a bob or two.'

'It just turned up one day... debt repayment in kind.'

Alistair Duncan sat down and then, as if to get his bearings, got up again and went and peered out of the window. 'Yes, of course, yes; there's The Solent and there's The Isle of Wight.' Satisfied southern English geography hadn't rearranged itself since leaving his car, he sat down again.

'Billy tells me you've a job for me. Commander, to tell the truth, I'm bored... retirement doesn't sit well... what can I do for you?'

The phone rang, Anne left the room to answer it. Duncan leaned over the table towards Sims and whispered, 'My wife was spiffing too, you know.'

Bereavement: a difficult subject to deal with, discomfit set in. Sims never good at handling it. 'She's... ...I take it she's no longer with us?'

'Yes... yes. Very much with us, just no longer spiffing. Magnificent would be more accurate. She's a year older than me: that puts her in charge you understand.'

'Are you sure that makes a difference? Anne's younger

than me... still in charge though.'

'You know, I've always put it down to her being older.' The wraps now lifted from his eyes; his vision clearer, he looked unsettled and got up to check The Isle of Wight was still roughly where it ought to be.

'Listen, I'm a commander in the British Royal Navy, she's a pregnant housewife... still in charge though. Her being a NID agent and an ace shot with a Beretta has an influence as well of course.'

'Yes, I can see that. In my case, I think I could have made Air Vice-Marshal and carried a machine gun... it wouldn't have made a blind spot of difference.'

'Rank and weaponry have nothing to do with it... Billy didn't say you were ex-Royal Air Force.'

'Pilot... Squadron Leader... damn good fun... mainly fly gliders now up at Lasham.'

'My old CO used to fly there... Lieutenant-Commander Maitland. Perhaps you met?'

'Simon... such a nice fellow... very upsetting... yes, very upsetting. Made the wife cry.'

This came from the heart, that much was plain. Sims warmed to Alistair Duncan. 'It's a small world,' he said.

'No, not really.' Duncan considered his words, 'When you think of it, the two of us in intelligence and were flying pals at Lasham. No, it's a very large world that often has quite small and connected populations in its odder corners, Commander.'

Anne returned, the caller not mentioned.

'Perhaps it shouldn't be me to bring the subject up, but has he talked you out of your car yet, Alistair?'

'Not yet.' he smiled, rubbing his hands together,

'Come on, come on... I'm impatient, shall we talk business? Can't stay long... I put the odd day in instructing at Lasham... students this afternoon... good flying day... thermals galore.'

Sims got straight to the point, 'How would you like to impersonate someone?'

'Tell me more.' Duncan looked keen.

'If you take the job, you are to double for the defector Gerald Radleigh... we get you to Denmark, you will then fly from Copenhagen to Zurich under the name Anisim Polzin... Radleigh's Russian name. You will book into a hotel not frequently used by Polzin for a couple or few days depending on flight availability. Whatever, certainly long enough to get seen, but, not by anyone who knows Radleigh well. From Zurich you fly to Heathrow as Gerald Radleigh using a passport under that name. Our people will be waiting and will take you, under wraps, to NIDii Unit 4 at Netley. You will remain there until we bring Radleigh in to replace you. That's it in a nutshell... interested?'

'Yes of course. Radleigh, has he a good tailor? Saville Row, perhaps?'

They both blanked.

'Tailor?' Anne queried.

'One has to look authentic. Opportunity to re-stock the wardrobe too good to miss... Billy's always generous with expenses... good for a bob or two... some good hotels in Zurich too.'

'You know the place?'

'Stationed there for five years.'

'Is that so?' said Sims. Handy guy to know, he thought. 'I know someone who'll know his tailor. I'll get back to you on that one. So, you are interested?'

'Of course... I told you, I'm bored. I'll talk to Billy and get myself ready.'

'We'll need you for a passport photo-shoot at Netley.'

'Name the day and I'll be there.'

Watching Duncan drive off, he slipped his arm round Anne's waist, 'One day I'm going to get me one of those.'

'Hmm. What do you think, Sims?'

'It'll have to be racing green... black soft-top. They've got a 3.4 litre, double overhead cam engine: unbeatable.'

'I meant Alistair, darling. Do you think he's a convincing pass for Radleigh?'

'So, back to the boring stuff.' Sims shrugged. 'Given I've only seen him through binoc's and on the snaps you took with the Photosniper, I'd say he's a dead ringer.'

She punched him, 'I do not take snaps, Sims Sherwood-Reeves.'

He ignored the thump, 'How about you?'

'Old school... Billy and Miles trust him... has been stationed in Zurich. Man of the world... sounds ideal, I think he's very good.'

'He thinks you're spiffing, by the way.'

'I *am*, and, for your information, I take photographs.'

'I know... good ones too.' XK120 now long gone, dust drifting and settling over the lawn, he continued to look down the drive.

'I've never seen you so smitten with a car before.'

'Wasn't thinking about the Jag.'

Already forgiven him for his snaps comment, she took his hand and squeezed it, 'Tell me.'

'If we get Radleigh back, we'll extract his Swiss bank account details from him. We could send in Duncan and see if we can't get the bad, black money transferred back to the UK.'

Despite her determined: her adamant resolution; regret crept in, 'I'm sorry, I should never have inferred you were a barrow-boy. Come inside, Darling... I'll take your mind off the Jag.'

'Yippee, bacon sarnie time,' he said, punching the air.

Anne belted him, pushed him through the front door and turned the key in the lock.

Jean was away visiting her sister in the village. Anne came downstairs and found Sims in the kitchen, 'You never asked about the call... it was Beatrise. She said the Brothers are pleased we trusted them with the money. She also said they are ready to move as soon as we give them the word.'

'Christ! All of a sudden it's hurry up time... we've got to get motoring, love.'

'How soon can we get going?' She was not going to let this trip out of her grip.

'Do you think you'll be able to manage in Korsør on your own?'

'I won't really know that until I'm there. To tell the truth I have no idea what my duties will be or how I'm going to be able to carry them out. Why do you ask?'

'I'd feel happier if you had a side-kick.'

'Anyone in mind?'

'Fiona... you'd make a deadly pair.'

'Hmm, she's very good... and communications are her speciality... good suggestion.' Anne filled the kettle and plugged it in. 'She's MI5, how do you think MI6 will take it if they find out?'

'I'll have to ask Billy first anyway... perhaps we'll give them a bit of their own medicine. They were operating outside their remit and territory over Buster. Maybe he can get her on NID's payroll. We'll need to deliver Alistair's passport photos to Mike... if Billy okays it we can ask her then.'

She frowned, she hesitated, 'I wonder what Alistair knows of those on Billy's list,' she said. 'Shall we ask him?'

'Might seem a bit over cautious... perhaps hold off for now... see how things progress... keep the list up our sleeve for a while. We don't need to start Billy's official commission yet... least said: least leaked.'

'You think he's a leaky type?'

'No, I'm just hedging.'

Tea brewed, she poured, 'Sims, we *have* already started Billy's job. I think you were right earlier, he knew you'd go for Radleigh if you got the chance. He's been nudging you in that direction all the time, *les Grands Amis:* he knew damn well you'd want to collect the whole set, too.'

'Yeah, he's a cunning old bugger... wouldn't put it past him.'

'The list of names is definitely part of it.'

Careful to be out of arm's reach, 'Took you long enough. An XK120, by the way, my spec for the bet.'

'Big stakes, Sims... *risky!*'

'Nah... sure bet... it's in the bag.'

*

83

'We are but one cog in the machinery of government. Intelligence is one, politics is another and, I suppose, history another. So, it follows that intelligence requires understanding politics, politics requires understanding history. Some will tell you intelligence is the first line of Britain's defence.' Captain Miles Stinton RN Retired, leaned back in his chair and studied Sims. Before him was a son without a father and he, a father without a son. His late son, Miles junior, and this young man their characters different in every respect except one: they both possessed courage.

Schooling Sims, he decided, was to be his raison d'être. He would educate and smooth rough edges: though never enough to obliterate his uncanny instincts. No, they must be preserved at all cost. As Anne says, he thought: *he makes things happen.*

They met regularly or, as regularly as work allowed. They met at Hell Head House, they met on *Alice Alacrity.* Occasionally, like today, at Stinton's cottage near Netley. When at Billy's, they only discussed work.

'Today, if I may, I'd like to clear up a possible misconception that Billy is in possession of. He, I believe, is correct when he states we were set-up by other British Secret Intelligence Services...' he paused, 'perhaps we should, like everyone else in the Racket, simply call them SIS.'

'Racket?' Sims queried.

'Racket; SIS; MI6; MI5; NID; the Firm; the Office or, even the Friends,' he rattled off. 'All different names for the same thing or sometimes different branches of the same thing.'

'And, Billy's misconception?' pursued Sims.

'Over the Buster affair... don't look surprised at Billy being *wrong,* it's an heretical notion I'm sure, and not a good thing to tell him, but, that's where he may be deluded.' Stinton, thinking of Sims' occasionally wayward tact and that he might be just the man to correct Billy on such a point, smiled. His mind cast back to the lad's stand-off with Billy following Anne's shooting. Nose to nose, Billy furious, Sims more so... Vice-Admiral versus ex-stoker, neither backed down. He had never seen Billy so angry. After Sims had left he seemed incapable of coherent speech for at least half an hour. His first complete and understandable sentences after coming round were, 'I'll keel-haul the stroppy bugger, Stinton, you see if I don't. I wish we'd never got rid of the *cat-o-nine-tails.* I'll strip him of his commission and reduce him in rank back to a killick stoker... *no!* lower than that; all the way back to a junior.' Calmer and a little later, he'd asked, 'What do you think?' Stinton, ever undisturbed and ready to persuade, smoothed things over. He talked to Billy quietly and sensibly until Billy Ruffian became, once again, Vice-Admiral John Jessop.

Sims said, 'He's very touchy about Buster... MI5 and MI6's involvement gives him someone to blame other than himself and NID's incompetence. He should have been on top of it.'

'Maybe, maybe... Billy asserts that MI6 were treading on MI5's territory and that *they* were both treading on NID's. Now this is the point: legally, and this may be a technicality perhaps, however, just as foreign embassies are deemed foreign soil even though they are within the three mile limit, it is possible to claim the *Ordzhonikidze* was foreign territory and therefore, the remit of MI6. A moot point I agree, but nevertheless a point. But, it might have been the point that got MI6 off the hook.'

Old lawyer Stinton: Old King Log, Sims thought. 'Did you study law?'

'Amongst other things, yes.'

'There's something else I've never got to grips with, why is Billy so against the demise of the Naval Intelligence Division? After all, they were shown wanting. If I were a top-dog in SIS, I would probably be pushing for it myself... might sound disloyal, it's more or less how I'd think with the evidence of NID's past performance in Portland in front of me.'

'Is it as simple as being down to our performance at the time? We have had many successes you know. To be sure, Billy knows we were lacking in that case. But, Sims, you must realise by now that good intelligence requires good instinct. Bureaucracy doesn't use instinct, it uses rigid principles and routine. What Billy fears most is Britain's first line of defence becoming overly bureaucratized. Your saga on The Isle of Wight is proof positive he's right - it raised many questions. You had little or no information or instruction, you worked your instincts until you were bleeding... worn to the bone - you came good, and Britain benefited. Of course some argue you were a loose cannon - which in fact to a degree, you were. And, if I may say so, still are. But, nevertheless, you were a loose cannon on our side... and that, young man, is a crucial fact which led to the raising of an important structural question: how much bureaucracy, instinct and loose cannonism do you allow? More to the point, if you agree there should a healthy smatter of each, how do you meld them successfully for Great Britain Ltd?'

'For convenience of this conversation, I'll assume that question is not a rhetorical one. So, for a kick-off, I suppose you'd avoid letting a bureaucrat rule the ship. Perhaps you need someone with a good dose of instinct, a dab hand at management and one who understands the limits of bureaucrats when the crap hits the whirly thing,' Sims replied.

Stinton smiled, 'That, I would say, just about sums it up. Though, I might add experience in matters government, espionage and diplomacy are useful too.'

'Bugger, that cuts me out... not that I'd ever want the job.'

'Not entirely... you have many of the requirements. I doubt if the eventual incumbent will be better qualified than you will be in a few years. However, I don't think it's a role you'd tolerate for long. No, you're not made for desk-life, Sims. Your job is where you are now. And anyway, your diplomacy is still a little short of the mark... better say, a long way short.'

'What about Billy? He must tick every box. He's got to be a good bet.'

'*Billy!* Good God no. You two are cast from the same mould: both fighters first. I've worked with him for years, many of them spent patching over the shipwrecks and debris he left behind him. No, not Billy, not ever. Great man in a fight, good instincts, more experience than most. It ends there, though. Billy knows his strengths. He'll do a grand job keeping the navy's interests well served.'

'So, where do we go from here? We can't just sit on our hands.'

'To some extent we do, we have to let things run their course. I don't think there is much influence we can bring to bear directly. It's possible, but long odds.'

'You'd better explain.' Sims said.

'Our cause has to be one of indirect influence. Surely you can see that you've already done this... The Isle of Wight again, lad. Anne told Billy you make things happen: and so you do. When something crops up, then you must do what you can to settle it.'

'Something like Billy's list you mean?'

'Exactly that. Chasing Billy's list could just reveal other pathways.'

'St. John Le Fanu. William Creasey, Laurence Heston, Charles Greave, and then, Peter Scammel, James Ross, Jack Passant. The first four left with Aston-Heyford at the defence meeting, as far as I know the last three are just three more on a list of names I know nothing about... perhaps this is a good time for you to tell me what you know of them.'

Captain Stinton eyed around the comfortable sitting room as if looking for an escape, 'For research of any depth you'd best talk to Shirley James MI5... she keeps tabs on many in the business.'

'You seem a little reluctant to give me a head start. Why's that?'

'Billy agrees with Anne, and so do I. Start digging for yourself. Start making things happen.'

'Perhaps I'll do that. Maybe I should kick-off with Shirley.'

*

Across the table, Fiona leaned, squinted over Shirley James' shoulder and looked at the list. She sniffed,' He's got that wrong, it wasn't a Defence Committee meeting.'

'Billy called it that,' Sims said.

'Don't care, it wasn't.' Fiona conceded a little, 'In a way I suppose it could be called that... but not a meeting of the Defence Cabinet.'

'I wasn't aware there were other types,' he said, loosely.

Shirley looked up, 'No, Fiona's correct, that one was Staff. Defence Intelligence Staff he should have called it... staff not cabinet members. And, it was an unofficial one at that... that's why there was a mix: the minister and staff. Aston-Heyford had been in the throes of reorganising the whole set-up. That's why he was in the chair.'

Fiona sat down. She added, 'Reorganising for his own ends... slime-ball.'

Shirley bit the end of her pencil, 'Some said it was necessary, but not with Aston-Heyford in charge.'

'Billy for one... what do you think, necessary or not?' Sims asked.

'Long overdue I'm afraid. We've moved from hot war to cold war. Things are changing, and it is possible we are headed to a new world of disorder. I'm not sure British Intelligence is ready for it... still run by an old-boy network. I'm afraid competence isn't a recruitment consideration... never has been.' Frowning, Shirley continued scribbling notes while talking, 'This is a very thin list, Sims.'

'I guess Billy's done some weeding out and pruning.'

'In one way or another, so have you and Anne,' said Fiona. 'First Throagh, then Aston-Heyford. Only Radleigh left and those on this list... we're going to see a few more bodies then, are we?'

'I doubt it... Billy says he wants them alive. Anyway,

for the record, I didn't touch Throagh or Aston-Heyford.'

Fiona sniggered, 'Yeah, all right then, tell us another one.' She tried to read him, 'You're happy with Billy still wanting them with a pulse when you've finished?'

'Not with Radleigh, no. He organised the guys from Riga who shot Anne...'

'Nuff said. You do know quite a few people say you hounded Aston-Heyford to his death, don't you?'

'They can think what they like. The important thing is the big ennobled shit isn't around any more. Anyhow, how do they know I had anything to do with it?'

'Billy reported Aston-Heyford's death to the minister... he had to. He also had to put your name forward as the person who reported it to him. They know you were in the cathedral at the time. It didn't need a bleedin' slide rule to put two and two together, love,' said Fiona.

Shifting, fidgeting nervously in her chair, Shirley, always uncomfortable with talk of shooting and retribution, pointed to the paper, 'Le Fanu, MI6... more diplomat than intelligence. A handy set of ears from what I can gather. Always on the move between embassies.'

'That about sums him up,' double sniffed Fiona. 'You should have added restaurants as well... that's why he's a fat git... slimy side of diplomatic, Sims... just my opinion, though I'd bet you'd want to punch him in the teeth as soon as you saw him.'

'Yes, even so, nothing ever doubtful about his dealings has come to light or even been suggested,' Shirley said.

Sims, asked, 'Can we write him off entirely? I mean,

why would he be on the list? Is he dangerous?'

'No, not in a physical way: it's not his *modus operandi*. He doesn't move in circles that need weapons training. I can only say what I said before; Winchester educated, more diplomat than intelligence.'

Sims grunted, 'Hmm, still doesn't answer why Billy included him. He didn't pick their names out of a hat.'

Shirley glanced over the table, 'He's on the list, Sims, because of closeness.'

'Christ, not that again?'

'He was very friendly with both Aston-Heyford and Radleigh... probably more so with Radleigh. In SIS, it's often there. Perhaps you ought to get used to it.'

'More so with Radleigh?'

'Very close... it was well known.'

'If I can stick my oar in,' Fiona straightened up and groaned, 'Apart from being a bender, I think he's clean... driven by a career in diplotelligencia.'

'No such word.'

'I know... sums him and a few others up though, dunnit?'

'So, you think clean eh? Well, I reckon he's on the list because he's a baddy. And, you reckon clean! Come on, money where your mouth is time, just how sure are you? Spill the beans, give us some facts.'

'Haven't got any... put it down to instinct... but I'll stake my virginity on it.'

'You're pregnant.'

'How clean's clean?'

Even Shirley laughed.

'Okay, let's move on: William Creasy?'

Fiona dived in, 'Career creep... I know him personally... MI6 and diplomat.'

'Barnacle, you reckon?'

'Yep, no doubt.'

'Close?'

'No. Another Eton arse licker though. Married... three
kids. Just a barnacle... nothing else.'

'No reason to be on the list, then?'

'No.'

'Yes there is, he's on it. To be on the list is enough.
That old bugger Billy knows something that we don't.
Do some more digging on him, please.'

'Peter Scammel?'

Fiona fidgeted, 'Could hardly go wrong in life... family
fortune.'

'How did they make it?'

'His dad's big in... ...big in being big I suppose.
Banking, African Investment Companies... you name it...
must be disappointed in his son.'

'Why?'

'Toss-pot in the old sense... permanently pissed.'

'Drinker, then?'

'Heavy. He's another one like the next on the list,
Heston.' Fiona stood up and smoothed the fabric of her
skirt, ' This bloody thing is getting too tight already.'

'Is everything going well?' asked Shirley.

'Yes, fine, it's bloody Mike... still in a daze, bless him.'

Sims put his head in his hands, 'God give me strength.
Here we have the nation's security at stake, and what's
the talk all about?... tight skirts and a husband who's
surprised his missus is up the duff after doing rude

things.'

Fiona laughed, 'Think it's rude then do you?'

'Disgusting... wouldn't catch me doing it. Listen, in the meantime while I'm waiting for God's guidance on whether I should have the two of you put down or not, can we for Christ's sake, get on?'

Shirley, admonishing, 'Children are very important, Sims. They are the future.'

'Aston-Heyford, Throagh and Radleigh were kids once,' he said, bluntly. He sighed, 'I'm so glad Anne couldn't make it today... ...Laurence Heston?'

Shirley's turn, she tapped the table with her pencil. 'An intriguing one... MI6 and had some interesting responsibilities in various embassies. He may have been tangled up in a scandal while at the Bern Station... something to do with money... may have tapped into someone's account. Swiss banks don't want this sort of publicity, they papered over the cracks. Never made clear what it was about. I can dig further if you like.'

'Yeah, an okay idea. Switzerland, good place to do it,' muttered Sims. Heston, might be useful in the future, he thought.

'He's also married... another Eton boy and then Cambridge... his wife drinks more than he does... day-time tippler, frequents most of the big London hotels.'

'May need to get her tanked up, then. Gin for gossip.'

'Oh, this one's my baby: beautiful James Ross.' Fiona looked wistful, 'Such a good looking piece. Goes for women too... tried to chat him up once in Paris... no chance... half a dozen models crawling all over him...

models my arse!'

Keen to get in, Shirley again, 'Beirut Station with Philby.'

'Previous contact with him?'

'Probably not before joining SIS... the only ex Harrow one amongst them. How much contact they had there is difficult to say, Philby may have preferred sticking to his own kind.'

Fiona, 'I wouldn't have minded sticking to our Juicy James.'

'You're MI5, what were you doing in Paris?... not your territory.'

'Don't miss much do you?' Fiona said. 'I'd been approached by MI6... they were on a poaching spree. I was invited over to see how the other lot work. Wasn't a problem anyhow, our embassies are British territory, remember? As an MI5 operative, I was entitled.'

'So, you didn't need to mention MI6, then?'

'Thought it best to, just in case you did a bit of prying.'

She's straight, thought Sims.

For Shirley, it was a hard stare she gave him, 'Fiona is one of us and above reproach. There are things you don't, and probably will never, know, Sims.'

'Have to keep my ears and eyes open,' he said, defensively.

'Best thing, if you want to stay alive,' said Fiona, without sign of malice.

Shirley tapped the table again, 'Charles Greave: Middle to upper grade Diplomat, SIS, Liaison with CIA, Eton, Oxford. In his forties, only recently married. Always kept his name clean.'

Sims grunted, 'When does Liaison become espionage?'

'That's a question I've often asked myself. We've handed so much to the Americans. I'm not sure we get the same in return.' From her expression, Shirley evidenced she knew more than she said.

'Not long ago, Captain Stinton was giving me a bit of low-down on the second World War. He said the USA's intervention had little to do with anti-fascism or support for lill' ole Great Britain against German might. He said they were, in part, shamed into doing something due to Ed Murrow's broadcasts from London during the blitz, and, on the other hand it was an opportunity for commercial endeavour; enterprise at its most bloody. Don't be over impressed with what you hear to the different, he said, read-up on the Marshall Plan and Lease Lend we're still paying for their help.'

'But, thousands of GIs were killed.'

'More or less what I said. Not much gets by old Stinton. He said: "dress that up as heroism and good triumphant over evil and nobody questions the human cost, and nobody in the Senate feels it necessary to mention the rewards".'

She, Fiona; 'I wouldn't trust the Yanks as far as I could throw a buffalo. The most important lesson to learn about them is they are on this earth solely for themselves, and the rest you hear is Hollywood bull shit.'

'You like them, then?'

'Oh, yeah.'

'Jack Passant, what have you got on him?'

'Interesting... a quiet man; listens carefully, only

speaks when it's absolutely necessary... MI5 and else-where,' said Shirley.

'Elsewhere?' queried Sims.

'Never been quite sure... elsewhere will have to do for now.'

Fiona scraped her chair from under the table and sat down. 'I met him a few times... chilly, dry skinned and austere. Ten minutes with him and I needed a stiff drink and stand by a hot radiator to recover... yes, definitely austere. No warmth... gives off a cold draught. It's like a ghost has entered the room.'

'So, says nothing *en passant*, then,' commented Sims with a suspicion of French accent.

Shirley smiled, 'True, I've always thought... can't say why exactly... I think Passant is the eyes and ears of someone outside.'

'Outside where?'

'The immediate defence circle perhaps. Could be outside intelligence circles. I really don't know. I do know something though, his background is sure to inter-est you... before Eton, he went to the same prep school as Radleigh and Ross. After Eton, Cambridge... Trinity College of course.'

'Never happen! At the same time?'

'No he's older. Before you ask, Durnford, Isle of Purbeck, Dorset... it's not actually in Durnford... next door, Langton Matravers. And, this leads me to some-thing else, there is a very curious thing about the list, Sims. There is another name that you would think would be on it, but isn't, and its omission sticks out very much... like a sore thumb.'

'Go on.'

'Commander Buster Crabb's MI6 minder. He was also a friend and confidant of Kim Philby: one John Nicholas Rede Elliot. He's not on it. That is curious, you know.'

'Why on earth did Billy not include him?'

'For some reason Rede Elliot seems to be an untouchable.'

'Have you more on him?'

'Oh, yes, plenty... like Radleigh, Ross and Passant, educated at Durnford preparatory school Langton Matravers, then Eton, then Trinity College Cambridge.'

'Jesus Christ! Trinity college, little more than a creche for practitioners of sedition. A traitor's gate into our diplomatic service. Didn't anybody make a connection and see it for what it is?'

'They were probably too involved scratching each others backs to notice,' said Fiona.

Shirley took up the story again, 'Here's a couple of other things; Rede Elliot was also Head of station Beirut, and he received the US Legion of Merit for services to 'Office of Strategic Services.'

'So, the yanks give out gongs for espionage do they?'

'He's never been accused of being a double or triple... he just seems untouchable.'

'Tell me about his connection with Philby.'

'Things were getting tight for him... a lot of dirt was surfacing. Rede Elliott was commissioned, as his friend, to extract his confession in Beirut. Rede Elliott claims he got a written but unsigned confession. He then returned to London and Philby defected more or less as soon as he was over the horizon. In the enquiry after, it is known Rede Elliott had said he felt he could not have prevented Philby's escape.'

'You mean to tell me he just buggered off and left him there?... hadn't he ever heard of a Browning 9mm? Eh, come on, that stinks.'

'That's what we all thought. At the time, the theory milling around The Office was that the British Government did not want Philby brought back to England as any ensuing trial would reveal too much... call it inadequacy... too much dirty laundry to be aired... or other under the counter deals etc.'

'Is that the *counter* that appears in counter espionage?'

'Could be, yes. Another part of the theory that went around was that Rede Elliot actually went there to persuade Philby to defect, and that was the sole reason for the visit.'

'It gets worse and worse. Where the hell are we headed?'

Shirley sighed, 'A new world of disorder, I fear, Sims.'

He scrutinised Shirley's notes for ten minutes or so, 'Notwithstanding Rede Elliot's omission, there's something else missing from this, we have connections of individuals with other individuals, what's missing is unifying linkage. You both have it that these guys are on the face of things, clean. Once again I have to ask, why are they all on the list?'

'I'm only a researcher, I don't get all the details. Even researchers don't have access to everything. Our work is mainly directed at activities outside Britain or to foreign embassies inside. Possibly the best answer is that they all were cronies of Aston-Heyford and they've in some way or another been connected in their past... that's the best I can offer.'

*

In the library he looked up from the paper he'd drawn a chart on. 'Sod it, I've all this extra information and yet for the life of me I seem to have ended up where I started. Anne, if Buster's a part of this, where the hell does he come into it all? For the life of me, I don't think he's just a bit player. He's got to be something much bigger. He was MI6... Rede Elliot was his minder. So there is no reason to assume he was unaware of the deception going on around him. And... and, don't forget, he'd done some espionage work in China, so I don't see how he could have remained ignorant... at least he must have been suspicious. And, if so, why didn't he report to higher authorities? NO, no, no, love, the answer is straightforward; he was complicit in whatever treachery was taking place, and, I'll bet my boots on it.'

She smiled at his turn of phrase, 'You may be forgetting complicity was rife at the top. Who could he have safely reported to?'

'Okay, good point, but, I still think he's a part of the chain too.'

'What, you mean absolutely intimately linked with the rest?'

'Yes, why not? In one way or another all the others seem to be,' Sims put forward.

'Previously I'd always thought of him, if not as an innocent person, an innocent victim at least. And, he may be... but we have to consider he may not be. He, as you suggest, may play a bigger role in all this. We must keep our minds open.'

'On another point, Shirley reckoned Passant was the eyes and ears of someone outside SIS. She didn't say definitely who... probably doesn't know.'

'It's possible she was having to hold back. I think it's time to use your instincts. Like you, I feel we might be missing something obvious.'

*

His instincts needed to be fed. The sky cleared, patchy sunlight dappled the long lawn. He got up from the *Bellerophon* table, stalked over to and peered out of the window. Craning his neck upwards, he said, 'Looks as if it might hold out for an hour or so... fancy a quick walk down to *Alice*.?'

'What about the foreshore... yes, let's go to the fore-shore. We haven't been along there for ages. I need the exercise. I'll bring my bins too,' she said, taking them from a drawer.

He took a deep breath, salt air and seaweed, 'Lovely stuff,' he said. Just the crunching of their footsteps: nothing said beside for half a mile or more. Sims borrowed the binoculars and stopped to look at the Royal Mail ferry on its way up Southampton Water. He watched its swirling wake. Deep down his subconscious made a connection: scribbled a margin note.

Anne hung back, extended her hand towards him, 'Come on, darling. Have faith, it will happen.'

Silent walking again: quietness and Anne. Zen moments on a smooth foreshore, ripples in the sand, grains in etched relief, empty mind, clarity.

Now he needed something else, also clear and unclut-
tered, another form of uncomplication. He took *Big Sylvie*
to the seamanship school, and then his Land Rover to
Buckland.

'Hello, Maggie.'

'Oh Sims, look at you. you look so well... how's Anne?'
Maggie turned and called, 'Derek! Come and see who's
here.'

'Stay where you are, Derek... if I'm lucky I might be
allowed in.'

'No not straight away, I want the neighbours to see
who we've got visiting.' Still on the doorstep, she gave
him a big kiss. 'There, that should do it, number seven's
curtains just moved, everyone will know within an
hour.'

The images Derek saw were those of a young stroppy
stoker he fetched from Chatham, a blood streaked and
battered Sims after his launch had been blown up; the
hospital bed and his seemingly bloodless body after the
shooting, 'My God, you've come a long way in a short
time, lad... you're looking so much better,' Derek said.

'Yes, I put it down to life with Anne and good friends...
I'm a very lucky ex-stoker.'

Friendship, good people, soft talk, tea and cake: there
are other kinds of Zen moments.

Finally; Anne at Spice Island Spices, he alone on *Alice
Alacrity*. She obeyed the helm and heeled; a gentle movement - smoothly, unhurriedly. She understood him and
what he needed. *Alice*, her rigging whispering, spoke
softly to him, 'Sims, my lovely son, stop thinking and

listen,' she murmured. He turned his face to the evening sun and did as bidden.

At Hell Head harbour, moored, he gave her mast his usual affectionate kiss before he left. A patch of wavelets ruffled the smooth dockside waters and skittered towards *Alice*: a soft breeze stirred her rigging, 'Good on yer, babe,' he said.

A ragged association made, he sat bolt upright: dislocated connections came to the fore. A jumble that needed ordering: Milton cemetery, Buster's grave... Billy Ruffian... Sir Anthony Blunt.

Anne awake and shaking him, 'It's just a dream, darling, you're here with me.' His nightmares less frequent now; just occasional, 'It's just a dream, darling.'

Swirling wake on The Solent... The Royal Mail - the royal male: Blunt. 'Anne, love, I'm okay... not dreaming, I'm okay. Listen, the first time you came with me to Billy's, he went to such great lengths to tell us about Blunt... do you remember?... where we shouldn't trespass... the inedible icing on the cake and all that! His royal connections. He wasn't telling us where not to trespass at all, he was pointing all the time. And babe, Buster's more involved in this than we think too. When we get back from Denmark, we've got work to do.'

'Sims?'

'Yeah?'

She turned on her side, 'I'm glad it wasn't a nightmare... I'm quite awake now.'

'So'm I.'

***

Chapter Seven.
Tanked.

'Bob, what do you think?... give me your opinion straight,' Billy Ruffian said, as though he had the slightest soupçon family loyalties and connection might have influenced Rear Admiral Sherwood's decision.

Bob Sherwood did not appear ruffled: he had half expected it. 'It's sound... no more nor less risky than any other clandestine insertion or extraction operation we've carried out. Getting so close to Riga will be a tough test on my subs and skippers, though. There's a pinch point at the exit from Riga Bay. At its narrowest just thirteen nautical miles across. This is where they are most likely to patrol... I'll have *Ocelot* lurking on station should we need assistance or a decoy.'

'What happens if you're cornered?'

'We think or blast our way out... both our sonar and our discipline are far superior and I'll have one of the rear torpedo tubes loaded with mines and the other with a defensive torpedo. Our subs are the quietest in the world. It will be a tough test from which we will learn real intelligence.' He turned to Anne and Sims.'If we need to sit on the bottom, we'll have to be precise where we are settling, the Russians, Americans and, I'm ashamed to say, the United Kingdom have been using the Baltic as a dumping ground for chemical weapons... fishermen regularly get them caught in their nets.'

'Why? That's disgusting. Why the Baltic? Why anywhere?' Anne asked.

'Who knows?' retorted her father.

An unpalatable subject: one to move away from. Billy turned to Sims, 'Admiral Sherwood's tactical reputation pushes my vote in favour... I'll back the project. And, to your credit, I should also add, to-date you have never let me down, lad. You have great instincts, Commander.' Billy now bowed his head towards Anne, 'And with you, my dear, at the helm in Denmark controlling his some-what single-minded tendencies, I have my confidence doubled.'

This, then, signalled the formal end to the meeting.

Lecherous old sod, thought Sims. 'With all that put to bed, how's *The Anne Sherwood-Reeves* coming on? I haven't been to Fox-Eastleigh's boat yard for some time to find out,' he said.

'Very well. Commissioning and ready for sea-trials in nine months. You, I hope, will perform the bottle bust-ing, naming and launching ceremony, Anne.'

'Oh, I'd love to. It will be such an honour, won't it, darling?' she said, with a slightest raising of her head, eyes narrowed and smiling at Sims.

With his hand laid on and then grasping Sims' shoulder, Billy cleared his throat, 'You're sure you're ready for the off then, young man? Everything ship-shape?'

'Yes, sir.' Billy's face looked gaunt. This is getting to him, he thought.

Billy leaned towards him, 'Duncan took me for three suits you know. God knows what else I've let myself in for. That man is... is... as sharp as a razor.'

'Well, he was not my choice. I feel obliged to remind you he was your suggestion.' Sims waited for Billy's answer. None forthcoming, he added, 'Perhaps this is a good time for me to tell you what I need.'

'It had better be essential,' Billy growled. 'I'm not in the mood for frippery.'

'My position is similar to Alistair Duncan's, it's about image... about being believable. Now sir, you patently believe image is important or you wouldn't have funded his new wardrobe.'

Billy slowly shook his head. 'Go on, lad.'

'It is my opinion, to be seen clattering about in a clapped out, tatty old Royal Naval Land Rover or driving around in Anne's Mini Cooper, is not right for what I'm trying to project... it's about time I had something much much better... a bit more up market. Something befitting a NID agent with a bag full of double agents and whole Soviet spy cell to his credit... there's my credibility at Netley at stake here. Christ knows what the recruits think.'

Good God, thought Anne, he's not going to, is he?

'Go on,' said Billy again - he looked almost distressed. 'What do you suggest?'

'It crossed my mind a Jaguar XK120 with a black soft-top, painted in British Racing Green might fit the bill.'

Anne stifled a gasp.

'If you don't mind, Commander Sherwood-Reeves, I'll

give my answer to that proposal when your wife is not present. Now, Bob, everything ship shape your end?'

'Perfectly so, sir. With your leave, the earliest we can depart is in four days time.'

*

'Billy was almost emotional when we parted,' said Anne, lying comfortably across the rear seat.

Her father looked round at her, 'Why shouldn't he be?... he likes you both.'

'He was just worried about coughing up for my Jag.'

She chuckled, 'You didn't really think he'd fall for that, did you?'

'No... just clearing the way for my captaincy.'

'Oh, come on now, how can it do that?'

'He promised me if I nailed Aston-Heyford he'd fight tooth and nail to push it through... the Jag's a reminder I'm after something still owing... Admiral Billy Ruffian has outstanding debts.'

'It won't work... it'll never work,' she said, firmly.

'Sure it will... trust a barrow-boy's instinct.'

Dad, still looking at Anne, smiled. 'Perhaps, if I can butt in here... Billy *has* tried for the captaincy and, as far as I know *is* still trying.'

'I know.'

'How do you mean, *you know*?' Anne dug.

'He told me when I asked where it had got to.'

'You didn't actually chase him up about it, did you?'

'Why not? He promised it. Anyway, he told me it was difficult and that because I was so young it would cause problems.'

'Billy Ruffian having problems? I can't see the day

106

coming,' she replied.

'That's more or less what I told him. You'll have worked it out he was lying through his teeth of course. He was just laying some more bait... said perhaps I needed to get the full set before Admiralty House would listen.'

'Full set of what?'

'God, where've you been for the last couple of years? Les Grands bleedin' Amis of course.'

'The old bugger!'

Bob Sherwood laughed, 'That was very fluent, Anne.'

'I've been in practice... married a stoker. They're fluent too, you know. What is the saying?... you can take the stoker out of the mess-deck but you can't take the mess-deck out of the stoker.'

'Get it right, it wasn't stokers and mess-decks, it was Taffies and valleys... anyway, commander stoker, if you don't mind, ma'am.'

Better than television, the admiral thought settling back in his seat.

'Please don't call me ma'am, Sims. My name is Anne.'

The significance of this comment lost on Rear-Admiral Sherwood.

'Seems a long time ago,' Sims said.

'Yes, it does,' she said, sitting upright, leaning forward and kissing him on the cheek.

Bob Sherwood looked puzzled. He'd missed something. Now, what on earth was that all about? he thought.

*

'I'm going to help Sims on a job. We may be away for

some time.' Anne laid out an A3 sheet of graph paper in front of Mo and Pearl. 'This covers the period when we're away and, it's also when you're most likely to need a little extra money... it's a danger point,' she said, pointing at a particular place in Spice Island Spice's cash-flow analysis. 'I've spoken to Sims and he's happy for us to lend you some money until around this point about a month and a half later,' she said, pointing further along the chart. 'You can pay us back then. I've brought a cheque with me... please bank it immediately... don't put it off... you're going to need it.'

'Shouldn't we be going to the bank?' asked Pearl.

'No, there's no need... this often happens in a new and growing business... you are quite safe. And, Sims and I are not charging interest. It's a pleasure to see you growing so well.'

'The question is, are *you* going to be safe, Anne, love?' said Mo.

'Perfectly.'

'Can you tell us where you're going?'

'No, I'm sorry. I'll come and see you as soon as we are back.'

Pearl looked up from the analysis, 'When you do, make sure you bring that sod of a husband with you. He hasn't been to see us in ages.'

'He's had a lot on lately.'

*

SETT - Fort Blockhouse HMS Dolphin

Neither by accident nor by discipline was it that Dusty arrived first; simple old fashioned competitiveness. Be there before the others, and at all cost be there before Sub-

Lieutenant David Mountford. In a classroom on the first floor of the diving tower, he sat talking with Harley, their Chief Petty Officer diving instructor. Harley queried, 'Your boss looks familiar... I'm sure I've seen him before. Can't place him, though.' He left the semi question hanging. These were Naval Intelligence personnel he was going to be dealing with, they might not take kindly to prying questions. "Push them through quickly... a shortened course; the priority is speed... there's something going on somewhere, no time to lose, you may have to cut a few corners," he had been instructed.

'You might well know of him. How long have you been here at *Dolphin*, Chief?'

'Four years... permanent diving instruction staff... close to finishing my time. I'll be here until I draw my last tot of neaters.'

'If you've been here four years, you could well have seen him, then. You'd remember him if you were an RPO... he had a habit of shooting them... well, maybe not actually shooting, just threatening to shoot one in particular... wish I'd seen it.'

'Got him... got him,' said Chief Harley, standing up. 'Can't think why I didn't connect him straight away... he was a leading stoker then. He's risen fast, what's he like to work with?'

'Shit hot.'

'Really,' Chief said, looking doubtful. 'He handles being a commander okay, then?'

'Yeah, really, no problem... as I said, shit hot.'

The Land Rover drew up outside, two doors slammed, Sims and Sub-Lieutenant Mountford entered the

Submarine Escape Training Tower administration buildings. 'This way, sirs,' called Dusty.

''Had a good breakfast?' Sims asked.

'No, sir. Not before the tank... didn't miss much, only rubbery scrambled eggs or *shit on a raft*.'

At a loss, all at sea, David Mountford placed a baffled look. Sims helped him out; 'Shit on a raft: chopped kidneys in thick brown gravy all dolloped on top of fried bread. Unbeatable.'

'I've had that - appropriate name.' said David.

'Morning, Chief. What have you got for us?' Sims said, looking at Harley.

'Good morning, sir. I've been given orders to do things at the rush... not the way we do things normally... it's easy to get escape training wrong... there've been a few near disasters and last year a fatality.'

'Kind of you to sugar the pill, Chief. Believe me, we'd prefer to do the standard course and do it the kosher way... but, no time for that... we've got to get moving... we're doing sea trials tomorrow... the people we'll be dealing with aren't going to hang around.'

'Understood, sir. If you'll permit me, I'll give a brief breakdown of what we're going to cover.'

Sims nodded, 'Go ahead.'

'Normally, we would go through escape equipment and how it operates, first. In your case we're going straight for the controlled ascent. For your first run you will have no equipment other than what God provides and you'll go from maximum depth from the mock conning tower... you do this one at a time. Now, have I got your attention, sirs? Remember this, during the ascent you do not hold your breath. The air in your lungs will expand... let it out naturally. I trust your lungs are in good working order. Again, normally, we would commence by gradually flooding the escape air-lock and getting students to control their urge to panic... or weeding those out with claustrophobic tendencies. As we are at the rush, this will not be done... your group will go straight for the ascent... there will be a team at the surface to assist if necessary.

David raised his hand, 'Wouldn't it be better if they were half-way down and waiting?'

'They'll have their eyes peeled, sir. They know the routine. So, to continue, you will all do a minimum of three ascents from maximum depth. If we get on well enough, we'll do another three each to make sure. On two of them you will use two different kinds of escape apparatus: namely, the Davis Submerged Escape Apparatus and the Steinkle Hood. We'll cover those after your free ascent, and before the three others.' Harley, uncomfortable with corner cutting, looked back at his notes and read their names and experience, NID, bound to be tough, he glanced at Dusty, done it before, at least one of them won't die. 'Getting back to your free ascent for a moment... let me make it doubly clear, as you rise the one hundred odd feet, the air in your lungs will expand. Let this out gradually as you ascend... don't try and hold it in, this can damage your lungs... If you have your trunks, I suggest, gentlemen, we move to the base of the tank and the conning tower.'

Dusty tapped Sims discretely on the arm: they held back a few yards, 'Can I have a quick word, sir?'

'Fire away. You haven't a problem have you?'

'No. Not me, sir. Well, it's said you took a bullet to the

right lung... I mean, do you think you'll be alright? Have you mentioned it to them?'

'Do me a favour, certainly not... they might have stopped me... wouldn't miss this for the world... thanks for asking... don't panic. If I'm still at the bottom when you come out, give me a tow to the top, will you?'
'Who's going first?' Chief Harley asked.

'Me,' said Sims, immediately positioning himself at the bottom of the ladder. 'You two sort it out between yourselves who's next.'

'I'm pulling rank,' Mountford said.

'I had a feeling you might, *sir*,' said Dusty, laying heavy emphasis on the last word.

Sims now married; wife with child; unusually cautious, had been to consult Surgeon Commander Monroe, the surgeon who had operated on him after his Isle of Wight shooting, 'When I was in the Far East I was unlucky enough to get shot in the back... the bullet entered my right lung.'

'Yes, I know, I remember.'

'What kind of problems might there be doing SETT?' Close to apologetic, he asked, 'Thought it would be a good idea to check.'

'Hmm, depends on the strength of the scar tissue. Worse case, it's possible you could suffer a collapsed lung... pneumothorax. This might happen because the expanding air in your lungs forces its way through the scar and fills the space between the chest cavity and your lung.'

Sims sniffed, 'Hmm, so, apart from then having my very own internal life jacket, how will I know if that's happened?'

'Most likely sharp pain following deep inspiration... that's one usual sign.'

'I have it in mind not to be doing a lot of deep breathing on the way up... any tips?'

'Almost force the air out of your lungs, Commander. Though if you simply allow the air to escape naturally, you should be fine. Whatever, don't hold you breath... *at all*,' he stressed.

'Okay, so if the worst comes to the worst, what then? Long term problems, or not?'

'No. Come here immediately... I'll stick a needle through your ribs into the air gap and draw it off. Regardless, Commander, I think it better you come and see me immediately after you've finished... we'll give you a thorough check over. Do you want this to go on your records?'

'Thanks, no.'

'Something told me you'd say that... best of luck by the way for whatever you're going to do after SETT.'

He's been around, thought Sims, obvious something's on the cards.

'How is your leg now?'

'Only the occasional tweak... you and your team did a good job. If any friends get shot I always tell them to make this their first port of call.'

*

A shortened experience: message received; HMS *Orpheus* to return half a day early. She slipped back into port and tied up alongside two other subs. Anne had got the message from her father. For technical reasons sea trials were to be shortened. *Orpheus* would cross over to Portsmouth dockyard the next day for dry-dock inspection and repair.

As soon as Sims was ashore, Anne slipped him away to their office. One and a half days of catching up were necessary - they would know how to handle this, later.

'It doesn't get any better when you're away... I thought I might get used to it,' she said.

'In a way, I'm glad. And, I'm glad you left out the *than*.'

Inquisitively, 'Okay, I'll fall for it... what *than?*'

'You might have said, "It doesn't get any better *than* when you're away.'

'Never happen.'

'You speak Chinese, too... something new to learn about you every day... come on, there's no point in us staying here, let's go home... what's Jean got in the fridge?'

'She's cooking now... Dad got a message to us to say you were returning. First thing she said: "He'll be starving, poor love".'

'What the hell are we waiting for? Let's go.'

'Not so fast, hold on a minute, darling. How are you? How do you feel? Any after effects from the tank?'

'Why?... should there be?'

'Sims, I know how the tank works and I know what injuries you've had... I was worried about the one to your back and lung.'

He drew her close, 'You didn't say anything.'

'Would it have made any difference?'

'It's not an issue that came up,' he said, deflecting. 'Anyway I went to see my surgeon in Haslar before and after the ascents... no problem.'

With her arms round his neck she said, 'Good prognosis... good news for the future.'

'Do you worry about that?'

'Always... you've taken a lot of damage.'

'Well you can stop worrying,' he said, nibbling her ear, 'I'm in good nick... it's official. They gave me something I'll be giving you later.'

'And what might that be?'

'A thorough going over.'

She laughed and squeezed him.

'I didn't want the report put on my records in case it was a bit negative.'

'Would you have told me if it wasn't?'

'Yes... and you know it.'

'Let's go home and see Jean and Harry. Then you can show me what one of these thorough going overs entails... I really can't imagine.'

*

'Let me look at you,' she said, walking round him twice.

'Jean, love, I've only been away two days.'

'Yes, I know *that!*... but submarine food...'

'All things considered it wasn't that bad... better than some surface ships I've been on... the skipper ate the same as us.'

Jean made him turn round, 'I'm sure you've lost weight.'

He gave her a long hug, and over her shoulder he smiled and winked at Anne, 'So, what you going to do about it?'

'Do you remember that steak and oyster pie you

always talk about... the one you had in Plymouth... down in The Barbican... at The Lord Nelson?'

'You haven't made one of those have you?'

'No, mine's much better.'

'I've died and gone to heaven.'

'Well, lad, how was your first taste of subs? And how did the tank go?' asked his father-in-law.

'Tank was interesting... climbing up the short ladder into the conning tower was okay. Then, the hatch was shut and the water flooded in... not a particularly nice feeling... not sure I'd like to do it for real. Then the pressure builds, clear the ears... deep breath, outer hatch opened, and out you go exhaling all the way to the top... seemed like forever. After that, the next two seemed a piece of cake... then we did another three later in the morning.'

'Who went first?' asked Anne, innocently.

Between mouthfuls, 'Actually, none of us.'

'*Explain!*' Waiting arms folded, head canted to one side. Half hidden smile; something was coming, that she knew.

'Oh, you know how it happens, we were dead lucky; there was this Wren 2nd Officer loitering outside chasing after Dusty... you'd know what they're like in the Strategic Supplies Office, bloody nuisances, always pestering lower deck ratings... she was typical of the sort... looked pretty gormless. So we told her it was a short cut to the NAAFI. Didn't need to exhale, screamed all the way up to the surface. My God their knickers look baggy fully inflated.'

Anne's narrowed eyes said, "I'll get you later". She

leaned forward, her mouth said, 'You're a lying sod!'

Better than television. He looked from one to the other. Skirmish over; no more on the subject, 'And, the sub, son, how did that go?'

'Yes, okay... learned a lot. What was it? Forty eight hydrophones, that's a hell of a lot of listening gear. I thought about transferring to boats once... glad I didn't, too cramped. I like being able to go on the upper deck for a breath of fresh air... this pie is superb... anyone want that last bit?'

'Yes, I'll have it,' she said.

'*Really!* you've had two bits already... you need to watch your weight... or you'll start to waddle.'

'Eating for two now... and anyway, oysters are good for the brain... they stop one becoming gormless,' she said, making a show of slowly cutting, chewing and hmming down the final tranche. 'There's a little piece of crust left, darling... shame to waste it. I'll have that too.'

Bob Sherwood smiled, game set and match to Mrs Sherwood-Reeves, he thought. Sims had been outflanked and needed rescuing. He said, 'And, your two partners?'

'Absolutely no problem.'

'Well, the news this end is, I've spoken to Admiral Jessop and it looks like we start flying out in two days. HMS *Odin* will be waiting for us. Better let your partner know, Anne.'

'Beatrise and Artis too,' added Sims.

*

Sims sat back in the armchair listening.

'Let us assume, and I'm sure you will... I'm sure that it *will* be the case... ...let's assume you get Radleigh back and safely installed in Unit 4. Be very careful you don't overcook him. It's easily done with certain... let's say, fragile types of subject. Try and assess how tough his character is before you start.' Miles Stinton said.

'Overcooking... nice term. You've done the interrogation stuff as well?'

'Of course, and used it. Never pleasant; sometimes essential... let us say, necessary in the extreme.'

'And, enjoyable if your name's Woodruff.'

'Hmm, unpleasant type isn't he? I have often wondered what he does outside work hours.'

'Probable keeps his hand in by inflicting pain on small animals... it's not hard to see him slowly toasting live hamsters... probably eats them to tidy up after.'

Stinton smiled, 'Back to the point, lad. I advise you to do the interrogation yourself. Get what you can from him before you return to Netley. He will be in no man's land on HMS *Odin*. He may not like the enclosed space and feel vulnerable. I think this will be your best chance. And, when you are returned, don't let Lieutenant-Commander Woodruff do it. He will most likely try to muscle in. He is not in charge. Radleigh will be in your care. Woodruff is not the boss at Netley; only a senior instructor and you, you mustn't forget, outrank him. Give your guards strict orders not to let him near Radleigh... perhaps tell them they may shoot him if he tries.'

'Dusty will like that.'

'Now, another word of warning. Beyond that which we need from him, there's much that could come from Radleigh and there will be old cronies and associates who will not want him to talk. I know security is good at NIDii Unit 4; regardless of how good it is, watch him.

We don't really know who is on our side at Netley.'

'We will do our best. He won't be there under his real name or his Russian one, and we won't be using Alistair Duncan's, somebody's bound to know it's not him. No, Mike Mason will do a passport, and he'll be entered on the books as Edward Godbehere, a good old Quaker name... and if I have my way, I'll have the bugger quaking till his teeth drop out.'

'I know it will be difficult, but, try not to let personal feelings enter into it, Sims.'

'Yeah, I know all that... he organised the guys who shot the missus... goin' to be difficult let me tell you. Really difficult.'

Stinton stood up and put his hand out to Sims, 'Good luck. I wish you the very best. And,' he hesitated, 'God speed.'

'Thank you. Good luck not necessary, neutral luck will do, or at least no bad luck.'

Captain Miles Stinton RN (Ret) watched Sims drive away. My son Miles and him, what a team they would have made, he thought.

***

Chapter Eight.
Whiskey Class.

They were known; they had form. Sims' graphic description of their recognisability an indelible imprint: 'We
would stick out like a tanner up a pig's arse.'

To be seen together would be an unforgivable error.
The obvious decision made, arrivals at Korsør would
be split up. Sims and Dusty first, followed by Anne
and Fiona, then, the following day, by Rear-Admiral
Sherwood and Sub-Lieutenant Mountford. Four days
after *Odin* undocks, Alistair Duncan flies in. Each group
would be picked up at a Danish NATO airfield and taken
south to Korsør naval base in unmarked cars.

They said their goodbyes at Hell Head, it was likely
they would not be together again until all were back in
England. Anne, tough, bright, cheerful, excited; that is,
until he'd been driven away down the drive and out of
sight - Jean stayed with her for an hour.

En route to Denmark, she sat with Fiona at the rear of the
near empty RAF Bristol Britannia. 'How did Mike take
being left at home?'

'Not happy... he's already having panic attacks over

being a dad... he's got strangely protective... feels a bit weird. Anyway, I told him this might be my last taste of action before the big arrival... not going to say no to this one... I shall miss him though... always do when he's not around. I love watching him paint... casual daubs, no apparent method... then the picture gradually emerges; perfect. He says he sees what to do by just looking at the blank canvas. He doesn't understand why others can't do the same.'

Missing husbands: a subject that needed changing, 'We might as well use the trip to brief me on communications.'

Fiona stood up and stretched. 'Don't know what I've got in here. It's already making its presence felt. Need to rearrange my innards.' She sat down again. 'Well, as long as everything's on hand, it should be a piece of cake. If it's not, we may have to borrow some gear and jury rig something. I'm not sure what you already know.'

'Very little... except for the radio on our launch and the need for messages to be coded.'

'Lucky sods, NID's given you a launch, have they?'

'Yes, *Big Sylvie*... very powerful... I love driving her.'

'*Big Sylvie*? Don't tell me... I don't need three guesses, one will do, Sims named her.'

'She's a pro' in Pompey... he says she's legend... beats Dutch sailors up.'

Fiona laughed, 'He lets you have a go, does he?'

The subject had slewed back to him. 'Insists on it... he showed our engineer the ropes. He wasn't very confident at first... a few master classes with Sims and he's now damn near as good as any of us. He has a great way of explaining things. He was driving his launch... we were in a spot of bother on our ketch...' she hesitated, '... how I first met him.' She halted. 'We'd better get on with communications, if we carry on talking about him, I'll be in tears.'

'That bad, eh?'

'Yes... always that bad. He was such a mess after his shooting.'

'Pity they don't serve drinks, we could get Brahms and Liszt drinking to our old men.

'Okay, love, very basically it goes like this: high speed coded transmissions are made, that's around one hundred words a minute, these are picked up by the sub and recorded on a Philips tape recorder, then slowed down and decoded. More or less the same procedure for sub to shore or sub to sub depending on the distance between them. So, with all the taping, slowing down, decoding, recoding and taping again,' Fiona took a breath, 'there's a bit of a lag between sending and receiving.'

Talking business: calmer, more control, 'Okay, I've got that. I remember father saying they didn't need to be on the surface.'

'That's right, they've got a stack of antennae for periscope depth transmission and receiving, and, they've got a clever device called an ALK buoy... they can tow up and behind them for use at greater depths.'

'Fiona, do you mind telling me how the hell an ex army girl gets to know all that? This is highly classified information... you must have been on some pretty special course or other.'

'Oh yes, I've done a few, specialised training didn't cover

it all, though. As you say, highly classified... had to nick some confidential documents and manuals... only way sometimes,' she said, with a sniff. 'I read a manual once, it was bloody near incomprehensible. So I rewrote it... got a hell of a bollocking. They got really snotty, said I'd no business having it in my possession... I told them to be more careful where they leave high security documents lying around in future, and then I told them they could do whatever they wished if they were sure they didn't want a quiet life... they got the message, couldn't do much about it then could they? God knows what they'd have said if they saw what else I had. *Secrets!* Those offices... stuff lying all over the place. Pretty obvious which were the important ones... *Top Secret* in red plastered all over them... no lucky dip time here, every one a winner. I mean, Anne, they're supposed to be highly classified documents, so what do they do? They advertise: let every foreign agent in the world know. Hey lads, this is our great security idea, we thought we'd make it easy for you... you know, make it obvious... the ones with Top Secret in red on them are... wait for it... *Top Secret!*'

She, feeling better, laughed, 'Was it really as easy as that?'

'Yes, really. Security bloody nightmare. It was assumed because you were part of the gang you were okay, nobody questioned your integrity.'

Anne was smiling quietly. She had been holding back how much to tell her.

'Nice to see you smiling again, love. What's so funny?' Fiona asked.

'I used to be the boss of strategic supplies in HMS *Dolphin*... all the security hoops we used to jump through... bit of a waste of time with people like you around.'

'You would never believe how easy it is. Come on, think back, how many in your office were you ever suspicious of... none, I'll bet. Was the receptionist ever checked out? I'll bet again, never. And, and yet, they have more freedom of passage than anyone. You know, I've got this lovely Schatz & Sohne subminiature camera... made in 1939... be worth a bomb one day... the shots I took.'

'Okay, before I have to turn you in, let's get back to communications. What about sub to sub and sub to surface by underwater telephone?'

'Works well, too risky though... easily picked up. Not a good thing if the Ruskies are listening in... about as subtle as using a megaphone in a seance.'

'I hope we'll have enough time for a good run round when we get there... can't wait to see Dad's face when he finds out how much I know and shouldn't. He used to get quite miffed if he thought I'd listened in to things.'

'Say if you want the full works and you'll be an expert by the time I've finished with you... it'll keep us busy and our minds off our old men.'

*

On the tarmac at NATO Air Transport Wing Aalborg, a black saloon, windows darkened, engine running, waited for Sims and Dusty. The message exited the short stub communications aerial on the rear of its roof: "Have expected arrivals." No formalities: passport control ignored, taken at high speed south. Twilight, misty and occasionally raining, willows and flat countryside. No stopping at Horsens, Vejle and Kolding, across the Little

Belt Bridge to Nyborg and then by ferry to Korsør.

Dusty commented, 'If it weren't for the place names, we could be in Suffolk.'

Sims grunted, 'Ganges boy, too?'

'Yes, sir.'

Arrival timed for after dark, they immediately embarked on board the waiting *Odin*.

A black pelagic monster as inky as the depths from which it had surfaced: HMS *Odin* wetted by recent showers, reflected the odd glint from distant dockyard lamps. The immediate area all but darkened, those lights still visible were dimmed, shielded, downward pointing, softly illuminating the gang plank. Commander Ben Robson, Senior Submarine Commander Baltic met them on the dock-side. Both men taken on board: Dusty escorted to his bunk by a leading torpedo man.

Operational lighting, dials, humming electrics, empty: the control room cleared of personnel, 'Should be an interesting trip,' Robson said. 'As usual, only two other of my officers on board have full operational details.' He carefully scanned Sims, 'Your Leading Seaman Miller, he knows?'

'Yes. He's good... watertight.'

'And Subby Mountford?'

'The same... both hand picked, both impeccable.'

'Your father-in-law I know,' he smiled, 'I guess he's okay.'

'Rock solid. He'll be here the day after tomorrow. How did you know he's my father-in-law?'

His smile was all in his eyes, 'It always pays to know what going on above and with above's family. We won't delay departure, we'll undock immediately he's on board. I'm very much looking forward to working with him again.'

'Again?'

'My skipper once. Experience with him in command got me where I am today.' Zero enlargement, Robson offered no more. It stopped there, an old habit, no more detail than necessary. Sparing with the facts and careful who confided in. No rule change for NID men or sons-in-law of admirals.

'Here's your pit,' the torpedo man said to Dusty, and sat on the bunk opposite. 'I've seen your boss before. Where d'yer reckon?'

Keeping shtoom, Dusty shrugged, 'Could be anywhere... it's a big navy. Lots of ships, lots of boats.'

'I know him from somewhere... I'll nail him by the end of this mystery tour... know where we're going?'

'Not a clue.' Dusty unpacked his kit. His pistol and shoulder holster lay exposed on his bunk.

'That looks a bit deadly... what is it?'

'Browning 9mm Hi-Power.'

'Can I look at it?'

'You are... from there is close enough.'

'I meant pick it up,' he said, leaning forward arm outstretched.

'Touch it and I'll bust your fucking fingers.'

'Easy mate, no offence meant... just asking.'

'No offence taken, just answering. In NID we call it appropriate response.'

'I reckon you know what's going on.. just not saying.'

'That's about it.'

Persistent; still pushing, 'You're clued up... seem all about, you've been on subs before?'

'Yeh, was a submariner till six months ago.'

'What then?'

'Not a clue... been in a coma... life's a complete blank.'

'Okay, I give in,' he said. Leading Seaman Foster wandered off.

'Good, fuck off.' muttered Dusty. It had been a long six months: NIDii; recruited into a top team; Whale Island with Lieutenant Hennerbury. Hennerbury, what a case, he thought. Cedric Hennerbury had tried, unsuccessfully, to get NID to release all three of them for the navy pistol team. He'd said, "You and Sub-Lieutenant Mountford, at each other all the time, got the right spirit, you're just what I need." He, Dusty, with no meaning of disloyalty, had pointed out, "The commander doesn't seem to be that competitive, sir." Hennerbury, putting his hand on Dusty's shoulder, had replied, "He doesn't need to be, lad.".

*

At the top of the conning tower, in the navigating position, there was adequate space for the five men. Moorings slipped, diesels throbbing, HMS *Odin* eased away from the dock. In the distance a car pulled up and parked. Sims focused his binoculars: Anne! She was there, binoculars too, looking at him. He raised his hand: a salute. He knew she'd come. She saw and waved out of the side window, 'Commander John Sims Sherwood-Reeves: not goodbye,' she mouthed. Just a few days, she thought. And for the first time she understood what it must have been like for her mother to watch her father leave port for anything up to eighteen months or more. God, how awful.

Soon, a grey dockside building blocked his view of her. He would try and put Anne out of his mind until the job was done. *Going to be difficult.* Later, still stood to the rear he watched the shores of the Langelandsbælt slip by. The island of Omø now ten nautical miles behind them, he took in what may be his last breath of fresh air for several days. Rear-Admiral Bob Sherwood stood up front with skipper Ben Robson reliving old days. Sims heard snatches of sentences, parts of phrases... Gdańsk... something dropped off at Liepājas... Sims would never know whether something fell off their sub or they had delivered something. The two men knew what they referred to; it wasn't a conversation for other listeners - old waters gone over or perhaps under, depths dived. The re-establishment of an old partnership. Now a name he recognised, Orel: Aleksandr Evstafyevich Orel the Russian Fleet Commander since 1959. The two men laughed... three boats and four anti sub frigates and they couldn't touch us. A great move of yours... unorthodox signalling, ejecting our rubbish out of the gash tube, so he'd know we'd been there... message sent. Another name recognised, this time a place: Tallin. Do you remember?... more laughter blown away on the wind.

Out of the navigation position, swiftly down conning tower ladders, close and secure the hatch. Twin Vee 16 diesel engines stopped, electric motors running. Bob Sherwood, eyes bright, looked ten years younger. Now for the quiet routine of life under water. A familiar closed space where he'd locked himself away after Alice's death. Tight discipline of the deep kept his grief at bay. He had set to pretending it was just another commission and she would be waiting when he returned. Two years later, commission finished and back home sailing *Alice Alacrity* alone, long overdue grief hit him: bursting waves of wetness. He stayed at sea for three days; accepted one day she was not going to suddenly appear and finally came to terms that her laughing face had gone forever. He resolved never to remarry, and for her and Anne, he was going push every limit and climb to the very top.

Sims, the instigator of the operation, naturally included in the select meeting. The pick-up and extraction attack team waited. Ben Robson invited the admiral to carry out the briefing.

'Gentlemen, we will rendezvous with HMS *Ocelot* off the entrance to the Bay of Riga. She is already on patrol in the area. We, initially however, shall dive and make for the northern tip of Gotland via Gotland's west coast... this, I hope, will throw off any lurking Soviets. I repeat, hope. It will also give us the shortest exposed route when we're given the off by our team in Korsør, and until that moment we will remain between Gotland and the isle of Gotska Sandon. We will travel through and be in their territorial waters, the Swedes have yet to be informed.'

Bringing the Swedes into the picture had not been in the detail discussed. Sims asked, 'When do you intend telling them, sir?'

'When we've finished the mission... and, only then if we have to.'

Sims smiled to himself. On *Alice Alacrity*, Anne had told him "he's become a commodore because he's not afraid to make decisions... good ones". She hadn't mentioned he breaks rules too... *good man!*

'This operation will involve considerable under-hulling. Travelling past Gotland we'll hitch a lift under appropriate sea traffic going to Stockholm then divert to the tip. At that point we'll be around ninety nautical mile from the bay... allowing for diversions or emergency recharge, estimated voyage time around ten hours .'

*

Lieutenant-Commander Andrew Markham skipper of the third sub: HMS *Onyx* stepped briskly into the sparsely furnished room, 'Good morning, ladies.' He looked them both over.

'Is that all? Good morning, ladies and that's it,' said Fiona. 'What have you got for us?'

'Just popped in to introduce myself... have a chat.. business first... I know this has all been organised at a bit of a rush, so we need to test communications.' He took his hat off and placed it on the table. '*Onyx* is okay with *Ocelot and Odin*... we use standard protocol and codes. The plan is for us to stay in harbour and for you to deliver your signals for them to us by hand... which we then transmit. Now, that's okay as far as it goes, but if we're called out... and NATO can do this at any time, you're going to need to signal us... we might be anywhere in the Baltic. Should add,' he said, 'the Soviets are carrying out extensive exercises up north at the moment. So, we could be called in five minutes or five days and be gone for two weeks.'

'What do you suggest?' asked Anne.

'Between your base here and *Onyx* we'll need to use

your frequency and code.'

Anne did not intend jeopardising the safety of Beatrise, Artis and the Forest Brothers by handing over their code book and frequency. Assertive; 'No, that's not at all possible. Only ourselves will use and control the code and transmissions with which we communicate with our people in the United Kingdom.'

Markham scratched his chin, 'Wondered if that would be the case. Okay, then, we'll have to use a one-off code and frequency... won't be used again... how does that do?'

'Sounds fine.'

'I'll get my signals man to sort it out... he'll come over later and we'll put it to the test.'

Fiona said, 'What's to stop us using the one-off all the time. Then we could slip this lump,' she said, slapping the case of their radio, 'into our car and call you from a pub.'

'Oh, dirty, dirty move, ladies' he said, smiling. 'On the subject of pubs, such a pity we're on twenty four hour readiness. I would have taken you both out for a noggin. Not bad stuff this Danish beer... miss my old local Oxfordshire brew, though: *Hookey...* that is.'

Fiona, a discerning beer drinker, dismissed the choice, '*Hookey!...* never heard of it. No, not had that one, what's it made of, straw and mangel-wurzels? Give me Fuller's London Pride any time. Anyway, we're both married,' she said.

'Ahhh, we must pity the uneducated... I feel obliged to inform you Hook Norton Ales are legend with people in the know. But I suppose until the next time I'm home, the Danish liquid will have to do. Okay, then what about this for an idea, how about a pint when we're stood down?'

She laughed, 'You don't give up, do you? I said, *we're both married.*'

He gave a *so what* shrug. 'I'm not,' he said.

'And, not only married, we're both pregnant,' said Anne.

'And her dad's the rear-admiral in charge of this little operation.'

'I know, such a shame... mustn't upset the boss, so, it looks like business only it will have to be then.'

Both women nodded. Andrew Markham collected his hat, gave a polite salute and left.

'He seems okay,' put in Fiona.

'Sub skippers,' Anne tutted, 'bane of my life at *Dolphin.*'

'I don't think I'd have worried too much... quite like what I've seen of sailors. Come on, love, no one to overhear, is this a good time for you to tell me our routine?'

'Yes, of course. It seems straight forward. We communicate with Beatrise or her husband Artis, direct. Don't ask me where they got it from, they've ended up with one of our navy's Marconi systems; I guess Stinton or Billy had one under the counter. Anyway, they flash broadcast to the Forest Brothers using their own bespoke code and frequency. Then, she gets back to us.'

'So, where's our code?'

Taking the battered blue book from her briefcase, she pushed it across the table, 'I've brought Sims' father's old seamanship manual. It's in here. He reckons it would confuse anybody... unfathomable he once said. Billy gave Beatrise an identical copy.'

'And,' she said, peering, 'what passages do we use?'

'I've book marked them. Please don't write in it. I treasure it, he gave it to me for a wedding present. You have no idea what it means to him. My good luck charm.'

Bound, battered and blue: title embossed on the front; title in gold on the spine.

MANUAL OF SEAMANSHIP

VOL.I.
1926.

Fiona read the bookmark note:

'Page 55 to 108; Bends and Hitches; Knots and Splices: Seizings; Ropemaking; Matmaking and Sailmaking. They're the relevant pages. Our call sign; *Catspaw.* Theirs; *Gateau.'*

'You said Beatrise likes cake.'

'That's not the reason. Chosen because it comes from a very special day.'

Fiona carefully opened the cover and read the adverts: The one for Balkan Sobranie Cigarettes made her chuckle:

"Wealth is relative" Willoughby remarked. "And I find that, to touch the Pater, there is one essential - that haze of cigarette smoke in which he sees himself as Solomon granting his favourite son his Saturday shekel." And, with a smile, he handed me his case of

Balkan Sobranie
One hundred shillings per thousand.

'Ten shillings a hundred! They were bloody dear even

then,' Fiona exclaimed.

'There's a lovely one a couple of pages in from the back from **F.P Baker & CO., Ltd.** They take half a page of advertising and have this very laudable business statement: *The foundation of our success has been the principle that in every satisfactory business transaction there must be a profit on both sides.*
They then forget to say what they do or sell... so charmingly inadequate. Almost Dickensian... Pickwickian.'

'We ought to give it a test run... I'd feel happier then. When do you reckon?

'Now's as good a time as any,' Anne said.

Fifteen minutes later the message came confirming they were in business. Between them, Beatrise or Artis would stand-by the radio twenty four hours a day until the operation completed.

'So much hanging on this for so many people,' Anne said.

Fiona squeezed her arm, 'Doesn't pay to think about it. In the end you learn to just get on with your bit and forget the rest. If you don't, it will overpower you, and, if that happens, nobody gains.'

*

Diesel does not have an aroma. It has a smell; not an attractive one. On ships it was one that Sims was familiar with, but never to the extent like that on the Oberon class submarine HMS *Odin*. It permeated the entire vessel. It's even in the wardroom, crews quarters and control room, he thought, it'll take some time... I'll get used to it.

This was normal living for the crew; a familiar component of every breath drawn. His father-in-law and Dusty, former submariners, fitted in immediately; as easily as a fried egg slotted straight from the pan into a sarnie.

'It gets right into your skin,' Dusty had told him. 'When I'd get home after a long patrol my mum used to put old sheets on the bed. Diesel fumes and other stuff came out of the skin at night and stained them brown.'

Sims assumed Dusty was telling a long and tall one and told him to fuck off; Admiral Sherwood confirmed the story as so. 'One shower a week, Sims, that's all... and that at the discretion of the skipper... water conservation a top priority on long patrols. And, you never know when an ordinary patrol is going to turn into a long one. So, just in case, it's water conservation all the time.'

From Gedser Point on the south eastern tip of Zealand, it took them twelve hours including battery recharge snorkeling time to reach the isle of Bornholm. There, it came to him suddenly. The immensity of what was happening; what he was doing. Returning from the forward torpedo room to the control room, he glanced up and saw skipper Ben Robson and his father-in-law, Admiral Robert Sherwood, heads bent over the plot table directing this multi million pound submarine on *his* mission; *his* clandestine operation. He stood for a few seconds taking it all in: British funded; British naval reputation in hock, and who, but a handful in Britain, knew of it? What of the personal reputations and careers at stake? Is this how Britain is really run? Small autonomous groups engaged in their own plots: what else is going on? And, *Jesus Christ,* I've pitched Britain against the USSR!... I am the first stoker to ever have done this! What an epitaph;

"Here lies the ex stoker responsible for starting the third world war; Commander John Sims Reeves RN", that is not something I fancy being chiselled on my gravestone. Anne would be furious. Fuck... shit, this had better come off.

The radio room door opened, 'Scheduled communication, sir.' Ben Robson quickly scanned it and handed it on to Admiral Sherwood. Then Sims read it and asked, 'We're at ninety feet, I didn't think we could receive that deep.'

'Salinity, Sims. We're in the Baltic... brackish water. In some places we can receive as far down as one hundred and twenty.'

'Got you.'

'We're going to come up to snorkelling depth to snort and recharge in an hour's time. We make Gotland in thirteen hours. We like to do it in the dark if possible.'

Ben Robson turned to Sims, 'Your man, Miller... submariner, knows the routine. If you don't mind, voyage out I'll assign him an action stations post. Return trip, I'm guessing you'll need him.'

'I sincerely hope so.'

'If subby Mountford wants some operational experience, he's welcome to sit in on things in the control room.'

'He'll love that... anything new, he's keen.'

Sub-lieutenant Mountford was everywhere; a kid at Christmas not knowing what box to open first.

In the quiet control room a listener interrupted, '*Malmo Star*, sir.'

'*Malmo Star*,' Sims mouthed at Dusty. 'what the fuck's that?'

'It'll be a ship, sir. It's like these listeners know them personally. They can tell what type of engine and make of nearly every vessel at sea.'

Sims looked doubtful.

'Straight up, sir. Each ship has it's own noise thumb-print. If you get a chance to listen in, don't miss it... you'll see what I mean, sir.'

Special lot, submariners, he thought.

'I knew a listener once who used to go ashore and get pissed with some of the ship's crew of vessels he'd heard. Said it gave an odd feeling when he recognised their ship the next time; knowing who was on it, probably what they were doing, and, all the time they wouldn't have a clue that he was there earwigging them.'

'I suppose you're going to tell me he knows where it's from and where it's going.'

'Yes, sir.' Dusty went over to the listener, then came back. 'From Rotterdam, going to Stockholm... scheduled service. By the way, sir, I've been given an action stations post... I understand that's no problem with you. But, if you don't mind, I'd like to keep my hand in and do a bit of watchkeeping as well... help the lads out... stop myself getting bored.'

'They'll appreciate that, go ahead.'

Bornholm to Gotland; the air change every snort a relief. Fresh air drawn in through the snorkel induction mast: stale air into and used by the diesel generators.

Sims had little to do but watch the routine of the control room. The occasional bouts of self-doubt, anticipation and tension controlled by wandering the length of the sub, poking his nose into every corner, quietly chatting to the crew in the motor room. Try how he might, it was still a tedious fifteen hours. Radleigh's pick-up being all that mattered and until that piece of action was in the bag, everything else seemed irrelevant and time wasting.

Gotland: more waiting: *Odin* at 150 ft. Another sonar report: 'Merchantman bearing 245°... single screw... ninety revs.'

'Another freighter, we'll take a look and a ride when she passes.' Pointing at the plot table, Bob Sherwood said, 'This one can take us some of the way till the next snort. Then we go deep and wait for another. Caution necessary, Sims, remember we're on someone else's patch. The Swedes are aggressive and they don't like intruders. They depth charge them. There's a long history of Soviet intrusion; strongly denied by Moscow of course.'

'I hadn't forgotten, sir. We're doing the same thing... intrusion, how do you square being on Russia's side. Soviet allies now are we?'

Bob Sherwood smiled, 'Hardly... for the moment we treat matters as if we have two enemies and we're in both buggers' camps.'

Tucked up underneath passing freighters and ferries, *Odin* made her way undetected to the stretch of water between Gotland and the isle of Gotska Sandön.

Another snort then ultra-silent again: sonarmen listeners using *Odin's* type 2007 long range sonar. It can track Soviet subs without being seen herself. With 2007 in use, ultra silent is essential: no mechanical maintenance to be carried out; no film show in the forward accommodation, both too noisy. Paper work only. *Silence is golden: silence is survival.*

One hour later the all clear given. *Odin* surfaces to periscope depth. An encrypted message situation report and instructions flashed to *Onyx*:

```
Message   Lieutenant-Commander   Markham
HMS Onyx Stop
Relay message to base - Inform Brothers
need three fishing boats total as cover
for  recharge Stop Pick-up coordinates
(57°  12'51.39 N  23°  56'43.80  E)  Stop
Arrive  in  24.25  hours  Stop  ETA  0400
Stop If first pick-up not possible then
24 hours later Stop
Rear Admiral Sherwood Stop EOM Stop
```

Ben Robson passed the order to the officer of the watch, 'Dive depth 100 feet. Set course 101 degrees. Speed twelve knots.'

Thank Christ, it feels like we're really on our way now, Sims thought. Just one day... I'll have that bugger Radleigh in one day's time.

An hour, and twelve nautical miles later, everything changes - in an instant. A detection: enemy subs. Action stations, dim red light illumination, ventilation shutdown, waiting, ultra-silent ultra-quiet listening time.

Tension during analysis.

Taking his headset off, a listener reports, 'Two Soviet Whiskey Long Bins, sir... unmistakable.'

Skipper Ben Robson takes the headset and listens. He nods and hands the set back.

Tracking them, the Sonarman calls again, 'Depth 150ft; speed six knots; Heading 176 degrees and constant.'

'Could be heading for Kaliningrad or Liepāja,' Ben Robson says. 'Sound signature recorded... unaware of us... probably finished their patrol and heading home.'

No sooner the words uttered and the listening sonarman calls again, 'Course change 245 degrees, sir, and closing.'

Bob Sherwood and Robson confer, 'Coming right at us.' Both men agree they would not have been heard or seen by them at this distance.

'Third sub, sir. Heading 135 degrees. Looks like it's on an intercept course with the Ruskies. Swedish, sir.'

They waste no time, Ben Robson orders a depth change to disappear under a thermal layer. Then, a little later they slip back up through the denser, colder water and listen: gather information. Again going deep, they drift down once more and hide - invisible and unheard by prying Swedish and Soviet eyes and ears.

'Third sub, definitely Swedish, sir. Draken Class... it's the *Springaren*.' The swish of its prop giving it away.

'No point getting involved... the Swedes will run rings round them. They claim 22 knots for the Drakens... we stick to our mission,' said Admiral Sherwood to Sims.

After a brief flurry of manoeuvres, the thumps of some warning explosions. The *Springaren* has made its point;

it is not to be messed with. The Soviets chased off, once more all vessels head for their respective bases.

All clear given, *Odin* rises to periscope depth; message sent with details of enemy sub contact and revised ETA. She dives and resumes her heading of 101 degrees.

*

'Fresh info... They're en-route for Riga. They've had themselves a couple of Soviet subs on their tail,' Markham told the two women.

Anne white-knuckle gripped the sides of her iron framed chair, 'How bad is that?' she asked, stifling a gulp.

'Oh, it's all good fun... all in a day's work. No match for our boys... pretty easy to avoid... noisiest subs in the world... slow too. So noisy they're unlikely to hear anything else. In the end they were chased off by the Swedes. Mind you, *Odin* will have to keep their eyes open, *Ocelot* reports plenty of activity.'

'How close is *Ocelot*?'

'Need to know... only,' he said, closing the door behind him as he left the office.

She turned to say something to Fiona. Fiona was already relaying the message to Beatrise. Minutes later, 'Message received, Anne. The Brothers will know within the hour, I guess.'

She wasn't listening, 'How much is plenty? Sorry, what did you say?'

*

Seventy five nautical miles towards the Bay of Riga, *Odin* surfaced to snorkel depth, signalled *Ocelot* and *Onyx*, and made her final snort and recharge until they were at the pick-up rendezvous. Conserving batteries imperative; speed reduced to eight knots. Outside the pinch point, speed reduced again to five knots, now to zero as they waited for a lift.

*

Andrew Markham returned. 'They've made their last snort. Unless they hit a spot of bother, it's probable we won't hear from them again until they're on their way home.

No news is good news, thought Anne.

Markham gone, Fiona asked, 'What the hell's a snort?'

***

Chapter Nine.
Abduction.

For the final leg, HMS *Odin* had tucked herself tight under Latvian freighter *Kupiškis* heading for Riga. The lift over, here, just a few miles from the coast, the water was shallow. *Odin* stopped both engines and submerged practically to the sea-bed. She listened to the freighter's engine getting further away and waited. Minutes later, the hull of *Kupiškis* would have disappeared into the darkness, its lights melding with those of distant Riga. The rendezvous coordinates were just three nautical miles away. *Odin* holding neutral buoyancy, inclined the forward hydroplanes a few degrees downwards and with motors at slow ahead, rose around thirty feet, changed course and slipped away for the pick-up point. Arriving, she came up to periscope depth and scanned the surface, 'We're bang on time... there's nothing... not a vessel in sight,' said skipper Ben Robson.

'We'll wait ten minutes... if there's no sight of them by then, we'll leave and rendezvous same time tomorrow,' said Admiral Sherwood. He would not risk a third. Old mistakes: third time unlucky and batteries too low.

Sims took over the search periscope and scanned all round, 'Nothing on the horizon... nothing,' he said.

Ben Robson cut in, 'There's another freighter leaving port... it's a good time to hitch a lift out of the area and then sit tight until this time tomorrow.'

'Time to go,' said his father-in-law. 'Don't be disappointed, lad. It was bound to take more than one attempt.'

Sims thought about The Forest Brothers and the unpaid risks they were taking, 'Hmm, how many can either of us afford to make?' he muttered, in reply.

Ultra silent means just that: ultra silent. Endless hours with no ventilation. Movements along the sub restricted. In the control room the heat build up from the sonar screens and lights, intense. Sweat; the other great leveller, officers and men, everyone dripping: from no one person a single complaint. They were a tight team, this was routine. Sonarmen listening, reporting, plotting contacts. 'Merchantman, 110 revolutions, heading 320 degrees, sir.' Helmsman tuned ready for instant response to orders given. The cooks managing miracles, meals taken at their action station. And so the quiet litany continued throughout the rest of the day and night until the next morning. A sleepless night for Sims.

In the early hours of the second day, three men in a grubby white van watched Radleigh approach. It did not look out of place among other parked fish vans. They waited for him to draw level. Stink can be an advantage. The day-time job of transporting fish to the smoking houses almost guaranteed it would not be searched: military patrols, mainly conscripts, did not like returning to base smelling of fish heads, innards and their uniforms sequined in scales.

He'd been drinking - enough for him to make the occasional veer to one side or other of the pavement. The three men had practised the manoeuvre, in seconds Gerald Radleigh was gagged, strapped, wrapped and heaved into the reeking rear of the vehicle. The van, a fairly typical example of the products from the Riga Autobus Factory, black fumed and popped its way to the docks.

Radleigh's disaffection with the Iron Curtain way of life had led him to dreaming of returning to Britain - I must be of value to MI6, he had thought, it might be possible. Dreams can come true, though, as in this case, it would not be in the way he imagined.

Among the fleet of other boats in the docks, the three fishing boats were waiting. The grubby white van drew up alongside one of them. In contrast to its graceful painted waist that swept to a high prow made even higher by the addition of extra bow planking, there was a paint flaky, flimsy looking wheel house close to the stern. The crew knew her as *Rita*: the authorities, as fishing vessel ЯД006. She looked as if it had been designed by a committee - a Soviet one: traditional Latvian boat builders for the hull and Russian garden shed designers for the steering hut. Soviet bureaucrats and Latvian shipwrights shouldn't mix.

Gagged and wrists bound, Radleigh was bundled quickly down the steps into its fish stinking hold. They told him, if they were searched and he made a noise, he would be the first they killed. His ankles were tied and he was covered with a cold, damp canvas sheet. For good measure, a few empty crates were piled on top of him. *Rita from Riga* would leave harbour with the other boats at the normal time and return with her catch ready for the morning market.

On this trip, Dāvis Lūž was an extra and unusual part of the *Rita's* usual crew. The delivery was his responsibility. He hoped Commander Sherwood-Reeves would collect the cargo... he wanted to shake his hand and say "thank you". Aunt Krista Bērzs had taught him the English words.

A few hours before daylight, steaming into a light wind and moderate sea, the smelly squadron left harbour and sailed deep into the Bay of Riga.

'What a din,' said a duty sonar man on *Odin*. 'We could run in on our diesels. No one would hear a bleedin' peep.'

Its starboard side facing away from the coast, ЯД006 and its two companions motored out further than the rest of the fleet. On the seaward side, at the bows, stern and midships, they hung three bright lanterns, their lenses painted green. *Odin's* engines stopped. Half a mile away a thin black object broke the surface - it left no wake. Skipper Ben Robson, still peering into the periscope, reported, 'I've got them... they're there... no mistaking it.' He stood to one side and let Bob Sherwood see for himself.

'Yes, yes. It must be them... well done, lad. Get alongside, Commander.'

'Thank fuck for that,' said Sims, slapping Mountford on the back.

'Well done, sir, well done.'

ЯД006 had not seen her until *Odin* manouevred close alongside and surfaced. Black as a breached whale she sat there, water cascading from her sides and conning tower. The two other *Brother* boats formed a cordon and clustered around her. *Odin,* ventilation turned on, a chilly blast from outside now cooling the sweaty control room, fresh air from the induction mast flushing the stale throughout the sub, diesel generators running, recharged for over an hour - this was the priority, not Radleigh. Hatches remained closed; ready to leave in an instant.

A pale tint in the eastern horizon, the first light of dawn not far off. Recharge finished; hatch open, Sims and Sub-Lieutenant Mountford were quickly on deck. Radleigh, roughly pushed down a rope ladder fell into a small skiff. It rocked as it bounced against the sub's superstructure. Radleigh slipped as he stepped towards the submarine. Sims grabbed him, Mountford grabbed Sims. Together they dragged him on board. Dāvis Lūž leaped onto the sub's deck, shook Sims' hand and said his "thank you". For a brief moment the two men, like old friends, clasped each other's hands. Sims slapped him on the shoulder, ' *No!* thank you, Dāvis.'

Dāvis grinned and clambered back into the skiff, 'Thank you,' he said, again.

Three green lensed lanterns extinguished, diesel engines thumping and clonking, ЯД006 and her companions quickly went on their way, casting their nets.

Cargo on board, Ben Robson gave the go ahead: he ordered *Diving Stations*. Crew all accounted for and inside, hatches shut and secured, HMS *Odin* flooded its tanks, and with its forward hydroplanes raised, once again they dived into the world of silent running, sweaty odours of damp clothes, diesel and boiled cabbage.

The chart table always screened from general view. Only Admiral Sherwood, *Odin's* captain, Sims and a few select officers knew where they were headed. Their course set, and with powerful electric motors running unheard by Soviet listeners, they were on their way back to the Korsør by the most direct route possible. Five hundred and sixty nautical miles if all went well. Twelve knots all the way. In a couple of hours under two days he could be with Anne and a shower in Kosør. Sims stood relishing the moment: *I've got the bugger.*

In the scrambling transfer to *Odin,* Radleigh was thoroughly soaked. During his slip clambering onto the sub's deck an icy wave had caught him full on - the shock of the near freezing water had made him gasp. Two seamen and Dusty with Sub-Lieutenant Mountford escorted him dripping to the stern torpedo room. No space ever wasted on a sub, the room doubled up as crew accommodation: they handcuffed him to a bunk.

Sims pushed the hatch open and called Dusty out of the torpedo room. He shut the hatch behind them and led the way into the next compartment - the motor room, 'Here's the routine, Dusty, we're going to play *good guy: bad guy.* Contrary to your character, you're to be the good guy. So, when you're with Radleigh, don't be too hostile, act friendly. Don't make it too quick or too obvious... take your time. If he talks to you just answer politely.

Gradually encourage him to make more conversation with you... you get the buzz? He's going to be uncomfortable in all that wet gear... he's bound to complain. We don't want him dying of pneumonia before he's dished the dirty. Offer to get him some dry clothing if he wants it. This is a not a bad thing to do - his familiar clothing, even wet, will reinforce his identity and his capacity for resistance. Just make sure the clothes he's given are at least two sizes too big for him - no belt, Dusty, no belt. When he stands up he'll have to hold his trousers up. And don't panic if I get a bit heavy... all a part of the game. Got it?'

'Yes, sir.'

'Right, in you go. Don't leave him alone. If you need me, call the control room. Tell the two lads they are, for the moment, relieved.'

Radleigh was shivering violently. Convulsive waves rippled and shook his body, 'I'm wet and cold,' he chattered. 'I've suffered pneumonia twice in my life, I need to get warm.'

An ideal time to start being a good guy, 'I can probably get you some dry clothing. Do you want me to?' he asked.

'Yes.'

'It would be quite useful if you said, please.'

'Of course, yes... please.'

Dusty moved to the telephone, 'Commander, sir, I'm worried about his condition, he's had pneumonia before... I think he needs a change of clothing... something dry and warm. And, possibly some food and drink.'

The two lads returned with the clothing and, with

Dusty, guarded Radleigh while he stripped, dried himself and dressed. After re-cuffing him to the bunk, they left.

'Are you hungry?'

'Yes, very.' A moment's pause, 'Thank you for asking.'

Dusty went once more to the telephone, ' I think Mr Radleigh needs feeding, sir.'

'Tell him the watches change in half an hour. There's a snack issued then. If he's lucky he'll get one.'

He relayed this message to Radleigh.

'Where are we?' he asked.

'We're in the stern torpedo room of a Royal Naval submarine.'

'Where are we going? he asked.

'Only a few know... we're never told,' answered Dusty. 'Are you warm enough? I could get you an extra blanket.'

'Yes... I would like that. Thank you.'

Radleigh finished his meal. Dusty left as Sims and Subby Mountford came into the room and secured the hatch behind them.

'I need to use the toilet.'

Sims looked him over, 'These two lads will take you there. Now get this; you don't just pull a lever and it flushes. There's a special sequence to follow. First, the toilets are small... cosy isn't quite the right word. You will find it easier if you drop your trousers in the passage and then back into the cubicle... better make sure it's not already occupied. When you've finished, you'll see a foot pedal press it... it will open the flap at the bottom and there's a hose to rinse the bowl. Make sure the flap is closed when you've finished. If not, and they should decide to blow the waste tanks out to sea, it will all come shooting into the passage. This has happened. If you were to be the cause of this, so help me God, I would make you clean up every last bit. Pay careful attention to what the lads tell you to do. It could save you a lot of heartache.'

Twenty minutes later Radleigh returned no smellier than he had gone. Despite the soaking and change of clothes, he remained smelling of fish heads and innards.

'I want you to listen to me and then over the next few hours think seriously about what I'm going to say to you. So, pay attention and listen up. Have I got your full focus?'

Radleigh, less comfortable with Sims, nodded.

'With Lieutenant-Commander Maitland's killing and my injuries I'm almost prepared to accept you were only indirectly involved. Please don't think I'm happy about it and everything's okay, it's just that I think you were only indirectly responsible. However, and this, mark you, is a very important however, you *were* directly responsible for my wife's shooting and for that I'm going to show you little mercy.'

'I didn't know your wife had been shot.' Radleigh now listened closely.

'Well she was... by one of the agents on the Viktor Abakumov. You must appreciate, I am very unhappy about that incident. I know you organised them, so don't even bother trying to deny it. On a lighter and more pleasant note, I'm delighted to inform you I accounted for them both. On a slightly darker one, give me one half-good reason and I shall account for you too. It would give me so much pleasure. When you've rested, you are going to tell me all about Commander Crabb and Lieutenant Miles Stinton. If you do so, I promise we'll take you back to Great Britain. If you don't,' Sims paused, 'we won't. Consider carefully what I have just told you.'

So Anne has not only shot someone, but been shot herself, David Mountford thought, ratcheting up the qualifications any future wife of his would have to have - number one priority, she would have to be a woman of action... *Superwoman!*.

Sims and David left the stern torpedo room.

Dusty came back in and took over, 'He told me he was going to give you one of his lectures. Now, you've heard his bit. Listen to mine. All I know is your name. Why we've got you I haven't a clue. I'll give you a word of warning. I'd go a bit careful how you talk to him... don't get on his bad side any more than you are already... he's got a bad reputation... he's a killer... nasty bit of work, one of the Naval Intelligence Division's assassins,' Dusty said, with "good guy" frankness.

For the remainder of the day and night, Radleigh did not rest easy.

A few nautical miles outside the pinch point of Riga Bay, HMS *Odin* snorted and signalled the lurking *Ocelot*. *Ocelot's* reply read:

```
Intense enemy activity Stop Six Whiskey
Class in the immediate area Stop Will
need assistance Stop  Have called upon
```

```
Onyx Stop Onyx en-route. Ocelot coordi-
nates follow.
```

Admiral Sherwood read the signal handed to him, 'To use one of your terms. Looks like we've got ourselves a spot of bother,' he said calmly.

Odin still at action stations from exiting the Bay of Riga changed course and headed for *Ocelot*. 'We'll creep up fast on the buggers,' said Ben Robson.

'Creep... fast, I didn't know that was possible.'

'Just watch me, Commander.'

Ben Robson and the admiral conferred, 'Decision made, Sims. We're going flat out for *Ocelot*, after thirty nautical miles we'll surface-snort to top-up and get their attention. Twin Cylinders are slow, so we'll burst through their ranks flat out. Slow down to let them catch up and see if we can drag them the forty eight miles to Gotland.'

*

'Signal from *Onyx*, Anne. Looks like she has to set sail in a hurry.' Both women rushed to the window. At immediate readiness, her gangplank and auxiliary power cable swiftly removed to the dockside, diesels roaring, mooring slipped, *Onyx* manouevred away from the dockside. It would take them twenty four hours to join the punch-up.

The signal from Beatrise came in shortly after *Onyx* leaving port:

```
Delivery made Stop
```

'They've got him, Anne. Your old man's only bleedin' got him. Christ, I wish the others were here... *come on*, you don't look particularly pleased!'

Certain that Onyx's departure did not bode well, Anne, pacing up and down, said, quietly, 'They've got to get back yet.'

*

Alistair Duncan poked his head round the door, 'This is a fine to do. They've given me an iron bed and I don't have a pass to get out of the base.'

'You know the rules Alistair Duncan, you're to stay out of sight. If you give us any bother, we'll have you handcuffed and put in cells until it's time for you to fly to Zurich tomorrow. I am not joking, Alistair. Furthermore, I will see that Billy takes back the suits you've conned him for. Now, that over with, meet my friend and partner for this operation. Alistair this is Fiona, Fiona this is Alistair Duncan our Radleigh doppelgänger.'

Fiona looked him up and down, 'Royal bloody Air Force,' she said.

Duncan took his time in replying, 'Do you know my wife at all?' Billy Ruffian had made a point of telling him that Anne had a hard streak and she was not someone to be messed with. To press home his point, Billy had described the accuracy of her shooting when she shot and killed Matrozis the late captain of the *Viktor Abakumov*. Fiona, he decided, deserved equal consideration. 'So, I leave tomorrow... where are we with the plan?'

'We have Radleigh on board and they are on their

way home. I should point out they may have encountered some opposition. *Onyx* has left harbour in a hurry. I believe this was in order to give assistance to *Odin* and *Ocelot*.'

'Not sure I'd like to be down there... not able to see the enemy... subs... at best iron coffins. Anyway, I understand the situation. You'll get little bother from me, girls. I'm ready for business.'

'Thank you very much for reminding me of the danger my husband and father are in, Alistair. I should have thought of that myself.. it hadn't crossed my mind.'

'And... and, we're not fucking *girls!* Call us that again and you'll never make the airport let alone bloody Zurich,' blasted Fiona.

Alistair took two steps backward. Fiona, alien; from a different race of people and a much altered world he thought he inhabited.

*

'We can see *Ocelot* and four Whiskey Twin Cylinders. The Soviets won't be able see us or *Ocelot*... out of range. She'll now sit deep and quiet until we're close.'

'Two unaccounted for,' said Sims.

Ben Robson again, 'If they're still in the chase, we'll hear them long before they see us.'

'Got to ask, said Sims. 'Why so noisy?'

'They've two missile launchers on the upper superstructure, just behind the conning tower. That's why they're called Twin Cylinder. They completely mess up the hydrodynamics... cause so much turbulence. That's where most of the noise comes from. Also, that upper-deck junk screws up the handling. They're fitted with

Shaddock missiles, the combined mass of these and the tubes make for a hell of a lot of weight to have so high up... makes them damn near top-heavy. Must be a nightmare to do a fast manoeuvre.'

'So, what do we do?'

'Give *Ocelot* a bit of relief. As I said, we'll break through the Soviet formation and lead them into Swedish hands. As soon as they're after us, *Ocelot* will know what to do. She'll surface, signal Korsør using a code that we know the Swedes have cracked... well not exactly cracked, we hope they are still unaware that we gave it to them.'

'The Swedes don't seem to like Russians, do they?'

'No, certainly not... as your father-in-law told you, they're not against depth charging them... they like to make a point.'

'Nearest soviet five miles bearing 025 degrees, sir.'

'Steer 320, speed 15 kts. Aft torpedo room prepare defensive torpedoes.'

'Sims entered, 'Unclip him and give these guys some room. Take him next door and strap him to one of the motors.' Sims grabbed Radleigh by the throat, 'Just give me one excuse and I'll see to you here and now.'

'We're through, sir. They're on our tail.'

'Nearest target two miles, sir.' Ten minutes later, 'Three miles, sir.'

'With all that junk, it looks like their max speed is around nine knots. Reduce speed to 10 knots.' An hour later, 'Reduce speed to eight knots.' Then, 'Depth 250 feet, stop engines, Ultra Quiet.' *Odin* heard the Soviets pass a few miles away and recede into the distance. They waited for two hours. Ultra silent, ultra sweaty.

*

Ocelot surfaced, snorted, and signalled the base at Korsør.

In the Swedish naval base at Karlskrona the duty telegrapher rushed the message to the officer of the watch. In minutes, depth charge carrying helicopters and aircraft were scrambled and sent to investigate. Ahead of the Soviet subs an array of Swedish helicopters hovered, lowered their hydrophones, and listened. Data gathered, signal sent to Karlskrona:

```
Red Rendezvous five minutes stop
```

They made for the intercept coordinates.

*

Hunkered down close to the sea-bed *Odin* heard and felt a succession of explosions, 'Time to go home,' said Ben Robson. *Odin* headed south for Korsør. Four hours later and well away from the action, she surfaced, snorted and listened. In these Baltic waters *Odin* carried a Swedish speaking telegrapher. He reported, 'Sounds like some damage has been done. One of the Soviets may have run aground.'

Before diving, the following signal flash broadcast:

```
Onyx to stand down and to return to
base Stop Ocelot to continue patrol
Stop Odin returning to base Stop One
Whiskey on the rocks Stop Others left
```

before closing time Stop

Action stations stood down, Sims returned and sat on a bunk opposite Radleigh, 'Have you thought about what I told you yesterday?'

Except for muttering: 'I can't tell what day it was, or is,' Radleigh was not going to talk.

'You are in a very bad position... not at all enviable. Now please understand this: for your information, the British Government does not know we've got you. What we are doing is known only to a few people in The Naval Intelligence Division and their instructions to me were to extract from you the truth about Commander Crabb and Lieutenant Miles Stinton. Cooperate and it will minimise your sentence... depending how much you tell us, you might even go free. If you do not, nobody outside a few people in NID will know of your disappearance. And, after being set up by your lot over Buster, they, I can assure you, wouldn't care less... think of it as NID's revenge on the last remaining member of Les Grands Amis.'

Radleigh did not like the sound of the word disappearance. However, he remained impassive and noncommittal.

'I have a sneaky feeling you don't believe what I'm telling you. I'm going to ask you once more and only once more. What happened to Commander Crabb and Lieutenant Miles Stinton?'

'I know nothing about either.'

'And that, I take it is your last word on the matter, is it?'

'How can I tell you what I don't know?'

'Fair enough... but I know you do know. The *Rihards Vāgners* docked a few hours before Buster went missing. You were importing drugs on that ship in exchange for secrets and the same case is true with the *Viktor Abakumov,* although that was for cash... this we know because we have photographic evidence of you assisting Aston-Heyford in lifting them from the sea-bed near Bracklesham. So, don't give me that bull shit about not knowing about Buster's disappearance. The *Rihards Vāgners* docking at that time was no coincidence.' Sims waited to see if he would respond - he didn't. 'Gerald Radleigh, I'm afraid your unwillingness to cooperate leaves me no option.'

He stood up. Dusty asked, 'Shall I get his meal, sir?'

'He won't be needing one.'

Radleigh blenched at this reply.

'Take his handcuffs off,' Sims ordered. 'Sit up straight, Radleigh.' From his pocket he took out a tape measure and went over to him without saying anything. He measured Radleigh across the shoulders, 'Now hunch your shoulders forward.'

Radleigh did as he was ordered.

'Nearly nineteen inches,' Sims muttered.

'What are you doing?'

'Seeing how wide you are.'

'Why?'

'Leading Seaman, go and fetch his old clothes!' Sims snapped.

'Yes, sir. Straight away, sir,' said Dusty.

'What's happening?' asked a paling Radleigh.

'Change of plan... it looks like you either don't know

anything - which I don't believe, or you're simply not prepared to tell me about Buster and young Miles Stinton. I don't intend taking you back to Blighty without your confession, someone might spring you... or one of your old cronies perhaps will manage to get you pardoned. That's quite possible isn't it?' Sims waved the passport Mike Mason had made. 'Nice photo, don't you think? This goes with you inside that nice little zipped pocket in the lining of your coat.'

Two Torpedo men came into the room and with unfaltering purpose started to disarm and unload a torpedo from one of the tubes. Radleigh looked on shaking and horrified - the penny was beginning to drop.

'Where?... what are you going to do to me?... where am I going?'

'Out.'

'How do you mean, *out*?'

'We've been circling back towards Riga... not long to go now... when we get there, just a few miles off the coast, we're going to eject you out of that empty torpedo tube.'

'You can't.'

Sims spoke to the two men, 'Eighteen or Nineteen inches across the shoulders. How wide's the tube?'

'Twenty-one inches, sir.'

Sims looked over at Radleigh, 'We can, and we're going to... you're a scrawny bugger... you'll fit nicely.' He turned to the seamen, 'I'll need you to give us a hand to dress him.'

'Make sure you get everything on him correctly... socks,

that sort of thing the right way round... not inside out... might look suspicious when they pick the body up if we've got it wrong.'

Radleigh struggled. It took the two lads and Dusty fifteen minutes to get the still damp clothes on him.

'We need to rope his ankles together so we can get him inside... we'll use something like a timber hitch... something we can slip off once his legs can't get in the way... you're seamen, you can work it out which is the best one to use,' said Sims, curtly.

Whether through fear or through the change into his cold and damp clothes was not certain: Gerald Radleigh began to shake, 'You can't do this to me... the Geneva convention forbids it,' he almost pleaded.

'Bollocks, the Geneva convention only covers acts of war... we're not at war and perhaps you've not worked it out yet, but just so you know, we're not in fuckin' Geneva either.' Sims beckoned to the two seamen, 'Right, now tie his wrists in a similar fashion and let's stuff him in.'

Radleigh was powerless, and struggle as he might, he was quickly shoved home. Before closing him in, Sims leaned over, 'When you hit the cold water, think of my wife and the twenty-five agents you helped to murder. We'll be down 200 feet, if you don't drown, you'll surface so quick you'll die of the bends. I'd like to make your death more painful, but I'm not allowed.'

Sims called the control room, 'Preparing to launch from port stern tube.'

The lights dimmed slightly and a sole red lamp flashed menacingly. One of the seamen started to close the tube door. Sims stood close by.

Radleigh screamed something almost intelligible. Sims caught the gist of it.

'Hold it lads. What did you say?'

He gabbled, 'I said Crabb isn't dead.'

'Bring him out... not too far. Sub-Lieutenant, go and fetch the admiral and skipper.'

Minutes later they entered the room.

'Radleigh, repeat what you've just said to me.'

Radleigh, twitching and fearful, looked desperate, 'By my life and everything dear to me, Commander Crabb is not dead. He defected to Russia on the *Rihards Vāgners* and is training their navy's frogmen in the Black Sea. He's married again... he has a Russian wife. So help me God, this is true. I have seen and spoken to them both.'

'What about Lieutenant Miles Stinton?'

'I swear I know nothing of anyone with that name.'

A bell rung. Sims realised his line of questioning had been in error, 'If I called him George Rankin would that make any difference?'

'Were they the same person?' Radleigh blubbered.

'Yes.'

'I didn't know that. Aston-Heyford killed him... he put Rankin's body in a diving suit and dumped it in Bracklesham Bay. He cut off his hands and head so that the body couldn't be recognised... it took a lot longer than he expected for the body to be found.'

'Drag him out and stuff the torpedo back in. Dress yourself, Radleigh,' ordered Sims. 'When you've done, you will sign a confession detailing what you've just told us. You know what awaits you if you don't,' he said, pointing at the torpedo tube.

Admiral Sherwood and *Odin's* skipper waited in the motor room for Sims. He came in and shut the hatch behind him.

'Those were extreme methods, lad, extreme methods.'

'Maybe, maybe. He was responsible for my wife's and your daughter's scar... know one thing, if he hadn't coughed, I'd have pulled the trigger myself.'

Admiral Robert Sherwood looked closely at his son-in-law, 'Take heed of what I'm going to advise, Sims: be careful of what you might become, lad.'

'I take note. Tell me, what button would you press or what trigger would you pull if ordered or you thought it necessary?'

'I shudder to think, son... well done. Congratulations.' He paused, 'The Forest Brothers: they kept their end of the bargain, didn't they? Billy thought they might not you know? Though, I think he would have kept his word and still backed you if they hadn't. Again, well done, son,' said Bob Sherwood.'

The barrow-boy in him spoke, 'Of course he would have. He's in it too deep not to.'

Ben Robson smiled and reached out to shake his hand, 'An excellent result, Commander.' With sub skippers respect is not a right. It must be justified.

***

Chapter Ten.
Doppelgänger.

Anne slipped two passports over the table to Alistair Duncan. He inspected them closely, 'They're very good. I take it Mike Mason made them up?' he said, simply, and taking in a deep breath. 'So, I am now, both Anisim Polzin and Gerald Radleigh. I take it I leave tomorrow as planned?'

'No, you leave now... in a few minutes. Please give me your real passport... we cannot afford a mistake.'

'I'd feel safer with it in my possession.'

'The deal is, we keep your passport with us. Sims will return it to you at Netley... Alistair, we discussed all this before we came out to Korsør. Why the problem now?'

'Always the same... pre-op jitters, I suppose. Looking forward to it, though. Just the same when I flew Mosquitos... Pathfinder Squadron, you know. That's how I got into intelligence. Always the jitters.' He handed over his passport. 'I'll be alright as soon as I'm airborne.'

'Alistair, you project a certain persona, and it's one that I believe to be at odds with that which you really are. There's a car waiting outside.' They both stood up. Anne went round to his side of the table. She stood in front of him, looked him up and down and brushed a fleck of something off his lapel. 'Now, take care... I know you won't let us down.' With that, Anne gave him a kiss on each cheek and a hug.'

Leaving the office, he turned, smiled, and said, 'Thank you... simply spiffing of you. Feel ten years younger... worth coming for in itself.'

'Fiona watched him out of the window, 'Not a bad old guy really... lays the RAF thing on a bit heavy. Gutsy lot, the Pathfinders... got to respect him. Did you know he's got the Distinguished Flying Cross and bar?'

'Yes. Sims said they didn't dish those out like Smarties at a kid's party. He asked him what he got them for... old Alistair changed the subject.' She paused and quietly said to herself, 'Sims will be old one day. No medals for what he's done, though.'

'Pardon.'

'It doesn't matter.'

'The old man again?... Sims that is?'

'Yes,' said Anne, leaving the room.

*

He, Sims, now habituated to the smells, was no longer aware of the all pervading smell of hydraulic oil, cabbage, sweat and diesel. Dusty told him, 'After a long patrol it's outside that seems odd. It's like swapping from taking sugar and then not in your tea... you need time to get used to it, then, which ever swap you're in, seems right. I like fresh air best, though.'

Sub-Lieutenant David Mountford could hardly contain himself. 'What a first mission... what a way to get off the ground,' he said, to Dusty. 'Next stage, find a woman like Anne.'

With other personnel within earshot Dusty didn't

165

answer; his look and slight head shake were enough, they clearly stated, "not a chance, pal".

Between bouts of interrogation there was plenty of time to kill. A golden opportunity to learn much about subs. Every crew member knew every valve and what they did. Sims learned these. On the hydrophones he listened to passing ships and began to appreciate the difference in sound each type made. He familiarised himself with the sonar system and then the two different periscopes - *attack* and *search*. When he slept, he dreamed of Anne, lungs full of fresh air sailing *Alice* on The Solent, and Jean's cooking.

Action stations were called twice. Both times just as he'd nodded off into a fitful doze. Each time the target was identified as friendly and action stations stood down. He found it impossible to return to sleep immediately and returned to thinking of Anne.

*

A maritime phantom: a modern day *Flying Dutchman*, *Odin* materialized out of the mist banks and tied up alongside the same piece of dockside she had left six days earlier - there is an aura brooding and sinister about a black, wet submarine.

The operation was not yet over; they were not to be seen in public together, she was not there to meet him. Radleigh handcuffed and escorted by Mountford and Dusty was taken to a small room in the same building as Anne and Fiona's.

'Keep a good eye on him, lads. I'm going to find the missus.'

Fiona said hello and discretely slipped out of the room. Anne hugged him tight, buried her face in his neck, quickly withdrew, wrinkled her nose, she said, 'Darling, you've smelled nicer. I love the beard though. Keep it.'

He started to move away, 'I'll get myself a shower before Radleigh fouls the bathroom up.'

'Sims, don't be silly, come back here... I don't really care what you smell like.' She hung on to him again. 'Well done, darling. I am so very, very proud of you.'

'Well actually, I didn't do much... Dad, Ben Robson and the crew... stunning performance. I did manage to find out about Buster though,' he said, nibbling her ear.

She nudged him, '*Well!* Go on.'

'Are you sure you want to hear this right now... you know, seeing as I chuck-up so much?'

'Stop being a sod, *right now*, Sims Sherwood-Reeves. Tell me this instant.'

'Buster's not dead, love.'

'*What?* Did Radleigh tell you this.'

'Yes, of course.'

'What, just like that?'

'Not quite, no... I had to ask him nicely... you know, say, please.'

Anne held him at arm's length, 'Where is he, now, darling?'

'Who? Buster or Radleigh?'

'*Sims!,*' she warned. 'Buster, of course.'

'He's married to a Russian and trains Soviet Navy divers... I don't know where exactly, somewhere on the Black Sea. I'll squeeze more from Radleigh at Netley.'

'Does anyone in the government know this?'

'I'm sure they do, love. I shall expect some visitors waving all kinds of restrictive orders when they find out *I* do.'

'If his grave isn't empty, who do you think is in it?'

'Might be empty... not necessarily, though... most likely young Miles Stinton - that's another thing for me to get from Radleigh. He told me what happened to Miles junior too. It's going to be difficult telling Miles senior... might get Radleigh to do it, and watch old Stinton kick fuck out of him.'

'What happened to him?'

'Are you sure you want to know?'

'Yes.'

'Aston-Heyford killed him, stuffed his body into Buster's diving suit and then did the dismembering bit.'

'Do you think he'd repeat that in court? They might not take your word for it.'

'We've a signed and witnessed confession and he said it twice, once in front of Dad and Ben Robson. If a jury wouldn't believe them, who else?'

'How did it go with you, love? You look tired. Everything okay below?'

'Yes of course... stop worrying. A bit sleepless, though. We were told you had some Soviet subs on your tail. Not a good thing to know.'

'Yeh... no match for Dad and Ben Robson. I'll tell you about it later. Let me go and get showered and changed. Even the bloody guard dogs are backing off.'

She laughed, and pushing her fingers over his stubble, 'Don't shave, Sims... I love it. It will match your chest.'

*

Fiona cracked the door open, 'Okay if I come back in?'

'Yeah, sure.'

'Well done, Sims. Can't say how chuffed I am. The lads are going to go bonkers... we're going to have to have a piss-up to celebrate, you know.'

'In good time, love. We've got to get the bugger back yet. We'll get him as clean as you can make a traitor. His suit's in a disgusting state. He got a dunking, got soaked... grease and oil all over it. He can't go in that. Need to get something else for him to wear. It's a good thing we're returning on a military aircraft.'

'I'll see if I can get him some flight overalls,' Fiona said. 'When do you need them?'

'Tomorrow morning at the latest. Mountford, myself and Dusty, leave midday. Mountford flying from Copenhagen to Heathrow to meet Alistair and escort him to Netley. Dusty and myself go military with Radleigh. You, Anne and the Admiral follow the next day.'

'Why not the same day as you, Sims?' asked Anne. 'I'd like to be there when you arrive.'

'Sorry love, I need you two by the radio in case there's a change of plan.'

'So, two more days?'

'Afraid so... then you can take some time off... put your feet up.'

'What about you?'

'Stuff to do, love... stuff to do.'

*

Alistair Duncan checked in at Copenhagen International Airport as Anisim Polzin and waited in the First Class Lounge. In English he asked the attendant whether he spoke French or German. He said a bit of each and that he preferred English. There was to be a departure delay of three quarters of an hour and complimentary drinks would be served: Alistair ordered the best. 'So good to be back in the cockpit again,' he whispered barely audibly.

During the flight he watched two smiling hostesses moving from passenger to passenger, he rued his increasing age. The thought passed. Left to my own devices again; no back-up. His mind wandered; why did I mention the Pathfinders to Anne, haven't talked about those times for years... where's the connection? Loneliness, perhaps? Different flight today, no throbbing Merlins on my wings, no slew to the left when the wheels unstick. No photos, illuminating flares, flak or tracer. Target reached, quick one hundred and eighty degree turn and head for home - more flak, more tracer. Even with the navigator sitting beside, always alone... watch out for the Luftwaffe. See our coast... concentrate, concentrate, Luftwaffe, easy to think you're home and safe. Always just me. The approach, touch down, shut down, relief alone. Again I had survived. Walk across the apron alone, debrief, always alone during and after a sorti. Little said, softly, quietly let people into my life again... never easy. Loneliness, was a place Alistair revisited each time he flew his glider at Lasham. Each landing a survival.

*

He walked briskly up to Leading Seaman Miller. 'Sorry to do this to another human being, I'm pulling rank, You're going to be strapped to Radleigh all the way home.'

'Sir, if he tries holding hands with me, I'll deck him.'

'And I'll turn a blind eye. Is he cleaned up?'

'As ready as he will ever be... he didn't think much of the overalls and long-johns.'

He found Anne and said goodbye. 'See you at Hell Head, love.'

'What happens then?'

'How long have we been married?... and you still have no idea? Let me give a couple of clues: Jean's cooking, put champagne in fridge, long bath... there was something else... been a week or more, forgotten what.'

She bit his neck, kissed where she'd bitten and then thumped him. Then a much longer kiss. 'Perhaps that might remind you.'

'Turn back the sheets?'

'You're getting warm.'

*

'I don't trust you, Radleigh... try anything when we get back and I'll shoot you. Now, are you listening? ...this is not an idle boast, I'm a fair shot. I don't care where we might be, who might be watching, I will shoot you.'

'He doesn't miss,' added Dusty, 'ever.'

'I'm chilled, I think I've caught a cold.'

'You certainly have.'

Radleigh had not hooked onto the alternative sense of Sims' response.

'There's an overcoat and gloves in the car should we need them,' said Dusty.

Sims threw their bags into the boot, sat in the front seat, the car pulled away.

Another bumpy flight for Radleigh; he looked queasy.

'If you're sick on me, I will take my revenge later,' Sims threatened. The RAF Bristol Britannia flew direct to Lee-on-Solent.

*

Two staff cars waited on the apron; Billy in one of them. 'Wait here,' Sims said to Dusty, and walked over to Billy's.

He wound down his window, 'Well done, Sims. Get him to Netley and lock him up safe, lad. I'll talk to you tomorrow at Tunworth.'

'Oh, okay, as you wish. You can wait that long to find out about Buster, then? Funny thing, I had imagined you might like to know sooner,' he said, smiling at his boss, saluting and starting to move away.

'Commander! If you know what's good for you, you'll come back here immediately! What do you know?... come on, lad... get in this car and spit it out.'

Sims climbed into the back seat with Billy. Memories of Derek the driver: chauffeurs have ears, he thought. He leaned over the front seat; 'Driver, do you mind getting out of the car and moving a few yards away to the other car? Chauffeur gone, he savoured and took his time, 'Buster is not dead, sir.'

'Good God!... Though I must say I had suspected as much. You know the Cabinet Papers at the time of the incident are subject to the fifty year rule, don't you?'

'You forgot to mention it, didn't you, sir. Now we know why.'

'Radleigh must have told you this. Are you absolutely sure he's not lying?'

'Absolutely. It would be a cool bugger that lied just

as he was about to be ejected from a torpedo tube. And, for the record, I suspect Radleigh isn't that cool. He also signed a confession and repeated it in front of Admiral Sherwood and the skipper of the *Odin*, Commander Ben Robson... how about that then, sir?'

Billy threw his head back and roared with laughter, 'Wish I'd been there, Sims. Wish I'd been there.'

'I have something else to tell you, that will best wait until Tunworth. And, if I may, I'd like to get Radleigh settled down in Unit 4 before I come and see you. I've got more squeezing to do while he's fresh.'

Billy studied him, 'Whatever you think best, lad.'

He neither spoke to nor looked at Radleigh. Billy drove away. To think I once hung that young man out to dry. Thank God they didn't get him. Where the hell would I be now if they had? he thought.

*

He sat in Stinton's cottage; Buster Crabb news related. 'Stinton, he was going to eject him from a torpedo tube... what have we let loose on the world?' said Billy, rubbing his hands together. 'The problem is, he's too young for a captaincy, how on earth can we manage it?... he deserves it.. I don't want to lose him.'

'Do you think that's likely?'

'I don't want to take the chance.'

Miles Stinton passed Billy a Pusser's rum and a beer.

'Stinton, where on earth did you get this from?'

'My local pub, sir,'

'What the rum?'

'No, the beer.'

173

'And the rum, Stinton... the rum?'

'I have contacts.'

'You've never offered it me before.'

'I never had it before.'

'So, it would seem it's from a recent contact... hmm, Sims would fit that bill. That boy sails close to the wind, Miles.' Billy smiled, and took a good pull.

'The nature of the beast, John.'

Far beyond twenty years together, they were now, at last, on first name terms.

As the Pusser's settled and freed up the system, Stinton chuckled, 'We fixed his records from stoker to lieutenant and then to commander... why not his birth certificate as well?'

'How do you mean?'

'Get Mike Mason to make a new one... make Sims three or four years older.'

'Ha! I knew you'd fix it. I just knew. He's got the makings of a beard now you know... looks older too. Happy days, Miles, here's to happier days.' Billy raised his glass and then took a gulp. 'Better than painkillers.'

*

A good hotel with an excellent kitchen, one chosen because Radleigh, as Anisim Polzin, had only used it when others were fully booked - the concierge and porters would fail to recognise this was not the man.

In his room he brooded over his meeting with Anne and Sims at Hell Head, and then Anne and Fiona in Korsør. They're a new breed... a new generation... a kiss on the cheek from one, and one who swears like a trooper. I think my day has run its course... time I settled down and stopped struggling to get in and out of that damned Jaguar. He now saw his XK120 as an ineffective symbol: a failed bid to cling on to a long gone youth. I shall sell it and use the money towards a new glider.

He thought it a shame he would only get to use two of his three new suits. 'Pity I couldn't visit a few old haunts... cut quite the man in these,' he muttered, carefully knotting and arranging his tie. Anisim Polzin's doppelgänger checked out of the hotel, took a taxi to the airport and checked in as Gerald Radleigh - his temporary metamorphosis complete.

In civilian clothing, Sub-Lieutenant David Mountford arrived at Heathrow in plenty of time for the arrival. In Zurich, KGB agent, Mitzlav Goretsky, flicked through the Heathrow flight departure list; he phoned his embassy immediately, 'There is a Gerald Radleigh listed as one of the passengers of a flight to Heathrow.'

'Has the flight left?'

'Yes. Three hours ago.'

'Why wasn't the list checked before?'

'You assigned us to another task. If you recall, your wife needed collecting from the station... sir, it's all recorded for you to see.' And others too, Mitzlav thought.

'It's possible there might be another Gerald Radleigh.'

'It might be possible, sir... let us remain hopeful.'

'God's turd,' he muttered. It was an odd phrase, one he had taken to using since a Swiss minister had given him a copy of Carl Jung's unfathomable missive on dreams - he had read it for diplomatic reasons - the

phrase, now a life long companion, being the sole benefit to come from the experience. What was going on in
Jung's mind, he had thought. A giant turd smashing and
dropping through a glass roof. And to think Jung had set
himself up to treat others. *'God's turd indeed!'*

Nikolai Zima, boss of the Riga Commissariat in
Peschanaya Ulitsa, was yet unaware of what was about
to descend on him and his new broom sweeping cam-
paign. The phone rang. Radleigh's NKVD maid gave
hint to the first chink in his plans, 'Anisim Polzin did
not come home at all last night... as I have informed you
many times, he has been returning later and later.'

'Let me know as soon as he gets in... tell him I want to
see him immediately.'

'Yes, sir.'

Zima fumed. I warned him about this... he's haunting
golubie krogs again. 'I will place him under curfew,' he
muttered. It will not be necessary to inform Moscow at
this point. I need him here.

Nikolai Zima, fretted. Agitation replaced bluster. His
horse had bolted, twenty four hours later Radleigh and
HMS *Odin* were more than halfway back to Korsør.

The following day, Zima had still not made it known
Radleigh was missing: maid Valeriya Vetrov telephoned
NKVD Moscow direct.

He jumped; the hot-line from Moscow rang, 'Where is
Anisim Polzin?' The caller waited for his reply.

Zima pushed a bluff, 'Against my strict instructions,
he has been up to his old tricks again.'

'Your instructions may have been strict: their execution followed less so. Find him today and report back to me immediately you have done so. You were a rising star, you had a good career ahead of you. It will be a good thing for you not delay his recovery.'

Zima uncomfortable with the past tense, organised an immediate search of the docks. From the seedier areas, suspects were rounded up; the severity of their interrogation matched that of Zima's increasing agitation.

The Moscow line rang again, 'Zima... Polzin flew from Copenhagen to Zurich. As Gerald Radleigh, he has flown to Heathrow, he is now back in London... he has defected, and you, his controller, had better return to Moscow and hand us your report. Today Zima... today.'

*

In the arrivals hall, Alistair Duncan did not see David Mountford until he had stepped in front of him and said, 'We have a car waiting for you, sir.'

Duncan started, recovered, and said, 'Decent car, I hope? One befitting this suit.'

David laughed, Alistair was serious and priceless, 'It's good to see you again, sir. Everything went smoothly, I hope?'

'Spiffing.'

'Netley next stop.'

'Can I phone my wife?'

'I'm afraid not, sir. Not until our pick-up is in Netley too.'

Sub-Lieutenant Mountford sat in the rear seat with Alistair. When we get to Netley, sir, I'm afraid I shall have to get you to wear this hood. We want to keep to a minimum those who know you acted as his double.

The old boy was tired and nodded off. Near Guildford he woke with a jump, 'Were you on the sub too?'

'Yes, sir.'

'What did you think to it?'

'I developed a strong respect for submariners, sir.'

'What do you think of Commander Sherwood-Reeves?'

'I have a strong respect for him too.'

'Do you think he'd drive a hard bargain?'

'Sure of it, sir. If I may, why do you ask?'

'I'm going to flog my Jag. He seemed to like it... might be just the person. Now the E-Type's out... might not fetch much..'

'If you'll permit a piece of advice, sir... I'd talk to Anne.'

'She likes cars?'

'Not that I know of... she likes the commander quite a lot, though.'

*

A dark windowed car drove them to Netley NIDii Unit 4. Sims hooded Radleigh before leaving the car. Secure in his cell, he said, 'Do not let Lieutenant-Commander Woodruff anywhere near him, Dusty. If he tries anything, tell him you need my permission for access. If that doesn't check him, threaten to shoot the bugger. He's an interrogator, he'll try anything. Though remember, you've got the gun, and interrogators are not used to questioning anybody who's pointing a Browning at them. All clear?'

'Yes, sir. Seems a nice type to put a bullet into, sir.'

'Exactly my feelings. David won't be long. As soon he's confirmed Radleigh's here he's been instructed to let Alistair go. We'll use the same staff car that we came in to take him home. When he's gone, you and David work shift and shift about on guard. Lock the doors. If I get time, I'll give you a break tomorrow. I have a few words to say to him. Well done on *Odin*, by the way... first class performance. You impressed Commander Ben Robson.' He looked at Dusty; took in what he was seeing. 'You look a bit knackered, you're going to need a bit of help guarding him. A couple of lads from your course maybe. Ones you'd trust. Any names?'

'They were all pretty good, sir. There was a leading telegraphist; Jack Foster. He was quite useful, so was Jimmy Potts, a leading stoker. I'd definitely partner him.'

'A stoker?... Bit odd isn't it?'

'Not seen from where I'm standing, sir.'

Sims smiled, 'Seems a long time ago.'

'Rumours got about a bit rapid. Plenty applying to join NID now.'

'Rumours?'

'About you, sir... could have been about Anne, though.'

'Yeah, that would be it... any idea where these lads are now?'

'Unit 3, NID pool, sir.'

'I'll get them up here as soon as I can.'

'How long is Radleigh going to be here, sir?'

'Not sure. Until I think he's squeezed dry.'

Sims would start the interrogation after Alistair Duncan's departure. He phoned Tunworth House. The housekeeper said Billy was with Captain Stinton at Stinton's cottage. Not the best place to tell him what else I have to say, he thought. Poor old Miles.

*

'Where's Anne?'

'She'll be here tomorrow, love,' he said, giving Jean a hug and a kiss. 'Dad may be a little longer... he didn't say... decided to do some official business while he's there.'

'Where's there, Sims?'

'Butlins... Clacton.'

Jean bustled around failing to conceal her concern: blurting, 'Is she alright?'

'Top form... you'll see for yourself in the morning. I've organised an early flight... she'll be tired. Don't worry, love.'

'You look tired too.'

'More hungry than tired,' he said, smiling.

'*Well*, as no one told me what was going on and when you were coming home... I haven't got anything ready.'

He looked distraught.

'Oh, don't look so sad, do you really think I wouldn't have something on stand-by?'

'What we got?' he said, giving her a squeeze.

'Well you can have either Easter Pie or Pork Pie with pickles, pickled eggs, chutney and piccalilli... there's cheese too.'

'Hmmm, don't think much to the *or* bit, how about Easter Pie *and* Pork Pie?'

He left early: before Anne arrived at Hell Head House. He drove to Tunworth and breakfasted with Billy. 'So, lad, what else was it you have to say?'

'There's a delicate matter... I need a bit of advice.'

'Go on.'

'Well, I managed to drag out of Radleigh a bit more about Miles Junior. He confirmed Aston-Heyford killed him. It seems he was butchered by our late lord after he'd stuffed him in Buster's diving suit. I haven't a clue how to broach this with Captain Stinton. I shall try to get it out of Radleigh where the hands and head are... and if it's him buried in Buster's grave in Milton cemetery. It's a difficult one, sir... can't imagine how Captain Stinton's going to react.'

'Sims, let us be clear about this, it's my responsibility to tell Miles senior... and let that be the end of it. You've done enough. Tell me when you think you can get no more from Radleigh. Then I'll go and see him.'

'I thank you for that, it wasn't something I was looking forward to.'

'But, you would have done it?'

'Of course, sir.'

Billy got up and went the sideboard, 'More coffee, Sims?... what's your next move?'

'Thank you, yes... after interrogation?'

'Um... Yes.'

'I have ideas... not sure yet. It might depend on what I extract. Can I tell you when I'm more certain?'

'Of course. How do you mean, extract?'

'I'll pull his bloody teeth if necessary.'

Billy chuckled and said, 'Caution, Sims, caution...

there are rules about such things.'

'Radleigh didn't follow the book, did he? Can't see why I should?'

'Nevertheless, lad... caution.'

'Hmm. By the way, I've told Leading Seaman Miller to shoot Woodruff if he tries to access Radleigh.'

'Sims,' he handed him his coffee, 'I do not know a single person that likes or respects that man... do you know that? Why do you think that can be?'

'It's simple, he's a pervert. He dresses up what he does by calling it professionalism... he gets a deep enjoyment out of what he does. God knows what his private life is like... might get on well with Radleigh.'

'Pervert eh? That's taking it a bit far, don't you think?'

'*No!* No I don't. When he's talking, he's so precise... too precise, like he's keeping himself in check; scared he might show his pleasure... though he'd probably call it job satisfaction. Sir, I'm not wrong on this one. He'll go too far one day and kill someone. I feel it in my bones... just know it.'

'Now that *is* going too far.'

'No it isn't, sir.' And, as a reminder there was still a fourth ring missing on his sleeve, he said, 'I'd stake my captaincy on it, sir.'

Billy had listened as much to his sentence construction as he did to what he'd actually said - Sims had used "sir" more than once. This hadn't been an idle statement off the top of his head. It was one of conviction.

Billy watched him drive away down the gravelled drive and out of the wrought iron gates; he mulled over Sims' words. He walked into his study, picked up the phone, dialled, waited, and then spoke, 'Miles, you recall Adian McClusky?' Billy listened.

'Yes, of course, a bad do. Black marks all round.'

'We may need to check the details of his death... it's possible it might not have been down to natural causes. There are copies of the pathologist's report somewhere? Miles Stinton said something, Billy listened again... 'It was something Sims said... I wasn't happy at the time, busy... Portland... let it go. You and I had better meet... your place again, I think.' Admiral John Jessop frowned, and, as if it was contagious, put the phone carefully back in its cradle. 'Hmm.' He pulled a book out the many on the shelf, opened it, went to the window where the light was better. Billy flipped through the pages and occupied himself not reading. He snapped the book shut and gave a tight lipped, 'Hmmm.'

*

'Jean, is Anne not back yet?' he called from the hall.

Jean showed her head at the kitchen door, '*Shush!* She was so tired, she's gone to bed these last two hours. She wants to see you as soon as you're home... best let her rest though.'

'She who must be obeyed, must be obeyed,' he said, starting up the stairs.

'I don't know where you two get your energy from,' Jean said, returning to the door. 'I'll get some lunch on... you'll probably both need it,' she sniffed, smiled, and went inside.

Drowsy, still half asleep, 'Sims, darling, is that really you?'

'Might I ask who else might it be?' he said, leaving his clothes in a heap on the floor and slipping in beside her.

'Just the milkman after he's finished with Jean,' she said, hugging him.

'Hang on a minute, that's my sort of line.'

'Catching,' she giggled.

First a gentle reunion, later they slept some more.

Comfortable waking moments. Easy wandering talk. 'Was Billy pleased?'

'You remember once calling him an old sea-dog with two tails? It was that all over again. Do you know, the old bugger already suspected Buster wasn't dead. Apparently, there's a fifty year block on the Cabinet Papers. It had slipped his mind to tell me. *Slipped his mind!* Gimme a break!'

'He plays you absolutely perfectly.'

'*Comment? 'Ow do you mean, my little baguette?*'

'God, I love your accent.'

'You didn't think much of it when I chatted up Marie-Claude and her mum.'

Anne laughed, 'Oh Christ, I was so jealous... so incredibly angry. I could have killed them both... and *you* as well, you sod. Do you remember what I told you to do after our tiff. How could you still love me after that?' she said, kissing his neck.

'Easy, you've got a gorgeous bum,' he said, turning her over gently biting it, then rolling her onto her back.

'*Sims!*' she gasped.

***

Chapter Eleven.
Listening to Blackbirds.

Outside the interrogation cell at NIDii Unit 4, a nesting male blackbird was singing. He knew it was a male; Anne had told him only the males sing, and then, only at nesting time. Sims listened for a few seconds to the liquid notes pouring in through the open window, then closed it. Sound proofed silence, and except for two chairs and a table, the cell was bare.

He opened the door and called, 'Bring him in, Leading Seaman Miller.'

Sims pointed to the chair opposite,' Sit down, Radleigh.'

'Thank you. It is good to be back in Britain. I wish you to know I will cooperate in anyway possible.'

'To make sure we fully understand each other, I thought it might be appropriate to bring this photographic evidence to today's meeting. The first pile are images taken by my wife of yourself and Lord Aston-Heyford retrieving the drugs dumped off Bracklesham by the *Viktor Abakumov*. This second lot were also taken by my wife, and as you can see, in the presence of Admiral Jessop, Captain Miles Stinton, and that man there,' he said, pointing. 'He is Assistant Superintendent Paul Bartrup of the British Customs and Excise. They were all taken during our retrieval of your booty. Now, the third, shows the results of the search carried out in Bosham Castle... there's a lovely view of the priest hole and its contents. I insist you take a good look at them all. Go ahead.'

Radleigh picked up each pile in turn and carefully studied each image. As he finished each one he stacked them neatly into their original order and sat silently looking at Sims.

'Not at lot you can say, is there?' Sims said. 'Even without espionage charges, treason, supplying the names of western agents to the soviets, etc, etc, there's enough evidence here to put you away for a very long time. Can you think of any reason why you shouldn't go on trial or be handed to the close relatives of those agents who died?... come on Mr Radleigh, speak up, any reason at all?'

'Is it possible we can come to terms?'

Sims glared at him and thought, the terms are these Radleigh you creep; one way or another you are going to die.

Sims killed the urge to strangle him on the spot. 'Of course we can. I give you my word.' He thought again; and in your case, *that* word of mine will carry no more integrity, be no more principled than yours has in the past.

Relaxing, Radleigh eased himself back into his chair. 'What do you want to know? I am ready to start as soon as you like.'

'Everything. You can start by telling me where we can find the head and hands of Lieutenant Miles Stinton.'

Radleigh dropped his gaze and took particular care of his phrasing, 'I wasn't there at the time. Throagh gave me the details. It was a ghastly mess. As I told you previously, Aston-Heyford had murdered Stinton a few days before at Bosham Castle. He had invited him down there for the weekend and apparently shot him in the head... he removed the head before dumping the body... a bullet wound would be counter productive to the issued story of Commander Crabb's accidental death. As I also told you before, he also removed the hands so their fingerprints could not be used as evidence of who the body really was. I think that bit was Phillip Throagh's idea... Throagh seemed quite proud of his involvement.'

'There are a couple of other points I need clearing up. A report I received from a first hand witness, said that Buster was in no fit state to dive on the morning he was supposed to have disappeared... he practically had to be carried to his car. How then did he get to the *Rihards Vāgners?*... he was seen to enter the water at HMS *Vernon*. It would be a pretty good feat if he swam all the way there in his condition.'

'Yes, it is well known Commander Crabb was an inveterate drinker... and being so, he sobered very quickly. And yes, he did enter the water at *Vernon*, though he then swam round to Spice Island, was picked up by Phillip Throagh and delivered to the *Rihards Vāgners* in a car. Throagh said it was all quite simple really, security was slack elsewhere, and everybody was watching the Russian cruiser *Ordzhonikidze.* And, Commander Sherwood-Reeves, just so that we get things absolutely correct, Crabb was not drunk the night before. That was a complete fabrication. I know this, I was there. He had

had one or two and it may have appeared he was drinking heavily, but, that was all part of Throagh's and Aston-Heyford's plan. It would give a credible argument for his disappearance, you see. Throagh was quite clever at these things and Crabb was a good actor. Aston-Heyford wanted me to assist them. I'm glad to say I couldn't, I had to return to Paris the next morning.'

'I suppose that brings me neatly to my next question. Where did they get the frogman's suit from? Was it Buster's?'

'Yes. Throagh fetched it from the *Rihards Vāgners* before she sailed with Commander Crabb on board. He helped Aston-Heyford to get the suit onto the corpse.'

'I remind you it wasn't just a corpse... it had been a person... Lieutenant Miles Stinton... one of our lads,' Sims said, menace leaking from every syllable. 'All these bodies were people until you and your cronies converted them into cadavers. You'd do well not to forget that when you're talking to me.'

'Yes of course. I apologise. After the *Ordzhonikidze* sailed, they took the lieutenant's body just offshore and threw him overboard in Bracklesham Bay. His head and hands were put in a steel box and taken further out to sea before being disposed of.'

'That doesn't quite tie-up with the official report. The fishermen said his head was still attached when they found his body but it fell off while they were moving it and they were unable to recover it. What do you make of that?'

'No, that was not true... definitely not true. They were pressured into making that statement.'

'Okay, what else? Please carry on...'

'Aston-Heyford was surprised it took so long for the body to be found. He knew little of the tides and local currents and was quite shocked when it was found so close to Bosham. It unduly worried him. He saw it as a perverse act of fate or nature to place it where it was so close to the castle. I have to say it made me feel quite odd too... it was like a ghastly horror film... as though the body was pointing its handless arms at the accused. Who knows, it might have gone all the way to Bosham if the fishermen hadn't bumped into it. You know, I could never reconcile Aston-Heyford's apparent superstition and religious leaning... yet he appeared to spend his life with the sole intention of defying fate and God.'

He took some moments to continue. Sims bided his time. Radleigh was coming forward with more than he expected.

'Commander, some people are simply misguided, others are evil. I believe Aston-Heyford was of the latter ilk. In later years, he and Phillip Throagh scared me... it is one of the reasons when given the opportunity, I agreed to work abroad.'

Why is he telling me this? Is he damning Aston-Heyford and Throagh while whitewashing himself? Christ! Next he'll actually begin to believe he voluntarily defected with us, Sims thought. 'If I accept what you've said as the truth, who is it in the grave at Milton Cemetery?'

'The lieutenant... at least Aston-Heyford said it was. It was a difficult time. Several close acquaintances and professional colleagues refused to confirm the body was Commander Crabb's. Aston-Heyford plucked and pulled every string he was capable of. I do not know for sure, it may have been around this time, or earlier, it was rumoured that Crabb had defected. The Cabinet decided it was for the best to endorse their previous communique and conclusions regarding Crabb's demise: that he died investigating the Russian cruiser.'

'Hmm. Okay, I want to move on for the moment. Who gave the names of the Baltic agents to the Soviets?'

'To be absolutely precise; myself, I handed them the document during a diplomatic trip to Riga. However, I didn't know what was in the envelope or the names of the agents until later... my role in this incident was no more than a diplomatic courier. Philby was the man who instigated it and supplied the information... he wanted or needed to demonstrate his fealty to Russia. Aston-Heyford was involved also. I'm sure there must have been more than those two involved. I never knew who.'

Sims wrote and studied his notes. 'I want to move on once more. It is said that Hugh Gaitskell was murdered to make way for Harold Wilson to take leadership of the Labour Party and that Wilson is a sleeping KGB agent. What do you know of that?'

'I know none of what I shall tell you from first hand accounts. What I know came from Aston-Heyford and Throagh. That which Throagh told me had probably come from Aston-Heyford too. Throagh had no direct contact with the political end of our affairs.'

What had been said so far Sims was certain was the truth or very close to it. There was too much at stake for Radleigh to lie. Whether he was surrendering all he knew, he was not sure.

'Go on, what about Gaitskell?'

'The implications were he was murdered by someone from our lot.'

'What lot would that be... Britain or Russia?'

'Forgive me. I see your point, Britain of course. It had to be someone who was able to get close. Hugh Gaitskell was infected with a virulent foreign disease. It is said Philby supplied the vial. He handed it to a British diplomat in Beirut. Who it was who administered the dose can only be one or two people at most. As I said, they had to be able to get close.'

Control your breathing... steady your heart rate... think as if you are shooting on Number Three Range, think of it as though Lieutenant Cedric Hennerbury was watching, Sims thought. 'Give me the names, please.'

'You probably haven't heard of them, but, according to Aston-Heyford it could only have been either senior SIS agent Jack Passant or John Nicholas Rede Elliot.'

Sims now chose *his* words carefully. He used the word talk to substitute for interrogate or interview, 'Interesting... we're making good progress with our talks. Interesting to hear Rede-Elliot's name again. Gets around doesn't he?'

'I'm not sure I follow.'

'Rede-Elliot was Buster's official MI6 minder wasn't he?'

A wash of concern flashed over Radleigh's face; his composure ruffled. 'Yes.'

'Was he at The Sally Port hotel the night before with Throagh?'

'Yes.'

'It would have been better for you to tell me up-front. there are issues of trust at stake.'

'Commander, I wish you to know I am going to retain two of the most sensitive pieces of intelligence I am in possession of until I have received a written guarantee of my freedom and that I will receive the full diplomatic service pension I am entitled to... backdated to the time of my defection. This guarantee must come from The Government.'

'I see. That is an understandable request. I expected no less. One thing more, couldn't Gaitskell have simply contracted the disease while travelling?'

'No. He had not been to any countries where it was known to be. No, Commander, it had to have been administered.'

Sims made a note of Radleigh's demand. He looked up, 'I want to move on to the supply of drugs. Briefly, how did les Grands Amis get involved?'

'Commander, do you mind if I stand up and stretch my legs? I am still stiff from our sea trip.'

Sims opened the window. The blackbird's song, an unbroken claim to territory, was answered by another a short distance away. 'Mr Radleigh freedom lies out there with the blackbirds.'

'Am I to take it you mean if I cooperate I can join them? I look forward to it, I have missed them and their song.'

Sims closed the window. 'Please sit down again and let us resume. The sooner we get this over the sooner you can go. So, les Grands Amis and their involvement?...'

'It was quite easy really, with our intelligence and diplomatic roles, we were able to integrate ourselves into the KGB network. Their policy and objectives were essentially the same as ours: to undermine the social fabric of the west. Addictive drugs were to be the vehicle. Les Grands Amis helped them to do this and made a good living doing so... the KGB didn't mind at all, there were rich pickings for them too, that way many of them paid for their dachas and a life that many in the West would be quite envious of.

'I am interested how you can talk so blithely of your... les Grands Amis, that is... your objectives. How do you square that with behaviour contrary to the interests of the country that raised and educated you? This is not a part of the interview, I merely ask out of personal interest.'

'Is it as simple a question as that? We were young, some would say arrogant. It was, in many ways, no more than the swagger of youth and if that was played upon, we were easy targets. Could it not also be a question of human design overcoming human conscience? Regardless of which side of what political fence they may sit, most philosophers would agree, in one way or another, human beings are flawed, Commander, deeply flawed. You may be surprised to hear I believe communism to be also flawed... I have thought so for some time. However, I had made my bed... and sleep in it I had to. Communism is an idealistic theory that ignores the fact that humans are deeply flawed... the human species are not ants, Commander. Only rigid oppression can make them appear as though they are. What idealists want is unobtainable. They want a world as they would like it to be. The world, however, has many different likes: this is what we have to deal with, isn't it?'

'That's an interesting answer. One I'd like to pursue one day. However, we must move on. So, enlighten me, from where did the drugs originate?'

'The Soviets were keen to support a trade in any part of the world that would harm the enemy. For our part, as long as the quality was of the highest order, we were not concerned where it came from. But, to answer your question, from Afghanistan mainly.'

'Not solely?'

'No, South America was another excellent source. Though they mainly supplied the USA.'

'And the route?'

'For the European market the South Americans delivered to Beirut, then by Russian freighters to the Black Sea. Regardless of where it came from, all of the raw produce was processed in KGB laboratories. Our portion was separated and sent on to Riga. I know Afghanistan supplied the KGB much of our product, but the actual route I'm unsure of, the channels could vary so much, through Turkey, Bulgaria, Montenegro. Smuggling with the cooperation of the communist state security forces was the norm, Commander. After processing and purifying it simply arrived on our doorstep in Riga.'

'Were you the only KGB suppliers to the United Kingdom?

'We were at first the only suppliers to London; never to the whole of Great Britain. The Russian and Bulgarian mafias, or security services as they prefer, are involved too. For our part, we gained a reputation for quality and reliable delivery. Mafia supply to these markets was often interrupted due to their inter-factional disputes.'

'What about the Italian mafia? Surely they must have

their fingers in the pie.'

'They have a vastly over rated reputation, I'm afraid. At best their organisation is chaotic. In the United Kingdom, extortion and prostitution are much more in their line.'

Radleigh yawned.

'Bored?' asked Sims.

'No, Commander, extremely fatigued.'

'Very well... let's call it a day. Are your quarters comfortable enough?'

'Adequate, thank you.'

'Leading Seaman Miller!' he called. 'Take Mr Radleigh back to his room.'

Sims went to the smaller room adjacent, turned off the tape recorder, connected a second recorder and then copied what had been said on to smaller reels.

At Hell Head House he unscrewed the brass plate in the centre of the *Bellerophon* table and placed them inside the cavity beneath. After refitting the plate he carefully filled each screw slot with fresh polish. 'I only wish I could have taped him when he screamed from the torpedo tube... I'd have played it every Christmas,' he said, to Anne.

***

Chapter Twelve.
He's Back.

It was still dim lit early when Sims woke with a start; his head clear, next step plain, he knew what he must do. He quietly slipped out of bed, showered without singing and left Anne in sprawling snuffling sleep. Jean not up yet, he grabbed a biscuit, then another and gave one to Harry, patted him, then drove straight to Netley.

'You're early, sir,' said Dusty.

'Yeah. We've a lot to do. Get him dressed, we're going to Oxford to get him suited up and then to London to show him off. Where's David?'

'He did the middle watch... kipping, he's grabbed an empty bunk... got his feet up.'

'Wake him... you're both coming. Dress of the day: civvies, side arms carried and made ready. And Dusty, stick a couple of pairs of cuffs in your pocket.'

'Yes, sir. Things livening up, sir?'

'I do hope so... finding things boring so far?'

'Not on your life, sir.'

'That's enough *sirs* for this time of the morning.'

*

Former intelligence partners and friends shouldn't mind early calls: James Fox-Eastleigh was about to get one,

'James, know a good tailor in Oxford?' Sims knew he had one there.

'It's seven o'clock in the morning and you want to know if I've a good tailor... how did it go?'

'Good... got him. How's Joss?... tailor?'

'Well done... she's fine... Hawksett & Burroughs Carfax. I've got an account there, so has father.'

'Give them a call and tell them someone is coming this morning who needs something urgent doing.'

'You'll need an account for that.'

'I've got one... *yours.* I'll pay you later.'

'They're not the fastest movers: very good, but not fast movers.'

'They will be today. I need a stitch in ultra quick time.'

'What are you up to?'

'Tell you when I next see you. Get on to it as soon as they're open, please... it's important.'

'Okay, when are we meeting?'

'God knows... soon as we can. Give Joss a kiss from me.'

He phoned Hell Head House, 'Hi, Jean, morning, love. Is Anne up?'

'Yes, young man, and she's not too happy about you leaving without waking her. She's out walking Harry down the foreshore... call back in ten minutes or so. And, you forgot to put the lid back on the biscuit tin; they'll get damp.'

'Sorry, love, that was Harry's fault... he's *so* disobedi-ent... what we got for dinner tonight?'

'I'll think of something. What would you like, something special?'

'Jean, everything you do is special.'

'Oh, Sims, that nice.'

Good, biscuits forgotten, he thought.

*

'Have you two eaten?'

Sub-Lieutenant Mountford stifling a yawn; bleary, 'No, sir, not yet.'

'Nor've I. Come with me, David... we'll get ourselves replenished... topped up. Dusty, your turn when we're back.'

Sims said nothing until he'd finished his first cup of coffee and eaten most of his breakfast. 'David, We're going to Oxford to get Radleigh kitted out. I could do it in London... I don't want him recognised until I'm ready. Then we're off to The Smoke... we'll take him to Claridges to get him spotted by the press. Both belt and braces, David... Riga and Moscow must think it's a voluntary defection... we can't leave it to chance. Got to do it quick, too much at stake for The Forest Brothers. We'll get back to interrogating the bugger later. By the way, well done on *Odin*... first class, both of you.' He finished another mouthful. 'I'm going to nick a pool car to ferry us around. When Dusty's tanked up make sure it's full of juice. Right, I'm off to phone Anne.'

'Hello, love. Nice walk? Cobwebs blown away?'

'I do not like waking up and finding you not there.'

'Almost gave you a shake... if I had done... I'd still be with you. Anyway, you looked so peaceful.'

'What made you leave so early, darling?'

'We have to get Radleigh seen by the press, and do it quick... can't hang around, love. When I call you from London, I need you to phone The Telegraph and tell them you have an exclusive... speak to the political editor. Don't tell them who you are...'

Still miffed, 'Good God, Sims, as though I would.'

'... just making sure, it's still early. Tell the editor Radleigh has always been one of our agents and has duped the Soviets big time. Tell him he is at Claridges... tell him to instruct whoever he sends to wait at reception and he'll be met. That's all you need to do.'

Always persistent, 'Why can't I come too?'

'We're leaving shortly... got to get on the road. I need you to do what I've asked.'

'Commander Sherwood-Reeves, I want to be there too. I want to be involved... Korsør was boring, just waiting... biting my nails. I can just as easy phone from London, and you promised we'd work together until it was absolutely unavoidable not to, remember? Or are you in so much of a hurry that your promises don't need to be observed? I'm waiting for an answer, Sims.'

'Ahhh, yes I did, didn't I... what the hell am I thinking of?... of course you can... I'm being dense. Get yourself ready, we'll pick you up at Hell Head. Bring your Beretta. And, phone Pat, please, and see if he can get the squad together at Claridges for a bit of assistance... tell them to carry side arms, they might need to shoot Radleigh. I reckon we'll be there by late afternoon.'

*

'An early start, Commander. Mornings are not my best time.'

'We're not chatting today. Listen, I have orders to gradually reintroduce you to society. They've left it up to me how we're going to do it. So, my way... understand?'

Radleigh nodded, 'Not in this dreadful outfit I hope.'

No, we want you looking your best. We're going to Oxford and we're going to get you a new suit made. While we're waiting, you're going to have your hair cut and a shave. While we are there, your name will be Doulton. In London you will revert to your own name.

'We *are* going to London, are we? Will I be able to call friends?'

'Yes to London, and no to calling friends. You're going to meet the press and tell them how between us we hoodwinked the Soviets. You will keep what you tell them to a minimum. Say to them you are going to write a book about your exploits and are not going to give the guts of it away at the moment. But, tell them if they play ball, they can have first shot at the serialisation. Then, when we've done with Fleet Street, we're coming back to Netley for the next stage of the game.'

On the steps of Hell Head house, Anne waited for them. Sims got out of the car and told Radleigh to do the same, 'Stay where you are, lads, I've an introduction to make.'

He pointed to the front door, 'In,' he said. 'Come on, love, you too.'

Radleigh, uncomfortable not knowing what was happening, shifted his weight from foot to foot.

'Anne, this is Gerald Radleigh the man who organised the two NKVD agents who shot you. Is there anything you'd like to say to him?'

Before she could reply Radleigh blurted, 'My dear, I

had no idea they might have shot you... that wasn't their brief.'

Anne, her voice icy, said, 'I have an unattractive scar on my shoulder... if I were to go sunbathing people would stare, and when I think about it I can't disconnect your involvement. It was very painful you know? Also, if you call me 'my dear' again I will shoot *you* somewhere very painful... just so you know what it feels like to have a bullet rip through your flesh. And, I will position the wound such that every time you use the toilet you'll deeply regret your actions.'

Jean had entered the hall unseen. She witnessed the conversation. She stepped forward, 'If I ever get you alone, I will see to you... I will see to you, by God. How dare you shoot my daughter?'

Radleigh stepped back in surprise, as did Sims and Anne. 'I... I understood her mother was dead.'

'She is, and I took over the love, care and responsibility her mother would have given her. So, Anne is *my* daughter. You'd better get him out of my sight, Sims. I'll mop out the hall when he's gone.' She stamped out off into the kitchen. Anne followed her.

To Radleigh, he said, 'Go and get in the car.' Sims waited in the hall for Anne to return. He wouldn't interrupt.

She came back wiping her eyes. 'Jean stays with us forever,' she said.

Radleigh was relieved to get away from Hell Head House and the danger lurking there in the form of Jean Calver. Despite Anne's threats he looked happier than he had done for many days, nevertheless, he remained silent for the greater part of the journey to Carfax, his hauteur broken only when passing notable eyesores. Didcot power station seemed to anger him particularly, 'A beautiful countryside marred by this unsightly monument. I used to walk these hills... always visible; always hideous.'

Despite his loathing Sims, much to his disgust, found himself in agreement with Radleigh.

He stood waiting. High class tailors smell different from high street clothing retailers. It was distinctive, why? he wondered. Hawksett & Burroughs was quietly busy. 'Good morning, sir. Have you an appointment?'

'Yes, I need to speak with your manager.' The assistant hesitated as though he would question on what authority. 'This very moment,' Sims added.

It was probably something in Sims' tone; he thought better of inquiring. ' Of course, sir. Your name, sir?'

'You won't be needing it.'

'If you would be so kind as to wait a moment, sir.'

Sims, disinclined to wait, followed him into the manager's office. 'That will be all,' he said to the assistant, gently but firmly guiding him by the elbow out of the door and closing it. He turned to the manager, 'Your name, sir?'

'Swanbourne... Mr Swanbourne.'

'You will have had a call from Mr James Fox-Eastleigh this morning?'

'Yes, I have... that is so.'

'For the purpose of this exercise, on no account are you to mention Mr Fox-Eastleigh's name to your staff and nor to the Mr Doulton you are going to outfit. You are not to enter the work you are about to do in your books. Send the bill to Mr James Fox-Eastleigh on a hand-written note... no copies made. Do it yourself. Is that clear?'

'Yes, yes, but this is all most irregular,' he tetched.

'We know... life outside this cosy world *is*.'

'Now, as I said, the man we have here is a Mr Doulton. He is to be fitted with a perfectly cut suit now... immediately... this morning. Can you do it?'

'May I remind you, we only make perfectly cut suits, sir. To do it in the time stated, we may have to alter one we are making for a customer, but yes.'

'Let's get going then. Oh, there's something else; do not put your label on the lining. Very sorry, advertising not allowed.'

'This is most irregular,' he muttered again.

'Mr Fox-Eastleigh's a regular customer I take it?'

'Yes... he and his father valued clients for years.'

'Let's keep it that way.' Sims, covering his name, showed him his Naval Intelligence identity card. 'We're not going to make you sign The Official Secrets Act... I'll come back personally to see to you if any of this gets out... understood?'

'Yes, sir.'

'I'm going to fetch him now. By the way, he'll need a shirt, tie, socks and shoes.'

'We don't supply shoes, sir.'

'Then send an assistant to get some, surely that's not impossible is it?'

'No, sir... of course, sir.'

'David, drive up to the front entrance. Anne and I will

take him inside. Unclip him, Dusty.'

Dusty removed the handcuffs. Radleigh rubbed his wrists.

'Right, you two, you can't shoot defectors on an empty stomach, park up and get yourselves something to eat and drink. Then relieve Anne and myself. Okay?'

'Yes, sir.'

Gerald Radleigh left Hawksett & Burroughs immaculately turned out. With the change of attire came a change in his demeanour. The bedraggled, sodden , self pitying wreck of a person on HMS *Odin,* now restored to full diplomatic superiority.

So that's the answer... every thing you need, Radleigh, thought Sims. The prestige that comes from a well cut suit and the world's your playground. I shall take great pleasure in handing your overalls back to you at Netley.

*

The tone and approach decided, Anne called The Telegraph, 'I want to speak immediately to either the editor in chief or your top political reporter, preferably one who can handle an exclusive and very big story.'

'They're both very busy at the moment, madam. Can I get you someone else?'

'Can I have your name please?... what I am talking about is not a matter for a bye-line... it is politically huge. I should warn you that you are not going to be popular if I'm forced to take this story to the The Times... your name please?' She quickly scribbled it down.

'Wait a moment please., ma'am.'

She heard a rapid and muffled conversation, then,

'Trevor Mitchell here... what have you got, love?'

'Don't ever call me love again,' she said, frostily.

'Sorry, ma'am.'

'The defector Gerald Radleigh is back in London. He's done the dirty on the Soviets. Are you interested?'

Trevor Mitchell held his hand up for silence; the office went as quiet as a busy newspaper office was able. He scribbled "Gerald Radleigh's back" and passed it on to the editor.

'Yes, we're interested. How sure are you of your facts? How much do you want?'

'No payment and very sure. Mr Mitchell, we cannot afford to wait. So, if, before the story is handed elsewhere, you have time to check recent flights from Copenhagen to Zurich under the name Anisim Polzin; that's Radleigh's Russian name by the way, and then check flights from Zurich to Heathrow for a Gerald Radleigh, you'll discover we know what we are talking about. Are you going to meet us or not? What is it to be?'

'Yes. Where?'

'Claridges. He is there under the name Doulton. Bring a photographer. If your photographer takes any shots other than those of Radleigh we will destroy his equipment... I want to make sure, you, he, and your editor understand this. Is that all clear?'

'Yes indeed, ma'am.'

Sims stood waiting near reception; near enough to overhear conversations. With Fiona sat near the main entrance and the rest of the squad at every other exit, Radleigh had little chance of slipping his leash.

Dusty and David sat a short distance from Radleigh. He, Radleigh, sipping carefully at his scotch. Dusty muttered, 'I'm a goody and he's a baddy... so what happens? he gets the effin' drink; no bleedin' justice. And, *and...* if he wants to go to the bog, I have to go with him.'

'Patience; it's your duty to Her Majesty... keep your mind on the job, Leading Seaman Miller. I'll buy you a pint this evening.'

'Mind on the job!... difficult with all this crumpet around... seen anything you fancy? Anything that might match Anne?'

'Leading Seaman Miller, may I remind you my mind's strictly focused on work.'

'Yeah, okay. I saw you clocking that bit in the blue silk.'

'She needed checking out. How are we to know she isn't a foreign agent.'

'What with a bleedin' poodle!'

'In future, pay more attention to your lectures. It's a perfect disguise... you've a lot to learn.'

'Not on the pistol range I haven't.'

'That was a low punch, Miller. A long way below the midriff... in fact, almost knee level. For that, I might just stop your leave for fourteen days.'

Followed by his photographer, Trevor Mitchell, political editor for The Telegraph fairly raced into reception at Claridges, 'I have an appointment with a Mr. Doulton.'

Sims stepped forward and, with his name obscured, showed him his Naval Intelligence identity pass. 'Mr Mitchell, if you value the odd exclusive, you will not mention our involvement until I, and only I, ask you to do so or give you permission. Is that understood?'

Mitchell nodded his assent.

'You should also understand that what we are doing today is only part of a much bigger deal. I assume you would wish your paper's involvement in that too?'

'Mitchell nodded once more.'

'Come with me.'

He turned to the photographer, 'Make sure I'm not in shot. Take your pics now and leave immediately.' They sat down. 'Mr Radleigh, this is Trevor Mitchell of The Telegraph. Perhaps you'll be kind enough to tell him a little about what you've been doing and about your forthcoming book.' He turned to Mitchell, 'I can give you twenty minutes, then, we have to go. No one else will get a look in today.'

Radleigh stuck to his brief. 'It has been a long and, at times, difficult assignment. As you are well aware, my name has been dragged through the mud. However, all was not as it seemed...' Sims got up and left them to it.

Anne ordered coffee. Sims sat watching both Radleigh and the time. 'I gave Mitchell twenty minutes.'

'He's enjoying all this attention.'

'Let him, he's got the tough stuff to come.'

'Sims, when The Government realises he's back, there's going to be so much to explain.'

'They won't know it's us who's got him.'

'At first maybe. Someone's bound to leak... someone *will* leak, Sims. Someone from our lot. The Government will then demand his release, or his handing over to MI5 or MI6.'

'I know... that's why we have to get everything we can from him before that happens. Here's the most important thing, by tomorrow Moscow will know all about it and the Forest Brothers will be in the clear and that completes phase one and a most important aspect of the entire mission... Dāvis has a family too.'

She squeezed his hand, 'What's phase two involve?'

'I guess we're going to have to sit back and wait to see what happens next.'

*

Heston waited until he had tipped back one drink and poured another. He could not afford to wait longer just in case someone stole his thunder. 'He's back,' he announced.

'Who's back?' questioned Scammel.

'Radleigh of course. You said there'd be much trouble, remember? You said he could never keep his mouth shut. You were right there, he's going to write a book... the *Telegraph* are going to serialise it. My, my, someone's in for a hot time.'

Jack Passant stood stock still, '*Rubbish*, how do you know... if he *was*, I'd know about it.'

Heston, as ever, gloating when first with the news. 'Well, your sources of intelligence aren't that reliable are they, Jack? Radleigh's back I tell you, read tomorrow's Telegraph. I got it from the horse's mouth... straight down my hot-line.'

'This is not possible,' Passant spat. 'He's a double, for God's sake.'

Heston laughed, 'Apparently, a triple actually. He's pulled a fast one over everybody including you and your lot, Jack. I'd go and sack a few straightaway.'

Out of earshot James Ross looked at Passant and muttered, 'First Phillip Throagh and then Lord Aston-Heyford. I put it to you Charles was hounded to his death by those two. Their hand is in this somewhere.'

'Our commander is not the problem! Take away his leader and without him Sherwood-Reeves will cease to function. After all he provides everything.'

'You realise what you're saying?'

'Yes, and you do realise we kill one person and two birds with one stone, don't you? Can't you see that?' Leaving the room, Passant turned to Blunt and stated, 'I can use your telephone.'

'I'm taking bets he'll come back looking like thunder... any takers? I'll give one hundred to one against Radleigh still being in Riga,' offered Laurence Heston

A towering, anvil topped *cumulo nimbus* drifted in: a thunderstruck Passant re-entered the room. James Ross took him to one side, and unheard by the others, said, 'You don't need to tell me. You are right... dangerous times and a time to act I think.'

Sewell butted into the general conversation and said with his usual aspirated "f" and flicked a hint of a "w" 'My opinion of him doesn't change, he's an educated fool. And, as he certainly *is* one, who knows, he may just have signed his own death warrant... I shudder at his idiocy, just shudder. How is it possible that the best education money can buy produces such a perfect example of utter foolishness? Wasted money... wasted money. What do you think, Anthony?'

'You may have a point, Brian,' an impartial Blunt replied.

Scammel, finding himself with a glass in each hand, emptied one and took a gulp of the other. He placed the empty on the polished table. 'Not everybody will be upset; Le Fanu will be *so* pleased.'

Blunt removed the glass and wiped dry the smear it left. Scammel, with a drunk's self-centred unawareness helped himself to another gin.

Passant spoke, 'Who is your *Telegraph* contact, Heston?'

'Jack, that is not a question you seriously expect me to answer, is it?'

'It could be a matter of national interest and security, so, yes I do.'

'Come off it. Don't you mean your security? You're getting nothing from me. Go and see your own men and ask them why they're so slack. My informants are mine.'

Without saying more, Passant left the room and the meeting.

'Well!,' said Sewell, 'he didn't even say goodbye.'

*

His picture prominent; Radleigh dominated the front page of The Telegraph. From early morning to evening their switchboard jammed with calls from government officials wanting to know how they got wind of his return, and literary agents and publishers wanting a slice of the action of the forthcoming book. The chief editor was called to a chill meeting at Downing Street; threats were made, he stonewalled. Radleigh's double defection was, as Anne had told them, a huge story. An old, hard bitten hack, would lose no sleep over mayfly ephemeral ministers' threats. They did not concern him. He had it within his power to destroy them and they knew it.

*

For public consumption, the Government claimed it to be a significant coup against the Iron Curtain intelligence network. Radleigh was lauded, hints made of honours to be bestowed in the New Year's list. Behind this Janus mask they were furious and demanded of MI5 and MI6 to know what was going on. They did not bother to ask the Naval Intelligence Division.

Secret Intelligence Service top brass were called to the Cabinet office, it was an insane meeting. Careers were at stake; tempers flared. MI6 furious, bellicose and insistent Radleigh was their property and MI5 was to hand him over immediately.

MI5, convinced this a double bluff, equally insisted that as Radleigh was on British soil he was rightfully theirs.

From the squad and his own reliable connections, the news quickly filtered through to Billy. He sat at Tunworth House chuckling. He was more than happy to let them squabble: his beloved Naval Intelligence Division had got one over on them. When the time was right they would know the truth. Then I will strut as they strutted. In the meantime let them tear at each other's throats. Billy Ruffian raised no sympathy. Let the walls be spattered with blood. Let the floors be awash... and let there be plenty of it, he thought. The bastards sat there smirking while the Naval Intelligence Division was keel-hauled, flogged, hung, drawn and quartered over Portland and Buster Crabb. They'll get no pity from me.

*

His habit was to open the newspaper without looking at the front page. Only when he had read the obituary column did he return and start at the beginning. He recognised the suit first, then, the person wearing it. 'Good Lord! It's Mr Doulton,' coughed Swanbourne, putting down the paper as though it had something nasty crawling over it.

'Who, dear? What is it?'

Sims' threat echoed; "I'll come back personally to see to you if any of this gets out... understood?" 'Nothing, dear, nothing,' he fluttered. Here was a man who, discounting the time the Vice-Chancellor of Magdalen College vomited on the fitting room floor, had little of interest happen to him in years. So sad he was unable to tell anyone.

'Who, dear?'

'I was just thinking out loud... a Mr Doulton,' he lied. 'He was a little overcome at the business. It was the material finishing again, you know it affects some people that way.'

'Oh... yes, dear. Do you remember the Vice-Chancellor of Magdalen College?'

'Yes, dear.'

Nigel Swanbourne's life had been stirred. Excitement and bustle of this kind never before entered the premises of Hawksett & Burroughs. In his office, he gathered his staff around him, showed them the newspaper, and implied it was a matter of national security and that it would be most indiscreet if not dangerous for them were they to mention the events the previous day to anybody. 'We have been touched by the world of espionage... people can disappear in the night,' he said.

Doddering, tottering, not a young person among them... a creak sounded. 'Did you say something Mr Bevan?'

'No, Mr Swanbourne... it was my hip. It does that occasionally.'

'You must get it seen to, customers might find it upsetting being creaked at.'

Swanbourne knew little to nothing about the world of intelligence matters, however, he considered himself a fine judge of the bespoke suit and its tailoring. And, of this matter it was evident British intelligence had not a clue - clearly, they needed educating.

As for the rest of the male staff of Hawksett & Burroughs, there grew a shifty, secretive swagger to their demeanour. Mr Beggs gripped and wielded his pinking shears in the manner an assassin might. The sole female employed at Hawksett & Burroughs, Mrs Mimms - accounts department; completely overtaken by mystery and vampism had looked at Beggs strangely - he found it disturbing.

Later that morning after dismissing his staff from his orderly, respectable office, Swanbourne sipped his tea, delicately nibbled a rich tea biscuit, and hand-wrote another note to James Fox-Eastleigh:

Dear Mr Fox-Eastleigh,

Thank you so much for calling in at Carfax this morning and settling your account so promptly – there was really no need to do this the very day after the fitting and completion. Also, I must apologise for not being able to give you more information about this rather sudden and unexpected visit.

On another matter, I have given much thought to your associate who escorted Mr. Doulton for the emergency fitting. If you are to see him again, may it please you to inform him that Hawksett & Burroughs could tailor him a suit that would make the gun he carries completely undetectable.

Yours Sincerely
J Swanbourne esq.
Senior Manager; Hawksett & Burroughs.

*

'Yes, thank you, admiral, Harry is well... and he stays here.' Jean put the phone on the table and called, 'Admiral Jessop is on the phone for you, Sims,'.

'Sir?'

'Sims, I've been thinking about our conversation regarding Woodruff and where, if you remember, you said he would go too far one day?'

'Yes, I do... and he will. He's twisted... for him interrogation is a vocation, not a job.'

'Well, lad, I have a feeling he has already done so. Some years back we had in our custody a suspect called Adian McClusky. He was supposed to be a sometime IRA, MI6, MI5 operative... God knows who he really belonged to. The point is, Sims, he died while under interrogation. The chief interrogator was our man Woodruff; he was a lieutenant then. The autopsy stated his death was due to natural causes. Apparently McClusky had been on the run from both sides, had lived rough and contracted double pneumonia and pleurisy while doing so. Lad, we were suspicious at the time. Due to Portland and other issues NID did not follow up on those suspicions. Now, the point of this call is that along with your many other tasks, I should appreciate you digging around a bit... see if you can unearth anything. See what you can bring to light, Sims.'

'I'll do my best.'

'I'm sure you will,' the old admiral said, putting the phone down.

***

Chapter Thirteen.
Kitty.

'You enjoyed yourself with the press, I see. Well, we got you the coverage we wanted. You are a huge celebrity now, and The Government is going to have to handle you very carefully. That, let me tell you, may be worth more than their guarantee of your future.'

'That was very clever of you, Commander.'

He had extracted most of the essential information from Radleigh. Without revealing Alistair Duncan's name, he quietly told Radleigh of his doppelgänger's route to freedom and that this was to be the official story: Copenhagen to Zurich to London. He gave him the boarding passes, luggage tags and the name of the hotel he stayed at in Zurich. Any mention of HMS *Odin* or his abduction would bring Sims to fulfil his promise of retribution. Fifteen signed and witnessed documents were made detailing Lord Aston-Heyford's, Throagh's and his own complicity in the defection of Buster on the Latvian timber freighter *Rihards Vāgners*; his meeting with Buster and his Russian wife near the Black Sea; Lord Aston-Heyford's murder of Lieutenant Miles Stinton, and the years of Soviet assisted drug smuggling into the United

Kingdom. Radleigh knew nothing of Aston-Heyford's slaughter of Pearl's niece Linda and the murder of Keith Salford. He had said, "Aston-Heyford was becoming increasingly deranged. He took to talking to himself and more than once confused me with Phillip Throagh. His deteriorating mental condition was the main reason I opted to leave when I did... I'm not surprised he took to killing. If he had not committed suicide, there would have been many more deaths."

Sims did not need recourse to his recently learned interrogation techniques. Gerald Radleigh was deliriously happy to be back in the United Kingdom and wallowed in the press limelight. He gave all; readily. Twelve of the signed confessions Sims kept in his own possession. Radleigh seemed oblivious of the danger he presented to old acquaintances: his presence back in society threatened them. The book he was to publish and its serialisation by The Telegraph amounted to little more than signing his own death warrant. Past associates and dark shadows gathered.

*

At Netley, Billy and Sims took a short walk to Southampton Water's edge: a short walk and a long conversation with many implications that Sims was unable to immediately interpret. Later he was to recall with clarity and understanding its meaning.

It was high tide. They stopped to watch a liner leaving port and retreated a few yards inland well before its wash slopped up the shallow shore and against the low retaining wall.

'He seems oblivious to the danger he's in. Surely a

man with his diplomatic background must be aware of that? He's got to be aware of the machinations of that level of politics, hasn't he?' asked Sims.

'Perhaps he knows he shot his bolt a long time ago. It may be he knows his days are numbered.'

'Sounds like he's committing a slow form of suicide.'

'Hmm, do you think we've got all there is to have?... we must squeeze him dry before he's assassinated... like you, I think it can only be a matter of time.'

Until Sims coughed up the bargaining plea for his captaincy, he would say nothing about the deal Radleigh wanted from The Government. 'All? I doubt it... the important stuff, yes. Enough to get him hung. And, we've shown MI5 and MI6 for what they are; Throagh, Radleigh and Aston-Heyford double dealing from within and right under their noses... what a bunch! No doubt a few of them are going to end up on the dole queue... we've given them more than a few red faces.'

Billy laughed. 'We've done that, lad. NID suffered greatly at their hands... more interested in scoring points against their own intelligence services than getting on with their direct responsibilities; their responsibilities to their country. It may sound contradictory to you, here am I saying they were more interested in scoring points, and I'm gloating over those we've scored. But, yes, it gives me more pleasure than you can imagine to see this happen. It means so much.'

'You said "their responsibilities to their country", which country would that be? Seen in a certain light, they may have been doing just that.'

Billy hrumphed. 'You've a point there. But Radleigh, Radleigh... what do we do with him now?'

He threw a glance at Billy, his old face seemed more craggy, more lined than usual - it lacked its usual colour. This observation that prompted him to say; 'It must have been hard work... difficult times keeping everything together after Portland and Buster's disappearance... must have been a hell of a strain. How on earth did you manage?'

'Strain, yes, it comes with the territory. A common enough phrase, nevertheless a fitting one.'

'I now have some little inkling of what you mean.'

'You've done so well, Sims. Threw you in deep end, didn't I?'

'Yes, that's a fact you did,' he replied, without malice. 'Forgiven?'

'Of course... if you hadn't, I wouldn't have met Anne. And, I've learned so much. It's been a bit of a nightmare time, but yes, definitely forgiven.'

'Thank you. That means a lot too.'

'Sometimes I feel I've done something positive for Britain and then, if I try to analyse what's going on, I'm not sure... its seems like there's a battle going on with no defined lines saying who is who... it's a bloody mêlée with no team colours and no effin' ref. All one can do is to keep chipping away at what one thinks is right...' Sims stopped for a few moments. '...perhaps I'm not making myself clear.'

'You're echoing my lifetime feelings almost exactly. As you progress through your career, and I'm sure you have one, some things will clarify; others will never. Politics is a turbid, turbulent arena, and the distinguishing line between friend and foe; ally and enemy, are often blurred. That is something you have to live with.'

A sudden gust blew along the foreshore. Not a particularly strong one, just with enough force to make one, with thumb and forefinger, grip one's hat by the peak. Billy staggered enough for Sims to need to place a steadying arm in support.

'Caught me off balance.' Billy said. He looked embarrassed. He gripped Sims' supporting arm, 'Young man, don't abuse time: there is so little of it; we, you, have so little of it. It's a commodity in such short supply. I want you to look about yourself. Ask, the question, where am I? Ask, why you are where you are. Only when you answer this honestly can you begin the most important journey of your life: the journey into knowing who and what you are. Fate has a habit of putting *you*, Sims, on the right track - you must always give Fate a chance and then assist her all you can. It is your job to do so. Listen to Fate. She will tell you what to do.'

There was an urgency in Billy's tone. Being off balance was catching: Sims uncertain of the deeper meaning to what he was hearing now.

Billy continued: 'Chance and circumstance... think about it, nobody forced you to be here today. Circumstance may have given you the opportunity, but, you are where you are because that is where your efforts have led you and that you haven't turned your back on your responsibilities. And, you haven't turned your back or run away for reasons you well know but may have found difficult to voice. You have remained because deep inside you know this is where you were meant to be.'

'I feel that sometimes, sir. Sometimes I feel it a lot. It can be a bit overwhelming.'

'It's called destiny, lad.'

They moved along the path to a nearby bench and sat down.

'Safer sitting than standing, young man.'

For the first time since he had known him, Sims saw Billy as being vulnerable; frail. He had never thought of him as aged; always wizened, tough, an elder without being old. The thought caught him out. For some reason he could not begin to explain, possibly through some subconscious connection, the feeling reminded him of an Icelandic patrol he'd been on once. Huge seas were the daily norm. When he stepped out on to the upper deck a blast of ice flecked spray had hit his exposed face. Maybe it was due to the similarity of the sensation; both sense freezing and body chilling experiences.

They sat for some minutes watching the shipping to and from Southampton's busy port. Billy changed subject. 'I've noticed, all but your enemies like you. You're affable, intelligent, yet, you don't seem to have many male friends.' It was an enquiry more than statement.

Sims considered this. Then said what he had often thought. 'Sir, I have Anne. When I am with her, I need not the company of other men; she is proof I am one.'

Billy chuckled. 'A wonderful answer. You are, as I have often thought, a very lucky man, Commander Sherwood-Reeves.'

*

Thin delicate sun of late afternoon filtered through the window, water colouring the books lining the wall. The library, unlit: warm fragrance of beeswax polish and mahogany: light and shadow. Shirley sat here by the

Bellerophon table clasping and unclasping her hands. Anne close by, 'You must speak to me... tell me what's the matter.'

She had arrived in a taxi and apologised for not calling. She had said she had not done so because they may have tried to get her to say what was wrong over the phone instead of visiting. She could not do this, what was on her mind was too important and needed to be said to their faces.

'I have to talk to Sims... yourself, of course, too. Anne, I'm going to resign... leave MI5.'

'Why?... why on earth, why?... tell me. How will the squad function without you? It needs you, we all need you. The squad includes us from NID now. And disregard, if you may, that we are fond of you, Sims and I truly appreciate what you do and have done. You are *so* necessary.'

'Thank you. I know much more than I've said... I've said so little... I'll wait for Sims to arrive.' She returned to wringing her hands.

Fresh air breezed in, 'Hi Shirl'... nice surprise, what's new?'

She got up and kissed him.

He said,'Wow, a kiss!... bit sudden, love... problem?'

Shirley, close to tears, biting her lip, did not answer.

'Look, love, we have to come to an understanding; I'm never going to leave Anne... you're just going to have to face facts.'

She managed a smile. 'Sims, the others must not know... ever.'

'Know what?' he said, glancing at Anne. She gave a

slight shrug.

'I've kept silent far too long. You have both risked your lives, and you, Anne, your baby... you will both be parents.' If what she uttered, wasn't entirely coherent; her mind at least was. She thought what she was doing was rational and felt right. 'I've kept silent too long. I know things... classified things... I know you understand I should not disclose these things.' She looked at her watch, played with her necklace... counting rosary beads; seeking absolution.

'It's late. We have plenty of time... take your time... you must eat with us and stay the night. It is no inconvenience,' said Anne.

'That's so kind... I'm normally so clear... not today.'

'I'll tell Jean we've one extra for supper. Sims, are you having a beer?'

'Only if everyone else is,' he got the message, looked at Shirley, 'sherry, scotch, gin, beer? You can even have a Pusser's rum... whatever you like.'

'I don't know what a Pusser's rum is... I think I'd quite like beer with a dash of lemonade... not a shandy... just a dash, please.'

Anne returned. 'A guest room is ready and supper's laid on. We've got all evening.'

'Now, love, what's on your mind?' he asked.

For a small, quiet, gentle lady and at complete odds with her size, she took a disproportionately large draught, 'Where shall I start?' She gently dabbed her lips dry. 'Well... well, this is I suppose as good a place as any,' she said, vacantly, while rippling through a pile of index cards stacked away in some mental nook. 'No, no, perhaps this is better. Yes, this is as good a place as any.' She took a deep breath and stopped wringing her hands. 'Well, many years ago when I first came into MI5, I worked with a woman called Kitty Jarvis... she was very nice and extremely clever. We got on well. Her husband had died and left her quite a bit of money; he had been something to do with Parker Pens. She had this lovely large apartment in Douglas Mansions. As I said, we got on very well and used to chat about lots of things maybe we shouldn't have. It turned out that before I worked with her she had been the personal assistant to Anthony Blunt: they were both involved in counter espionage for MI5. Just imagine that, Sims, Anthony Blunt a Russian spy actually active in British counter espionage. Anyway, while Kitty was his assistant, she had shared an office with the defectors Guy Burgess and Donald MacLean... they used to take her out to dinner. She got to know them well and they talked her into using one of the rooms in her apartment for meetings of sensitive military intelligence matters. In many ways she seemed to be an innocent. It's possible she was completely taken in by them. Unless of course she knew what was going on all the time.' Shirley took another swig of her beer.

Nothing particular about Kitty to raise interest; no alarm bells clanging. The name Kitty Jarvis meant nothing to him. Anthony Blunt, however, was reveille time, now add to that the names Burgess and MacLean, it was a wake up call of the first order. *Action stations!*

Sims sat up straight. 'Okay, always interested in those three, who wouldn't be?' he said. 'Lots of people must have worked with Blunt. But, Kitty Jarvis... any reason should we know or care about her?'

'Not necessarily... not on the face of things. But, the point is, Sims, she was Buster Crabb's aunt.'

Sims jumped up almost knocking his beer over, '*Christ!* Please tell me you're not joking.'

'It's the truth, Sims. And, it wasn't just Anthony Blunt and Burgess and MacLean. Gerald Radleigh was associated with them through another meeting place, The Cavendish Hotel.'

He looked at Anne. 'Radleigh kept that quiet.'

She, lips parted, trying to take in the ramifications of the news. Its implications would be complex. 'So there *is* a connection, darling. You always felt there was.' A slight and involuntary shiver passed over her. There were times when Anne felt she'd married a psychic.

'Cavendish Hotel?' Sims asked.

'I'll come to that in a minute,' Shirley said, taking another pull at her beer.

'Why should what you're telling us... why does this mean you have to leave MI5?' asked Anne. 'I don't understand that.'

'Let me finish, and I'll tell you... It's a long story... I'll cut it down. Buster was out of work. He had a cheap room at the Cavendish, the owner, Rosa Lewis, managed to get Buster an interview at an exclusive art gallery and antique shop called Cameo Corner. He got the job and was there for around a year. His aunt Kitty bought several paintings from it. Well, later, in the bar of the Cavendish, Blunt introduced himself as the owner of Cameo Corner to Buster. Kitty said that Buster hadn't, until that point, realised that Blunt was his boss. But, I don't think that could have been the first contact he'd had with him. There were often parties at Kitty's apartment... Buster must have been at least to some of them, so he must have had contact with Blunt, Burgess and MacLean there... as well as meeting Radleigh.'

'Good God,' exclaimed Anne.

'I always thought Radleigh and Blunt hated each other... The Cambridge Apostles and les Grands Amis... big enemies,' Sims said. 'What happened to all that?'

'Kitty said that he and Radleigh didn't get on any better than they had done at Cambridge. They agreed to tolerate each other... it was an association of convenience for two like-minded people, that, or a business arrangement.'

'But surely other people must know about this... why should you in particular have to leave? There have been all sorts of accusations flying around.'

'Unless one is in the know, the connections are not obvious. What I've told you isn't actually secret... it may have been hushed up... brushed under the carpet. No, the secret part involves Kitty, she's still alive. She lives with her daughter now in St. Albans. I know officially someone else apart from you is digging over old ground, Sims. MI5 are going to interview her. That's the secret part. It is very hush-hush. What is going on, Sims?'

'You once proposed that maybe we're moving towards a new world of disorder... it might be something to do with that. Or, it could be just the old world fitted out with some new togs and the same dirty tricks going on underneath.'

'Where there are human beings there are always a few dirty people doing their dirty tricks,' Shirley said.

'Are you sure it's just a few?' He reached over and took her hand, 'Any idea who's doing the interviewing?'

'Only one of them: Jack Passant. Do you remember? He was on Billy's list... do you think he's setting you up again?'

He shook his head, 'If you mean Billy, no, not at all... he's being as open as Billy can be. The list is his way of telling us to watch our backs, who to look out for.'

Anne looked up from her jottings and doodles, 'You said you thought Passant was the eyes and ears of someone outside. Who do you think it is?'

'I used to think it was Lord Aston-Heyford, but, Passant is still with us, and as far as I know information is still being passed on. If I'm correct, it could spell danger. I have recently thought it could be Rothschild. He was a regular visitor at The Cavendish and at parties at Kitty's apartment... and I know he loaned Blunt money to purchase pictures.'

Sims, well aware that Shirley knew more than she was saying, said, 'Billy and someone else I know reckoned if we peered too far into his affairs we would find ourselves in very murky waters.' He muttered, 'Murky waters and grubby money'.

'But why would it spell danger?' Anne asked.

Shirley looked concerned. 'Please, Sims, I know what you are like... don't think of going down that route. You'd get little or no protection from The Government.'

'Why on earth not?'

'Sims, many of them have become rich since becoming ministers... you must ask yourself *how*. Don't you see, Billy would be powerless to help. It's as though these bankers own the world.'

After breakfast the following morning Anne spoke in

soft toned confidence to Shirley, 'Now, we've all slept well. I have had a little time to digest what you've told us, but, I have a problem understanding the difference between your involvement in the squad before and the squad now.'

'Anne, I don't want to know or not know things any more, I'm tired. Years of uncertainty; what if Aston-Heyford had suddenly appeared having found out about the squad. I doubted my courage to resist interrogation and then I would have exposed Pat, yourselves and the others... there are families with children involved now.'

Anne moved closer to Shirley and took her hand. 'In the past, you worked with the squad because of your conscience, and that is what is driving you now... it's why you've come to see us: it's your conscience telling you what to do... what you believe to be right. How will you feel a few months after you've left... rested... knowing you could have helped? What we do is the squad's vocation; our vocation; your vocation. You *are* tired... you have a right to be tired... see a doctor, get him to order you to rest... take a holiday, Shirley darling, and make your decision after. And, please remember this, we all doubt our ability to do the right thing if it came to it... those doubts mustn't stop us, must they?'

*

The interrogation block was quiet: Radleigh's cell empty. 'Dusty, where is he? Where's fucking Radleigh?'

Easy going Leading Seaman Dusty Miller, less so, stood to attention. 'He was removed from our custody in Unit 4 early this morning... signed orders from Admiral Jessop, sir.'

'Who came for him?'

'No names, sir, just a release note from the Admiral. It was pukka, sir. Sub-Lieutenant Mountford phoned Tunworth House and spoke to the admiral himself: he confirmed it.'

'Who was it? Did they sign for him?'

'Yes, sir.'

'Who has the release chit?'

'The sub-lieutenant, sir.'

'Go and fetch him quick.'

Sims took the release note. An unreadable signature followed by MI5 in brackets. He pocketed the receipt, 'I'm off to Tunworth House to see the admiral... that's where I'll be if you need me... catch up with you both later. Stand down the other guards... chance for you both to catch up on a bit of shut-eye.'

They watched him drive out of their compound at NIDii Unit 4., 'I'd like to be a fly on the wall at that meeting,' said Dusty. 'It's pretty obvious he and Anne knew nothing about this... why's that do you think? All a bit shady... maybe you should have called them, sir.'

'I found myself in quite an awkward position, Billy was insistent I was not to. I feel as if I've let them both down.'

'Not a nice feeling. I'm glad I didn't have to deal with it. Buggered if you do: buggered if you don't.'

'Exactly.'

*

'Before you get what you've got to say off your chest, let me say in my defence, I couldn't justify holding him any longer I thought it best to let him go.'

Perhaps it was Billy on the defensive, apologising to him that did it: he'd had the wind taken out of his sails. Sims was not angry, and not being so, surprised him. He took it much better than he thought he would. Driving to Tunworth House he had considered many likely outcomes. Radleigh's face had been plastered cover to cover, all the front pages of every major Sunday newspaper. The headlines: "Radleigh Ruse Rips-off Russians." - "Gerald Radleigh - A Modern Day Hero." - "Two Timing Radleigh Three Times the Soviets.". Only The News of the World thought the reading public would be more absorbed by "Vicar in Three Way Sex Tangle with Parishioners".

If Shirley was correct and someone from MI5 was digging around, it did not bode well for Radleigh's survival. It couldn't be guaranteed they were intent on protecting him from the Soviets. He was a danger to someone in their lot as well. Surely Billy must understand this.

'You may have a death on your hands... and this time, not of mine or Anne's doing.' Sims stared at the old admiral, 'At the moment, I am at a loss... I don't know how to help you if Radleigh is assassinated, and that in my opinion is very likely to be the case. We can't keep the lid on over our role in all this... it'll come out sooner or later. NID and yourself will take the rap again... you do understand that, don't you, sir? It will be a repeat of Portland and Buster all over again... egg splattered across your and NID's faces.' Sims threw an old Billy line back at him, 'I hope you can survive in this awful world, sir.' Building, he added, sincerely, 'I will miss you if you can't.'

'Sims, listen! I'm gripping the blade of a double edged cutlass. You have extracted much good information from him, there's little more he could give us of any worth. Look, if we'd kept him in our custody and he'd been got at... and that's always possible, we'd have taken much punishment. If, on the other hand, we hand him over and he gets assassinated, it will be on someone else's watch. I agree, there would still be a lot of mud thrown at us and interesting questions we would have to answer, but, not anything like the amount that would come our way if it was done on our patch. There are those in The Government who would have preferred Radleigh to stay where he was... you've ruffled the waters, lad. The Naval Intelligence Division will come good out of this. The Government, they fear an enquiry... their dealings may come to light. We won't suffer, Sims. We will *not* suffer.'

'Hmm, I can see all that... and I hope you're right... and that's all very well, but, why not tell me? Don't you trust me?'

'Oh, lad... *oh, my lad,* I trust you. I trust you to punch as high as you can and then beyond... you are a fighter, I couldn't risk you making a fuss.'

'So, now we just go back to the day job, then... nine to five... nine to bloody five.'

'*No Sims!* Now we go underground.'

*

He found Anne in the library. 'Radleigh's gone.'

She stood up. 'Not *dead?*'

'No, just taken... MI5. I've just got back from seeing Billy, that's why I'm late... he was expecting me. He'd authorised his release.'

'Why didn't he tell you first?' she said, angrily.

'He told David Mountford not to contact me. He thought I'd make a fuss... he's right, I probably would have too. It puts a question mark on Mountford, though. He hasn't learned where his loyalty lies.'

'Oh, come on, are you sure you're being fair, darling?'

'Possibly not. It's early days for him. But, I'm sure what you, Dusty and I would have done in the same situation.'

'Don't make any hasty decisions or judgement about him. He's a good man, Sims, and he thinks the world of you. Think how he must be feeling.'

Sims hrumphed. 'Anyway, the Soviets are a bit steamed up about all this. Billy thought it best to get him off our patch. Let the rest of SIS have the headache. Radleigh is really lapping up all this limelight. Either his ego is so huge and he doesn't believe anyone could hate him enough to kill him or he actually thinks he's bloody safe. And, with his diplomatic background I don't see how he can believe that. I reckon he knows he's doomed and probably prefers the idea of being buried in England. Think of it this way, even if some gang in SIS, or just outside, don't get him, it's for sure his days are numbered as far as Moscow's concerned. Anyhow, Billy's probably done the right thing.'

***

Chapter Fourteen.
Thick Haar.

Thick, hair dewing haar had blown in shortly after they docked. Hull, uninviting, tonally dull, matched the prematurely greying blond hair of the woman walking along the narrow wet street. She stopped at one of the terraced houses and knocked first on the window that opened directly on to the street and then on the front door. To a similarly aged woman who answered the door, she pointed out a section on the rolled up newspaper she carried. An agreement seemed to be made and she was let inside. Door closed, they hugged, kissed and now spoke Latvian.

'Krista, at last.' Vita Gaida wiped away the tears hanging on her cheeks, 'How long has it been?'

So many memories to deal with; Krista unable to answer, shrugged.

'My house is your house. You must stay here as long as you like,' Vita said.

Krista Bērzs eventually found her voice, 'I heard the sad news about Peter.'

'Yes, we have both lost our Englishmen now.' A moments silence. 'Are you hungry?'

Krista shook her head. 'I've been well fed... the crew were very kind.'

'Then, you must rest now, and when you have, we have so much to talk about.'

'I am not tired... I don't need to rest, I've done so little on the voyage over here. We can talk now.'

They sat either side of the small coal fire. Vita hugged her knees. 'Why did they let him go? I thought they would have put him on trial at least.'

'I don't think they would have risked getting him from Riga just to set him free in England... that is not possible. Dāvis has met the commander and his wife... he said they are special. He trusts them. No, something political has happened. Something out of their control.'

'Have you come all this way just to tell me this?'

'No, I've come to kill him myself.'

'But if you're caught the Brothers will be in danger.'

'It *is* dangerous. The Brothers agreed I should do it... I will be very careful.'

'Won't they miss you at your school?'

'I will not be missed... I no longer teach... I have married one of the Brothers and we live a long way outside Riga.'

With no sense of criticism, Vita said, 'I didn't think you'd ever marry again.'

'I wasn't married to Thomas.'

'You were in the eyes of us all,' Vita said, poking more life into the fire and placing another shovelful on top of the glowing coals.

Krista stretched her legs out almost straight. 'It's not a normal marriage... we have done it for this operation... to get me out of Riga and out of sight... he *is* a good man, though.'

'Do you need us to get you a weapon?'

'No. I have my own pistol... a Tokarev. It's old but in good condition.'

'So, Krista, what do you need from us? A passport?'

'I have a Swedish passport. All I need you to do is change these American dollars into Sterling. And, let me stay here when I return to catch the freighter back to Riga.' She opened her bag and took out a thick roll of notes. 'These are some of the dollars the commander sent us.'

'Does Beatrise know?'

'No.'

'Do you want me to tell her?'

'No. It is only natural she will be questioned about his death. She and Artis mustn't know.'

The two women sat silently watching the fire. Vita then rose and drew the curtains on the gathering gloom of the late afternoon. 'Shall we have some more tea?' she asked.

The kettle whistled. Vita brought the tea pot in and placed it beside the fire, 'In England we let it brew for four or five minutes.'

'How do you manage with Peter gone?'

'I have a small pension, and there are other contributions. I receive money from Naval Intelligence. This is always in cash. I am not rich, but I have enough to keep our operation open. And, as you can see, I can keep warm... coal is very cheap.'

In this tiny terraced house in dingy Hull, the two women sat drinking tea while discussing a traitor's murder.

'How will you know where to find him?'

'He is most likely to be in London.'

'It's a big place.'

'Yes, it is. First I will go to Portsmouth and wait there and read the newspapers. Gerald Radleigh likes the high life and publicity. I shall find out where he is from the news.'

'I don't understand, why Portsmouth?'

'I must make an homage to my Thomas... he once told me that in an English pub you can talk about any subject you like and no one will tell the authorities.' She, lost in a happy memory, smiled. 'He also told me that sometimes the beer is not very good and there's a lot of rubbish spoken in English pubs, but that was a part of their charm. Dāvis told me of a pub in Portsmouth... it has a lovely name. So, I shall go to The Golden Bell and think of my love and drink to his memory. I'm sure Thomas and I would have gone there one day. It is in Charlotte Street... number sixty. Then, when I feel the time is right I shall go to London.'

'You may need help. I'll ask Pamela to go with you.'

'No. Pamela is too precious to you. I think I can manage. If I need help, I promise I will let you know.'

*

The phone rang on the long wooden counter of Spice Island Spices. Pearl answered.

'Pearl, love. It's Arthur... Arthur Adams... from The Golden Bell.'

She interrupted, 'Arthur, for God's sake, I know your bloody voice by now, and, for Christ's sake, I know where you live. Perhaps you've forgotten, I used to live there myself once. How's Molly?'

Arthur winced. 'Sorry, love. Have you got Sims' telephone number handy? I've put it somewhere and can't find it... Molly's fine.'

'Problem? Is there a problem, Arthur?'

'Don't know. Knowing him, I'm not taking any chances. He comes in for a pint now and again with Derek... no telling when the next time's going to be, though.'

That evening at Hell Head House, Anne answered the call, 'Oh, hello Arthur, this is a surprise. How are you and Molly?'

'Fine... can I talk to Sims?'

'Wait a moment, I'll get him.'

'Arthur, you old bugger... got a problem?... now I know it's unlikely, customers started liking your beer? Wouldn't know how to deal with that, would you? Derek been in lately?'

'No, he's not. And, young man, for your information, I keep a bloody good pint. If you came over and drank more of it you'd know that.'

'So, what's up then?'

'Might be jumping at shadows... there's a woman with a foreign accent been coming in every night. Not a pro... looks a nice sort. She said she was Swedish.'

'What's wrong with that? Might be your lucky day. These Swedish parties have a reputation to live up to. Just make sure Molly's not around. You do know what to do, don't you?'

'Sod off. Bloody matelots, I don't know why I bother,' he muttered. 'Anyway, there's a guy called Sven who comes in for a drink when he shouldn't, he's Swedish and *he* says she's not Swedish... probably Latvian... that's what he said, and he should know being a Swede. Just thought you might like to know, that's all.'

'What time does she come in?'

'Most lunchtimes and then evenings after eight.'

'Which bar?'

'Either.'

'Has she mentioned my name?'

'No.'

'Have you?'

'Yeah... well you know, I like to tell the story...'

'Hmm. I'm coming over tomorrow lunchtime. I'll go into the saloon bar... if she's not already in there, my lads will get her to join me.'

'Right. I'll see you then. Try not and make a mess.'

'If she's legit, you know straight up, how about I put a good word in for you?'

'Fuck off.'

'That is no way to talk to loyal customers, Arthur. Carry on like that, and I'll give you a year before you go broke.'

'Customers like you and it won't take a bleedin' year.' Arthur put the phone down.

Dusty and Sub-Lieutenant David Mountford entered The Golden Bell through the front door into the quiet public bar: Anne and Sims through the side door and into the saloon bar. Krista was already there talking to Arthur. David came down and took her left side, Sims her right. Dusty closed and blocked the door from the public bar. Anne, barred the door to outside. Arthur thought better of staying in the line of fire and disappeared to the other end of the bar - spy stories were for telling, not being in.

'Put both hands on the counter, please.' The two men either side of her took hold of a wrist each while Anne checked Krista's pockets and removed her pistol.

Sims said, 'It's strange who you come across in saloon bars... different type of person. But, you're not an ordinary person are you?... ordinary people don't carry guns... they don't need to.' He took the pistol from Anne and released its magazine, 'Tokarev, unusual for a Swedish lady to carry one of these. I wouldn't bother showing me your passport, I know you're not Swedish. Why are you here?'

Krista remained unruffled, that she would be picked up was always a possibility. She stared at him and then Anne. She looked at the scar on his forehead, realised who he was, and said. 'You are correct, I am not Swedish. You're the commander, aren't you?' She switched her gaze to Anne, 'And you are his beautiful wife. Dāvis described you both.' Still looking at Anne, she said, 'I can see he was very accurate in his description. He also said it was very good shooting when you killed Matrozis. He was very impressed with you both.'

Dusty gave Sub-Lieutenant Mountford a raised eyebrow "so now you know" look.

Krista turned round to face the bar again only to find Arthur was no longer there. 'I thought so, Arthur must have telephoned you.' Now to Dusty and David, 'Were you on the submarine too?'

They both looked at Sims for approval. He nodded; they nodded.

A Latvian woman posing as a Swede and carrying a Tokarev. Sims thought a bit of clarification was in order.

'You're either a well informed Soviet or one of us. How is he?'

'If you mean Dāvis, he is fine and my name is Krista Bērzs.'

'That wouldn't be hard to find out... what was the *all clear* signal the fishing boats gave to the sub?'

Krista relaxed and smiled. 'Three green lights on the side facing away from the coast... we sent three boats in total. Radleigh almost fell and got washed away. I taught Dāvis to say "thank you" and you both shook hands on the submarine... I wrote the notes for him. I am his auntie. My fiancé was a British agent captured and killed by the NKVD. Radleigh, Aston-Heyford and Philby gave his name and many others to them.'

A story Billy had told them indelibly printed on her mind. Anne stepped forward took the gun and its magazine from Sims, pushed the magazine home, checked the safety catch was on, and gave it back to Krista - an act of faith from someone who had been lucky enough for her man to survive. She gave Krista a hug. 'I am so sorry about your fiancé... we heard the story.' Stumbling a little, 'I was in Korsør. It's nice to meet the person on the other end of my messages,' she said, giving her a kiss. 'But, you still haven't told us why you're here.'

'This is going to be better done over a pint,' Sims said. He called up to the public bar, 'Arthur! *Arthur!* Any chance of some service down here?'

Arthur scanned the saloon for blood and bodies. He looked disappointed. His stock in trade story of Sims' shooting on The Isle of Wight was wearing thin - fresh epics were needed and would be welcome.'

'The lady's innocent, we're going to buy her a drink

to say sorry.'

'Krista stared at Sims and Anne; from one to the other and back again. 'I always thought I would meet both of you. I am so pleased.'

'Does anyone else know you're here?' asked Anne.

'No. Not even Beatrise and Artis.'

'You seem to be avoiding the question,' Sims said, 'why are you here, Krista?'

'I wanted to find out why you let him go. It must have been political. I wanted to know who the Forest Brothers are dealing with. Whether we can we trust you?'

'You can trust the four of us. It's politicians who can't be trusted... and, that goes for those in Britain, USSR, Latvia, United States... anywhere. The problem we have is not just with our government, it's with the other intelligence services; MI5 and MI6. If you want to get home safely, don't talk to anyone but us.'

'How do I talk to you?'

'Have you a good memory?'

'Yes.'

'Then memorise this number; Hell Head six, six, six.'

'That is very ominous, Commander. The sign of the devil,' Krista said.

Anne laughed, then smiled at Sims and said, 'And, considering who married into our family; very appropriate.'

Sims dismissed David and Dusty. 'Okay, you two, make your way back to *Dolphin*. I'll get in touch later.'

*

'Okay, Krista, they've gone now, what's your plan? You didn't come here carrying a Tokarev just to ask why we'd released him. So, once again, why are you here?'

'It was Radleigh that helped kill the very best man in the world. I've come here to kill him. To do what the politicians won't do,' she said, simply and without emotion.

'Krista,' Anne interrupted, 'you don't need to get involved. You have done your bit by helping us get him back to the United Kingdom. We are certain there are many people after him... Soviets; people from our own country who will be worried what his book might reveal. Members of MI5 and MI6... maybe some from our organisation. Please go home, Krista, it is our opinion Radleigh will not stay alive for long. It's just a matter of time.'

Sims took hold of her hand. 'Listen, love,...'

'My Thomas used to call me that.'

...we're going to say nothing to our superiors and we are going to let you keep your gun. Don't do anything foolish. Take note of what Anne said. And, remember this: we want him dead as much as you. He will not do a deal with Anne and myself.'

*

Leaning on the rail of the Gosport ferry, Dusty said, 'He's getting cagey... didn't want us there for whatever they're going to discuss.'

'Probably the less we know the safer she is. It's not official don't forget. But, yes, he's been a little reserved. Just a little bit distant. I think I should have phoned him before I let Radleigh go.'

'You were following orders... Billy told you not to. Doesn't do a career a lot of good disobeying admirals.'

'That's all very well... But, I feel I should have done. I fear he doesn't totally trust me now. I think you'd have let him know what was going on regardless of who told you not to.'

'Maybe, we'll never know. Anyway, it's different for me, I'm not a commissioned officer... less to lose. I reckon it was a hard ask to get right. Hard lesson to learn.'

They continued watching the water slip by. A pastime all matelots are proficient in: just watching water and waves.

David broke the spell, 'How do you get it back?'

'What?'

'His trust.'

'Time, I guess. We've only just started. We'll come good.'

'How about you? Are you going to trust me still?'

'I have to... you're my boss,' he said, smiling, and then after a slight pause added, '*sir*. Anyway, you need me... I'm the better shot. Someone's got to look after your back.'

*

At Tunworth House, Billy, always pleased to see Sims, ordered coffee the moment he saw the Land Rover enter the drive.

'You didn't bring Harry with you?'

'I would have done... Jean, our housekeeper, wouldn't let me... she's scared you'll hang on to him.'

'I remember her. Fierceness seems the order of the day with Hell Head's women. He's found a good home, I think.'

Coffee served, Billy asked the purpose of the visit.

'I need a float, sir. Best it comes from your scran bag of dirty money. Needed for unofficial operations.'

'How much?'

'Anne reckons five or six hundred to kick-off with.'

Billy scoffed, 'To kick-off with... this sounds bad, lad. It isn't for that bloody Jag is it? Not trying a different tack are we?'

'No. Trust me. These are for legitimate expenses, sir.'

'Trust you! How do I know I can?... she said you had a barrow-boy's instinct. Between yourself and Alistair Duncan you've just about cleared out my kitty. And, another thing, expenses for what? And don't hedge round the issue. I want a straight answer, Commander.'

'Surveillance duties.'

'Is this to do with my list?'

'More or less.'

'Good Lord, what sort of answer is more or less?'

'It means just that... we may get led to places we can't account for at the moment. To do that would be an act of divination, and, as I've yet to master the knack, I'll have to stick with more or less.'

'You always were a cheeky bugger, Sherwood-Reeves. I want receipts; genuine ones.'

'Anne will see to it. She has an accountant's instinct.'

'How is she?' Billy asked.

'Blisteringly good... top form. I'll tell her you asked.'

'Yes, please do.'

*

Sims called the two men into his office, 'You're going to get your hand in on a bit of surveillance... tracking skills. I want you to follow Krista Bērzs everywhere. Any out of the ordinary movements, let me know immediately. Here's some cash... Billy wants receipts for everything. Don't talk to Arthur Adams, he likes to chat...' He exhaled slowly, '...to anybody and everybody. And, take these, your alternative identity passes and passports with you. I'll tell you when to start using them.'

Driving back to Gosport Dusty said, 'This is your chance... we'll come good... time to rebuild.'

'If we do okay, maybe.'

'We'll do fine, sir.'

'I may have the Queen's commission, however, since joining NID I no longer feel qualified to be called "sir".'

'I reckon you're possibly worrying too much?'

'Is that possible? We work for British Intelligence now. Our record is important.'

'With respect, we work for Sims, Anne and Billy at the moment... the rest of NID and British Intelligence haven't got a clue what we're doing. So, I can't see how our performance can affect our records. Anyhow, if Sims didn't trust you, he wouldn't have given you the job.'

'I hope you're right.'

'I am.'

'Thank you.'

*

Before the phone rang three times, Sims had grabbed it. 'David, what do you know?'

'Last evening she went to The Golden Bell as usual and then returned to her digs; not far from the station. She had taken bed and breakfast there. The landlady is English, local woman. She said it was nice to have the business off season. We were just in time, sir. She checked out this morning and took the 1000 train to

London. Dusty's on her tail, I'll catch up with him later. I asked the landlady whether Krista was coming back. No arrangements had been made. And, sir, Dusty will call you or Anne at *Dolphin* or at Hell Head House and let you know where I should meet him. I'd better get off now and catch the 1200.'

'Okay, well done. David, from now on, you and Dusty are to use your other identities.' Sims put the phone down. 'Bugger,' he said.

'Bugger, what?' asked Anne.

'Krista's done a runner to London. She didn't take our advice... she's going to get him herself... make sure the deed is done. Only the two of them; she's going to be difficult to keep tabs on.'

'For all we know, she might have needed to go to London to go home.'

'No chance... never happen.'

'You speak Chinese too, I see.'

'Like a native, the missus taught me,' he said, vaguely. 'Better check your Beretta over. Things are getting steamy.'

*

At Hell Head House Anne jotted down the number of Dusty's phone box. When David Mountford called from London she gave him this and Dusty's report.

'He has got Krista in his sights. She travelled on the underground to South Kensington, walked about half a mile to Chelsea and it seems she checked in to a small and fairly ordinary hotel there: *The Mulberry* in Mulberry Walk. Unless she moves off, he'll stay near the phone box in the street until you arrive.'

'Very well... I've got that. I'll call as soon as we've news.'

*

For Nikolai Zima it turned out not as bad as it might. He sat for an hour listening to his Moscow controllers blast him for his inattention to Radleigh and his movements. He asked a straightforward and simple question of his interviewers: how was it, they with all the resources at their disposal, were unaware of Radleigh's undetected and continued loyalty to Great Britain? It was a brave, if not desperate, question to have asked and, by asking, he saved his neck and had earned and been given a second chance by Moscow. It was a great relief; it may after all be possible to redeem himself. The given chance was not without its risks. He was to travel to London, join the Russian Embassy there, find Radleigh and despatch him. Make a clean job of it he had been ordered. If you do you can return to your post in Riga.

He would not be required to carry a weapon while travelling. A side arm was to be supplied by the embassy: not a Soviet made one; a British Enfield service revolver, was to be used. His lack of familiarity with the model just a small point of concern; to be certain, he would need to be within close range. He would have preferred a Makarov.

Serving there as a mid-ranking diplomat some years before, Zima was no stranger to the city. Paris, London, New York; these were postings to thirst for - Riga was not. Nevertheless, Riga could be a stepping stone to better things. A good job done there and the clean killing of Radleigh might be sufficient to get him placed in one of these three corners of heaven.

Zima, in an undisciplined moment, had considered defection. On reflection, if Moscow were prepared to send him to eliminate Radleigh, would they not do the same for him? All thoughts of re-establishing the drugs trade route were now abandoned. From here on he was going to stick strictly to his diplomatic brief - apart from, that is, this short period as an undiplomatic killer.

*

If she saw him, she would recognise him, Krista had met him in The Golden Bell; Dusty was careful.

Though she had not seen him, Krista played safe. She booked in and paid for her room in advance and as proof of identity used a second Swedish passport - one she would destroy later. The phone call she had made from South Kensington underground station was brief. 'Collect me in one hour from The Mulberry Hotel, Chelsea.' Krista did not unpack. She sat in the small reception and waited.

Sub-Lieutenant David Mountford walked quickly up to Dusty. As they shook hands, a grey Austin A40 Farina drew up to the entrance to The Mulberry Hotel. Krista quickly threw her valise into the rear seat, climbed in alongside it and the car made off. She saw both of them: Mountford and Dusty saw her. As the car drew level, she gave them a little smile and a wave. They'd lost her.

Dusty had been quick enough to get the registration number. While scribbling it down, he said, 'She won't be back. You going to call Hell Head or shall I?'

'I'll do it. You see what you can find out from The Mulberry.'

'Anne Sherwood-Reeves,' she said.

'It's David. We've lost her... picked up by a car... drove off in a hurry. She saw us both as she was going... waved and smiled as she went past.'

'Best check into The Mulberry yourselves and wait for Sims to call.'

Dusty returned. 'She checked in as Margit Håkans-dottor, using more than one Swedish passport, I wonder how many of those she's got.'

*

Krista leaned over the front seat, 'Thank you Michael. It's so nice to meet you at long last. You remind me of Thomas. You look so much like him.'

'Yes, I know. Everyone says so. And it's nice to meet you too. We think of you as family.'

'We didn't marry.'

'You would have done, though. Wouldn't you?'

'Yes.'

Little more was said until they drew up in a narrow back street in nearby Fulham.

*

'Look, don't you and Dusty worry about it. It was a rush job... you did your best,' Sims said, and put the phone down.

'What did he say?' asked Dusty.

David told him.

'He's right. It *was* a rush job. No time to organise anything. If she'd taken a taxi from South Kensington, I could have lost her then.'

David looked doubtful.

'Look, Sims and Anne live in the real world. They know we're short staffed. What did 'Tracker Dog' say at Netley? "Minimum of six trackers and vehicles nearby and stand-by." David, we had none of these things.'

*

'Do you remember meeting Inspector Adstock when we test fired Throagh's Beretta? I'm going to give him a call.'

Sims sat drumming his fingers waiting for Adstock to answer.

'Inspector Adstock here.'

'You may remember me from a shooting in Richmond... Commander Sherwood-Reeves.'

'Ah, you were a Lieutenant then and just Reeves, right?'

'Spot on,' said Sims.

'Sounds like you've moved on a bit.'

'Could say that. Any chance of a bit of assistance?'

'Such as?'

'How do I get some info on a vehicle registration?'

'Your lot should be able to get you that.'

'Don't want them to know.'

'Still trailing doubles are you?'

'In between getting shot at, yeah.'

'Give me the details and if you're still alive in an hour's time, I'll give you what we've got. I'll call you back later.'

Sims grabbed the phone before Anne.

'The number's registered to a Christopher Hammond,

Adderbury, Oxfordshire... red Ferrari. He lost his license speeding through nearby Deddington... it's now insured in his wife's name... Sophie Hammond.'

'Christ! Too awful to contemplate. Fancy being driven around by the missus in your own prize Ferrari. Must be a nightmare.'

Anne, eyes narrowed, shook her head.

'Anyway, it looks like your guy either got the number wrong or they're false plates. Don't ask me to check the addresses of all grey Austin A40 Farina owners, not enough manpower. Sorry, that's as far as we can take you. If you're in the area, call in for a tea. Can't stop chatting... work to do.' Astock put the phone down.

'Bugger, false plates.'

'Sod it,' said Anne. Then asked, 'Something wrong with my driving?'

Lost ground to make up. 'No dear... absolutely not. Never feel safer than when you're at the wheel.'

Jean poked her head round the door, 'Do you want your tea in here or in the kitchen with me?' she asked.

'Kitchen's fine with me.'

'And me,' said Anne.

'Looks to me like you've got a bit of a problem, Sims,' Jean said. 'What is it, love?'

'I've hit a brick wall, babe.'

She laughed, said she was feeling her age, and that she didn't feel like a babe any more.

'Come off it, you're a mere lass.'

'I'm far too wide across the hips to be called "mere" any more.'

'Top cooks are not meant to look like stick insects. It gets the kitchen a bad reputation... suggests the cook can't stomach her own grub.'

'I'll believe you... anyway, why don't you phone that nice Mr Harvey... he's sensible.' Jean's advice was to the point, but came out not quite as she meant it to sound.

Anne laughed.

'That's a bit cruel. Am I to take it you think I'm not?'

'No, dear. We all get stuck sometimes, don't we? Though, I generally find it's more often men than women... that's all, love.'

Anne laughed once more.

Jean felt she was painting herself into a corner and excused herself saying she had urgent things to do in the nursery.

'Actually, she's right. If the squad aren't already on Radleigh's heels, they'll know who is. If we know where he is, we know where Krista's likely to turn up. I'll tell the lads to stay where they are for the moment.'

He called David, 'Get yourself booked into The Mulberry for at least another couple of days. If we can find where Radleigh is hanging out, we can be pretty sure it won't be long before Krista's sniffing around.'

***

Chapter Fifteen.
The Lover's Brother.

'Archie Abbot's located him, Sims,' said Pat Harvey.

'Where?'

'Not far from Aston-Heyford's place in Chelsea.'

'Can Archie hang around for a while?'

'He's hellishly busy... tired as well... been on the case solo.'

'We'll relieve him as soon as the lads get there... they've hired a van. Better give me the address.'

'Our MI6 man, Le Fanu... his place.... Rochester House, Chelsea Square.'

'Chelsea *and* Le Fanu, that's convenient. That was quick, how the hell did he know to track him there?'

'He's smart... uses his nut, found out who on Billy's list was in town at the moment... Le Fanu was first in line.. he hit lucky straight away. Press were already there... faster off the mark than us; just a little embarrassing.'

*

'Anne, *please* will you stay here and man the phone? And, I need to nick your Mini. I'm going to London. Archie Abbot's found Radleigh's burrow. He's staying with Le Fanu. I've jotted the address down on the note pad by the phone.' He waited: the expected resistance did not come.

'I don't like it... but, yes, okay,' she said, looking doubtful.

'Is that all?... no protest?'

'You need someone here. There's no one else is there? This time we have to split duties.'

'Don't worry... I don't think Krista's the type to take a crack at me.'

'No, I'm sure she wouldn't. You had better go, darling, before I change my mind.'

'I'll call as soon as I get there... I reckon to book in at The Mulberry with the lads. I forgot to ask Mike Mason for a new Identity Card and Passport... it's going to have to be Piers Monsoon again. Please, darling, will you stop grinning, and then will you give them Le Fanu's address and tell them to park the van within easy sight.'

Still smiling, she said, 'Piers, I have a feeling that's why he was on the list. Billy knew they were connected. Both MI6. Both in Paris. Both probably at the same time.'

'Hmm... spot on.' He gave her a quick kiss, told her there was nothing funny with being called Piers Monsoon and he would have preferred Kevin Mongoose. He gave her a longer kiss then left.

Anne went to sit with Jean in the kitchen.

*

'Mr Monsoon, your wife called, sir. She's already booked for you.'

'If you could show me my room,' he asked, 'I need to unpack and go out straightaway.' In his room he checked his A to Z. Le Fanu's cottage no more than three hundred yards as the crow flies and five hundred or so by the streets. I'll go on foot, he thought. He threw on his shoulder holster. Before sliding his Browning in he checked its magazine was full, actioned the slide and flicked the safety catch to on. He put on his leather jacket and then slid a spare full magazine into a zipped side pocket. After phoning Anne, he left.

He scanned left and right. 'Mulberry Walk,' he muttered, 'not a tree in sight.' He quickly walked the short few paces to the end of the road and turned up Old Church Street, turned right into South Parade then right again down the west side of Chelsea Square. So, we have a treeless Mulberry Walk and a Square that's actually a rectangle, he thought, fuckin' brilliant. It was with no great observational effort he spotted the green Bedford Dormobile van the lads had hired. Le Fanu's house just as obvious; a small gathering of press hacks and photographers clustered around the columned doorway to the red brick facade.

Archie was in the van with the lads, 'Glad to put me plates of meat up for a mo',' he said, as Sims slid the side door open.

'Hi all... prime parking spot... how did you fix it?'

'Archie showed them his MI5 pass and told them we were Radleigh's security guard,' said David.

Archie smiled, 'It was one of Mike's... not a real one.'

'He also took the copper's number and told him to fuck off or he'd report him,' laughed Dusty.

'Archie, do you want to get off and get some shut-eye?' Sims asked.

'No... I'm alright for the moment... you and your lads

need someone who knows their way around the streets. Radleigh's been out for a stroll a couple of times... goes round the common opposite... he's lapping it up... press following him like he was dishing out free fags and beer. The heat's going off the story a bit... less of them flocking than before.'

'If you're staying a while, I'm going to have a look round the back... see you shortly.'

History may well one day determine whether Sims was in the right place at the wrong time or the wrong place at the right time. It would depend from whose point of view the question was to be considered. For Nikolai Zima there was no debate about his celestial positioning: it was well out of kilter. It could not have been more ill-timed - whichever of his Fates were on duty, she had it in for him that day. The embassy had tipped him off as to Radleigh's current whereabouts. His decision he made in a rush. He would go to Chelsea Common, a small rectangular piece of grass in Chelsea Square that inhabitants thought of as countryside. He would go there and observe Le Fanu's pied-à-terre. If the opportunity arose, he would strike Radleigh from the cover of shrubs. All he needed to do then would be to get back to the diplomatic safety of the Russian embassy. For their part, they were unconcerned if he were to be caught: they had him listed and documented as a Latvian patriot: a terrorist.

As Sims turned the corner from South Street into the narrow alley that serviced the row of houses facing the common, a car drew up temporarily blocking the entrance. Walking towards the car was Krista. From the opposite direction on the same side of the street, Nikolai Zima walking towards them stopped. With a surprised look he stepped backwards. Krista made for her Tokarev. The driver, unaware until that point, that there was a problem, quickly exited the car and drew his pistol.

Krista fired one shot; Zima was down and finished. Nevertheless, as a precaution, Krista then pulled the trigger twice more.

Browning drawn, Sims ran up and levelled it at the driver, 'Don't move. Throw your gun into the back seat.'

Krista leaning on the car, said, 'Don't shoot him, Sims.'

Sims went round to her side of the car and grabbed her arm, 'Come with me, Krista. We've got to get you out of sight.'

'He was from the commissariat in Riga, a Russian agent. Aren't you going to arrest me?'

'Babe, we're on the same side.'

'Then get in the car... and you Michael,' she ordered.

'Okay, get the hell out of here. But drive normally... don't attract any more attention than you've already done,' Sims said, scanning the road for onlookers.'

Michael the driver said, 'I know the routine.'

'Okay, turn left here and then take a right when I tell you. Drop us off well past the hotel and go and get rid of the car. Come back on foot to The Mulberry Hotel in Mulberry Walk. Later I'll get you both to wherever you want in my car.'

'Krista, please act as normal as a Latvian killer school teacher can, and pretend to be with me. And, please don't force me to shoot you... my wife would never forgive me, she likes you.'

'And, you, how about you?'

'You're okay, babe.'

'Thank you,' she said politely, and put her arm through his.

'I'm going to trust you not to run away. Please wait for me here. I'll be back in five minutes or less.'

*

'Looks like Sims is coming in a bit of a hurry-up,' said Dusty, looking out of the rear window.

Sims violently slid open the van side door. 'Just bumped into Krista... and she's just bumped off a Russian agent she knew. All shit's going to break loose. So scarper, get the hell out of it... *Go!* Go immediately back to *Dolphin*. I'll sort The Mulberry out. What are you looking at? What are you waiting for? *GO!* That includes you Archie... thanks for you help, mate.'

*

Back at the hotel she was still there, in the small lounge he ordered coffee for them both, 'Would you like something stronger to go with it?'

'I think a brandy would be nice.'

'Any particular brand.'

'I don't know, I've never drunk one before... it seems the right thing to do.'

He smiled, 'It will go well with the coffee.'

Sims watched her take a large swig; more than was good for her. She caught her breath, gave an impolite cough. Her eyes watering a little, she asked, 'Should I have drank the coffee first?'

'Not necessarily. Perhaps though, as it was your first

time, maybe you should have drunk less than half the glassful in one go.'

Krista wiped her eyes and relaxed a little. 'Commander, he deserved it.'

'What made you do it for Christ's sake, why the hell did you shoot him? I know you *are* aware he was not Radleigh?'

'I know *that*,' she butted in.

'Well, who was he then?'

'Nikolai Zima... I told you, from the Commissariat in Riga. He presided at my wedding. Ours was the first one to take place after he took over the job. It was a public relations stunt. He wanted to appear friendly to us natives... it made my new husband and I feel sick. I'm not sure why he was here. Perhaps they must have sent him to get Radleigh... he saw me, Commander. If I'd not shot him and he'd reported me, so many would have suffered. I don't think there was anything else I could do.'

'I shouldn't worry now: he's telling nobody. Your secret's safe with him. Now, listen to me. Go, Krista... get back to Riga... like we told you, someone else will do for him. You've done enough.'

'No I haven't. I'm not going to lie to you, Sims, I cannot go while Radleigh is still alive.'

'Well, at least lie low... see if I'm not right... it doesn't have to be you... you still have our number?'

'Hell Head six, six, six.. how could I forget it?'

'Call us if you need help.'

Michael walked in.

'Michael, we're going to take Krista back to where she's staying. Then you and I are coming back here for a chat.'

*

In his room at The Mulberry he sat two beers and two scotches on the table, 'So, you could have stopped her... easily shot her... but, you didn't. At the time I had no idea you were connected... you were fucking lucky, mate. I might have thought you were after her... you were about to get a bullet. Come on, if you think about it, it was a reasonable action for me to consider. But, then she'd done Zima and she could have taken you out and didn't... only one conclusion to come to; you were in it together.'

Michael Mondot said nothing.

'Krista, I like her... so does my wife. We've indirectly worked with her before. She's a smooth operator. Looks the proper Latvian school ma'am... butter wouldn't melt in her mouth. Packs a Tokarev, though. And, by all accounts, can use it,' said Sims.

'She was trained by a good teacher.'

'Who was that?'

'My brother.'

'Ahh...' Sims, said. 'Things are beginning to tie up. You're SIS, that's for sure. Are you official?'

'Sometimes. At the moment, no... I'm MI6 and vengeful.' Mondot started to relax his hands towards his sides.

'Don't move until you've answered my next question... are going to drink those or not?'

Monton smiled. 'Yes indeed, A beer and a scotch I need this. Maybe doubles next round.'

'Your lot's got the grander budget, I'm not paying for effin' doubles... Billy'd go mad.' Sims put his hand out, 'I don't know where the boundaries lie, but, with respects to this little do with Radleigh, I guess we're on the same side. My name's Sims... Sims Sherwood-Reeves.'

'Michael Mondot,' the other man replied. 'It's not just Sherwood-Reeves. It's commander, isn't it?'

'Yep.' Sims paused, 'Anne and I were very sorry to hear about Thomas.'

'Yes... it's a risk we all take.'

Michael sank half his beer in one draught and followed it by half his whisky. 'I said I needed that,' he said, after a brief cough. 'Don't drink much... thought my lot was up that time. It's not nice staring down the loaded barrel of a Browning... thanks for not completing the pull through.'

'God knows what made me hesitate. Just had a feeling it was the wrong thing to do. It makes me break out in a sweat thinking about it... you were close... very close... a gnat's cock away from being late.'

Mondot drank some more. Sims sat back looking at him. 'In a normal world I would expect Krista to be well on her way back to Sweden by now. What do you reckon?'

'If all goes to plan she should leave tomorrow.'

'I've news for you, she's not going anywhere until Radleigh's spoken for. I know this because she's just told me so.'

'It's difficult helping someone like that.' He took another huge mouthful. 'She's very obstinate.'

'I've a wife like that. Krista's a good ally... depending how you wish to view it, a safe or unsafe pair of hands, I think. What do you think she'll do back in Latvia?'

'Resume her quiet married life I suppose.'

'What, retiring?'

'Oh no. She'll never retire completely. Thomas' disappearance marked her for life... no, no, she'll never give up the chase. Hers is a bigamous marriage, she's also wedded to the idea of a free Latvia. I hope she sees it.'

'Hmm... what about you?'

'For the moment, I'll continue to help Krista. Then, back to official MI6 stuff. When Radleigh's been dealt with, there'll be no one except Philby to get... he's so well surrounded that's going to be nigh on impossible. So, I'll play the waiting game again. I waited for Throagh, Aston-Heyford. They were both linked in some way or other to Thomas' death. Never had the pleasure of pulling the trigger on either of them: pity. Perhaps you ought to go after Philby as well as les Grands Amis.'

'That's well down the list of things to do. First, Radleigh's got to be sorted and then I've got to find out why my boss, Billy Ruffian, thinks Adian McClusky was murdered and find out who was responsible.'

'Sims, if I can be of assistance with anything, let me know.'

'You may regret saying that.'

'I don't think so,' he said raising his glass to Sims.

'I'm short handed, if you want to give me some back-up perhaps you could try and keep Krista out of trouble for a few days, and keep tabs on Radleigh. I'm going back home until some of the heat's off. Krista's got our number.'

'Sure anything.' Michael finished his scotch. 'I'll walk back... clear my head a bit.'

'Clear head!... no such thing in these times. Okay, if you're going to help, throw what's left of your beer down your throat... no time for walking, I want another chat with Krista.'

Sims paid for his room in advance in cash and told the receptionist he wasn't sure when he'd be returning but it would be any time in the next few days.

*

'Earlier you said you wouldn't go while Radleigh is still alive. Listen, I'm not asking you not to. All I'm asking is don't kill him yet. He has information we need. I don't know what it is, but I know it's important. Krista, please take some time off. Anne and I helped you. Now you help us by not getting in the way. I'm not making threats, I'm just asking. How about it?'

'I can't stay forever, my money will run out, and eventually I will be missed. I cannot wait more than two weeks. I will need to catch my boat then. I can't just take any boat... it has to be the right one. That's my problem, Sims.'

'I understand. Look if either of you find out where he is, please let me know straightaway.'

They nodded.

*

At Hell Head House he held her at arms' length, 'Anne, the smelly stuff's well and truly hit the fan, love... Krista shot and killed a Soviet agent in broad daylight in the middle of Chelsea. I thought we'd better split the scene straight away... the lads should be back in *Dolphin*.'

'*Christ*, Sims... how? Why? Were there witnesses?'

'Not that I know of... there was some old scrote much further along the street... I don't think he was capable of

263

registering much. Didn't even look at us when we passed him.'

'Who's we?'

He gave her the full story.

Anne turned round from looking out of the window, 'Radleigh won't be able to stay at Le Fanu's place with the Soviets on his tail. MI5 will have to move him to a safe house.'

'Probably have already done so and that's going to make it difficult for the squad and the lads to find him. I've got to get to him, love. He knows a bunch of stuff he hasn't coughed up yet.'

'They might have moved Radleigh but they won't have moved Le Fanu. You need to find him and persuade him to tell you Radleigh's whereabouts... he's influential, he'll know.'

'Spot on,' he said. 'I'm going back to The Mulberry... see what I can find out.'

*

Press presence zero. He walked to the end of the road and glanced to where Nikolai Zima had assumed a posture not possible in life; a crumpled and abandoned marionette. No police scene of crime men. No sign of the recent slaying. Sims returned to Le Fanu's door and pressed the bell. The speaker clicked. A metallic voice asked, 'Who is it?'

'Commander Sherwood-Reeves Naval Intelligence Division. I need to talk to you. You must be aware Gerald Radleigh is in extreme danger.'

'Come in.'

Le Fanu, rotund and pampered waited in the hall.

'Come in to my study and please make yourself comfortable and sit down. I'll be with you in a moment.'

Sims did not sit as asked. If he was going to need to move quickly, he preferred to do so while stood upright and ready.

Le Fanu returned with Gerald Radleigh in tow.

'*Christ!* I thought at least you'd be hidden away somewhere... a safe house.'

Radleigh looked creased and anxious. It was plain he hadn't been sleeping well. '*Safe* house, you say. Are you sure anywhere's safe from my pursuers?'

Sims looked at Le Fanu, 'My men handed Mr Radleigh here over to MI5. You're MI6. How come you ended up with him?'

Radleigh gave a light cough and interrupted, 'MI5 saw that I was politically too dangerous for them to have on their books. They realised Admiral Jessop had dumped a load of trouble on them. You might say I'm *the* poisoned chalice.'

'So how come MI6 took you on?'

'They didn't... my very good and old friend St. John Le Fanu has done what no other has the stomach to do. Commander Sherwood-Reeves, I think my days are not long... my book will never see the light of day.'

He, Sims, glanced at Le Fanu. Fiona's words: "I'd bet you'd want to punch him in the teeth as soon as you saw him." - it was not so. If everything was above board and just as Radleigh had said, then, Le Fanu had taken a big and probably career wrecking risk. Sims gave him the benefit of doubt and found he did not want to punch him in the teeth or anywhere else.

'So, Commander, you see... we're in a bit of a fix,' said

Le Fanu.

'How come the press have lost interest so quickly?'

'They don't know I'm here. I did a flit in the middle of the night. St. John let them come in and see for themselves I had gone, and then I flitted back very early in the morning.'

'There is also the unfortunate killing we had a few hundred yards away... they shifted their attention to that. Do you know anything about that, Commander?'

'No.'

'Very interesting: the victim was Russian carrying an English service revolver, yet, the bullet that killed him was of Soviet origin. What can one make of that?'

Sims shrugged, 'Well, you have my word I shall keep quiet about your presence here. I take it you still require the deal you wanted... pension backdated and all that?'

'Yes, though I don't think it will make a lot of difference to my outcome. Also, Commander, The Government is not going to respond quickly and I am short of funds. I cannot live off the charity of my friend here.'

Le Fanu broke in, 'Gerald, you are welcome to stay as long as you like.'

Sims looked at them both, 'Give me a few days... I can't promise anything. Please stay here out of sight. If I phone I'll call myself Jason.'

***

Chapter Sixteen.
Cash Transfer.

Billy Ruffian threw his hands up in the air, 'This is risky, Sims. Why on earth do you want to do it? Why not leave him where he is? He's not our problem anymore, lad. Let him be for god's sake.'

'It seems everything we do is risky. That's not a good enough argument for me. Anyway, since when have you given up taking risks? *Christ*, I'd like a good look at your unpublished record... I bet that would tell a tale or two.'

Little more than a twitch, Billy smiled and then frowned, 'Yes, that's all very well, but taking Radleigh back to Zurich... anything could happen. I cannot give this idea the go-ahead.'

'It's perfectly sound. And, if I may say so, no more risky than taking several million pounds worth of submarine and its crew into Riga Bay to pick him up in the first place. And, if you ask me, it's just a bit unjust you giving me a list of names to sort out, and then binding my hands firmly aft while I attempt to carry out what you've asked. Sir, you once told me staying a stoker would open few doors. Well, let me tell you, even commanders find it difficult opening doors with their bleedin' hands strapped behind their backs.'

'Calm down, lad. Just give me a good reason why.'

'I can give you more than one. But, try try this for a starter: neither of us know how much cash he's got stowed in Zurich... it's not going to be a few pence, you can bet on that. If he gets killed... no, let's put that a bit different: *when* he gets his comeuppance, that money will stay locked in his account forever doing nobody any good but a few Swiss bankers. These ackers are best put to good use in the United Kingdom.'

'I'd be the first to agree with that. Even so, why should *he* agree to do it?'

'He's short of funds... he told me so. I don't think he'll like the idea, but he *will* go along with it. Listen, sir, Radleigh knows his days are numbered: he'll comply.'

'I don't understand your reasoning. Why should his impending death motivate him so?'

'Difficult to say. I get this feeling talking to him he knows he's made mistakes... he's very fond of England, you know. I don't think he's sorry for his political beliefs. Just doubtful of the way he exercised them... how he put them into practice. I think I'm right: call it instinct.'

'Well, you've always had good instincts, lad, I'll give you that.'

'Then why not let me follow them? At least you could let me find out if he'd go along with the plan. His presence, fingerprint and signature at Hoffmann Bank are essential. So, if he refuses, the plan's buggered anyhow. Even Mike Mason and Alistair Duncan couldn't get us round that one.'

Billy chuckled, 'Anne said you had a barrow-boy's instinct for a deal. Alright, swing out a sounding line and see what sticks to the wax... sound him out, Sims, and maybe, and only maybe, we'll go from there.'

'Okay, thanks. Now, here's another reason to do it. Laurence Heston was involved in some sort of banking scandal at Berne. Let's see what we can find out about that while I'm there. But, perhaps you already know about it, sir.'

Vice Admiral Billy Ruffian Jessop turned round from looking out of the window, smiled, and said, 'You're getting very good, Commander.'

'Might be a captain soon,' Sims said, getting up to leave.

*

He found her at the bottom of the garden muttering about slugs and poking around in a flower bed. She looked up, 'Did you give him my undying love, darling?'

'The bollocks I did.'

'You're jealous.'

'Rubbish.'

Ritual skirmish over, kisses exchanged, necks nuzzled, she asked, 'Success?'

'Partial. He's allowing me to sound him out before going any further. He's getting cautious, love. A bit unlike him. Strain's getting to him.'

'*What!* to Billy? Never.'

'I think so. Unless he's holding something back.'

'Now, that's more like it. When are you going to ask Radleigh?'

'I'll try for tomorrow... phone him this evening.'

Anne took his arm as they walked back to the house, 'Call sign... *Jason...* Jason and the Golden Fleece. Very appropriate, darling. What on earth made you come up with that?'

'Just popped into my head when I was talking to him and Le Fanu. Barrow-boys are good at fleecing. Been thinking about all that gold in Switzerland for some time now. Quite pleased with it, actually... you know, good line.'

She nudged him, 'You're not thinking of keeping some for yourself, I hope?'

'Haven't made my mind up yet.'

*

Three arm chairs pulled up around the fireplace.

'You'll need cash if you have to do a sudden dash.'

Gerald Radleigh looked doubtful.

'It *is* risky, Gerald,' said St John Le Fanu. 'What he suggests is correct, though. One day you're going to need money. And, you will have to be there to release it... listen, he's right, Gerald.'

'If I agree, what's your plan?'

'False passport out and return... you'll use your own in the bank. Just in case it's escaped your notice, I'm taking risks too. And, so that I have some confidence you won't do a runner, I hold your true passport until we need it... that done, you'll hand it back to me.'

'That's all there is to it?'

'No, there'll be discreet watchers tailing us... making sure we don't get into trouble.'

'The same two from the submarine?'

'Yes, and possibly a few others... they're very good. Your account, is it the only one you have in Switzerland?'

'Yes.'

'Any others in Europe?'

'A small amount in one in Paris.'

'How much is small?'

'Eighty or ninety thousand, I guess.'

Sims smothered a fit of choking. 'If you consider eighty or ninety thousand as small, how much is in Zurich?'

'In Swiss Francs, something in the order of the equivalent of seven and a half million pounds Sterling I wouldn't wonder.'

Le Fanu did choke. Recovered he said, 'Good God, Gerald, that's an awful lot.'

'Was that all from drug smuggling?' asked Sims.

Radleigh hesitated.

'Might as well tell us now. I'd hate to have a shock later. I want to know what I'm dealing with here.'

'I had a very broad remit when I worked in the British Embassy in Paris. My role included smoothing out all kinds of diplomatic dramas; *faux pas*... some of them monumental...' Radleigh stopped mid-stream. '...getting two sides of an international dispute together for an unofficial meeting. It was a good life,' he said, quietly, and took a delicate sip from his glass.

Sims waited. Mind racing, time viscous. Wait, wait, he thought, this is like squeezing the trigger... wait until you know the moment's right. No one tells you when that is. You just know it. It's going to be worth it: *wait*!

Radleigh took another sip and continued, 'There was an incident at the Bern branch of Hoffmann bank... that is also my bank in Zurich. An embassy man called Laurence Heston...'

'Excuse me, went down the wrong way,' gagged Sims

over his drink.

'... have you recovered, Commander?'

Sims nodded.

'Heston, had been an MI6 agent for many years. His work, not unlike mine, covered many areas. It appears that MI6 held deposited money in two accounts at Hoffmann Bank. The first was the main MI6 international slush fund and the biggest held by any of the branches of British intelligence. It also appears that no one in the higher echelons of MI6 had any idea how much was there. Well, let us say, if they did know, they did not reveal they knew.'

'Why two accounts?'

'One was official... used for world-wide MI6 work... smoothing paths, oiling wheels, old fashioned bribery etc. The other contained funds syphoned off from the official account... MI6 bosses certainly did not know of that one. Who could tell if funds drawn from the first account were for legitimate purposes - receivers of bribes rarely sign receipts, Commander. Nevertheless, the second account, with its deposits and interest, grew to hold a substantial amount.'

'How did Heston get involved?'

'There had to be two signatures to make withdrawals from the official deposit and both signatories had to be present at the bank. Possibly because of his banking connections, young Heston was chosen to replace an embassy official who died. Heston is a smart man, it didn't take him long to realise that something was amiss. He found out about this second account and in one way or another managed to gain access to it. He then took an inordinate amount for himself.'

'Did others know?'

'It's possible.'

'Then why not blow the whistle?'

'I know you are a French speaker, Commander. It was down to *Le Piston,* Commander, *le Piston!*'

'As good as my French may be, that's not a term I'm familiar with... help me out.'

'In political and diplomatic circles in France, everyone understands *le Piston.* One discovers something compromising about one's associates and one stores it away as insurance. That, Commander, is why there is so much high-level corruption in France. They all have the capability of taking each other down. It would have to be an immaculate group of men to break the stalemate. Such men do not exist in France.'

'Does this go on with our lot?'

'To a lesser degree, yes.'

'How did Heston move the money around?'

'He simply enlisted the help of his friend Peter Scammel and his father... his father had banking interests in Africa.'

That's two more ticked off Billy's list. Two birds with one stone, thought Sims. 'You're being remarkably forthcoming. Why?'

'I need your help, Commander.'

'Hmm, okay, let's go back a bit. How did you get involved?'

'I was well known at Hoffmann Bank. It was common knowledge I had diplomatic influence. They asked me to intervene.'

'I don't see that. As far they were concerned, Hoffmanns had two cash rich legitimate accounts, why should they worry?'

'I doubt if they did at first. And only then, when Heston got horribly drunk and made some inappropriate statements about his wealth in front of both MI6 and bank officials, did they show concern. MI6 decided they couldn't touch him... *le Piston* at work, you see. It doesn't mean they weren't angry; they were actually beside themselves. But, what could they do? To go public would leave them with a nasty stain on their reputation, and, as for Hoffmann Bank, it doesn't pay to have a misappropriation scandal hanging over a reputable Swiss bank. They asked me if I could help. I investigated and persuaded MI6 it was better to let Heston keep his gains and say nothing. I didn't need to advise them to keep him well away from financial matters in the future.'

Radleigh took another sip. 'I advised both parties to keep the second account open. To use some of it for its original purpose, and let some of the money be transferred over time back to the original account. For this service of mine I took, on behalf of les Grands Amis, a commission of twenty percent... some four and a quarter million pounds of what is in my account in Hoffmann's at this moment. Hoffmann Bank was very pleased with the arrangement.'

'Do you mean to tell me they fiddled twenty one and a quarter million pounds without being clocked?'

'Oh, it wasn't really that difficult, Commander. They were bright, yes, but no more than that. All systems have a soft underbelly, you know. And, Heston had the luck to have this one laid at his feet.'

'And Scammel?'

'He is the son of a banker, obviously he would have

taken a cut too.'

Sims sat thinking and then looked at Le Fanu, 'Mr Radleigh will not be able to stay here forever... it won't be safe. If I can arrange it, he might be better off returning to Netley for a while until the Government sort out whether they're going to comply with his demands and see to his safety.'

'At the moment I feel as if I'm a threat to St John... I don't like that, he's done enough. So, yes, I think back to Netley for the moment is a better thing.'

'I'll see if I can get clearance and let you know. In the meantime, just keep out of sight, please.'

*

'Fancy coming up to see Billy?'

'Yes, of course.'

'You can tell him about your undying love while you're there.'

'How do you think he'd take it?'

'Pretty well, I'd imagine. In his boots, I know I would.'

There are short smiles and longer ones. Anne, gave him a *very* long one, 'That's nice, darling.'

*

'Well, sir, that's two off your list: Heston and Scammel. And, you never heard anything of this?'

'I heard whispers, just whispers, lad. You've done well.'

'Twenty one and a quarter million,' gasped Anne. Sims had not given her the details of his meeting with Radleigh and Le Fanu. She looked at him astonished,

'What did you say when you found out.'

'Nothing, just choked.'

Billy politely ignored her exclamation and question. 'You said two off the list: Heston and Scammel... and not Le Fanu. Why not? He's on it.'

'Fiona thinks he stinks. Myself, I'm not sure. I can't see what he has to achieve from sheltering Radleigh apart from ruining his career. He seems to be behaving like a good friend ought... I'm going to reserve my judgement for now.'

'Do you remember my words when I handed you the list, Sims. "They are suspects, not condemned criminals". You may be right, he may be innocent. If he is, he may be the third off the list, lad.'

'Anyway, Radleigh has seven and a half million pounds in his account at Hoffmann Bank. That has to be worth going for. And, I don't see any good reason why we shouldn't take our expenses out of it and repay your slush fund. With the rest we could buy another 'O' class sub if we wanted... there's enough to fit it out with gold plated taps and then bows to stern tubes with Axminster carpets too. We could call it *HMS* bleedin' *Opulent.*'

Billy laughed. Anne giggled, and, not for the first time in their married life, wondered what she had hitched herself to.

'Get a plan together, Commander,' said Billy Ruffian.

'Is that a yes?'

'No, a strong maybe.'

'You won't like this, but, first I want to get Radleigh back to Netley... he's in agreement. He knows he's not safe in public at the moment. We need to do this now, sir. Anne and I will get the plan together as soon as he's there. I know NID will be vulnerable... I think we have to do it.'

'Go ahead. Keep him out of sight and out of Wood-ruff's way, lad.'

'Yes, sir.'

*

'Do you think he'll go for it?'

'If you mean Billy, yes. I think he's already decided to,' Anne replied.

'If all goes well in Zurich, how and where do you reckon the money ought be transferred?'

'Banker's draft to an account in London. That will be the quickest... only don't lose it on the way home.'

'Two.'

She looked puzzled, 'Two what?'

'Two accounts, he's not having it all... Jag to pay for.'

'Seriously, Sims, or I'll be forced to bash you.'

'*Nice...* will I whimper?'

'Sod off,' she said, looking out of the side window so he couldn't see her smiling.

Sometime later she said, 'You're quiet.'

'Thinking what the split ought to be... it's got to be attractive enough for him to go for it. Even if he agrees to us getting seventy five percent, he still ends up a million-aire. Should do the trick.'

'What are you going to do with the balance?'

'Not a clue. I'll have it put in our name. Think of it as a future bargaining chip.'

'Will that be legal?'

'Couldn't give a toss. Look at it this way, when you've got over three million quid in the bank, everything's legal; legality's up for sale, love. Anyway, it's his cash he can do what he likes with it, and if he chooses to put in our hands, it's his choice. All above board and legal. No extortion... a straightforward business deal.'

'I'm not sure anything's straightforward with you, darling,' she said, laughing and leaning over to bite his ear.

'I'm pretty sure Radleigh will go along with it. When he does we'll have to move fast. I still have Radleigh's passports, one in his name and the other as Edward Godbehere his Quaker name. We'll have to get one for Alistair...'

'*Alistair!.*'

'Yep, he knows Zurich inside out... might be useful... possibly essential... can't have him travelling as Gerald Radleigh, can we? And then we need one each for David and Dusty. I'll have to use Piers Monsoon again... when this is over I'm going to get Mike to make another, this time I'll choose the name. God give me strength, enter stage right: Piers bloody Monsoon again.'

She laughed, then, 'What about mine? We're not known in Zurich.'

'You sure you want to come?'

'Absolutely, think about it, Commander Barrow-Boy... I want to make sure you don't run off with the cash.'

'Bugger, thought I'd slipped the leash.'

'*Well!* Can I come or not?'

'Okay, should be an in and out job. It'll be nice to have your back-up again, love.'

'Did you miss me on the sub.'

'Yes... and you'll never know how much.'

Now and again, a small smile flitted across her face.

278

They were still flitting as they turned into the drive of Hell Head House.

'Sims, Alistair doesn't need another passport. Surely, it would be better if he travels under his own name. He might need proof he isn't Radleigh.'

'Hmm, you're right, of course.'

'And, there's another thing, you've not mentioned his money in Paris.'

'Been thinking about that. It's not petty-cash. We might go there first. Next couple of jobs: get Radleigh to play ball with the accounts, then get Alistair and the lads together.'

*

'This way, you are buying your future... your security. It's two accounts in London or nothing. To make sure you've got the picture, let me repeat, we go to Paris first and then Zurich. The first London account will hold seventy five percent of what we bring back, and you will have zero access or rights to that one. The second, you and I will both be signatories. Each cheque drawn will need both our signatures.'

'Why the two of us?'

'I need your cooperation. There'll be over a million pounds in that account, if you are the sole signatory you could bugger off and do as you will. No, let's be clear, for the short term, you and I work together on this one... dual signatures... that's *my* insurance. When the Government come up with a deal for you, I'll drop out and it will be all yours. That's the deal. Mr Le Fanu is witness to what I've said. Yes or no?'

Radleigh knew he was caught.

Le Fanu said, 'As the commander says, you will still be a millionaire, Gerald. You're not in a good position otherwise, twenty five percent of something is better than nought percent. You'll still be a millionaire, Gerald. You must see that.'

With a hopeless shrug he uttered, 'I agree.'

'Right, pack some things, suits etc. We're going to Netley. When we get there, you will write a letter to Hoffmann Bank and tell them what you want. Tell them that you wish to withdraw all funds. Tell them you require two banker's drafts in the proportions we have agreed and made out to the London accounts. I'll have this letter couriered to Switzerland as soon as it's ready. We can't trust the confidentiality of French banks, so we just fly in, march in, do the deal, and march out. The same courier that takes your letter to Hoffmann Bank will also take possession of the drafts and see them safe to the London bank. I hope we understand each other, Mr Radleigh.'

'Yes, it seems I have little option.'

'Better get packing, then.'

*

'David, you look the part, you'll be logged as a government official. You're going to courier a letter from Radleigh to his bank in Zurich, then, you'll courier the drafts to London. We're giving them a couple of days to get things ready before we arrive. Dusty, you've the look of a thug about you, can't put that in your passport, though. Nor, submariner... same thing really. Better go as a maritime advisor.'

'Sims, Switzerland doesn't have a navy,' Anne

laughed.

'I *was* bleedin' joking.'

Sub-lieutenant Mountford broke in, 'How about something appropriate for Swiss trade and something Dusty understands... perhaps put him down as a clock watcher, maybe?'

'For that, I will take revenge on the pistol range, sir. I've tried hard not to humiliate you in the past... it's gloves off time from now on.'

Sims heard Alistair's XK120 enter the drive, 'My car's turned up.'

Greetings over, Sims stood up, 'Right, down to business. Alistair, you David and Dusty are to go direct to Zurich a few days earlier than Anne, Radleigh and myself. Check into a hotel and check out Hoffmann Bank... keep a close eye on it, at least one of you watching during its opening hours. See if there are others watching it also. The Soviets know his money can't be moved without his presence. I can't see them missing that trick, there's a good chance they'll be on the look out.'

Anne raised her hand, 'Can I butt in?'

'Of course.'

She looked at David and Dusty, 'Lads, you are new to the game, please listen to Alistair, he knows Zurich and the ropes... use his experience. I'm sure there's a lot... so much, we can all learn from him.'

'Thank you my dear, young people do tend to think we oldies, idiots, don't they.'

'I don't think that, sir,' said Dusty. 'You got to stay in a hotel and was fitted out with some smart suits. We stayed in a smelly sub, got chased by some Russians and didn't even get a pint of beer out of it. No, sir, you're a lot smarter than us, I'd say.'

'Speaking of suits, do you think Billy could go for another one or two, Anne? Possibly three?'

She smiled, 'Good God, Alistair, you might just be pushing your luck there. He's already shudders at the thought of the hotel bill you presented him with. How much was that meal the last time you were there?'

'My dear, I had to act the part, and for what it was, it was worth every penny. Gerald Radleigh does not do things cheaply... one must always act the part.' He turned to Dusty, 'This time you'll be staying in a top-hole hotel with a restaurant to match... I'll show you what good food is all about. If the chef is still there, he does this marvellous *entrée* of *truffe paté* and *foie gras.* You would be forgiven for thinking the combination a little rich, but not so... perfectly balanced.'

Dusty rubbed his hands together, 'Fancy starting with truffles and the other stuff before we get into the big dishes.'

'One doesn't start with an *entrée,* it is served between the fish course and the following course. While there, I shall see it my duty to school you, young man.'

'I'll be a willing student, sir.'

'Can we get back to business?'

'Sorry, sir.'

'The hotel, Alistair, how close to Hoffmann Bank?'

'Directly opposite across the square.'

'You have, as you know, a more than passable resemblance to Radleigh. I want you to go and enter the bank regularly. If the Ruskies pick you up all the better. They'll soon find out you're not the real one. When the real Radleigh arrives, they might not want to risk making fools of themselves again. On that point, I just need you to act as decoy, I want you and Radleigh to wear identical suits.'

'So, I can get another?'

'It looks like it.'

Alistair Duncan clapped his hands, 'Wonderful, top-hole, spiffing. I'll need some shirts as well.'

*

Billy smiled but did not rise when Sims was shown in by the house-keeper. He handed the sheet of paper to the old admiral.

'It's a complex operation, we shall need plenty of funds, sir.'

Billy looked at Anne's estimate, '*Good God*, what have I let myself in for? If these weren't Anne's figures I'd say you had included the cost of that damn Jaguar.'

'No time to lose, best to cough up and let us get on with the job... we'll claw back what we're owed later.'

'You're confident about all this, Sims?'

'Absolutely.'

'Bloody Duncan's taken me for another suit.'

'No option... he's got to closely resemble Radleigh. So, sir, are you giving the go-ahead or not?'

'I spoke to Miles... he thinks I ought to.'

'What about you, though? You're the skipper.'

'I may not be the best person to make judgement at the moment, lad. I'll go with it. Do your best, Sims.'

'I always do, sir. I'll be on my way, then.'

***

Chapter Seventeen.
Marjorie Monsoon.

'*Marjorie? Marjorie* bloody *Monsoon?*' she said, throwing the passport onto the *Bellerophon* table.

'Careful, you might scratch it. Napoleon might have walked on that very spot,' Sims said, getting up and gently buffing the place where it had landed.

She glared ferociously at him. 'You absolute... sodding... bugger, you.'

Sims had positioned himself on the opposite side of the table before sliding her passport over to her. 'Look love, if we're to sleep together in the same hotel room, we can't *but* go as a married couple. Surely, you can see that? And, as I'm travelling as Piers Monsoon I had give you the same family name.'

'I'm not sleeping in the same room as you... I'll, I'll sleep with Alistair.'

'Please yourself... I bet he's got a wrinkly todger.'

She couldn't help herself, she sniggered, 'But why Marjorie, Sims?'

'Not Marjorie *Sims*... just Marjorie. I mean that'd be stupid giving you a blokes name. Anyway, I like alliterations; *Mrs... Marjorie... Monsoon.* It's got a nice flow to it.'

'I suppose this is petty revenge for my teasing so

much over Piers bloody Monsoon.'

'Yep. Took a long time, but, yep. Crap name, innit?'

She stood frowning at him; one of her special frowns: the kind that make admirals apologise.

He realised he'd pushed her a bit too far: he was in deep shit and knew it. He tried a recovery move, 'Had nobody to frown at me like that on the *Odin*... really missed that.'

'Oh Sims, did you really?' she said, coming round to his side of the table. He held his arms out to her. He'd left his guard wide open. She had suckered him and gave him a devastating punch in the ribs.

'Fuckin' ouch,' he said, dodging backwards and regretting having taught her exactly where to place the hit.

'If you ever call me Marje, Sims Sherwood-Reeves, I shall sodding shoot you.'

'I don't think you would,' he said, backing away.

She recanted, 'No, I probably wouldn't. But, I *would* cut off your meat ration.'

'*Jesus!* how long for?'

She looked at him, not frowning, 'About half an hour,' she said, smiling.

He was still backing away.

'Stand still, Sims. Stay where you are.'

She put her arms round his neck and kissed him. 'Quits now?'

'Yeah... okay.'

'Are you sure?' she said, rubbing his side.

'Yeah, yeah. What you doing in half an hour, Marje?'

*

Gerald Radleigh had said little during the flight. In the taxi into central Paris he broke his silence, 'I think it best I first call the bank and tell them what we want, and that we'll be there for 1130 to sign and take possession of the draft.'

'Why 1130?' asked Anne.

'This is France, everything stops for *déjeuner*. The manager will want to process us as quickly as possible... he probably will have lunch appointment with some rich client. He won't want to delay it... this is France, Mrs Sherwood-Reeves, they have great respect for their stomachs. Their day is made up of three important gastronomic events: *petit déjeuner, déjeuner* and *dîner*. To miss the first is unfortunate, to miss either of the other two is to lose one day of their lives.'

Henri de la Tour du Pin, *le directeur d'agence bancaire* and pompous *fonctionaire*, protested.

Gerald Radleigh calmly and firmly said, 'Monsieur, we have known each other many years, have we not? I have urgent business. I must have the bank draft, *la traite bancaire,* this morning for 1130. I am not closing the account, merely using it. I must remind you, it is my money not yours. You must do as I say.'

He continued to protest.

'Now, let me give you an ultimatum: either you do as I say, or I will have every British Embassy account that is held with you transferred to *Credit Agricole*. I will be with you at 1130. I do not want to be kept waiting,' Radleigh put the phone back in its cradle.

*

Henri de la Tour de la Pin might have been modelling smiles: he had mastered and displayed his entire range from smirk, ingratiating to broad and many minor variations in between.

'That wasn't difficult was it?' said Radleigh, as he checked and signed the documents. 'All in order. *Bon appetit, Monsieur.*'

In the waiting taxi he handed the envelope to Sims. Sims handed it on to Anne, 'Now you're a courier too.'

'Seems such a long time ago,' she said, leaning on him.

*

In Zurich, he pointed at the register, 'That's Marjorie with a 'J', please,' Sims informed the concierge.

'I am so very sorry, madam.'

'It's an easy mistake to make... one person in particular makes them daily,' she said, glaring at Sims. Her face said everything, it radiated, "I am never going to forgive you for this, Sims Sherwood-Reeves".

David and Dusty were waiting. 'They picked him up, sir. Alistair's first visit to Hoffmanns and they hoisted him off... *first visit!*'

'Where is he now?' She looked concerned.

'In the restaurant. He spends quite a bit of time in there, sir.' said David.

'We'll join him... I'm starving,' said Sims. 'You two escort Mr Radleigh to his room. We don't want him and Alistair seen together. If you've not eaten, order the full works from room service. And, I suggest you let Mr Radleigh order. I'm sure his international experience has taught him a thing or two.'

The three of them entered the lift. Anne and Sims clearly heard Dusty's comment to Radleigh, 'See if you can outdo Alistair... the stuff we had last night! We were at the table for at least two hours. He's built like a Maltese racing snake... can't see where he puts it all... bleedin' incredible.'

They made their way to the dining room. She tugged on his arm and stopped him.

'Darling?'

'Yes, love.'

'We are just about to take seven and a quarter million pounds from an account in a Swiss bank being watched by Soviet agents, aren't you just a *little* bit worried?'

'Not really, no... got bigger things to worry about.'

'Such as?'

'Your revenge and what we're having for dinner.'

'I don't think I'll be able to eat much,' she confessed. She squeezed him, 'I'll think about the revenge later, Piers.'

Alistair was on spiffing form, 'They were so obvious, I spotted them immediately... parked right outside the front entrance. I went into the bank and when I left they bundled me straight into the car... nearly creased my trousers.'

Alistair raised a finger in the air and wagged it sideways indicating Anne and Sims. A waiter smoothed up and from the bottle on the table poured them each a glass of heavy Cabernet Sauvignon. 'This is a particularly good one... discovered it during my trip from Copenhagen.' He took a careful sip.

'Well, in the embassy I asked them what they thought they were doing and who the hell they thought I was. The cheeky blighters said I could choose, Anisim Polzin or Gerald Radleigh. It was a great game, Commander, so much fun. I said that I'd read about him in the London papers, wasn't he once one of their agents: they didn't think much to that. Then I suggested perhaps if they'd like to take my fingerprints they'd discover I wasn't who they thought. I told them my name and demanded to be allowed to speak to the British Embassy. Naturally, I knew they wouldn't go along with that. Nevertheless, one could see they were a little unsure of themselves. They brought Radleigh's dossier in, took my prints and quickly realised they'd made a most embarrassing and quite large mistake. Apparently the agent who had done the questioning was the KGB's main man in Switzerland. He was horrified at his error. To pave the way for my future sightings by his men, I told him I had business at Hoffmanns which would require me to visit there several times a day over several more days. I also told him that I hoped his men wouldn't repeat the same mistake. Having wrong-footed him, the long and short of it, Commander, is that I did a deal with him. In exchange for not reporting this incident to our embassy, I said I would accept a gift of some sort. So, at this moment, I have this case of very expensive vodka in my room and another box of the finest caviar... Caspian Sea Beluga, Commander, Beluga.'

Sims turned to Anne, 'And, you call me a barrow-boy! I've nothing on this guy... absolutely nothing.'

'Alistair, I assume you're going to share the booty

with us when we get back?' Anne asked, smiling.

'That depends, my dear, are you going to share the money with me?' Alistair might not have asked the question if he'd known how much they were collecting. On this matter, only Anne, Sims, Radleigh, Le Fanu and Billy were in the know.

*

That evening they met in Sims' and Anne's suite.

'Commander, I should like to know your plan? said Radleigh.

'That is why we're gathered here. Tomorrow, Alistair will visit Hoffmann Bank more than once in the morning. He will make contact with the Soviet watchers... smile at them... speak to them. Pass a few minutes with them, telling them how pleased he was with the quality of the vodka and give them a bottle each as a "no hard feelings" gift. On your second visit, Alistair, just a wave, more or less ignore them. Now, the third visit will be the one we're here for. Mr Radleigh and myself will go into the bank and do the business. To make sure the Soviets do not recognise Mr Radleigh going in, Anne will distract them... ask them the time... something. You'll have to *ad lib*, love. David, when we are ready to leave Hoffmanns, I'll signal you and Dusty. Cause a minor disturbance... just a minor one: nothing too violent. Then it's everyone back here. Now, for safety's sake, Alistair is to make one more trip that morning. While he is doing that, we'll get on our way to the airport. Alistair, as a gift for your incredible service to the Royal Navy... despite your ex RAF status, I'm going to give you the go ahead to stay a further night here at Billy's expense... I'm sure you don't need me to tell you how to abuse this privilege.'

'Damn it all, not abusing, Commander, *savouring*.'

Sims, involved in detail, talked to Alistair, David and Dusty. Anne sat beside Radleigh. He turned to her and said, 'Disregarding for the moment his desire to eject me out of a torpedo tube and generally wishing me dead for the harm I may have indirectly caused yourself, for which I deeply apologise, I have, despite our opposing ideological sides in events, developed a strong respect for you and your husband... both of you. Now, perhaps you will permit me for enquiring, but where did he get such acuity?... such *intense,* almost flippant, understanding of the moment?'

'Mr Radleigh, that is a question I have often asked myself. If you were to ask him, he would likely tell you it was because he was once a stoker.'

She looked over the table at Sims; her sod. Anne discarded the lingering idea of wreaking revenge on his being. Instead, she formed another plan.

Sims and David were talking head to head. Alistair coughed for attention: a polite RAF cough. 'Commander, are you armed?'

'This is not a diplomatic mission. We might have been searched in customs... we couldn't take the risk... I feel naked.'

'I did wonder if that would the case.'

Sims could feel there was more, 'And?'

'I took the opportunity of visiting an old contact. Fortunately, he was still in business. I use the term "business" loosely, Commander. In my previous time here, we had done each other many favours.' Alistair paused.

Sims thought: shady ones at that. He wondered, if there was a noun that covered such things as shady favours? I'll have to ask Anne. Perhaps *shavours,* he thought. He glanced across at her. She had been looking at him and smiled. Deep inside him, in his subconscious, resident sod yelled *"Yay!"* and vigorously rubbed its hands together.

'So, Commander, I took the opportunity of ordering... well not so much ordering as renting enough side arms for us all. By the way, I think it would be a good thing for you to meet him before you leave to hand them with the unused ammunition, back. He will appreciate that, I know. And, *you* never know, Commander, if *you* and he might need each others services in the future.'

'Unused! Are you expecting us to fire a few off, Alistair?' asked Dusty.

'As I told you at dinner last night, young man... we are boy scouts all... and therefore we should be prepared, Dusty, always *be prepared.'*

'Okay, what have you got for us?' Sims asked.

'All the same model and ammunition.' Alistair never used the contraction "Ammo". 'They are the best I could get at short notice: Makarovs; nine millimetre. They are a useful weapon, and seeing you are all, except Anne, using Brownings, I thought them the best alternative.'

Sims gazed at the old man. 'Alistair, I had this feeling you'd be useful.. I just knew it. We could do with you lecturing at Netley.'

'Billy and Miles Stinton have asked me before: I'm afraid I prefer teaching people to fly, to enjoy themselves. I'm not sure if ours is a trade I want to teach. Many fall by the wayside, Commander.'

'Maybe in a good cause.'

'Who knows?... maybe.'

Gerald Radleigh looked away.

Sims stood up, 'Big day tomorrow. Early night required for everybody. We'll meet 0900 for breakfast. Okay, off you go.'

Anne watched them leave. She closed the door behind them and locked it. 'Should that have included me? Did you mean me as well?'

'Depends on who you want to sleep with. Alistair looked quite excited when I told you were going to share his bed. Might be a shame to disappoint him.'

Just the hint of a frown. 'You didn't really tell him, did you?'

'Sure. He drove a hard bargain. In the end we settled for twenty quid.'

She giggled, 'You should have charged thirty... we could have gone out to dinner.'

'No, no, wrong again, that's what I had to pay him.'

*

She stumbled and leant against their car, busied herself removing something stuck to the sole of her shoe. She tried scuffing whatever it was against the pavement. Anne smiled at the driver - she had their attention. It was easy, a few others milled around entering and leaving, first Radleigh, then Sims entered Hoffmann Bank.

'You received my letter of authority?'

No names were exchanged in public: security and

confidentiality at Hoffmann Bank forbade it. 'Certainly, sir. Everything is in order. Please come with me, it is better we conduct this in my office.'

Few words exchanged. Radleigh was handed the draft and covering documents. With his back to the manager, he opened his briefcase inserted the documents, closed it and scrambled the six combination numbers. He turned round, 'It has always been a pleasure to deal with you. The French could learn a lesson from you.'

'I assume you do not like the French, Mr Radleigh?'

'Quite the reverse, I adore the French, their culture, their appreciation of fine wines and good food. I adore everything except their ability to organise and manage an efficient banking system.'

'Then I trust and hope this is not the end of our association, Mr Radleigh?'

'No, of course not. World commerce would die without Switzerland's neutrality and Hoffmann Bank's efficiency to conduct the benefits. It is but a short and necessary readjustment to my affairs.'

From the foyer Sims nodded and thumbs-upped David. He walked briskly towards the car. Ignoring the pedestrian crossing and dodging the heavy traffic, Dusty ran across the road. It was close, his timing perfect he slammed into David right by the car. They hadn't counted on the assistance of the Swiss police. A whistle sounded.

This was not an incident they could afford to be involved with. Another mess was not required. Picking-up Alistair had cost their boss dearly - a speedy return to Moscow threatened. Zurich was a good posting - the car and agents slid away from the kerb-side.

Sims escorted Radleigh back to the hotel and placed him under Anne and Alistair's custody. 'I'm nipping back... the lads did a good job... a bit too good, cops involved. Better see if I can help.'

Dusty looked puzzled; David was doing his best to confuse matters by using his grammar school French; the two policemen looked exasperated.

Sims strolled past, halted and returned. 'Excuse me, I couldn't help overhearing,' he said, politely. 'I'm happy to interpret if you wish.'

'Sir, please tell this man, if, once more, we see him attempting to cross the streets of Zurich other than by the official crossings, we will arrest him.'

They checked Dusty's passport and let him off with just the warning. Mike Mason had done a good job.

'Right! David, you are now the group's official courier.' Sims handed him the briefcase. 'Handcuff this to your wrist. The rest of you, get packed, and while you're doing that, Alistair will take me to see his armaments man. David, as soon as Dusty's packed both of you take a taxi to the airport... it doesn't matter what it costs, get the next available flight to London... first class if necessary, no! as you were, be sure to make it first class... you'll be certain of a ticket. Anne, Mr Radleigh and I will follow. Dusty, at Heathrow pick up your weapons from left luggage and keep your eyes open. Don't wait for us. David, you know where to deposit the drafts. If there are any problems with British customs, use your real identities... just in case they were to check. Anne, settle the bill for the rooms, please. *Bonne chance*, lads.'

Their taxi pulled up close to the Zurich main train station.

'It's but a short stroll from here,' said Alistair. 'A small side street off Zürcherstrasse. Should you not know this, Commander, arms are everyone's right in Switzerland, and nearly everyone has one. I once read in an intelligence paper that Switzerland has more guns per head of population than any other country in the world, and yet, curiously, there's very little gun crime. Now, the man we're going to meet: Peter Frohlich, is a very useful contact to have. He is a legitimate gun dealer by trade with a not altogether legitimate side-line in weapons of assassination or, more pertinent to our situation, untraceable to us. Peter is more or less tolerated by the Swiss intelligence service. Nevertheless, one needs to know him well before he comes forward with offers of supply.'

Peter Frohlich beamed and shook Alistair's hand, 'Mr Duncan... Alistair, it's been many years. Too many years. And your associate? Who have we here?'

'To be trusted, Peter. To be trusted. British Royal Navy I'm afraid, but, nevertheless, to be trusted. Peter, this is Commander Sherwood-Reeves of the Naval Intelligence Division.'

'I am very pleased to meet you. Isn't NID to be closed down?'

'Christ! That's got around quick,' said Sims.

'It's a very large world that often has quite small and connected populations in its odder corners, Commander,' said Alistair.

'You told me that once before.'

'Yes. I remember. It was an instant truism of my own making and is still relevant today, Commander.'

Frohlich had yet to find philosophy profitable. Only for modern philosophers is there money in it he had told his son. And they, he had added, have reason on their side. And, no matter how unfair it may seem, *reason* has taken sides with them. 'Alistair, you must tell me the purpose of your visit.'

'That is simple: to return what is yours, to pay our dues, and to introduce my colleague here. He is a handy person to know in England. He has useful contacts.'

*

'Frohlich? Is that his real name?'

'No, I don't think so. In my opinion, he's of Hungarian extraction. Frohlich is a good name to pass as Swiss.'

'What makes you think he's Hungarian?'

'We did some work together... took arms there. Through Austria into Hungary... difficult work. With this particular job it was never about profit with Peter. There was an angry passion at work. I put two and two together.'

'I'm still not clear why you thought it necessary to bring me along. Can't see myself coming back to Zurich... too far from a decent coast line.'

'Young man, It seems we have known each other long enough... can I call you Sims?'

'*Christ!* About time.'

'Touching on Zurich, you are here now: so why not in the future? If one year ago I had asked where you might be in a year's time, would you have said Switzerland?'

'Okay. I get the point.'

'Before I met Peter, I would not have believed I would one day be landing a small aircraft up-slope on a snow field high in the Austrian Alps near the Hungarian border.'

'*Jesus*, really?'

'Going, it was quite a task fully laden... small aircraft. And, contrary to what you might think, even though we were lighter, taking off unladen was even more so. Downhill takeoff and a fair catabatic wind developing.'

'Catabatic?'

'Airflow down the mountainside... cold air rushing down into the warmer valley below... anabatic when it flows uphill. We hadn't quite made take off airspeed before we plunged off the edge.'

'Hell, Alistair. What then?'

'Pushed the stick forward - airspeed up and in control... marvellous little aircraft.'

'What kind.'

'Feiseler Storch. World War Two: German.'

Sims's appetite wetted. His thoughts cast a couple of years rearward to his first trip to Tunworth House with Simon Maitland. They passed Lasham airfield and he had asked if it was difficult to learn to fly.

'Alistair?'

'Hmm.'

'How about you teaching me to fly?'

Gliders or powered?'

'Both.'

'I look forward to it.'

'Drop me off here. Let's arrive separately. I'll walk the rest of the way... see if the coast is clear.'

*

Hell Head House.

'Sir, You gave me a sealed envelope which I handed in, and the manager gave me a sealed envelope in return with what I assume was the receipt. How did you know the receipt would be for the correct amount?'

'They're an old school bank. Totally reliable. But, as a precautionary measure, when I set up the accounts, and there were two as a matter of fact, I let him have a very long look at my Browning.'

'How much did we bring back, sir?'

'Need to know, Dusty. Need to know,' Sims said, tapping the side of his nose.

***

Chapter Eighteen.
No More a Ruffian.

They were young and easily bored.

'Food will never taste the same,' said Dusty, reassembling his Browning - he'd given it a thorough strip down and clean. 'Old Spiffing's got life taped. Knows how to live. What he doesn't know about wine and food... I've a lifetime's learning in front of me.'

'I feel a bit out of sorts, like an odd sock. It's a bit of an anti-climax after Zurich.'

'Is that what they feel like?'

'What?'

'Anti-climaxes... socks.'

'You know what I mean.'

'No, I've never felt like an odd sock or anything else odd.'

'You're being obtuse.'

'Never felt like a triangle either. Though, as a matter of interest, I did have a girl once who had anti-climaxes.'

'One doesn't have an ant-climax, it is something that *is*, or, one feels.'

'She did. We'd be on the job and she'd fall fast asleep... anti-climax... definitely.'

'That's narcolepsy.'

'*Never!.* Is that anything like leprosy?'

They busied themselves; David reading the newspaper, Dusty putting a final polish on his gun.

'Perhaps Anne knows what's going on.'

'Yes, I'll call her.'

*

'All she said was, "Come to Hell Head House". We'd better get going.'

Dusty topped up an empty magazine and clicked it home into the butt. 'Wonder what's cooking?'

'In general or by Mrs Calver?'

'Mrs Calver. English cooking versus continental... what's your choice?'

'Horses for courses,' answered David.

'That's continental, then.'

'How do you mean?'

'French grub.'

He laughed. 'That's almost very good.'

*

'Did Sims ever mention Adian McClusky?'

'Not in detail... just in passing,' said David.

'He died under interrogation at Netley Unit 4. Busy yourselves, find out what you can. Watch Woodruff, he was the interrogator. Sims thinks Woodruff may have gone a bit too far. Billy asked him to quietly reopen the case when he had time. He's busy at the moment on other things... maybe it's a good chance for you both to find your own feet... but, go careful.'

'What can you tell us, ma'am?'

'Anne, will do nicely... McClusky was picked up by

301

the Special Boats Service and handed over to one of our subs off the southern Irish coast. Officially, he was in a bad way when Unit 4 received him and he soon after died of pneumonia plus other complications: the latter not being detailed. Perhaps it might be a good thing to discretely check out a few people who were around at the time. Don't go too far with your digging without consulting Sims. He's also looking into it himself.'

'Do you know what boat it was that took delivery?' asked Dusty.

'HMS *Oberon*.'

'Yes, I can see why you asked that,' put in, David. 'Netley's a bit of a closed shop... difficult to ask many questions without giving the game away.'

'*Dolphin's* a good place to start, then.' said Anne. 'I'll also ask father if he has anything to put in the pot.'

The door opened. Dusty leapt to his feet. '*Mrs Calver, spiffing...* let me give you a hand with that?'

*

On her day off they met in a car park in Woking, well away from the eyes and ears of the squad. There were matters of security the issue of which Shirley did not want the squad or herself to be implicated in.

'Adian McClusky was never a member of the IRA, Sims. He may have infiltrated them and it may have appeared he was in the thick of their actions. He trod along the shadowy border of MI5, MI6 and organised crime. It is often difficult to know which group some operatives belong to. He was ex SAS and a very fit man. It is difficult to believe he would have succumbed to something like pneumonia following a few days exposure. He was trained in survival.'

'Anything else?'

'Do you remember me telling you about Heston and a problem in Switzerland?'

'Yes, of course.'

'McClusky was there at the same time. I'm not sure for what purpose. There are often *handy men* on call at our embassies. What I have also managed to glean, is that he was sent there shortly after the Heston incident came to light.'

'This gets more and more interesting, love.'

'I'll keep digging, Sims. I have to be so careful, though. But, that's about all I have at the moment. How is Anne?'

'Blisteringly good. I'll tell her you asked.'

She wound down the side window and called to him as he walked away to his car, 'Sims, I almost forgot, Passant was somehow involved.'

He leaned in the window. 'Now, that is also very interesting. That name, always worth a little dig at, babe. Now, listen, go careful.'

*

'Radleigh's disappeared again,' said Heston, third drink in hand. 'Le Fanu says he doesn't know where he is.'

'How do you know what Le Fanu is saying?' snapped Passant.

'I asked him, Jack... asked him. Some of us talk to people... hold conversations.'

'He wasn't taking calls.'

Sewell had to have his say, 'Not to you, Jack. Perhaps

you shouldn't have called him a "fat pimple". Appropri-ate, though undiplomatic and badly timed.'

'I didn't say that.'

'We all heard you, Jack.'

'You shouldn't have been listening. This is all completely irrelevant, what I want to know is how did Radleigh get back here?'

'*Read all about it,* Jack. Read the bloody papers,' laughed Heston. 'And, when it's out, read his bloody book. You never know, you might get a mention. Signed copy might be nice.'

'I have read all the readable newspapers. Every damn one of them... too simple. Somebody assisted him.'

'Perhaps it was our rum drinking friends, cack-led Scammel.'They did for Aston-Heyford and Phillip Throagh.'

'No, not that navy lot. International operations... way outside their league that's for sure,'

Passant glanced a slight frown at him, sat down, and for the rest of the evening remained silent and in deep thought.

*

'So, no hitches... no bends, no splicing necessary? And no bodies, lad?' Asked Billy Ruffian.

'Nothing major... no limbs needing re-attachment. Alistair's a star turn... worth his suit, shirts and meals.'

'Hmm. And, where's the money deposited now?'

'In two bank accounts at Coutes London. And, sir, I advise it's left there until further notice.'

'Come on, lad, why?'

'Bargaining chip, sir.'

That's "sir" twice, thought Billy.

'I shall get Radleigh to open a third that only he has access to. We, that's him and I, will transfer some funds into it to keep him afloat. That done, he's on his own... off our backs.'

'Do it as soon as possible.'

*

'Le Fanu.'

'Jason.'

'How is my friend?'

'Okay, I need to talk to you.'

'I am at home now.'

'Okay, give me a few moments.'

*

It took him less than five minutes to get to Chelsea Square and Rochester House. St John Le Fanu opened the door and let him in.

'He has funds now. Very well off... cash rich. We can't cold store him any longer,' Sims said.

'Am I to assume Zurich went well, Commander? Or, shouldn't I ask?'

'He's only going to tell you himself, so, why not me? Both Zurich and Paris without a hitch.' Sims looked around the apartment. 'Is there anywhere apart from here, he can go?'

'No, here's best, bring him here... very early in the morning.'

'Same time as the milkman?'

'Yes. Just before... say five o'clock.'

'Consider him on his way.'

*

'Radleigh is off our hands, sir.'

'Where is he now, lad?'

'Le Fanu's place.'

'Which one?'

'How many's he got?'

'Several, I'm not sure exactly.'

'Well, for the moment he's in Chelsea... the lads have just delivered him.'

'That *is* a relief. We've got his money and got rid of him. Well done, lad.'

Sims made a mental correction. *I've* got his money, he thought. Got it wrong there, Billy.

*

'Admiral, there's a Mr Passant for you.'

Before answering, Billy held the phone to his chest for a moment; he pressed the record button, the tape recorder spools began to turn; let the other man do the talking, he thought.

'Admiral Jessop here.'

A man of few words, Passant said, ' I need to talk to you privately.'

'And, the subject?'

'Your protegé Commander Sherwood-Reeves and his wife.'

'We can talk now. Passant, let us be clear, harm just one hair of their heads and I will lay great retribution on you... we can talk *now*.'

'No, I wish to talk where we will not be overheard.'

'I say again, we can talk now... securely. I give you

my word it will remain confidential.' The spools kept turning.

'If I sound overly cautious, it is because that is my nature. And, I've been too many years in politics: I need to be certain. I will not discuss this matter over the telephone.'

'Very well, where and when?'

'Can you make Dorset, 1200, the The New Inn at Church Knowle. I eat there after taking my weekly walk, they do a good lunch.'

Unusually chatty, thought Billy. 'I'll be there.'

North of Southampton the traffic was heavy. It took his driver nearly two hours to reach Church Knowle and The New Inn. Billy had decided he would not eat with this man. A long and deep hatred of Passant had many years ago put paid to taking lunch with him or those he determined as vermin. 'Park and wait here,' he said.

In the pub's small pull-in, Passant's car was parked facing the road. He leant against the radiator cowling, hands in pockets, ankles crossed.

Billy strode up to him and without shaking his hand, said,'What's this all about, Passant? I got the distinct impression you were making not so hidden threats against Commander Sherwood-Reeves and his wife. Let me tell you straight to your face... I am aware this may not be a way you normally deal, but I will make what I have to say to the point: now, if you harm one hair on either of their heads I will come after you personally... and I will bring a gun.'

Passant did not move. He simply glared at Billy and said, 'Don't threaten me, Jessop. You're in no position to.' He smirked as though he was party to something Billy wasn't.

'Oh, don't be under the foolish illusion that what I just made was a threat. No, I made you a promise, and, I always keep my promises. So, be quick and tell me what's on your mind.'

Passant stood upright and tossed his car keys from one hand to the other. 'Your commander is digging into areas he ought not to.'

'My commander is doing what he has been told to do. He is carrying out my orders.'

'Then, perhaps, for his safety... let us say, both their safety, you ought to countermand them.'

'I do not need your advice on how do to run the Naval Intelligence Division, nor will I ever require your advice on how to clean up the British intelligence services.'

'You think we need cleaning up do you?'

'You're in a terrible mess and know it. Remember this, Passant, harm just one hair.'

Billy's driver watched the confrontation. He hoped Billy would not be long - he, Tony Morton, was in his sixties and liked to get home early to his tea and telly. He saw Passant drop the keys he'd been fiddling with and bend down to pick them up. The next two events were virtually simultaneous: first, Billy was violently flung sideways, then, Tony Morton heard the rifle's report. Instinctively, he looked behind him. A small white van that had been parked a couple of hundred yards up the road was driving away. He looked back to where Billy had fallen. He appeared to be struggling to get up and made a desperate grab for Passant. He then collapsed back onto the ground and lay still.

Passant ran into the pub and called an ambulance.

Unable to soak up what he had just witnessed, Tony Morton sat dumbfounded.

*

The phone rang; Sims answered. It was Billy's house-keeper, 'Admiral Jessop has not returned... he said he'd be home by tea-time. Usually if he's going to be late he would always call.'

'He could just be held up.'

'No, he seemed preoccupied. And, he asked me to make his favourite supper.'

Sims scratched his head; this was an odd call, 'So, he's not returned from where?'

'He said he was going to Dorset.'

'Did he say why?'

'No, but I know he received a call from a Mr Passant just before he left. They a had a short chat. The admiral looked angry and left straightaway.'

'You're sure about that? You're sure it was Passant?'

'Yes, I usually answer all incoming calls in case he's busy.'

'I'll do what I can... please let me or my wife know if he comes in.'

*

Sims told David Mountford where he was going and drove the short distance from Netley to Captain Stinton's cottage. 'Took a gamble on you being in,' he said. 'didn't want to phone.'

'Don't stand there on the doorstep,' Stinton said affably. 'What's on your mind?'

'Had an odd call from Billy's housekeeper. She's say's he's late and would normally let her know. She said he had a call from Passant just before he left. What do you think he's up to?'

'With Billy?... God knows.'

Stinton's phone rang. He came back into the room. 'It's your Sub-Lieutenant Mountford, he says he has some urgent news for you.'

'Sims here... what's your problem, David?'

'Sir, Admiral Jessop has been assassinated in Dorset. He was with one of those on the list, Jack Passant... he didn't do it. Rather, it was unlikely he would have done it. He was stood right next to him and in the open.'

White with anger, shock and sadness, Captain Miles Stinton RN (Ret) poured two large rums. I think we both need this... Sims, let us drink to the passing of a great man and a good friend. Then he leaned over to him, grasped Sims' wrist and said, 'Many years ago when I hadn't known Billy long, he came out with a gem. I've never forgotten it. He said; "Wherever politics is involved, truth will be jeopardized. Whenever politics and security are in the mix, security will always be compromised." It is a doctrine I bring to the front on all important occasions, I have lived believing it all my subsequent career. Before I listen to anybody or trust them, I consider those wise words. I advise you to remember them and do the same.'

'God knows, he must have made many enemies... political or professional. But...' Sims stalled. '...for

Christ's sake, he was a top admiral. Who on earth would shoot one of those?'

'Someone who was told to... not necessarily an enemy. Because when it comes to enemies, all is political. Remember, professionals, like yourself, are not our enemies, they're the ones who carry dark politics out. Sometimes they're just jobbing killers.'

Sims only half listening, 'I know, I've killed three or four myself. Do you have any idea who issued the order?'

'No, but I do have an idea you must go careful, bide your time... take a leaf from the SAS: watch - wait: watch - take note; watch and repeat. Note every move regardless of perceived significance. Play the waiting game, Sims. Take a leaf from prospectors too; look for small grains of gold amongst the gravel... get enough until you've an ingot: and don't make your move until you have that ingot. Then, if possible, act... for both of us. I think we will miss him very much,' Stinton said, taking a steadying pull of his rum. Minutes passed. 'You must bear in mind that in furthering the investigations into his death you will be delving into an arena where you cannot be protected. These are deep and dark affairs of state, Sims. There will be a vacuum at the top of the Naval Intelligence Division. Wait until we see who fills the gap. If he's friendly, then, we may be able to act. And bear in mind the pending amalgamation of the security services... there may be no NID shortly. Admiral Jessop's removal will make this easier for someone to rule.'

'I don't see how I can let this rest. He told me we were going underground. Somewhere there's a clique in the know. They mustn't get away with it.'

A deep and grieving parallel: the memory of his own head-strong son. 'Sims, listen to me. Think of Anne, think of your child to be, think of your family. *Listen!* Billy told me that at some time in the future, they have every intention of extending the Cabinet Paper's fifty year rule regarding their discussions on the Buster Crabb affair by a further fifty years. How he knew about this I do not know. But I do know this; for them to seek this extension, it has to be big. The clique you are talking about is no ordinary mob of gangsters. Gangsters they may be, but, they get away with it because they are the government. They are the system. And, who do you think they may be protecting that needs this affair hushing up until 2057? Who might that be? *Who?*'

'Not that establishment lot again?'

'Without a doubt, lad.'

Sims stood up and extended his hand. 'I must go and tell Anne before she hears it on the news.'

'While you're doing that, I'll go and tell his house-keeper... they were very fond of each other.'

'*Jesus!* I had no idea.'

'For many, many years... they kept it well hidden.'

*

He did not call Anne. A phone call was not the way to tell her. Besides, he needed to collect himself. He wasn't sure he could utter the words.

He called his father-in-law instead.

'Good God.' Silence; then, 'Sims, come with me down to *Alice*. Drive to Hell Head Harbour. Don't go home first. What I have to say to you I don't want overheard.'

For the second time that day he was given this piece of advice; '*Listen*, tread carefully.'

Sims shrugged.

Bob Sherwood read the shrug; 'What has happened to Admiral Jessop is serious in the extreme. I can tell you, it *will* be covered up. Politics and Intelligence are like icebergs: most of what goes on, their bulk: submerged... hidden from view. They say that seven eighths of an iceberg is underwater, in politics it's more like ninety nine one hundredths pushed under the carpet. Without Billy, you are neither big enough nor powerful enough to do anything about it. You say Stinton said "play the waiting game". Those are wise words. Don't rush matters... your day may come. Remember, I said, *may*... it also may not. Don't prejudice everything by rushing. Be clear about this: *Billy is dead*: precipitous moves will not bring him back.'

A young angry man spoke, 'At least if I get the man who did it, it would be some small compensation, wouldn't it? It would send some sort of message wouldn't it?'

'Yes, it would, and that's what I'm afraid of. The message would be a clear one: Commander Sherwood-Reeves is on the warpath, he must go too. As things are, they may think by cutting Billy out they neuter those underneath. Let that be the way they think. Do you remember when your launch was blown up? You were wise and let them think you were dead... you laid low. Play the same game, lad.' He watched for his reaction. 'Sims, you are as much my son as Anne is my daughter.' Bob Sherwood placed his hand on his shoulder, 'I could not have wished for a better liaison. Please... please, don't rush.'

'I promise I won't rush... I *am* going to do some thinking though.'

She cut a shallow angle across the low swell: a light subdued pitch and roll - they headed home to Hell Head Harbour. Dark clouds were gathering in the west. *Alice* and The Solent in a sombre mood. She, *Alice,* overheard everything said. Her rigging sighed the accompaniment while to herself she sang *Blow the Wind Southerly*... careful, for all our sakes go careful.

*

She knew the moment he walked into the room something was badly wrong. 'What is the matter,' Anne asked, standing up. 'Tell me what is wrong.'

He walked over to her and took hold of her shoulders. 'There's no easy way to tell you this, love.' He drew her towards him and held her tight. 'Billy's dead, love.'

She took a step backwards and stood stock still her hands cupping her nose and mouth: she whispered, 'How, Sims, how?'

'He was shot while outside a pub in Dorset... must have been long range high velocity... no accident. He was with Passant... that means definitely no accident. At the moment, that's as much as I know.'

After many tears Anne looked drained. 'Rough; tough; aggressive; all those things and more, Sims. Sometimes wrong; he set you up with the Russians. He knew he shouldn't have done that and he regretted it. But, I think he was a good man, a very good man. Above all, he was loyal to Britain.' She began crying again. In despair; 'How can we have hope in such a terrible world? What are we bringing our child into? What hope is there for the human race?'

He had no instant answer. Instead he took her hand and led her to the library, 'Come on, love, come and listen to something.' In his own moments of grief it had been his only remedy: music. In that few paces he chose the piece he must play. 'It won't take long. If it's played correctly, just a few seconds over seven and a half minutes.' Again, taking her by the hands he sat her down, kissed her on the forehead, and placed the record on the turntable; the second movement of Beethoven's piano concerto No. 5; the Emperor. He sat beside her holding her hand. Not a word spoken until the end.

He lifted the stylus arm, 'Far, far from the other end of the world of awfulness, cruelty and evil, *that*, Anne, is the beauty the human race is capable of. Please try not to despair: there *are* good people too... even Emperors have to die.'

***

Chapter Nineteen.
Dragunov SVD.

'I wondered how long it would be before you turned up,' Surgeon Commander Monroe stood up and shook Sims' hand. 'Bad do... never met him personally.'

'He was a good man... I'm not happy about it. Was it quick? Instant?'

'No. The surgeon at Dorchester Hospital said he fought with all his might... there were other complications that weakened him. They operated... the team used all their experience to no avail. His body was brought back here to Haslar for the autopsy.'

'Do you have the bullet?'

Monroe knew this was coming. 'Yes. You do understand Naval Intelligence will probably want it.'

'That's why I'm here.'

'I know you're one of them, but you're not the Naval Intelligence I had in mind. I was referring to those higher up in London.'

'I get your point. Please let me have it for two days, then... stall them, lie to them if necessary... *please!* Just two days.'

'I know you won't let me down, Commander Sherwood-Reeves,' he said, taking a plastic box from his drawer and handing it over.

A door knocker altogether unique; an ensemble of polished brass cartridge cases. It's central boss, two back-to-back welded trigger guards from scrapped .303s. It's receiving plate a brass butt end also from a Lee Enfield .303. Sims used it. The crisp sound echoed down the hall. Les Goodwin shuffled up and opened the door. 'Sims, what's the matter?... Christ, you look serious.'

'I am. These are serious times, Les... Billy's been murdered.'

Les reached for support: the door frame would do. 'What the fuck's goin' on?'

'Don't know yet... need your help. I didn't want to come and see you at Whale Island,' he showed him the bullet, 'best you tell me what you can about this, here at home.'

'Come on through. I've got a little workshop out the back.'

Sims placed the bullet on the bench. 'What d'yer make of this?'

Les took a *vernier gauge* out of its box; checked the diameter; checked the length, and on a delicate pair of scales noted the weight and then, rolling the bullet around its length, noted other dimensions Sims was not sure of. Through a bench microscope he inspected the rifling. 'Thought it was,' he said. 'Dragunov SVD. 7.62 by 54 mm; twist rate 320 mm... four right hand grooves. New issue... came out in '63. Long range Russian sniper rifle. Specially made for marksmen. Russian marksmen with these aren't part of the usual sniper squads, Sims, they're attached to platoon level cannon fodder groups. This, my lad, is not just a battle field rifle with a scope fitted, it's purpose built. A fine piece of work... first of it's kind in the world. Extended chrome lined barrel, rifled for only 547 mm. Carries a flash suppressor; skeleton stock and a PSO.1 scope ... great bit of work. We've got nothing like it.'

'You get all that just from looking at a bullet?'

'Yep. why not?'

'Forensic, Les, bleedin' forensic. You've seen one before, then?'

'Had one in for evaluation... like I said, very, very good.'

'Where is it now?'

'Don't know... no idea,' he said scratching his head. 'They took it back... only had it a week.'

'Who's they?'

'Naval Intelligence Division. You going to tell me more?'

'Outside a pub in Dorset... his body's in the mortuary at Haslar... that's as much as I know. Keep what I've told you under your hat.'

'I reckon there's going to be a bit flak from this.'

'Yeah... there is. Les, knowing you, you must have kept some of the fired rounds to check the rifling... you wouldn't miss that trick, I know.'

'Of course.'

'Where are they?'

'Whale Island.'

'Can you bring one home? Just need to check.'

'I'll take that one and do it there if you like.'

'This doesn't leave my possession. I've only got it for

two days.'

'Okay, lad. Come back tomorrow dinner time. I'll make an excuse to come home... it'll only take a minute or two.'

'Best not say anything just yet to Cedric, okay?'

'Okay.' He paused. 'Sims?'

'Yeah.'

'Go careful, lad.'

'Yeah.'

*

Les placed the killing round on a soft felt pad under the lens, leaned over the microscope and studied. He then placed the test round from Whale Island alongside and compared them. He sniffed, 'Both fired from the same rifle, stake my life on it. Rifling marks from different rifles are like snow-flakes, each one different... just like finger prints. No doubt, same rifle. Take a look.'

Sims looked. 'Can't see how you can tell.'

'You'd tell if they were fired from a different rifle... take my word on it.'

Sims set up Anne's short tripod and her camera fitted with a close-up extension. 'Can you set them up so that it's obvious they came from the same gun... you know, rifling marks and that sort of thing.'

'Les arranged the bullets and on two pieces of paper and drew pointers to the relevant identifiers. Sims adjusted the bench light.

Les said, 'That should do it... obvious to anyone in the know.'

'Pal, I've known you too long to doubt your word. Remember, not a squeak to anyone... not even to Cedric...

and thanks once again.'

*

He parked the Land Rover immediately outside the front entrance to Haslar Royal Naval Hospital. 'Your bullet... I'd appreciate it if no one knows I've had the borrowing.'

'Commander, I've done you a favour in letting you have it, are you going to tell me what you've discovered? One of our top admirals murdered incites more than a little curiosity. We were talking in the wardroom, apart from sea battles, natural causes or accident, no one could recall anything similar happening before.'

'Nothing to be said in the wardroom. Scout's honour you'll keep it to yourself?'

'Absolutely.'

Sims did not intend to implicate Les or Whale Island and Lieutenant Hennerbury; 'The rifle used was a Dragunov SVD. They're the best sniper rifle around... Russian. Now here's a twist that will incite a bit more interest and speculation: under a microscope I compared your bullet to another Dragunov round in my possession... it was fired from the same rifle. You'd like another twist perhaps?... the rifle was one from NID's collection. So, apart from designing and manufacturing the gun, the Soviets had nothing directly to do with his killing.' Sims got up to leave. 'I really appreciate your help, Commander Monroe. For the moment that's all I can tell you.'

'One of our own men? What on earth's going on?'

'Since getting involved with NID, that's a question I've often asked myself. I'll see myself out,' he said leaving.

Before he got to the door, Monroe checked him. 'He went to the meeting armed, you know. An old Smith & Wesson. Did he normally go around armed? Do you think he expected trouble?'

'Yes, I do. And, I'd like to know why?'

*

Through his defences the vacuum that death leaves made itself felt: immense characters leave an immense void: an unwritten legacy to their companions. He was in need of more time with Captain Miles Stinton. The shock of what had happened was setting in. Sims needed the comfort of Stinton's long term friendship with Billy. He imagined it would somehow assuage his sense of great loss and waste.

While Stinton poured a couple of drinks, Sims said, 'I'm finding it very difficult to come to terms with. It's like going to Pompey dockyard and finding HMS *Victory* been taken away in the night and scrapped or, they've removed Nelson's Column and broken up it for hard core.'

Miles Stinton handed him his glass, 'I should have said something earlier and I apologise for not doing so... but you must appreciate it was a shock to me too. However, if it's possible, don't feel too bad about his death... it was only a matter of time... only slightly brought forward from what it would have been. In some ways I'm glad it was over with quickly and not slow and lingering. I wouldn't want him to have gone that way.'

'You're going to have to help me out here.'

'Billy had an advanced cancer... I knew about it some

time ago; we hoped for a remission and kept our fingers crossed. It seemed at one time he was winning and we looked forward to his role in the new SIS organisation, then, he stopped responding to treatment... he deteriorated rapidly. Billy wanted it kept quiet. It was diagnosed shortly after he'd decided to move to London. When he found out he gave up the idea. It's a great pity he didn't last long enough to sail in the *Anne Sherwood-Reeves*. It's also why he conned you into taking Harry.'

'Conned?'

The memory made Stinton give a brief smile, 'He said it was an inspirational moment. He was quite concerned about leaving him behind if he didn't survive... Mrs Braddock, the house keeper is not fond of dogs. Then, there *you* were, he said, about to leave just as the plumber's van turned up. Anne had told him you had a flint hard part equally matched with a soft one. You were a push-over he said.'

'The rotten bugger! He said it was from a dog's home.'

Stinton chuckled. 'Do you regret taking him?'

'No, not at all.'

'Then you must agree, some cons can be acceptable, can't they?'

'Hmm, maybe. In that case, if he wasn't going to move, he had no need to give me the *Bellerophon* table.'

Stinton shrugged, 'Maybe, and then again, no. For the reason he gave you about moving; a whitish lie. No, because it was a gift he thought he owed you.'

Sims pondered all. So, "other complications", that's what Surgeon Commander Monroe must have been referring to, he thought. 'The fact that he had cancer doesn't mean it's not murder though. It doesn't mean we can say "that's all right, then" and sit on our arses as though nothing happened.'

'No, it was murder alright.'

'I'm *going* to have them.'

'All in good time, lad.'

'How much time have we got?... Anne and I could be unemployed soon... then how are we going to find out who did it... time's short.'

'Sims, get one thing straight... you will never be unemployed. The other SIS organisations will want you.'

'But if NID goes so may the scent. And, that's crucial seeing as he was killed by his own beloved Naval Intelligence Division.'

'*What?*' Stinton, wide eyed, stood up. 'What did you say?'

'Someone from NID nobbled him.'

'Is that guess, Sims?'

'No, a fact. In one way or another someone in NID killed him or was heavily implicated. I know this to be true. Please, don't ask me how... there are others I don't want to incriminate.'

'And, you're absolutely sure?'

'Yes. Completely and absolutely.'

Stinton sat back down and poured himself another rum. The bottle he offered to Sims was refused.

'Billy's death can only accelerate NID's end,' Sims said. 'Like I said, time's short. If we're going to do anything, we've got to motor and motor fast.'

'The new regime may be on our side.'

'And they may not... I don't want to wait to find out.'

'Why not give it a little time. We'll soon be able to tell

how friendly they're going to be.'

'Okay, how.'

'We'll see if they keep Anne on the payroll or, how quick they are to release her and her services.'

'If we wait, the scent will get colder. I'm not of a mind to wait. I have a feeling I need to talk to Mrs Braddock. How was she when you went to Tunworth?'

'Upset, of course. It was a shock. She knew about the cancer. She'd prepared herself for his death. It was still a shock, though.'

'I'm going to go up there to see her.'

*

'Three years ago, he offered to marry me. I refused. I thought it might harm his reputation marrying his house-keeper.' Mrs Braddock took Sims' hand, 'He thought so much of you and your wife... he said you were uncanny. You *will* find who done it won't you?'

'I'll do my absolute best. That, I can promise you. You might have to help me, though.'

'I'll do what I can.'

'Has anyone been here yet for his papers or been asking questions?'

'No.'

'They will. There's not much we can do to stop them taking everything... I'd have liked the time to go through the whole lot.'

'It doesn't matter if they do. Admiral Jessop always had duplicates made of the really important ones. They wouldn't know about those.'

'Someone knows about them... the person who made the copies.'

'Yes, that's me. I did much of his secretarial work. I think it best you take possession of them. You'd best take the tapes of his phone calls as well.'

'Did he tape the call with Passant?'

'Yes, of course... most calls were taped. And like the papers, he saved all important ones... he was going to write his memoirs.'

Billy had once told him their calls were completely confidential. So, the old bugger was lying through his teeth, he was recording all the time, he thought. 'Can we hear it now?'

Sims listened to the last words he would ever hear the old admiral utter. Clearly, Passant had blackmailed Billy into the meeting: "Your protegé and his wife" was enough evidence. 'He was protecting Anne and myself,' he said.

'He thought the world of you both... you may have made him angry once or twice, but, he saw much of himself in you... he doubted he would have time to get you the captaincy he promised. He regretted that.'

'Mrs Braddock, where are the duplicate papers now?'

'We will have to go to his solicitors in Alton, Kenward and Kenward. I used to deposit them there every week. In light of his cancer, I have had power of attorney of his affairs for this past year and, I am, with Mr Kenward, an executor of his will.'

'Would you be so kind as to arrange a meeting? Initially, just to introduce my wife and myself. I have a feeling I need to make out a will. Please don't mention this in front of my wife.'

Before Sims left Tunworth House he asked, 'How will you manage?'

'He left me well provided for. I shall want for nothing but his company in the evenings... oh, and the songs he used to sing,' she said, quietly.

'Billy *sang?*'

'He collected old shanties. You know, he and Stinton got quite drunk one night... shortly after you had cleared up the Soviet cell in Portsmouth... they sang '*Billy Ruffian*' together. They did it so well. I'll never forget it. He had such a fine voice... the voice of a long past era.'

*

'Passant is clammed tight. He's sticking to his story. MI5... they're suggesting a couple of possibilities, one, Billy's car was followed from Tunworth to Church Knowle, or secondly, the real target was Passant and that Billy just got in the way. The second is the one they prefer, and seeing as Passant probably set it up, it would be wouldn't it? I had a word with Billy's driver, he says he didn't spot anyone on their tail... but, I suppose, why should he? He wouldn't be on the look out for anyone.'

'Would the assassin have to have been a good shot?' Anne asked.

'Pretty fair. They wouldn't want to take the risk of missing. Better change "pretty fair" for pretty good.'

'We know SIS operatives are all trained on side arms, how about rifles?'

'You said *all*, possibly not all. Shirley said Le Fanu didn't move in circles that needed weapons training... not sure if she meant that literally or not.'

'Then perhaps we ought to check those on Billy's list

of names for specialist training. Maybe Shirley can dig a bit deeper into their backgrounds... see if anything stands out,' Anne said.

'You make a good point, but how do we know they're someone on the list... I guess that's the sticking point.'

'I think the list is a very small list because Billy had already narrowed it down, Sims. In fact, you said so yourself once. A conspiratorial group wouldn't want everyone to know... they'd want it kept to a select few.'

'The select few on the list and maybe a couple beyond maybe,' Sims said.

'I don't think Billy was playing games. So, I ask myself if that's the case why didn't he include any others? In my opinion he knew there might be some but simply didn't know who they were.'

'I'll go along with what you suggest. I'll get Shirley to do some more digging... she always knows more than she says. One thing for sure, love, Passant wasn't the target, he was the lure.'

*

Sims listened to the shipping forecast.

"A gale warning has been issued at 1200 GMT for: Fisher, German Bight, Humber, Thames, Dover, Wight, Portland Plymouth.

Wind: Northeast six to gale eight: increasing force nine or ten later.

Sea State: Moderate to rough.

Weather: Wintry showers.

Visibility: Poor".

With the Met's gale warning, Sims had run down to *Alice*

to check her moorings and put out extra fenders. 'Bit of a blow coming... just wanted to make sure you were nice and comfy,' he whispered to her. He gave her a final look over, chatted for a few minutes to a couple of club members and then ran back to Hell Head House.

Anne found him snooping in the kitchen. 'Pat phoned. Shirley's done some more digging... interesting. James Ross, ex-army lieutenant and top marksman. He shot at Bisley... you might have competed against him, it would have been around the same time.'

'Don't remember him there.'

'She's been busy. She's been checking out Woodruff, he's a marksman too.'

'Yeah, in some ways I can see that... so precise - control freak.'

*

Dusty knew exactly where to start - the dining hall: post tot-time. Two *Oberon* class submarines were tied up down in the docks. Their crews would be billeted ashore in HMS *Dolphin's* accommodation. It didn't take him long to get some useful answers. He sat down at one of the long dining tables.

'Know anyone here who's crewed the *Oberon?'* The submariner next to him shook his head and asked the next person along. Two or three down the row a hand popped up, 'There are several,' he said pointing at various tables.

He visited them all, showed them his identity card and told them to move to an empty table at the end of the hall.

'I'm eating my bleedin' dinner,' said one.

'Don't fuck me about, I eat twats bigger than you for breakfast. Get off your fat arse and take your grub with you... NOW!'

The group sat down.

'You the one that shot the RPO?'

'No. He was a killick stoker... he's my boss... I'm still waiting my turn.'

'Did he really kill two agents on The Island?'

'Yes. And he got rid of a couple more on a freighter, as well. Enough questions... I need answers.'

If they had harboured thoughts of obstruction and truculence, those thoughts had evaporated.

'Okay, are you listening? Adian McClusky, any of you do the pick-up off Ireland?'

Elbows and forearms still on the table, two, briefly, from the wrist, flicked their hands upwards.

'The rest of you, thanks, and back to your places. You two stay here with me.'

'Tell me about McClusky.'

'Not much to tell... just like most mystery tours we hadn't a clue where we were. We surfaced and picked up this guy and a couple of SBS escorts. We didn't know his name then. Supposed to be IRA we find out later... didn't have much of a paddy accent, though. Next, we dock at *Dolphin*, he's taken ashore, we refuel and straight back on to patrol. That's it, nothing more to tell.'

'Did you see him?'

'Oh yeah. I was on the on-deck party when we picked him up... did it at night.'

'What condition was he in? Did he look in a bad way

at all?'

'No, nothing... pretty fit bloke I reckon.'

Dusty looked at the other submariner - stoker, 'And, you, Stokes, what do you reckon?'

'I was duty watch in the engine room when they brought him on board... saw him during the trip back, though... plenty of times.'

'And... was he damaged goods?'

'No. No way. Apart from being chained up, he was in perfect nick. Rabbited away like a good un. Except about what he'd been nabbed for. Kept quiet about that.'

'Thanks, lads. If you're in the NAAFI tonight, I'll stand you a pint or two.'

'Straight up?'

'I said so, didn't I?'

*

Sims picked the phone up. 'David? What have you got for me?'

'I've been trawling through records at Netley. Woodruff is the longest serving member there. Each time he's been listed for a new draft it's been blocked... no reasons given. Not getting any further down that line, I then thought I'd check the civilian worker records and found one who had been there at the time... a Peter Shadbolt, retired ex matelot. He lives not far away, so I visited him... he gave the impression he knew more, but, seemed reluctant to talk. I couldn't understand why he was so reticent, possibly something to hide or told to keep quiet about. He may need your persuasive touch, sir.'

'You two buggers have been busy... well done. When I get a moment I'll come up and we'll see him together.

By the way, has Dusty told you about his findings?'
'Yes, sir.'
'Looks pretty smelly, doesn't it?'
'Certainly does, sir.'

*

In Bursledon they pulled up outside a few uninspiring local council houses - pebble dashed and austere.
'Worse than married quarters,' muttered Sims.
'Number five,' said David.

Peter Shadbolt answered the door.
'We can interview you on the doorstep or inside... it's up to you,' said Sims.
'Inside.'
'What branch were you in?'
'Sick Berth Attendant.'
'Not thick, then?'
'Hope not, sir.'
'No need for "sir", you're a civvy now.'
'Habit.'
'Is it your habit to cover up for somebody?'
'Not sure I know what you mean.'
'Right, let's start from the beginning. Adian McClusky died while a Netley. What's your take on that?. We know you worked in Unit 4. and we know you were there at the time.'
'All I know, he was supposed to have escaped one night.'
'Escaped? How?'
'Gave his interrogator the slip and ended up in the oggin in the dark... caught pneumonia and died.'

'Who was the interrogator?'

'Not sure.'

'Peter, you're holding back... you might as well tell us what you know now and not later. This investigation is not going to go away. So, cough up. I know who the interrogator was and so do you. Your options are straight forward, tell us everything you know and save yourself a lot of hassle. Because, if later we find out you know more, I'll do you for obstruction. What was your job at Netley?'

'Amongst other things, I looked after the medical records of the patients.'

'Come on, Peter, they weren't patients and you know it. Now, these "other things", what were they?'

'I occasionally assisted during interrogations... keeping a medical watch on those that needed it.'

"Why would they needed watching, Peter?'

'Well, you know...'

'No, I fucking don't know. That's why I'm asking you.'

'Well, sometimes they needed to recover from administered medications. What they were I don't know... I just kept watch.'

'What were you doing the night of McClusky's accident?'

'I had a load of work to finish in the medical department: I stayed late.'

'Still think you're holding back. Did you see anything? Hear anything?.

Shadbolt hesitated.

'Look, we are members of the British Intelligence Services. We can take you in if you don't buck up.'

Shadbolt didn't take well to the idea of this. His demeanour changed. He sat upright in his chair.

'There was a lot of noise. I stepped out of the office for a moment to see what was going on. Lieutenant-Commander Woodruff, he was a lieutenant then, was struggling with McClusky. McClusky looked petrified. He broke away from Woodruff and ran away in the direction of Southampton Water.'

'Go on.'

'About an hour later Woodruff returned and fetched a Land-Rover. Not long after that, he returned with McClusky lying in the back.'

'Was McClusky alive at that point?'

'Don't know... he wasn't conscious.'

'How do you know?'

'I went over and helped Woodruff get him inside.'

'And then?'

'Woodruff told me to leave.'

'Anything else?'

'Hmm... Woodruff was as soaked as McClusky, and the next day the chief shipwright was draining down a dinghy hadn't been secured properly and was within half an hour of being adrift on the ebb tide.'

'How long after this was McClusky pronounced dead?'

'Same day.'

'Okay, Peter, what's your opinion of all this?'

'I found working at Unit 4 it didn't pay to have opinions. Woodruff said I was to be neither judge nor jury on matters of state security.'

Sims stood up, 'We might be back. Say nothing to anyone... that includes Woodruff: especially Woodruff if he asks.'

Time to do some thinking: he let David drive back to Netley.

'Any questions? You must have some.'

'Why should McClusky be petrified. It doesn't make sense. Woodruff would have hardly been a challenge for an ex SAS man.'

'Unless, of course, he was already ill. But, you're right, why petrified? Petrification's not on the menu with SAS lads.'

'Do you want us to keep investigating, sir?'

'Dead right I do... you're doing well. Getting interesting stuff... keep digging, both of you.'

'Thank you, sir. And, sir? I beat Dusty on the range yesterday.'

Sims laughed. 'How did he take it?'

'Badly, sir.'

'Was that the first time you beat him?'

'Yes, it was so good. He checked the targets over and over again. He even borrowed Les's vernier gauge. It was worth joining NID just to witness his anguish.'

Sims laughed again.

A few miles down the road he said, 'I hate to have done that, the poor old bugger has had the frighteners put on him and then we go and give him a bigger scare... not nice.'

'Could we have done him for obstruction, sir?'

'Not a clue, lad.'

***

Chapter Twenty.
Haar Today Gone Tomorrow.

Anne called into the kitchen, 'That was Billy's house-keeper, Mrs Braddock. She arranged a meeting with Mr Kenward: one-thirty, Thursday afternoon. I told her we'll pick her up.'

*

On the way to Alton Mrs Braddock thought it prudent to advise them on Kenward & Kenward's apparent organi-sation, 'Please don't be put off by the clutter, he can lay his hand on any file he wants to.'

'If Billy trusted him, that's good enough for me,' said Sims.

*

From his appearance sat comfortably in his padded leather carver, Benjamin Kenward of *Kenward & Kenward Solicitors Alton*, might well have been sat there from the moment the building had first opened three hundred years earlier.

It was to be a short meeting of introduction. Old Kenward liked to see who he was dealing with.

'As executor of Admiral Jessop's will, Mrs Braddock has requested that she would like you, Commander Sherwood-Reeves and Mrs Sherwood-Reeves to be granted full access and, if necessary, possession of all his naval documents. This is to include those of sensitive nature from his work with the Naval Intelligence Department.'

On the surface, that was about the measure of the meeting. Business concluded, Sims asked Anne and Mrs Braddock if they would allow him to speak with Mr Kenward in private. Though she frowned, Anne diplomatically led the elder woman from the room.

'Now, Commander, I see you have something on your mind?'

Sims handed him a signed letter of authority. 'These are my solicitors in Richmond. I would like you to take over my affairs... there are deeds to three properties lodged there. Two are in the Richmond borough and the third is in Spice Island, Portsmouth. Also, I would like you to prepare my *last will and testament*. Naturally, the beneficiary is to be my wife.'

Old Kenward hrumphed, 'Wise of you, intestacy: lengthy, costly and rarely has an equitable outcome for those deserving benefit. I take it this is your first will?'

'Yes.'

'And your wife?'

'She's never mentioned the subject.'

'She ought.'

'Not a good time.'

'It never is, Commander.'

*

In the phone-box, Patrick Harvey pressed button 'A' to make the connection. He heard the money rattle down the chute and hit the cash box. 'Sims, I remember you telling me of a Lieutenant-Commander Woodruff.'

'Yeah, that's right. A senior instructor at Netley... go on, what about him?'

'Second visit to MI5 headquarters in as many days. Thought it might interest you.'

'Christ! what's he up to? He's supposed to be on leave. I take it he was in uniform?'

'No, in civvies. The only reason I knew it was him, I heard Jenkins on reception say his name. After he'd gone I went and double checked the register... definitely him. He had a meeting with Passant... Ross was there too.'

'What, at the same meeting?'

'Yes. And, looking back through the register it's clear the two visits he's just made were not his first.'

'What are those buggers up to? Can you keep your eye on them, Pat?'

'I'll do my best... do you want me to get Shirley on to them both as well?'

'Sound her out... if she's happy, give her the brief... who are they meeting and for how long... you know the routine.'

'Things hotting up?'

'If not now, they will be shortly.'

'Any clues about Billy?'

'Yes. This one's for your ears only... don't tell the rest of the squad yet. Billy was murdered by someone from SIS... maybe NID.'

'*Fucking hell!*'

'I remember you saying that before.'

'Sims, you've got to go careful.'

'Everybody in the know's saying that.'

'Anything I can do, anything. Just give me a nudge.'

'Okay... should have kept your mouth shut. Keep close tabs on Woodruff and Ross, if you will. Woodruff may also be involved in some dirty dealings over McClusky's death.'

'I'll get on to Shirley right away.'

'Ta... be seeing you.'

*

'Can you meet me?'

'Sure, Pat, where?'

'Your stompin' ground.'

'How are you coming?'

'Train. Arrives Portsmouth 1215. Can't stay long got to get to Guildford for 1600.'

'We'll be waiting.'

*

He poked his head inside the Railway Cellars. With a couple of destroyers, four frigates, the aircraft carrier HMS *Albion* in port and it being a pay week, the Cellars, a lunchtime session in full swing, was throbbing.

'Too crowded... The Golden Bell it is then,' said Sims.

Sat in the saloon bar Pat looked around and said, 'The mythic Golden Bell. I often wondered what it was like. Big Bertha, Niklāvs Matrozis... dodgy cliental.'

Arthur Adams carried in a plate of sandwiches.

'Comes from having a dodgy landlord. It got that *mythic* reputation from the cost of Arthur's sarnies and crap beer.'

'Leave it out,' said Arthur returning to the public bar.

He called after him, 'Arthur, we needed somewhere quiet for a chat... we knew it'd be empty here.'

'Bugger off.'

'Must be juicy to come and tell us personally. So, what have you got for us?' asked Anne.

'Interesting possibilities... certainly a few questions raised. Fiona, as you well know, is a communications buff. As such, she occasionally backs up the scouring squad if they're short handed.'

A querying look: Anne raised her eyebrows, 'Scouring squad?'

'They check for phone taps and radio mikes... that sort of thing. She gave me a call to say she was going to do Passant's office the next day. Passant, it so happens, was there when they arrived. She told him they needed to give the office a good stripping and it would be better if they had it to themselves. She did the scour and gave it a clean bill of health. Before leaving, it had been her intention to plant a couple of her own transmitters. As bad luck would have it, Passant returned as she was installing the second. She bluffed her way round it: very cool. Apparently she said "Well, what have we got here?" and made out she'd just discovered it. Passant insisted he should keep it. She stood her ground saying they would need to look at it and they would give him the result of their analysis along with the device in due course.'

'She got away with it, then?' asked Anne.

'Just: by the skin of her teeth, it seems. Passant didn't seem happy that his private secure conversations might have been witnessed. Fiona's not only cool, she's smart. Back at base she substituted some duff soviet components into the transmitter and took it back to Passant's office. While waiting for him, she calmly removed the first transmitter and stowed that in her tool box. When Passant arrived she told him the one she found was unservicable and security had not been compromised, and in future he should have his office swept clean more often. He asked her who might have planted it. She said she wasn't detailed to counter espionage and left it at that. There is a slight point of concern; Passant has been doing a little digging into her background.'

'This is bad... will she be safe, Pat?' asked Anne.

'She knows what's going on, she'll keep her eyes open. Anyway, while it was installed, the first one picked up some interesting conversations. One in particular caught her attention... between Passant and your man Lieutenant-Commander Woodruff.'

'*Never!*'

'Absolutely no doubt. Woodruff was very agitated and said he wanted out... wanted no more to do with it.'

'With what?' asked Anne.

'We're not exactly sure. It's fairly obvious, though, they've worked together before. Passant insisted that he wanted *it* again... before you ask, he didn't say what. Point blank, Woodruff said no. Then, Passant got nasty and threatened to release a confidential autopsy note. He said he had kept the original, and, if Woodruff didn't go along with his request he'd make sure the contents found their way to NID and others.'

'Was Ross there?'

'Doesn't appear to have been there this time or, if he was, he kept mouse quiet.'

'It's got to be about McClusky. I'd give my left knacker

to get a copy of that.'

Anne winced.

Patrick Harvey opened his brief case, 'McClusky... you're dead right and you can stay intact. Passant was scheduled for a monthly departmental meeting... usually they're about three or four hours. While he was away, Fiona, Archie and Allan did a quick search. It took Archie less than two minutes to open the filing cabinet and desk drawers. Fiona's got this fabulous little camera... a Schatz & Sohne.'

'I know,' said Anne.

'She took several shots, they put everything back in order and left. This is the result.' He handed over a crisp, perfectly focused enlargement.'

'*Jesus!* Will you look at this, Anne.?'

'We need a medical doctor to interpret it,' she said.

'I know just the man... he'll keep quiet too.'

'He's good is he?' asked Pat.

'I've got two legs to stand on due to him and his team... he's good alright.'

'What do you reckon it is that Passant wants Woodruff to supply?'

'My bet, a Dragunov SVD long range sniper rifle, and probably a few rounds as well. It was the model that killed Billy. Probably the same gun from NID's black museum at Netley.'

'So, who pulled the trigger?'

'Not sure... I have an idea, though. Any more of these?' he asked, waving the photo.

'Plenty. How many do you want?'

'How many you got?'

'Six, here... more if you want, and here's a copy of the

tape.'

'Six is fine. Well done Fiona.'

'If Passant *was* talking about needing the Dragunov a second time, what do they want it for? Have they got someone else...' She had stopped mid-sentence and put her hand to her mouth.

'Don't panic, love. We'll impound the entire arsenal at Netley. Look, there are plenty of rifles that would do the job from the range Billy was shot at. But, Passant doesn't want any old gun, if it is the Dragunov he wants, he wants it for very specific reasons... one, because it's Russian made and there are very few of them around.'

Anne still gripping Sims' arm could not trust herself to speak.

Pat asked, 'Come on, Sims, cough up, I don't get your take on all this.'

'I think Passant is scared Radleigh told Billy, and possibly myself, things that concerned him and some of his previous little bits of nastiness. He's either guessed or worked out who got Radleigh back from Riga and it's just possible he's also heard rumours of the Zurich trip. To use one of Alistair Duncan's phrases, Passant could well be in a flat spin. In short, he's crapping himself and needs to get rid of the key witnesses. Now, the point is this, if he uses Russian weaponry, he can claim Billy's shooting, and any others, were Soviet inspired revenge killings. And, if it's ever traced to NID, the dirt drops on Woodruff's doorstep... and I reckon Woodruff knows this. That's my best guess at the moment.'

Pat sat drumming his fingers on the table while Anne remained silent.

'Do you want that last sandwich, love?'

'No thank you... how can you possibly have an appetite?'

'Ex-stoker... how about you, Pat?'

'No, go ahead,' he said, equally unsure how, considering the circumstances, Sims could blithely munch his way through the best part of the whole plateful.

Arthur came down, 'Everything okay?'

'Sarnies not bad... bread's only three days old and with enough mustard you couldn't tell the beef was off. Yeah, so, all in all, things are on the up here at last.'

'Bugger off... and for your information it was pork,' he said, mooching back to the public bar.

'Ross,' he said, finishing off the sandwich.

'That's all?' said Anne. '*Ross*.'

'Yeah, Ross pulled the trigger. Ex-army, lieutenant, marksman, possibly seen action. Need to know his day to day whereabouts , Pat.'

'What about, Passant?' she asked.

'We'll get the lads on to him... tracking his every movement. Can you spare anyone?'

'I'll check Archie and Allan. Fiona's getting a bit large... confined to barracks. It'll keep her out of the limelight,' he said, tailing off. '...tracking's not Mike's forte. He can look after Fiona.'

Anne tapped the table top, 'Remember on Billy's tape, Passant said he went to Church Knowle after his weekly walk. Do you think he still goes there? I mean, if he does, he can't feel very threatened. It would be almost an admission he wasn't the target, wouldn't it?' she said.

343

'He'd be bleedin' stupid if he did. If he's a keen walker and likes the area, he may stick to somewhere nearabouts. His old school's not that far away. He might choose somewhere near there for his constitutional... old schools and habits die hard, love.'

*

Surgeon Commander Monroe read the autopsy sheet, 'Scopolamine, Mescaline and LSD. Nasty little cocktail, Commander.'

'Why would they be present in his blood?'

'They are all inducers of psychosis and are better known as truth drugs. If you want to know their effects, we'll need to talk to a colleague of mine from the psychiatry section. Is this information classified?'

'Yes. But does he need to know the details?'

'No. I suppose not,' Monroe said. 'I take it this is to do with Admirals Jessop's death?'

'In an indirect way, I suppose it is, yes.'

'Let's type out the list and see what he says.'

Lieutenant-Commander Evans handed the list back to Sims, 'To answer your question, Commander, the side effects could be many and varied. It depends very much on the mental stability and condition of the subject they were administered to. Needless to say, they are not three drugs I would ever mix as a cocktail. They all are capable of inducing severe psychosis and, all of them can induce panic and fear varying in magnitude from extreme to intense terror. If, and I suspect from the manner the question was slanted, they were used as, let us call them, *truth drugs,* then, they could have left the subject with permanent damage... especially in the case of LSD. On its own that one is capable of that... as a combination with the other two, I hesitate to think of the mental state of the patient.'

Walking back to Monroe's office Sims thanked him for all his help today and in the past.

'It's difficult to say thank you in a more positive way without it being construed as bribery. However, I'll take the risk... do you like sailing?'

'I love it and don't get enough time doing it.'

'So, you wouldn't construe it as an inducement if I invited you to come sailing on our ketch... she's a lovely old boat... *Alice Alacrity.* And, Jean, our cook at Hell Head House is five star Michelin.'

'It would be a great pleasure... all this is a nasty business... glad to give any help I can. I remember your father-in-law coming to thank me after your shooting. Quite overcome with relief he was... good man.'

'One of the very best. I struck lucky there. Anyway, glad to have got that cleared up... I'd been meaning to ask you for some time. Now something else though, the report says there was an amount of fluid in the lungs... sea water. What do you make of that?'

'You say the official report claims pneumonia and attendant complications as the cause of death. There's fluid on the lungs with that and I think it's possible that's why they chose that interpretation of the facts. If you want my opinion, though, I would say Adian McClusky drowned under the influence of those drugs, Commander... *drowned.*'

*

Michael Mondot's list, short enough for him not to need to write down: the sole name *St John Le Fanu*. Him, though, not for killing, but watching and studying.

When all others had turned their backs, Le Fanu had succoured Gerald Radleigh in his hour of need. *Strong bond*, Michael reasoned. Le Fanu would do it again.

MI6 records of their personnel were thorough and not for general staff or public consumption. Mondot did not need to pull strings to gain access - there was an active squad in MI6 too.

Michael studied the dossier. Le Fanu owned two other properties in England. On a long lease he rented out a modest riverside house near Windsor. In the quiet Oxfordshire village of Duns Tew for a few weekends in every two or three months The Grange came to life: Le Fanu entertained those he thought might be politically influential and, like his prized asparagus, worth his cultivation. The rest of time he kept a husband and wife as custodians: gardener and housekeeper. Thursday, their day off, and invariably spent at Banbury market.

Mondot had for many weeks known what he must do: Thomas had been his brother. There was too much at stake in Latvia for him to let Krista complete her mission. She was too valuable. No, this was to be his job. The Riga station had to be kept alive. Since Thomas and his group's disappearance Krista had kept the entire operation afloat. She must return home, and soon.

From the White Horse public house Gerald Radleigh

walked back through the village. It was a nice day. His vision of England. The England he had missed so much when living abroad. He didn't hurry and took time to soak up the clean air. Strolling past the entrance to the old Manor house he glanced at the ancient Cotswold stone dovecote, then he passed the church gates and opposite them, on its triangle of grass, the hollow elm tree that marked the turn to Middle Barton. He heard playing children call it The Cross Tree.

This is a nice village, he thought walking up the drive to his death.

At the rear of The Grange, he turned the corner to the kitchen door - sandwiches would be waiting.

Radleigh, two fingers holding a cigarette stopped short of his chin, the act frozen: as if giving a smoking benediction,

'This is for Thomas and all the others.' Michael Mondot pulled the trigger. Gerald Radleigh, *bon viveur*, millionaire and last surviving member of *les Grands Amis*, crumpled backwards onto the yellow gravel.

Rats, rabbits and pigeons are considered vermin: the occasional gun shot is not unusual in the countryside. The retired head mistress working in her garden opposite ignored the report, nor, back aching, did she bother to stand up straight and watch the grey Austin A40 turn right out of the gates and head for the Banbury to Oxford main road one mile away. Reaching it, Mondot crossed over, drove through the little village of North

Aston, then, over the river Cherwell and the canal at Somerton, past the US airbase at Upper Heyford and arriving at Ardley he turned right for Bicester and then to the anonymity of Greater London.

*

'How did you get my number?'

'Many fingers in many pies, Commander,' said political editor, Trevor Mitchell.

'If The Telegraph calls something's got to be up. Okay, what's the buzz?'

'Playing coy, Commander? or, have you really not heard?'

'Stop fucking around. Heard what?'

'Your Gerald Radleigh's dead.'

'*Christ!* How? Where?'

'My, my. You really didn't know did you? Shot this afternoon... Duns Tew, Oxfordshire.'

'Oh, come on. You don't think I did it do you?'

'Yours is a dodgy business to be in. Thought you might have heard something. In Claridges you said there's more to come.'

'Yeah, just for the record, so you don't go wasting your time, my wife and I were at a business meeting all afternoon... cast iron witnesses.'

'Okay, I'll buy that. Any snippets on Radleigh we can quote?'

'Plenty of snippets. Might be a while though. You'll have to wait until I write my memoirs.'

'Can we quote you?'

'Only as a reliable source.'

*

'Radleigh's dead.'

'Who did it?' asked Captain Miles Stinton.

'Be assured it was neither Anne nor myself.'

'Do you know who, then?'

'No,' Sims truthfully answered. Although, he had a fair inkling it was one of two people.

'Looks like he was jettisoned just in time. Where did this take place?'

'One of Le Fanu's places... Duns Tew... Oxfordshire. That's as much as I know.'

'Ahh.'

'If you don't mind, ahh what?'

'Billy and I were talking about Le Fanu once. He had a feeling he had a place somewhere around there. You'll know a lot more soon enough, Sims. Perhaps you ought not to do any more digging in Radleigh's direction for a while. Somebody's bound to think you were involved. Keep clear for now, lad. that's my advice.'

'Yes, I'd already decided to do just that.'

He put the phone down and thought: that old bugger Billy knew all the time that Le Fanu had a place up there... why the fuck didn't he just come out and say so?

He found her in the library. 'Radleigh's bought it... someone's shot him this afternoon.'

'Krista?'

'Possibly. Though if it was her, God knows how she found out where he was.'

'Michael Mondot could have told her.'

'Michael Mondot could have done it, love.'

'Yes he could, couldn't he?' she said, frowning

thoughtfully.

'What d'yer think?'

'It's going to get busy, darling. That's what I think, but, you know that already.'

'Le Fanu may think I did the deed. I'll have to get hold of him and put him properly in the picture.'

*

'Mr Le Fanu, let me make it perfectly clear, it was not me who killed Gerald Radleigh. And, furthermore, I do not know who did. He had information I wanted. It was not in my interest to murder him.'

'Are you going to investigate into who did?' asked Le Fanu, quietly.

'It is not my first priority. That's finding out who killed my boss, Admiral Billy Ruffian.'

'That's an honest reply, Commander. Do you think there's a connection between Gerald's death and the killing of the Russian a few streets away?'

'It's always a possibility... but, as I said, I really don't know who did the deed.'

'Are you getting anywhere with the admiral's death?'

'I have a few suspects. I know the weapon used and I know where it came from... there are missing bits in the story.'

'You must be aware of Kim Philby's defection from Beirut. And I know you are familiar with the Berne incident and the Hoffmann bank. There might be some gaps filled in if you connect the two and do some searching. That's as much as I'm prepared to say, Commander.'

*

'It's done. Go home now.' He paused while he listened. 'On Thomas' grave I swear it. I shall destroy your Tokarev.'

*

The two women shed their parting tears hours before. Now, they hugged briefly, then, Krista Bērzs opened the front door of the small terraced house in Hull and made her way to the rendezvous. Swirling sea mist again, she brushed the thick droplets of haar clinging to her greying blond hair and chanted her mantra over and over again, 'It's done, Thomas, it's done. It's done, my love, my love, my love.'

In a small cafe close to the docks, she sat waiting for two seamen from the ship that had brought her to England weeks before.

'It's done, but not over, Thomas, my love.'

***

Chapter Twenty One.
Arrest.

Admiralty house - London.

He looks a tough old bugger, thought Sims, taking a chair and sitting down at the table opposite his interviewer.

'Commander Sherwood-Reeves, my name is Admiral Stockley-Grantham I am a senior admiral in the British Navy and *the* most senior member of the Naval Intelligence Division. In due course I will join and also be a senior member of the new integrated intelligence service. For your information, Admiral Jessop told me you were loyal and trustworthy. In accordance with his opinion of you, I feel I can safely say without fear of your disclosure to others of NID's top brass, I was the sole person other than Admiral Jessop to officially know of the cabal's existence.'

'I once asked Billy...'

'His name was *Vice... Admiral... Jessop...*' Stockley-Grantham staccato snapped.

'Not to me he wasn't. No, he was Billy and a friend of mine. We were on first name terms.'

'You called him *Billy* to his face?'

'No, not exactly, he once overheard me call him that at a distance: not one of my better moves. Usually it depended where we were... and then, sir or John.

However, my wife and I will always think of him as Billy.'

A minute's silence. Whether out of respect for the dead Sims wasn't sure. Stockley-Grantham, now watching Sims closely, said, 'In Portsmouth, he staked you out.'

'I know, we got over that.'

'As I said a few minutes ago, he said you were loyal.'

'Hmm... and as I was saying, I asked him who was at the top of our lot. He never gave your name. I got it from elsewhere.'

'It's never been a secret.'

'Then never a widely shared piece of information either.'

'Commander, you asked for this long overdue meeting. Here we are. Please tell me what you want.'

'An easy one to start with... let's kick-off with, who is my immediate boss now?'

'I am.'

'Is that for general consumption?'

'No.'

'Still rats in the woodpile, then?'

'Yes.'

'If you're my boss, what next? Does Anne stay on the books?'

'We saw you as an essential partnership... a team. So yes. At least until the merger. After that, it's difficult to say what will be and what will not.'

'You know she's pregnant?'

'Yes.'

'You know, no doubt, there are two others in my

squad?'

'Yes. I also know there's another squad in your squad.'

'Do they know you?'

'Not personally.'

'I shall have to inform them.'

'Yes.'

'Okay, so what next with business?' asked Sims.

'I should have thought you could have guessed.'

'Find out who killed Billy.'

'Precisely.'

'I'm doing that already. I'm also looking into the death of Adian McClusky.'

'I know.'

'And, Gerald Radleigh had more to give.'

Stockley-Grantham quickly looked up from his notes. 'Hmm. How do you know?'

'He told me. He wanted a deal with the Government... protection; back dated pension etc, etc.'

'He'd probably have got it too. He could have done a lot of damage.'

'I think he knew that... so did others. I reckon they wouldn't have wanted him to do a deal, though. They'd just wanted him silenced... out of the way.'

'What do you think? How would you like to have seen it happen?'

'Oh, I'd love to have been the one who put a couple of rounds into him. But, there are others that have done that for me. My job was to obey Billy's last order... get what I can from him. Fat chance of that now.'

Admiral Stockley-Grantham nodded, 'Do you have any idea who might have pulled the trigger?'

'No.'

'Hmm.' That hint of doubt: Stockley-Grantham didn't sound completely convinced. 'Anything else?'

'Yes, sir. So, where am I at the moment? Previously I answered to a vice-admiral, and now, a full one. Did he mention he owed me my captaincy?' Sims had made a point of ownership and right: not "*a*" but "*my*".

'Bi...'

Sims smiled, 'So, you called him Billy too, sir?'

'...Everyone who knew him did. Vice Admiral Jessop did bring the matter of your captaincy up. It was of concern to him.'

'What's your feeling on the matter?'

'You're too young... you deserve it... you deserve a medal for what you've done. You will probably never get a medal... you may get a captaincy and beyond if you bide your time.'

Sims sensed it was deal time, 'I've never been much good at that.'

'So I understand. You do know you're listed for an intelligence role after the merger, don't you?'

'I hope they have the decency to ask me first. I may not want one.' He watched Stockley-Grantham's reaction.

'The Royal Navy will need all the support it can get, I would like you in it, Commander.'

'I would like a captaincy, Admiral.'

'Is this why you're here?'

'No, just making a point, sir.'

'Point taken, Commander.'

Stockley-Grantham writing notes. Sims cleared his

throat, the admiral looked up at him. 'Is it within your power to order the exhumation of Buster's grave? If it were to contain the body of Lieutenant Miles Stinton, it would mean he could be buried properly... albeit minus head. And, if we were able to do that it would mean a great deal to his father.'

'Ah, yes, Captain Stinton's son. Captain Stinton a good man... very good man. I never met his son.'

Sims sat patiently waiting for the answer to his question. Stockley-Grantham grunted, 'I could have some influence on getting the matter raised, but not the final say so. That would have to come from The Government. And, Commander, I must tell you, they are not going to give the go-ahead for that. The Cabinet papers on Commander Crabb's disappearance are subject to *the fifty year rule*. So, for the moment the grave and the remains contained within it stay as they are.' Stockley-Grantham, concerned at a Sims tangential move, warned, 'I would advise you it would not be a sensible move to dig him up yourself.'

'Billy thought that the block on the papers would be extended by a further fifty years. Now I have a theory that when consumption of Cabinet papers is deemed not to be in the public's interest, you can be sure someone's arse is being covered. So it follows if another fifty is tacked on, it's covering a pretty big arse.'

The admiral permitted himself a smile. 'Navigating your way through half truths and lies pushes one into believing nothing that you hear or read: I sometimes even doubt what I see is real.'

'I think I know what you mean,' said Sims. 'Sometimes I think it better to listen to the gaps; spaces; full stops. What people say is just words.'

Stockley-Grantham sat and scrutinised the young man on the other side of the table. 'He said you were loyal, Commander. Loyal to whom?'

'Those I think deserve it.'

'Country?'

'Not first on the list, no. My family first, close friends a close second... then country. I have to tell you I've not been impressed with everybody I've met in British Intelligence. Most of them are not in it for the right reason.'

'Commander, the new integrated intelligence service is as much about ridding ourselves of the old boy network as it is about efficiency and saving money. Money that could be better spent. It was this old boy network that Admiral Jessop worked to eradicate. He never belonged to any other network than his own. First and foremost, though, I believe his allegiance was always to his country.'

'It was. Great Britain was very dear to him.'

The admiral sensed more, and waited.

'I'm interested in why I've not come across you before. Some time back, I, with my wife, attended a staff defence meeting. Why weren't you there?'

'Even admirals can catch influenza, Commander.'

'You should try Pusser's Rum... it's a cure all... possibly even leprosy. It might have even made half the buggers attending more acceptable.'

Stockley-Grantham grunted, 'I shall try and remember that.'

Until the depth of the present mayhem had been sounded, after the wax inspected and the condition of the bottom determined, he had held back from mentioning *Operation Zurich*. How much Billy had kept Stockley-Grantham informed was an unknown. Let's find out, Sims thought.

'Who do I go to for cash, now? Who's my banker?'

'Me... your wife is an accountant I believe?'

'Yes, and a good one too.'

'I will need accurate accounts.'

'As I said, she's good, she's scrupulous, and she's responsible for exposing Aston-Heyford's game.'

'So I understand. And with that, Commander,' he said, collecting his papers together, 'I have other matters to attend to. I hope we have a reasonable understanding of our relationship.'

'More or less. It's a pity I didn't get more from Radleigh. What we did get, Billy thought was very, very important for NID. One other matter, now the *réglement des comptes* has taken place, please keep in mind it was not me that killed Radleigh. I had bigger fish to fry, but, I can tell you this, those that killed Billy are going to get more than a light battering.'

'So, you think a settling of scores over Admiral Jessop's death will take place?'

'If I have my way, definitely. I hope I'm there at the time.'

'Tread warily, Commander. And, I didn't hear that last statement of yours.'

'I will be careful, sir.'

Stockley-Grantham looked at his watch and held back from rising from the desk. 'Commander, a ship's decanter has a wide base to give it stability in rough weather. Peculiarly, but for the same reason, society needs stability at the top. In other words, it requires it to behave in the opposite sense. If that stability at the top falters or fails, expect trouble... from every quarter. In the western world those at the top rarely assassinate equals. It's not a game that's played. It makes them vulnerable too. Neutered; removed from power, yes... murdered rarely. Commander, you will be wise to remember what I am about to tell you, and I do so with no intention of supporting a cover up. Now, *listen to me*, I do not believe Admiral Jessop was removed by the establishment. I think it unlikely, but there are some who are saying we cannot write off the possibility it was retaliation by the Soviets for assisting and accepting Radleigh back into the fold.'

He stood up. 'This time I really must leave. However, one last point, there is a very good reason I want you in the new SIS. Despite all evidence, the general population does not wish to believe the world around them is unstable and chaotic. Tell them: show them: demonstrate unequivocally the magnitude of this disorder and greater disorder approaching, and they close their eyes and ignore you. So, what do *we* have to do about that, Commander?'

Sims about to answer was drawn short at mid-breath intake.

'Perhaps you will first permit me to give my opinion: what we do is we fight the multitude of hostile disruptors on the public's behalf. So, the choice is a simple one, Commander, you join us, or join them. And the membership to their club and the subsequent rules to follow are easy: *you don't have to do a damn thing.'*

'Are you certain there are only two options.'

'Possibly not. The two I've given, though, are the important ones.'

'I'll think over what you've said, sir.'

'We'll meet again soon, Commander.'

*

'You're still in. At least until the merger.'

'Tell me more.'

'It's early days, I think he was being straight. He is convinced Billy was not got at by the establishment.'

'If not them, who and why.'

'Something and somebody involving NID... that's all we've got to go on. For the moment, I'm going to run with the not establishment route.'

She looked doubtful. 'We haven't got a lot to go on.'

'We've got plenty. We've got the list.'

Anne remained silent.

'And, old Kenward reckoned he had papers that shocked him.'

'Might be easily shocked.'

'Possible.'

*

Anne had looked out of the window set to one side of the main door at Hell Head House. She quietly walked to the study and collected her Beretta, inserted the magazine and released the safety catch. Next, she went to the library; Sims was writing there.

'I sense a bit of trouble looming... on the front steps, darling.' she said. 'They look official.'

He took his Browning from its case, made it ready, slipped his shoulder holster on, slid the gun into it, then put on his uniform jacket. Finally, he squared his gold braid peaked hat. 'Might as well use all weaponry,' he said.

The three looked heavy duty. He told them to stay where they were. 'Who are you and what's your business?'

'NID Special Regulatory Branch, sir. Sir, you are thought to possess the two Tokarevs taken from the Soviet agents you killed on The Isle of Wight. They are not logged into NID's inventory at Netley. We assume you have them.'

'In my job, it's not illegal for me to possess firearms.'

'That's true, sir. We have to cover all contingences.'

'What contingences?'

'Gerald Radleigh and another, were shot using a Tokarev. If you are in possession, you are to hand them over to us immediately. And, sir, until we prove that neither of them were used in the shooting, we are ordered to place you under arrest.'

Two of them stepped forward. Sims stepped sideways and backwards and drew out his pistol. Anne, Beretta levelled stepped out from the darkness of the doorway. 'One step further and you're dead. You are not going to arrest my husband. Place your identity cards on the step in front of you and then retreat down the steps. Do it *now*,' she shouted.

Sims put his side arm back in its shoulder holster. 'Better do as she says, lads. She doesn't make idle threats nor does she miss.'

Her unwavering pistol gripped hand rendered his

advice unnecessary. Harry joined the confrontation, positioning himself in front of Anne and showing an unhealthy amount of teeth.

'He's just as lethal as my missus,' Sims said. 'The last person he bit had to have quite a large lump of his leg surgically removed after old Harry here had a go at him. He's got it well and truly in his mind that his part in matters such as this is to provide a sort of preoperative investigation... very good at it... bit nasty to watch, though.'

'You're not making this any easier for yourself, sir.'

Sims checked their identity cards. 'No, you listen to me. I'm going to make it easy for *you*. While Anne covers you, I'm going to phone Netley and check that you're legit. If you are, I'll fetch the two Tokarevs and all three of you are going to print your names and sign a receipt for them. And, that receipt is going to contain their serial numbers. Is that okay, have you got it? Then, you can go and do your test firing and see that neither of those guns were used. Just get one thing clear, though... you are not taking me with you... got it?'

'How did you know the commander has the Tokarevs? Who told you?' asked Anne.

The youngest of three answered. 'The commander displayed them at a lecture, ma'am, and then showed us students what a mess they can make of a leg.' He turned to Sims, 'It was a very good lecture, sir.'

'Hrumph,' Sims said, going inside with their identity cards.

'I want you to answer my question fully. *Now,* are you listening? *Who* sent you?' Anne demanded.

'Orders from our senior officer. Someone else must

have instructed him... we don't know who.'

Interesting, the young one's on our side, thought Anne. Good lecture, Sims.

'What is your name?'

'Regulating Petty Officer Masters, ma'am.'

Sims returned. 'Okay, it seems you're pukka... sign here.' He handed over the guns. 'Don't damage them... they're special. And, in case you don't know,' he said, handing them the magazines, 'these are needed to put the little pointy things in... they're called bullets by the way. You'll have to supply your own rounds of course. I used mine all up pumping them into Radleigh.'

'Is that a confession, sir?' said the most senior looking of them.

'Oh, for fuck's sake bugger off, before I give Harry or my missus the go ahead.'

'Gosh, that felt so good. Not something I'd do normally, darling. It did feel good, though. Next time I won't be so restrained... might pull the trigger... arrest my husband, how dare they?'

'Probably haven't heard the last of this, love.'

'The young one, Masters, is on our side. He might be useful.'

'You don't miss much do you?'

'It doesn't pay to... I've got you to look after. Us accountants have a very broad remit. First lesson at college; beware barrow-boys, they're nothing but trouble.'

'Getting regrets?'

She had lost the skirmish. she caught hold of his arm, 'Don't say things like that, Sims... please, ever, ever, and no, never regrets.'

'Below the belt?'

'Just a bit, darling. Things are going to get rougher, aren't they?'

'Yeah, just a bit,' he echoed.

'You know, it's going to be interesting to see what they come up with. If you remember, we were up in Alton with Mrs Braddock fetching Billy's papers from Kenward & Kenward when Radleigh was shot. We won't say anything for the moment... someone's jumped the gun. Let them have their head.'

'We'd better go and see old Kenward before they get to him, darling. When they find out where we were they might just try and make him change his testimony.'

'What are you suggesting, getting him to sign a deposition of the facts?'

'Yes, and at least three copies of it too... Dad can have one of them... we'll see how they'd try and get round that one if they dare.'

*

'Commander Sherwood-Reeves, people have tried to bully me before. And, I must tell you they have never succeeded. I could have chosen to practise in London, instead, I chose to work in my father's business here in Alton because I love the countryside. That, as I have often said, does not make me a yokel.'

'But are you happy with signing the depositions?' asked Anne.

'Of course... to be sure. On the day in question and the time in question you were both here. That is not in doubt.

I have a good memory, and the appointment is entered in my diary. We'll have the depositions endorsed and countersigned by my partner and witnessed by a responsible member of the public. If I may advise, we should have five copies made instead of three. Of the two extra ones, one will be lodged here and the other elsewhere. One cannot be too careful in these matters. Particularly so in light of Admiral Jessop's passing. Despite what has been written in the press, I have assumed it was no accident.'

'You assume correct,' said Sims.

'While on the subject of that brave man, it was his wish that I should be granted probate of his affairs. To this end, I can inform you that you are both to receive bequests. I am not able to tell at this time what they amount to. However, they will be made public at the right time; the reading of the will.'

*

Hot under the collar, Sims stalked into the library. 'Another time wasting exercise... God, aren't those buggers past masters at it. I've been summoned to a preliminary inquiry at Netley... looks like I'll have to attend. '

She smiled. 'Should be fun to watch, I'll come to too.'

'You'll be better here holding fort. Anyway, you won't be allowed in. This is where we need you. I'm also leaving my Browning here in case they try and take it from me. I'll go and see old Miles for some tips.'

'Will I be allowed into that one?'

'He'll be pleased to see you.'

*

David Mountford met him in the car park. 'Sir, they've given us quite a grilling. We didn't say anything of our business.'

'Well done. What did you say?'

'I told them we had received direct orders from Admiral Jessop not to reveal our purpose.'

'What did they say to that?'

'They threatened me with a court-martial. They said their authority over-ruled the late Admiral Jessop's. I apologised and said in that case I would have to wait for your authority.'

'Perfect... well done, David,' said Sims, slapping him on the shoulder.

Sub-lieutenant David Mountford looked happier than he had for days.

A senior captain sat at the centre of the three inquiry officers on the opposite side of the table from Sims.

'I am Captain P. Rook. On my right is Commander J Vickars and on my left, no doubt a familiar face to you, NIDii lecturer, Lieutenant-Commander W. Woodruff. The nature of this meeting is that of a preliminary inquiry. For your information, we have interviewed Artis and Beatrise Podnieks in case there is a connection.'

For a vanishingly short moment, Woodruff's composure broke - for him, he appeared ruffled. Sims clearly aware of an ephemeral frisson leaked by Woodruff. Had they slipped up and given away something he was not happy about? Why bring this up other than to see my reaction? Sims thought. How should I react? Ask the question: Beatrise was the interpreter for the Matrozis incident. So, why shouldn't he admit to knowing her.

'Wasn't Mrs Podnieks the interpreter on the Viktor Abakumov?' He watched their reactions: nothing significant.

Captain Rook nodded to the secretary. 'Start taking notes.'

As he was speaking Rook bounced his pen on the table. Not as cool as you'd like to appear, Sims thought. I'll see how far I can push you.

'The purpose of this preliminary inquiry is to gather facts about the death of Gerald Radleigh. We know he was shot with a Soviet made Tokarev. The identical gun... I should say, the same gun was used to assassinate a member of both the Soviet Commissariat in Riga and of the NKVD; one Nikolai Zima. What do you know of this.'

'Not much more than he was shot with a Soviet made Tokarev. The identical gun or the same gun was used to assassinate a member of the Soviet NKVD, Nikolai Zima,' Sims threw back at him.

'Your facetiousness will not help your situation or this inquiry at all, Commander.'

'Preliminary, sir,' retorted Sims.

Rook, showing the serrated edge of irritation, said, 'What?'

'You said it was a preliminary inquiry, not an inquiry... easy mistake to make, sir.'

Rook's pen fairly rattling now. 'What do you know of their deaths, Commander?'

'Only that they are dead and were shot using a Tokarev, and, of course, that other piece which you've just told me... I won't bother to repeat that bit, sir.'

'Let us get to the point, where were you on the day of the murders?'

'It's difficult to say, I might not be able to account for my time on that particular day and, if I could, there might not be corroborating witnesses... I've been very busy lately. In my spare time I do quite a bit of sailing. And, it's not good form to keep a diary of one's movements in case it's stolen by the enemy. The enemy's all around us, sir,' he said, looking at the three interviewing officers in turn and settling on Woodruff for a long enough to send him a little message: "We know your game, Woodruff.".

'It appears you were not at Netley.'

'That's not unusual. I have other duties.'

'Outline these other duties to this inquiry... this *preliminary* inquiry.'

'I am afraid that will not be possible, they are of a sensitive intelligence nature.'

'Are you prepared to say who instructed you in these duties?'

'Of course, that's common knowledge, almost in the public domain; Admiral Jessop.'

'Admiral Jessop is dead.'

'Well, I am aware of that, sir. However, until I know who has officially replaced him and that person has been briefed by me and I have then received his orders, they will remain the late Admiral Jessop's and my own affairs. They are of a highly confidential nature, sir.'

Woodruff leaned over and spoke to the Rook.

'Lieutenant-Commander Woodruff makes a valid point in that due to the forthcoming amalgamation of the intelligence services, it is quite possible Admiral Jessop may not be replaced.'

'Someone somewhere is surely going to continue the work he undertook. Surely whatever state secrets he was party to or currently involved with are not going to be ditched into the nearest dustbin. No, I don't see that... he'll be replaced by someone, even if he's from the army, God forbid.'

Commander J Vickars gave a slight smile.

He's home team, thought Sims. He doesn't want to be here... brought in at the last moment... this is a rush job.

Rook brought the meeting to a close, 'If you have nothing to add to your statement, you are free to leave. We will return the Tokarevs to you when they have been test fired.'

'And that little process is going to do nothing but waste more Admiralty money, sir. In the meantime I wonder if you could give me a little information?' It was time to send a message to Woodruff.

'Go ahead,' said Rook.

'While in custody here at Netley, Adian McClusky died. Can you tell me who headed the inquiry into his death?'

There could be no doubt this time, Lieutenant-Commander Woodruff looked as though he had swallowed the contents of a spittoon.

Got you, you bastard, thought Sims.

'Is this important to this inquiry?' asked Rook.

'No... just a private venture, sir,' Sims said, holding Woodruff's gaze.

'This is not information I have to hand... it should be on record somewhere. Where was the inquiry held?'

'Here in Netley, Unit 4. Internment and Interrogation.'

*

Patrick Harvey called, 'Hi, Sims, how are things?'

'Apart from being arrested for killing Radleigh; pretty boring.'

'Look, I'm afraid it's calling from phone boxes again. Can you call me back?'

'Pat, what have you got?'

'A witness, an old boy, says the Soviet agent killed in Chelsea was shot by a woman... grey or blonde. Anne doesn't have a wig does she?'

'Witness! That old boy was barely living. I didn't think there were any.'

'So, you were there then? You're being defensive. So, it must have been Anne, then.'

'Fuck off. No it bloody wasn't. You know damn well I was around at the time. Keep this strictly under your own hat... tell no one else, Pat: she was at home taking calls from myself and the lads when he was done in.'

'Interesting! The witness says he saw an accomplice; male. You sure it wasn't you?'

'You sound like a copper.'

'And, you sound as if you know who it was and aren't going to tell.'

'Maybe, Pat. Maybe.'

'Why the secrecy?'

'Let's see if any scum rises to the surface, shall we?'

***

Chapter Twenty Two.
The Sherwood-Reeves Debt Collection Agency.

The high ceilinged square room echoed slightly as the three naval officers entered. Sims' chair had been placed facing and a few feet from the table. The senior of them: Captain Freemantle, spoke.

'This is an extraordinary tribunal: not a court-martial, nor is it a disciplinary meeting. I wish to make it clear you are not charged with any misdemeanour. I repeat, this meeting is of an extraordinary nature.'

Freemantle turned the page and sought his next words. 'Following his unfortunate accident...'

'Accident, my arse,' exclaimed Sims.

'Since his unfortunate accident,' Freemantle crisply repeated - he had expected troublesome outbursts. 'Admiral Jessop's papers have been thoroughly analysed. There were, by nature of his rank and position within the Naval Intelligence Division, many issues not of general knowledge to all in the Admiralty. It is one of these unknowns that has caused this meeting to be convened.'

Good old Billy, thought Sims. First fire from the hip, then sweep the bits under the carpet. He inwardly smiled: must have been one of the few carpets with a forty-five degree slope.

Freemantle peered at Sims over his half-moon gold

rimmed glasses. 'You should know, I have expressed the wish for my personal and following statement to go on record in that, I have much admiration for your conduct and bravery on The Isle of Wight. Also, your role in the closure of a former spy-cell.' He took a deep breath. 'However, the manner in which you received your commission *was* highly unorthodox, irregular *and* most importantly, illegal. This does not imply in any way you were responsible in the matter. The responsibility lies entirely at the feet of the late Vice-Admiral Jessop.'

Hadn't got the guts to get at him to his face: had to wait until he was dead... spineless bastards, thought Sims.

Freemantle looked at each of the other two officers in turn. 'Accordingly, after much consultation and deliberation, you are to be stripped of Her Majesty's commission.'

'Back to Killick Stoker, then? Just like that!'

'No. Further to you being stripped of the commission, you have been medically discharged from Her Majesty's Royal Navy. This is to be backdated to your discharge from The Royal Naval Hospital Haslar.'

'How are you going to get the overpay back?'

'As this mess was not of your making, we have decided this is not a legal issue. The excess pay is to be considered in lieu of your separation payment. You will receive a disability pension appropriate to your rank on leaving the service.'

So that's how you treat your men, thought Sims. 'So, I'm a civvy, then?'

'Yes.'

'From when?'

'As you were just informed, let us say, from the date of your discharge from Haslar into the care of Rear Admiral Sherwood at Hell Head House.'

'I am to believe then, that since that time I have definitely been a civilian?'

'Yes.'

Hmm, interesting, thought Sims. 'And, that includes the operation I conducted in Zurich?'

'Zurich?'

'So, the old bugger, Billy, didn't write that one up, then?'

'Zurich? Perhaps you would be so kind as to enlighten us?'

'I escorted Gerald Radleigh to France and Switzerland to recover funds he had in accounts held in those countries. These funds are now deposited in the United Kingdom.'

The tribunal, heads together, conferred.

'The legality of those funds must be in question, I assume the intention is to hand them over to the British Government.'

'The smaller portion of the funds was in no doubt obtained illegally. Mr Radleigh was in possession of that. So, as he's dead, you'd better get yourselves a good medium and find out where he stashed it. The very large remainder was obtained legitimately and from a legitimate source. Which, by the way, was handed fairly and without pressure to me... there are plenty of witnesses to that.'

'And, what do you intend doing with it?'

'I intend keeping it. All four and a quarter million

pounds of it. It'll help make up for the crappy pension you were prepared to pay me. See me as my own debt collection agency.'

'If it is money obtained by Gerald Radleigh and then obtained by you, it must rightfully be ours.'

'I don't know where you get your advice from... wherever, sack the buggers. You see, actually, it's not your money at all and never was. So you'll get none of it. MI6, completely out of control, and, as usual not knowing what day of the week it was, had no idea of how much cash was being hijacked from their overseas slush fund. The money I have was commission paid to Mr Radleigh by a Swiss bank for diplomatically smoothing things over and it was, I repeat, willingly handed over to me. Everyone in MI6 may deny knowledge of the syphoning off, but, I'll bet you someone at the top did it. What a good story this will all make. I know just the guy to go to at The Telegraph.'

'What has been discussed at this meeting is of naval concern only. It is expressly not to be divulged to parties outside these four walls.'

Our man leaned forward, planted his hands firmly on his knees, and said, 'Bollocks, I'm a civvy now, you said so yourself. So, *fuck off*. You have no jurisdiction over me. *Christ!* this feels better than threatening to shoot an RPO.'

Sims stood up and threw his hat on the table and, as he left the meeting, he said, 'I'll keep the jacket for the moment, it's nippy outside. I look forward to receiving the discharge paperwork... don't expect a quick reply, I'll be busy, I've some shit stirring to do and four and a quarter million quid to do it with. Just call me ex mess-deck lawyer number one.'

*

Seated, Anne waited in the entrance lobby. 'You've forgotten your hat.'

'No need for it. I'm an unemployed civvy now, love.'

'What?'

'They've given me the big elbow and, for some reason, think that's going to shut me up.'

Anne turned and quickly walked in the direction Sims had come.

'Where're you going?'

'To get your hat... it's *famous!*'

*

Room empty, table cleared except for the gold braid peaked hat. She stalked to the table snatched it up and snarled at the young escorting lieutenant, 'My husband, myself and this hat belong together. His dismissal is not going to happen.'

She stomped back, 'Take it,' she demanded.

He hesitated.

'Take it, Commander Sherwood-Reeves. You *earned* it.'

*

'It's a blocking tactic. They're trying to silence him,' said Rear-Admiral Sherwood.

'The Tribunal, who were they?'

'Admiralty administrators led by a Captain Freemantle.'

'Hmm, don't know him.'

'I'm not surprised... bureaucrat. Not our navy, Richard.'

'Any of them from Admiralty Legal Section?'

'No, the legal department kept well clear, and, were well advised to do so. Now, The Tribunal, that's another matter: they *were* ill advised.'

Admiral Stockley-Grantham nodded. 'The point is, Bob, who is behind it and why?'

'Someone who doesn't want my son-in-law chasing their wake.'

'He has friends in high places you know. I think a visit to The Defence Minister is in order. The commander cleared up that Pompey mess on his watch... pleased him enormously. He won't have forgotten.'

*

This is a bad do, Admiral. What do you suggest?'

Stockley-Grantham, urged without hesitation, straight to the point, 'Reinstate him, Minister. He's loyal and we need men like him.'

'Could he not operate for British Intelligence as a civilian?'

'Not him, no. Regardless of what he might say, the sea and the navy are in his blood.'

'Very well, I'll memo the Admiralty for a full reinstatement... it might also be a good thing for someone to make an apology. Let's get those legal boys in the Admiralty earning their money. Talking of which, what's the position with Radleigh's fortune?'

'As far as I know there were originally two accounts. Seventy five percent of the total retrieved was deposited in the first and under the sole control of the commander.

The second held the balance and required the joint signatures of Sherwood-Reeves and Radleigh for payments or transfers. Later, a third account was opened in the name of Radleigh alone. This is where Sherwood-Reeves has been particularly smart. From the two initial accounts he transferred the exact amount of funds gained from drug importing and therefore illegally gained. His opinion being, if The Government wanted that, they could deal directly with Radleigh... this amounted to a little over three million pounds.'

'And, the total recovered you say, was?'

"Seven million three hundred and fifty four thousand pounds, Minister.'

'*Good Lord,* are you saying Sherwood-Reeves ended up over four million to the better?'

'To be precise, Minister, four and a quarter million.'

'*Good Lord!*'

'Exactly, Minister. Sherwood-Reeves is a handy man to have around.'

'Indeed he is. Do you think he'll hand it over?'

'Why should he? Le Fanu confirmed with a signed deposition that it was gifted to the commander without coercion. And, the money itself was legitimately earned commission. The Inland Revenue will of course take a fair proportion. In Le Fanu's deposition, he also thanks the commander for being so helpful to his long-term friend Gerald Radleigh. Minister, this man is important to us. If his exploits on The Isle of Wight were known publically he would be a national hero. Sherwood-Reeves has been treated unfairly. His trust in the Admiralty and SIS is low... he'll keep it as an insurance policy.'

'I can't say I can fault him for that.'

They sat looking at each other across the minister's desk.

'And the Tribunal, what about them?'

'For the moment leave them be. Someone suggested his commission was illegal and they, being the bureaucrats they are, took it up. My recommendation is, The Admiralty overturns the decision and you back their decision.'

'And this will satisfy Sherwood-Reeves?'

'Not quite, Minister. My bet is, he will ask for his captaincy. And, if you really want him to remain in the Royal Navy and SIS, you'll recommend it be granted.'

'Are you sure we can afford him, Admiral?' he said, smiling.

'Remember The Isle of Wight, Minister.'

'I have not forgotten. Individual... heroic. You'll keep his wife on, of course?'

*

'Don't worry, we're millionaires now. That cash is ours.'

Anne, stomped up and down the library. Her anger turned to tears, *'Money!* I'm not worried about money. Your dismissal will not stick. You earned your commission... Dad is furious. He's at a meeting with some pretty powerful people at Admiralty House. You'll be back as a commander by the end of the week... you mark my words: commander again by the end of the week.'

'Nope. You're wrong there... wouldn't accept it even if they offered it.'

She looked horrified. 'Why ever not, Sims? It means so much.'

'Captain or nothing,' he said, grinning. 'Barrow-boy,

remember?'

Her tears now laughter, she shrieked, *'Really?* You'll hang out for that?'

'Why not? The buggers are wrong footed... ...what are you staring at?'

'You'll do it, won't you? You'll get it too. Sims, I've just realised I shall shortly be married to a captain. Captain John Sims Sherwood-Reeves. *God!* That sounds so sexy, darling.'

'Yeah, I know,' he said, advancing towards her. 'Just get one thing straight, though, we're not giving up the loot.'

*

Anne greeted him from the topmost step, 'Alistair, it is so nice to see you again... you're looking so well after your trip.'

'Copenhagen... Zurich... back in the cockpit; gave me a new lease of life. I feel top-hole, my dear. Or am I not supposed to call you that? I'm not sure what to call young ladies these days... things have changed.' he said, looking around to see if by any chance Fiona might be nearby.

'There are some people I would take exception to calling me that. But, they would be people I didn't like. Now, let's go inside and talk business.'

How would my wonderful barrow-boy handle this? she thought. Make him comfortable and get him some refreshments... Billy said he was sharp, he's old school, though, he won't want to upset a lady. 'Alistair, darling, you must take tea with me. Jean has it all ready and waiting... you mustn't disappoint her.'

Being called "darling" had rendered him almost defenceless. Far from being calculated, she had uttered it unwittingly... it was a term of endearment she used with those she was fond of. Nevertheless, unwittingly uttered or not, he was temporarily, completely and overpoweringly charmed and blinded by her.

Alistair's habit of checking his bearings came into play, he wandered over to the window and scanned the horizon. He returned to the table and sat down. 'As I told you on the telephone, I'm going to sell my Jag. Sims seemed to be fairly keen on it. So I thought I'd sound you out on the matter. That's why I wanted to make sure Sims wasn't here when I came.'

She frowned. 'Did he suggest this?'

'No. He knows nothing about it.'

'Then, why do you need to talk to me? Why don't you ask him?'

'Well actually I'm following David Mountford's advice. He suggested I spoke to you... he said you were quite fond of Sims.'

'Much more than quite fond, Alistair... and I must tell you I'm still quite lost as to why you've come to me.'

'Mountford suggested I ought to.'

'So, you two think I might be a softer touch, is that it?'

'No, no... after thinking about Mountford's comment, I wondered if you might prefer to surprise him... make it a present.'

A fuller understanding of Alistair's sharpness came into focus. Anne thought, the cunning old sod. She said,

'Alistair, that's such a sweet thought. How much are you asking for it?'

'Well, considering its condition, I couldn't accept a penny less than nine hundred and ninety pounds.'

Sims had once told her, "never accept their first offer". She would use that, and the few trumps she held up her sleeve; mercilessly. 'Oh, much too much... what a pity. You set me thinking after your call so I phoned up a few garages to enquire about prices and what I should look out for. I must say, as beautiful a condition yours is in, that price is way over the top. And, what with the baby coming, we're going to have to be so careful. I'm so sorry. Look let's just forget it and enjoy our tea. And, please don't tell Sims... he would just pine. So, tell me, how's your wife. She'll no doubt be pleased with the extra money.'

He coughed. 'Actually, she doesn't know I'm about to sell it...' He had slipped and about to slide further and deeper. 'I'm going to put the money towards a new glider.'

Hmm, Anne thought, Sims wouldn't miss this one I know. 'Oh God, that could be awkward if that slipped out when we meet... I'm so thoughtless at times. Do you think she'd be angry?'

The old Mosquito pilot looked as though he'd had a bad landing and lost his undercart. 'Well, hmm, look, why don't you make me a sensible offer?

Got you... 'Oh, I'm not sure... the kind of price I could afford to offer would be an insult. No, Alistair, let's forget it and have some more cake. Would you like me to pour you some more tea?' She sat back and thought: me, *barrow-girl*.

Alistair, now uncertain of his position, got up and once again looking out of the window craned his neck left and right... he needed to spot a familiar landmark. Something that correlated with his plot. He feared he was lost.

'You haven't got it in mind to meet my wife, have you?'

'Actually, Sims and I discussed inviting you both down for the week-end when we've some spare time... we could go sailing. We wanted to thank you for your help with Radleigh... you did such a good job. And, I'm dying to meet her. We must have lots in common; so much to talk about.'

Maybe she could be stifled. He tried one further ploy, 'Abigail and myself never talk shop... never; not allowed under The Official Secrets Act, you know. Not pukkah to do so, my dear... the country's security at stake and all that.'

'Oh, come on, Alistair, how many in SIS don't talk to their wives, lovers and friends about matters of state security? None of them, I bet.'

What is it about the eyes that show defeat? The face and body may appear positive and resolute. The eyes, however, fade dull and register the victims impending doom.

'Oh my gosh,' she exclaimed, with her hand to her mouth, 'I just thought, I shall have to keep quiet about the money you earned from Billy... I assume you haven't mentioned that either?'

'No, I haven't yet.'

'I suppose you were going to? Or were you going to buy her a nice present... women love diamonds you know.'

'And, similarly, men love Jaguars.'

'Yes, yes, but not at any price. There has to be a limit, Alistair. An E-Type only costs twice that much. I could borrow the extra from father. And, the XK-120 only cost just over twelve hundred pounds new. Since then we've had the XK-140 and for the price you're asking we could have one of those.. their top speed is one hundred and forty mph: that's why it's called the XK-140. Alistair. Sims would accept one readily, I'd bet. I'm sorry to have to tell you, the bottom's dropped right out of the XK-120 market. Sims would never forgive me paying anywhere near that price. I couldn't possibly go above three hundred pounds our budget just wouldn't stretch that far. Perhaps you'd best keep it and forget the glider... have some more tea, darling.'

'Couldn't you make that around four hundred and fifty?'

Around, she thought. Does that mean he'd accept a lower sum? Yes, what am I thinking of, of course it does. 'Alistair, I'll make a conditional offer of three hundred and seventy five pounds, and that will definitely have to be that.'

'Conditional?'

'Yes, conditional in that it has a full service by a reputable garage and a complete set of new tyres.'

'Good God... Billy said you had a hard streak in you... I had no idea how hard.'

'Have we a deal, Alistair?'

'Yes, I... I suppose so... you'll keep this quiet, won't you?'

'Of course... and not a word to Sims... he'd go mad if

he knew I'd spent that much.'

'Of course.'

*

'Admiral Jessop was killed *because* he was dying. That is my sincerest belief.'

'*That*, you are going to have to explain,' said Sims.

'I know Billy had certain information. He had hinted at it... I consider myself to have been his closest confidant, yet, there were issues of national security he never divulged to anyone... and that even included me.'

'Kept it close his chest, then.'

'Yes. Billy knew something. In my opinion this involved the very highest and dirtiest dealings of the present and former British governments. That, of course, is speculation on my part. But, in my defence, over the years I have gleaned snippets of information, pieced them together and then coupled them to events. For instance, Billy was present at a top level security meeting the day after the death of Hugh Gaitskell. There were people at that meeting who knew Philby might defect.'

'How right they were.'

'Why did they think that? How were the two events connected? Do you know Billy had actually met Golitsyn; Anatoliy Mikhaylovich Golitsyn the Russian defector. He identified Philby, along with many others as Soviet agents... he was correct in every case.'

Billy had told Sims this, 'He briefly mentioned him... gave Anne and myself a little background... never said he'd met him, though.'

'That's often the way Billy worked.'

'Okay, I can accept he may have heard or known

something not for our ears, but why kill him now? Why not before?'

'Look, Billy knew he was dying for some time. You can be pretty sure he wasn't going to go out with a whimper... that wasn't his style. No, no, I think he threatened to reveal something unless he got something valuable in return... something valuable to him.'

'Go on.'

'Ask yourself what a dying man might ask for? That is, I should say, a man like the admiral who possessed values and integrity. Perhaps, in our minds, we should not picture the wishes of an ordinary man, but, it may be better if we should think about what Billy would ask for? That's the crucial question. What would Billy ask for?'

'He didn't seem particularly religious. So, absolution's out... must have been something close to his heart.'

'Exactly. And what might that be?'

'You said *that*. So, it's a thing not a person.'

Stinton nodded.

'Jesus! It can only be something to do with NID or, I suppose something like rebuilding the Bellerophon. But if push comes shove, I'll settle with NID, he wanted it's and his name cleared over Portland, Buster and the truth about both told... can't seriously think of anything else.'

'Sims, that's the conclusion I came to as well.'

'So, what he asked for scared the shit out of someone or some bodies.'

'Definitely.'

Soft late afternoon sun filled the small sitting room. Sims glanced up and out of the window. 'I'll have to be on my way soon.' he said, 'Anne will be expecting me.'

'How is she?'

'She's fine... in good form. Worries a bit, though.'

'About you no doubt.'

Sims gave a slight nod. 'I offered to give the job up and resign. She said, we've got to see it through... doesn't stop her worrying though.'

'Understandable.'

'Do you think Billy committed what he knew to writing?'

'Most likely.'

'Any idea where that might be?'

'No. I was hoping you might.'

'If he didn't confide in you, he was hardly likely to tell me, was he?'

'Don't be so sure of that. You are young; I am old. He would have wanted to pass it on to someone who could see the job through.'

'Well, as I said, I must be off.'

'Before you go... a question I must ask: something that's puzzled me for a long time... why are you so accurate? How is it possible?'

'Hmm... don't know for sure... there's a calm, an instant in time of alert relaxation: an inner conviction tells me when. This then, is the time to pull the trigger. It's as if I already know the result, as if it's already happened, and I'm just part of a predetermined process.'

'Time only travels forwards, Sims.'

'Are you sure about that?'

*

'Miles come up with anything, darling?'

'He has a pet theory that Billy threatened to reveal something unless NID finished up with a clear name.'

'He could be right. Billy was always close to losing his temper when discussing it. The Naval Intelligence Division meant so much to him... he told me he thought Britain's security would be compromised without NID being around. He once said to me, "NID keeps Britain on an even keel." We'll miss him, Sims,' she said, looking away. 'What do you think?'

'If you mean Billy, he's left a bit of hole behind him... going to take some filling. If you meant Miles, I think he could have hit it right on the button. I asked him if he thought Billy had written down what he would reveal. He thought I'd have a copy if there was one.'

'Why?'

'Something about me being young enough to complete the job.'

'Do you think old Kenward has got it?'

'It's not impossible. Whether he'd tell us, that's another matter... tough old bugger, wasn't he? I've thought about having my legal stuff handed over to him.'

'What sort of stuff?'

'Property titles... you know, that sort of thing.' He moved to the window and looked towards The Island.

He was looking at a break in the woods and a small field between; she knew this. 'What else?' she asked, quietly.

'Come on, babe, give me a break. You don't think I haven't made a will do you?'

'Sims...' she was unable to finish the sentence.

'Don't panic, love. Just a precautionary measure.'

*

'It's good of you to see us at such short notice,' said

Anne. 'We'll be as brief as possible.'

'Don't concern yourself, Mrs Sherwood-Reeves. Now then, what's on both your minds... I assume it's something to do with the Admiral Jessop affair or is it about Mr Radleigh?.'

'Diectly, Admiral Jessop; indirectly Radleigh perhaps.' said Sims. 'We have a simple question. Apart from his will and the other papers of his, were there any others? Perhaps even more sensitive than those you handed over to Mrs Braddock and myself.'

'There were indeed. However, I cannot allow you to see or take possession of them. There were, once again, five witnessed copies. These were bound and sealed. Admiral Jessop distributed four of those, to where I do not know, and the fifth, and original one, he kept in his possession.'

'Are you in a position to tell us what they referred to, Mr Kenward?' asked Anne.

'Only that they were the minutes of a meeting, and that the signatures endorsing them were those of very important people.'

'Must have been more than hush hush,' Sims said.

'It was astonishing... the like of which I could hardly believe.'

'And you can't reveal the detail?'

'I am sorry, no. Client confidentiality must be guarded at all costs.'

'Thank you for your time and help,' Sims said, shaking his hand.

*

Anne sat up and shook him awake.

'What's a matter?... are you alright?'

'Yes... perfectly. I couldn't sleep... I'm wide awake.'

Sims yawned, 'Therapy time, you always sleep well afterwards.'

'Actually, darling, I was thinking about something else.'

'Sod and bugger it.' He yawned again.

'Sims?'

'Great, you've changed your mind?'

'No... later. I was thinking about Miles hoping Billy might have handed you a copy of the minutes.'

'And?'

'Well he might have done.'

'Not to my knowledge he hasn't...' he yawned again, 'is it later yet?'

'*NO! Listen!* Why did Billy give you the Bellerophon table. Apart from the reason he said, and don't forget you yourself always thought a museum ought to have it, *why*? In my mind, there has always been this "*why*" over the table. It's such an historic piece. Perhaps Billy's top copy of the minutes is there.'

'Come on, honey. You were there when we unscrewed the plaque... there was just the cavity and the note.'

'I know that... I know *that*. But Billy has almost always seemed to code the information he's given you. I don't mean he was playing games with you. It's as though he has put things just out of your reach, and if you climb high enough, you are worthy... you are the man he hopes you are.'

'Keep going.'

'I was thinking about the box Les made for your Browning and how cleverly the opening device was.

They used to put that sort of mechanism in old writing bureaus... Aunt Catherine has one. Press a panel or side and it reveals another compartment.'

'Maybe he gave it to her to stash... no bugger's going to get past that old bat.'

'Be serious. It's possible there's another compartment in the table... I think we ought to go and look.'

Screws removed, he lifted the brass plaque clear. Anne put her hands inside the shallow recess and pressed each side in turn. Nothing. No click of a catch releasing; nothing.

'Let me have a look,' Sims said.

With the rounded handle of the screwdriver, he gently tapped each side and base; the reflected sound, iron hard. 'All wood... solid wood, love. Hand me the torch please.' He peered inside. 'If he'd regularly used a catch or something there'd be evidence of wear or some sort of discolouration. Good try, love.'

She took the screwdriver from him and proceeded round the table tapping every inch. 'Solid,' she said. 'Oh, well...'

'Don't be too disappointed, it was a bloody good idea... not at all implausible,' he said.

'Still, I'll bet you Miles was right... I bet Billy gave you something... perhaps it's among the papers you picked up with Mrs Braddock.'

'Maybe. Come on, love, enough for tonight, you'll get cold.'

'I *am* cold, darling. I need warming.'

***

Chapter Twenty Three.
Three Birds - One Stone.

'Sod the weather,' said Anne. 'Let's take *Alice* out, let her stretch hers limbs... she's been in harbour too long, and you need a break.'

'You up for taking the helm?'

'*Of course...* I'm fine.'

For two hours he worked hard, sweating every last ounce of performance out of her sails. Squalls blew through, white horses and rain soaking their faces. In the aft cockpit he sat down with Anne. 'Want a break?'

'No, I'm enjoying myself... get your thinking done.'

Half an hour later they tacked. While resetting the main sheets, he said, 'Got it.'

'Got what, darling?'

'Where do you buy your seeds from, love?'

'Thompson & Morgan... a very old firm. Why?'

'Billy once accused me of sowing dragon's teeth. I wasn't then, I was letting some lurking poisons hatch out of the mud. If they're sowable they must be seeds. Do you reckon they'd stock them?'

'I should know what that's about... can't remember,' Anne said. 'Greek wasn't it?'

'Billy said it was... Cadmus, "sow dragon's teeth and

foment dispute". Good old Billy.' Sims looked up to a towering cloud in the sky above. As though Billy was sat comfortably in its billows, he shouted, 'God bless your soul, sir. That's just what I'm going to do. Turn this lovely old girl round, Anne. Let's go home.'

During a brief shower, goose-winging with the brisk wind fully astern, *Alice* plunging into thick heaving swells, bunched up her frilly white bow wave - she looked forever as though she'd hitched up her skirts and, showing her petticoats, was making a dash for cover. *Alice* was happy, this is what she had to give. She loved her children. Her daughter was safe with him: and he had felt and listened to her gentle but insistent urging.

*

'Dragon's teeth, darling. I need to know more,' she said.

'Billy once used me as bait: Passant used you and myself as bait for Billy. Own-back time: let's lay down some dubby and catch ourselves a shark or two.'

'Still not entirely clear, Sims.'

'Passant, Ross, Woodruff: I'm going to foment dispute... get them at each other's throats. Then, we'll take the *Royal Box* and watch the show. I'll start with Woodruff.'

*

Showing him into his office, Sims thought: and now to sow my first gnasher. He leant forward, elbows on the desk.

'So, Passant's got you firmly gripped by the bollocks, Lieutenant-Commander. Making you jump through hoops, is he? I almost feel sorry for you... he's a nasty bastard and no mistake.'

'Commander Sherwood-Reeves, you are not only talking crudely, but in riddles, and I was never good at those. What are you attempting to convey?'

'Go careful. I outrank you. Don't forget to say "sir".'

'I apologise, sir,' Woodruff said. A quick glance at his face told all: he despised Sims' low birth status, elevation to officer class and him being one rank higher than he.

'We'll start again. Passant's got you jumping through hoops. Now, before you repeat you were never good at riddles, listen to this.' Sims played a copy of Fiona's tape. Woodruff, visibly disturbed, shifted uncomfortably in his chair.

'What was *"it"* you wouldn't supply? The Dragunov, maybe? If you've looked you'll have noticed it's no longer in the armoury. I've had it removed and placed somewhere safe. Oh, by the way... you'll be very interested in this; it was the very rifle, NID's own specimen, that fired the round that killed Vice-Admiral Jessop. And, Lieutenant-Commander, all has been ballistically and scientifically proven.. What do you reckon to that, then? What on earth can it have been that made you murder one of your own, and our navy's finest admirals?

Some composure regained, Woodruff coldly said, 'This is a ludicrous conversation, Commander.'

'No it isn't. It's all very straight forward. You see, Admiral Jessop had a list... a list of names of people involved in various misdemeanours. Actually, you weren't on that list to begin with. Yours came along later. On this later list there were only two marksmen, you and James Ross. Now, as the Dragunov was in NID's possession and you had one of the two keys to the cabinet, it's not looking too good for you is it. We wouldn't want to appear unfair, so, just to be certain, we'll be paying James Ross a visit shortly... that's just to make sure it wasn't him... we've got to get our facts straight, haven't we?. However, that's all pending. The other big question is why did Passant threaten to reveal McClusky's original autopsy? What was in it? And, why did he think doing so would make you change your mind?'

'I don't know the detail... there were errors. Perhaps it needed amending.'

'How do you mean errors? Little slips of the pathologist's pen unforgivably and inexplicably mentioning, Scopolamine, Mescaline and LSD? All, in case you don't know, can induce extremes of psychosis. But, silly of me, of course you'd know that... tools of the interrogator's trade, aren't they? A medical man I know called it a nasty little cocktail. The point is though, and one you still haven't answered, why would Passant threaten to reveal this autopsy as a frightener to you. Strange, isn't it?'

'The autopsy didn't mention those things.'

'I agree, the official one didn't. But, this original one did,' said Sims, handing Woodruff the clearest of evidence from the little Schatz & Sohne. Sims pointed to the section on the blood test. 'See what I mean, Scopolamine, Mescaline and LSD. And, if you look at the implied dosage you'll see for any one of them it's way above the prescribed limit for use in interrogations. Poor old McClusky, somehow he managed to self-administer all three all at the same time and in overdose quantities too. Tut, tut. But then, he wasn't an expert, was he?'

'I know nothing about that autopsy report and I know

nothing about Admiral Jessop's killing. What Passant said to me in that private meeting has been misinterpreted. I repeat, I know nothing and am innocent of the implications you are making.'

'We can't prove anything, I admit. But, we know this, you, Ross and Passant are all old boys from Durnford. That's how you're connected. We also know that Passant and Ross were involved in some shady dealing over MI6 funds and that Admiral Jessop was about to reveal the details. Exactly, where you fit in that little lot, we've yet to discover. However, I've got over a million pounds I'm prepared to spend to find the truth about my old, and well loved, boss. I bet you, with a bit of financial inducement Ross will tell all. So I'm going for the sure bet and Ross is it. Now, for you, here's the rub, the Naval Intelligence Division is a thorn in SIS's side. They don't like us, Lieutenant-Commander, and will stop at nothing to make certain we're not represented in the new organisation. So, take this on board, they'll go with Ross' story whether they believe it or not.'

Woodruff, white round the gills, found a sensible measure of control and remained silent. In the circumstances the safer thing to do.

'We'll know if you talk to Passant. Do it and I'll drag you in so quick you'll get friction burns. And, when I've got you in Unit 4, me and my lads will give you a dose of what we think you gave McClusky. That's a promise, Lieutenant-Commander, a promise. As I said, we can't prove anything at the moment... so, you're free to go. I can't get away for a few days, but, once I'm free and I've spoken to Ross, no doubt I'll be back. Now, bear this in mind: my boss was older and a touch more diplomatic...

I'm still young and fire from the hip... got it?'

*

'Hi, babe, any cold beer in the fridge?'

'You look pleased with yourself... tell me.'

'Well, I fed him a load of fact mixed together with quite a dollop of fiction. Perhaps not exactly fiction, call them guesses I'd be prepared to stake money on.'

'And?'

'He looked worried and stayed silent.'

'What next?'

'I'm going to see what else I can get from Le Fanu and then possibly Michael Mondot.'

*

'Mr Le Fanu, I'm a little stuck. Stuck in one of those story gaps I spoke to you of.'

'It must be very hard for you to do your job, Commander. So many closed doors. There's much snobbery in SIS. Your origins won't suit them.'

'Naval or social?'

'Probably both.'

'What about you?'

'I admire bravery, Commander. But, tell me, why should you trust what I say?'

'Not sure really. I confess Gerald Radleigh wasn't a favourite of mine. You, though, acted like... well, like I think friends ought.'

'That might be being a little naïve.'

'I guess I have no option than to be so. Everything I do, every corner I turn takes me somewhere unknown. I use what common sense and ken I have, then, it's up to the Fates and whatever mood the Gods are in. In the new, aren't we all naïve?'

Le Fanu chuckled. 'I suppose we are, yes. That's a very charming and philosophical way of putting it. I can see why Gerald thought you were a decent sort?'

'Did he tell you what I threatened to do to him on the sub? I wasn't exactly being decent then.'

'He was of a forgiving nature, Commander. In more ways than one he was also trapped in something he couldn't get out of... both in his body and by a mistake in his youth... we've all made them. But, and you may find this hard to believe, Gerald was never a killer. That I'm sure of. The two agents on the *Viktor Abakumov* weren't instructed by him to shoot your wife. It was their decision to act the way they did. Their brief was to recover what they could from Bosham Castle and, if possible, to harm Lord Aston-Heyford. He was appalled when he heard what had happened.'

'Most of this has not been made public. He must have told you.'

'Yes, indeed he did. This room was his confessional. It was likely to be his last confession he made here and he knew it. He said, I want to get a breath of English air before I die... that's all I ask for. I sent Gerald to Duns Tew to get that last gasp of freshness, Commander. What else could I do?'

'So then, if you were his confessor, you must know Buster Crabb isn't dead?'

'I suspected so: Gerald confirmed it. It was something bandied about amongst senior security people for many years.'

He chose not to pursue the matter whether Radleigh had been a killer or not. He had his opinion and Le Fanu another. Sims needed to reach *gap filling* time.

'Mr Le Fanu, I'm going to tell you what I think about Admiral Jessop's killing. I'll cut to the chase. James Ross was the shooter... that I'm pretty sure of. The question is why? That's where I'm stuck.'

Sims was not going to beg for help. His instinct told him he didn't need to. Le Fanu was clearly in grief for his old friend: he would set Sims' compass bearings for him.

'I referred earlier to many closed doors, Commander. I do not believe it is the way things should be done. It is not the way we should operate.'

Le Fanu went to the sideboard, gestured to a bottle, 'I know it's early, would you like a drink?' Sims waved the offer aside. 'Do you mind if I have one?'

Le Fanu poured a large brandy for himself, took a sip and once more sat down.

He lightly sniffed and dabbed his nose with a handkerchief. 'Gerald's biggest fault was his ego, and this, I must tell you, defended a huge inferiority complex. A complex maybe developed at home or later at school, and the latter is I think the more likely. Nevertheless, he carried it for no good reason that I ever discovered. So when Lord Aston-Heyford called him a fool. He could not have committed a mistake of greater grossness. Gerald told me this is why he informed the Riga Soviets of the whereabouts of the priest hole and the combination to Bosham Castle: all done in a fit of ego inspired anger, Commander.'

Sims knew this but kept quiet... let him talk, he

thought. He's on a roll.

'You might think this inferior opinion of himself might lead him to be a snob... it often happens that way. This would be an error, though. He certainly lived a good life in Paris. An ideal place for him. He felt sufficiently culturally distanced from the natives for his complex not to show. Now, Commander, after what I've just said, this may sound like a contradiction: my good friend Gerald did not have *a* complex, he had many and they would come and go like the seasons. He was, to put it simply, *entirely* complex. But, no snob.'

Letting him roll on was all very well, but, Sims felt they were going nowhere, and so, before Le Fanu had poured more brandy inside himself, he felt it best to push ahead. 'Did Gerald know Ross?' It had been no lapse of concentration or softening of attitude that caused Sims to use the familiar. 'And, what do you think to my suggestion of him being the shooter?'

'Yes, and, perfectly plausible.' Le Fanu took another sip: slightly larger and longer this time.

Okay, thought Sims, he's getting ready for the big tell. One more swig and it'll be a sledge run... non-stop, wall to wall spilled baked beans.

'I must be clear, I will not put my signature to any of that which I will tell you.'

Sims nodded.

'After Kim Philby defected from Beirut there was quite a spring cleaning of the staff there. In the aftermath of the clear-out, Ross was sent to Berne. He later assisted Passant who had been sent to uncover the measure and magnitude of the MI6 Swiss fund fraud. While they were doing this they discovered or realised no one knew its real extent. So, Commander, they helped themselves to a good portion of it and each of them deposited their share into other Swiss accounts. That way there could be no record of their dealings reaching the ears of the British Government... Swiss banking secrecy, you see. They hadn't been clever... it was simply too simple for them to get wrong. The corollary, Commander... Ross and Passant got away with it... scot-free, absolutely scot-free.'

'How do you know this? Were you in it as well?'

Le Fanu smiled and sipped some more. 'Oh no, Gerald told me. He knew far more about the affair than he told you, Commander. When Gerald helped sort the diplomatic mess for Hoffmann Bank, he insisted he was given every bit of relevant information. It must have been difficult for them, they conceded though, and to guard their reputation, Hoffmanns shopped both Ross and Passant: not that they are aware of it. But Gerald had all the facts and decided to keep quiet... as quiet as Gerald was able to, that is.'

'Why, if he let Heston's role be known, didn't he shop the other two?'

'He couldn't shop Ross for fear of implicating Passant, and he was the much more powerful operator. Gerald knew the extent of Passant's power and influence: he wasn't going to waste such a valuable asset. Information of this kind is useful stowed away for a rainy day: it can calm a tempest. In SIS and the diplomatic service rainy days and tempests are frequent, Commander.'

Le Fanu returned to the sideboard, again offered Sims a drink, again refused. With a full measure he sat down once more.

'So, you see, in the final analysis, Swiss banking secrecy does have a soft under-belly... a chink in its armour... strange that this should be its very own secrecy, don't you think?'

'So, you're telling me that nobody, other than Gerald, knew Passant and Ross had dipped their hands into the kitty?'

'One man did, Commander. And, that man might have been going to blow the whistle.'

'Got a name to fill a gap?'

'Adian McClusky.'

Time slowed. His breathing slow, regular. Heartbeat dropped below sixty beats per minute. Sims thought it the moment to deviate lightly from the truth. He heard his own voice as though it was someone else speaking, 'Don't know the name... what can you tell me about him?'

'Adian McClusky was a handy man at Berne. He had worked variously for MI6, MI5 and God knows what other organisations. Gerald said he was an honest and brave man. I think he was attracted to McClusky: that would have increased his indiscretion... he could be indiscreet at times. Sometimes his enthusiasm for the shocking got the better of him and this is possibly how McClusky ended with the knowledge he died with.'

'Do you think that's why McClusky died?'

'There's a whiff of suspicion about the circumstances, don't you think?'

'I do.'

'McClusky could have also found out about the misdealings from a man called Laurence Heston... perhaps not so much a man as a drunk. McClusky, though not a drunk, liked a drink. They were on a night time binge when Heston talked. Whether McClusky told Heston what he knew is uncertain. What is certain though, shortly after McClusky was recalled to London.'

'Did Gerald ever manage to get evidence of their accounts?'

'Believe me, that wasn't a trick he was going to miss, Commander. He had manouevred Hoffmann Bank into such a position they could hardly refuse.' Le Fanu got up as though to pour himself another. This time he opened a drawer. Sims heard a click; in case Le Fanu had released the safety catch on a side-arm, he quickly stood up and levelled his Browning in readiness. Le Fanu turned round with a sheet of paper in his hand. He gaped, the paper flip-flop floated to the carpet.

'I'm sorry, but for Christ's sake if you're going to make clicking noises, do at least let me know in advance or at least let me see what you're clicking. When you've had as many bullets in you as I have, one gets quite twitchy at such noises.'

'I don't use weapons, Commander. And, let me tell you, I think you may have fallen in with the wrong types.'

Le Fanu picked the paper up and handed it to Sims. He then thought it better to have another brandy after all.

Sims sucked a deep breath in. In front of him he had every detail of Ross and Passant's Swiss bank accounts.

'Mr Le Fanu, once more I'm at loss: why are you prepared to hand this to me? It's dynamite.'

'Put it in your pocket with your gun... it's a copy. You may keep it.'

Le Fanu slowly walked to the window and gazed out across Chelsea Square. Still looking he sniffed and said, 'Passant was the reason Gerald and myself had to separate. He tried to blackmail us.'

'You said, tried. If you separated because of his threats, doesn't that mean he was successful?'

'He wanted far more than our separation, Commander. He wanted to control and influence us in our diplomatic and SIS roles. He also wanted money. I had powerful friends and used them to the full: they applied convincing pressure on him to let matters lie. Those same friends organised Gerald's position in Paris.'

'So, let me get this absolutely straight, you're hoping I'll deal with Passant for you?'

'Yes, Commander.'

'Fair swop,' Sims said, waving the paper at him.

'We have an arrangement, then?'

'Of course! You have no idea how useful this is going to be.'

'I think I do,' said St John Le Fanu.

Sims stood up to leave. He put his hand out, 'Sorry about pulling the Browning on you,' he hesitated, 'and, Mr Le Fanu, may I say I am also very sorry for your loss: I have lost people too.'

'Thank you very much, Commander. I believe that to be sincerely given.'

*

'Let me just hold you, babe. *Christ,* I miss you when you're not around.' He gently sniffed and nibbled her neck and ear. 'You've been working in the garden again.'

'How can you tell?'

'The sun brings out your fragrance.'

'Is that a polite way of saying I smell?'

'No, it's not. Smell doesn't have a turn-on effect.'

'I still turn you on, do I?'

'Always, and all the time, babe.'

'That's nice.'

'Want to see what I've got?'

'Sims, we're married, I know exactly what you've got.'

'For the first time in our married life my little female replica stoker, I *was* talking about something else. St John Le Fanu was more than forthcoming... have we got ourselves some seeds to sow. Take a look at this?'

'God, Sims, this is...'

'*Dynamite*! I know, that's exactly what I said to Le Fanu.'

'How's the best way to use it? This is far too important to waste.'

'We get the squad in on this one, bound to have some good ideas... time for The Running Fox again. You feel up to travelling?'

'God, I wish you'd stop worrying, darling. You're getting as bad as Mike. *Of course* I'm up for it!'

*

In The Running Fox the astonished comments ran from Pat's, *bloody hell*, to Fiona's earthier contribution; *fuck me!*

'We need some thoughts on the best way to use this. You guys know MI5 and MI6 better than Anne or myself. Any ideas?'

Archie laughed, 'Use it carefully... think of the first

rule in bomb disposal and mine clearance; make sure it doesn't go off in your face.'

'This is as dangerous as plutonium,' said Pat.

'*Hang on,* hang on. Sims didn't ask what it was or how dangerous it is,' said Fiona. 'He asked for advice. So, let me throw this in the ring if I may: how about plonking a copy of it on Passant's desk and see what happens. He's going to crap himself.'

'Brilliant,' said Anne. 'Don't you think we should add a note from Woodruff telling him if he reveals McClusky's original autopsy, he'll let the world know about the Swiss accounts? That should get them locking horns.'

Sims said, 'We'll post it from Netley. I'll get a sample of Woodruff's handwriting and, Mike, how about some creative writing?'

'No problem... get as big a sample as possible.'

Allan Johnstone stood up. 'So, Passant gets this in the morning post, what then?'

'We tag them, I guess,' Pat said, looking at Sims for approval.

He nodded. 'Please.'

'Can't we do something for Ross at the same time?' Anne asked.

'Good point. Mike, can you make that two letters... both from Woodruff. We'll work out what to say on the way home.

*

'You must be tired... are you?'

'Just a bit... we'll have a good rest when this all over. We'll take a break. Why do you ask?'

'You're much more serious lately. Don't lose your humour, darling.'

'Things are hotting up, love. The job's winding up. We'll get back to normal when it's over. Billy's murder's something that sits a bit heavy.'

'Yes, doesn't it. I still can't quite believe it.'

They arrived late at Hell Head House. Jean was waiting for them. 'I've something nice in the kitchen.'

'Jean, darling, you should have been in bed hours ago.'

'So should you, my girl. Eat first, though, you need to keep our baby fed. And, you're resting tomorrow... that's an order. I'll not stand any nonsense.'

Sims said, 'I'm going to have a beer with this pie.'

'Your humour may be on the wane... thank God not your appetite. Now, if that were to disappear, I would be really worried. So, what next?'

'Possibly another beer and then some more pie.'

'I meant with Passant.'

'Let Mike do his bit, and while he's doing it, I'm going to see Michael Mondot.'

*

'There were enough people on his tail. We can eliminate Krista... I hope she got back okay.'

'Yes, safe and sound,' Mondot replied.

'*Safe?*'

'As safe as she'll ever be.'

'Hmm, you know you're one of those I would have included on the tailing list? Probably heading it.'

Mondot said nothing: *nothing* said everything.

'I'll keep my trap shut,' said Sims, standing up and offering his accepted hand.

'See you around, Commander. And, thank you.'

'Yeah.'

*

'Michael Mondot did it.'

'Did what, darling?'

'Radleigh.'

'I'm not surprised... I thought he might get their first. We're keeping quiet about this, then?'

'Yeah.'

***

Chapter Twenty Four.
Collision Course.

'Who gets the first letter?'

'Okay, a quick answer to a reasonable question... I reckon Ross.'

'I'll go along with that.' She left the outstanding question hanging. There being no enlargement from him, she sighed and said, 'You have to give me *why*, Sims.'

'Passant has stacks of power and influence. He had a death grip on them both. He pulled the strings and Ross pulled the trigger. Woodruff supplied the gun... we're damned certain of that. I want to leave Jack Passant to last... let the bastard sweat buckets.'

'So, Ross gets number one?'

'Yep. I'll post it soon, but not until I've had a word with Stockley-Grantham.'

'How's Woodruff been behaving himself?'

'Pretty well. The lads have been taking it in turn in the switchboard office... he hasn't made any calls out. They've got Jack Foster and Jimmy Potts to help follow him any time he leaves Unit 4. Dusty reckons he doesn't have the same confident air about him these days.

'If he only knew what's about to hit him. Do you think he'll run for it?'

Nope. I'm guessing he doesn't know what to think... his manual doesn't deal with the kind of crap he's in. He'll just sit tight for now. He'll wait to see how the wind blows.'

'You're sure of that?'

'Can't be... it's what I'd do in his position. Look, love, when you're trapped in the dark and you don't have the coordinates of where you are, or how the land lies, or who's on your side, there's not a lot else you can do, is there?'

'I suppose not. Is this how you felt on The Island, Sims?'

'Until you found me... pretty much.'

Anne got up and sat close beside him.

*

'I haven't long. So, to business. What is it you require?'

'I would like a couriered letter taken to Hoffmann Bank in Switzerland. It must come from The Government and have all the correct signatures and seals. I have the details of two accounts. I want them blocked... frozen.'

'Are you sure they'll do that? I doubt if they'll be easily scared.'

'If they don't cough up, we'll threaten to expose a few details they won't want us to. We must insist Radleigh's name is mentioned in the first letter of instruction... that should concentrate their minds a bit.'

'Is this personal or SIS business?'

'The latter, sir.' Sims handed him a sheet with the account details on it.

'Whose accounts are they, Commander?'

'Jack Passant and James Ross. It's money they filched

while supposedly investigating the MI6 slush fund fraud. Do you think you can get The Government to play ball, sir?'

'Yes, I certainly do.'

'Sir, this has to be done under the strictest of security... let's use a term I learned on the *Odin... silent running* all the way. Here's a little extra you'll like. I am as certain as I can be that Ross pulled the trigger on Billy.'

'*Good Lord!* Are you serious?'

'Yes. There is another person involved in the killing too: a Lieutenant-Commander Woodruff. I have him under close observation. He supplied the Dragunov, Passant acted as lure, and Ross, a marksman, pulled the trigger.'

'I'll take this personally to the minister... this will please him... he went out on a limb over your reinstatement as commander, you know. Now, tell me what evidence have you got?'

'With Woodruff, I have pretty much incontrovertible evidence that in a fit of over enthusiasm he killed Adian McClusky while under interrogation. He then gained a falsified autopsy report with the assistance of Passant. Secondly, he is one of two key holders to the armoury at Netley. It was this NID Dragunov SVD used in the shooting of Admiral Jessop. I have this confirmed with a ballistic report from a test firing.'

Stockley-Grantham came out with his now almost stock retort, '*Good Lord!*'

'Permit me to continue,' said Sims. 'I have a taped recording of Passant demanding something again from Woodruff... it looks like he was attempting blackmail. We believe he wanted use of the Dragunov a second time. Ross, we know, has embezzled MI6 money: as has Passant. Furthermore, Passant is guilty of withholding evidence, namely, the true autopsy findings. You told me you didn't think Billy's killing was at the behest of any group on high. I now think you're right, and if you want my opinion he was killed because they were crapping themselves that McClusky had said something to him or even that Radleigh had.'

'The Dragunov, why did he want that again?'

'Simple. To kill me. By using a Soviet weapon twice, it could be construed as a Soviet revenge killing for Radleigh's double defection.'

'Why connect it with Jessop and yourself.'

'The only likely way Passant and Ross could know about Radleigh being part of a NID operation is that Woodruff told them. He'd been trying to worm his way into the new organisation. He might not know how we got him back, but he would know we'd got him at Netley. So, a revenge killing would be a reasonable argument for them to put forward.'

'What now?'

'Let the letter to Hoffmann Bank take effect. I'll have a team tail them.'

'Why don't we just arrest them?'

'Governments don't seem to like messes: old or new. Lets see what occurs, sir. Let's see if they settle their own scores: a *reglement des comptes,* sir, *leur comptes.'*

*

If he valued his freedom, the letter said, he was not to inform Passant of its existence. Passant was not to be trusted. It also said, he, Woodruff, had the account details coded and in safe keeping, and that Passant was trying to blackmail him into supplying the Dragunov once more, and this implied Passant would get him, Ross, to commit another assassination. Admiral Jessop's killing was merely the beginning, it said. Passant had them both over a barrel. It would not end with two murders. Holding the account details was the only defence he had against someone of infinitely more power and influence. It suggested a meeting somewhere to discuss their way out of the problem: Ross to decide where and when.

*

When he received notice of his Swiss account blockage, he had an inkling it was over - the spree would end: if not that day, very shortly. It was not until he spoke to Hoffman Bank and they said they would not reveal their precise source, but, it came on the highest governmental authority, that Ross knew he would be visited shortly and his liberty ended. In hiding, his money in England would soon dwindle.

For an army officer, killing, if required and ordered, was a part of the job. Privately ordered assassination of one's own countrymen was not. He knew that there was truth in what Woodruff had written. If necessary, Passant would want more killing carried out to protect himself. Ultimately, Passant would only see to his own safety: he had the power and connections to swim clear. Ross was now aware that with taking MI6 funds he had signed his own death warrant. With nowhere to flee, the spectre of prison loomed: he settled that incarceration was never to be an option. Ross prepared for the moment they came to take him and the method of his own end. He thought meeting with Woodruff was clutching at straws, even though, with nothing to lose, he called him.

'We are both trapped,' he said. 'Passant has us both, that much is clear.'

Woodruff assumed he referred to the Dragunov.

'Meet me at Worth Matravers. I hope you can extract us both from the mire,' Ross said.

Dorset Coast South of Worth Matravers.

'Do you remember having to go swimming down there? So cold... all weathers, all seasons... so bloody cold,' said Ross.

'It was to make men of us old Bandy and his wife used to say.'

'An awful man and headmaster. He didn't mention making us killers as well as men, did he?'

'I haven't killed anyone,' Woodruff said, defensively.

'Not directly, maybe.'

'Look, Ross, you suggested we meet here. Talking old school days over isn't what I came to do. I'd sooner forget them.'

Ross looked behind them. 'I think we've been followed.'

'Oh dear, Commander Sherwood-Reeves has been on to us for some time.'

'You kept that quiet.'

'I'd hoped Passant might have stepped in and cleared matters.'

'Little chance of that, I'm afraid. He'll be busy looking after his own affairs.'

Of the treasure of stories told since the first: *Gilgamesh*, many have been capable of ambiguity and mishearing by the listener. This one, a story featuring a dragon's tooth, written by Anne and Sims was to join the hoard.

Ross looked out the rear window again. 'I know you know my secret: Passant's too. We know your secret as well... I think the dam is about to burst. We've had it,' Ross said, bleakly.

'Yes, it's worrying'

'I've always suspected it may come to this... they've frozen my account.'

Woodruff stared blankly out of the side window barely listening to Ross's words nor, therefore, realising their portent. 'Killing an admiral... life imprisonment. Yes, just like that bloody school: life imprisonment... it was a rotten way to start, wasn't it?'

Ross listened to the inanity of Woodruff's words. He could see nothing helpful was coming from him. 'What did old Bandy say? "Seek your own solutions to the problems you make". I think this is for the best. They'll get us one way or another' he said. Ross firmly gripped the hand-grenade, pulled the pin then released the lever.

The brilliant flash seen - reddened, flesh frosted windows splaying outwards, a second later the explosion heard and felt.

Dusty shouted, 'Fuck a duck. What's going *on*?'

'Something we'll be too late to do anything about,' said, Sub-Lieutenant Mountford, already up and running down the slope to the cliff edge.

'Sir, sir... stop. Stop now. Stop, fucking NOW!' said Dusty, grabbing his partner's coat.

They were still three hundred yards away from the

wrecked and smoking car.

'What? What?, Mountford shouted, coming to a halt, snatching free and running again.

Dusty tackled and brought him down, 'We need to keep out of it. We'd best to keep NID's nose clean, sir. They're sure to drop it on their lap... which means Sims and Anne's lap... let's go for fuck's sake... come on, shake out of it, sir.'

'Yes. Okay, you're right,' he said, rising and staring at the disintegrated remains of the car. 'There's nothing we can do.'

Dusty tugged his coat, 'Well, come on, let's put the decision into practice, then... let's scarper before we're spotted.'

*

'Hey-yup,' said Sims. 'The lads are here... looking a touch serious, too.'

David Mountford opened the batting, 'They're both dead, sir.'

'Steady, David. Who are both?'

'Ross and Woodruff, sir.'

'*Jesus*,' said Sims.

'Better give us the full story,' said Anne.

'Woodruff received a call early this morning from Ross. He left Netley... we followed him. He met Ross at Worth Matravers in Dorset and got in his car. They turned down a lane... Winspit Bottom Road.'

'More a track than a road,' said Dusty.

'When it looked as though we were nearing the coast-line, we took a small track to the left... I thought we could watch them from the cover of some trees. I'd taken our binoculars. They stopped in full view. They seemed to be talking normally... no violence. Woodruff looked and pointed down to the shore. I doubt if they were stationary for more than five minutes. Then the car seemed to erupt in a flash of light. We started running towards the car... Dusty had the presence of mind to suggest our best course of action was to leave immediately... keep NID out of it, sir. That's about it, we came straight back here. There's was no way they could have survived.'

'Anything to add to that, Dusty?'

'Not really, it's just as the sub-lieutenant said... hell of a bang... bits of body and car flying everywhere.'

'Well, that's two more off the list. I'd like to have got that bugger Ross myself, though. Still, that's history now. Lads, you know the routine, anyone asks questions, you know nothing. And, well done both of you.'

*

'What next?'

'Cry havoc, take advantage: then watch from the *Royal Box*.'

'God, that's a bit Machiavellian,' gasped Anne.

'Sod all to do with him, babe... original, all mine.'

Jean called, 'Sims, there's an Admiral Stockley-Grantham on the phone for you.'

'Sir?'

'Your hand in this do, Commander?'

'No, sir. Not directly.'

'I have your word?'

'Yes, sir.'

'Hmm... you said, not directly. Indirectly, then?'

'I may have stirred things a little.'

'A little?'

'Maybe more than a little.'

'Hmm. Any more to come?'

'With any luck, sir.'

'Hmm. I'm putting a lot of faith in you, Commander.'

'I hope in the end it will be seen as having been well founded.'

'Hmm.

'Are the janitors on to it?'

'Yes.'

'I'd like to know their findings.'

'Hmm.'

*

Breathless, Laurence Heston practically fell into Blunt's apartment, 'Ross's dead... car blew up by the coast in Dorset... not far from his old school... somebody else with him. They haven't identified the other person yet. Naval officer, they say.'

Passant said not a word.

'Didn't you hear, Jack. Your old partner Ross is dead. Surely that raises some feeling?'

'I'll use the phone,' he said to Blunt.

'Ross is dead. What do you suggest we do?'

'*We?* I don't need to do anything,' said the banker on the end of the line. 'You must do what ever's necessary to save your own neck, Mr Passant. Don't call me again.' The line clicked and went dead.

'Damn him,' Passant said, quietly. 'Damn him, damn Ross, damn Woodruff and damn Sherwood-Reeves. His hand is in this. His grubby tar-stained prints are all over it.'

Only a few late workers were in the building. Passant signed in, ignored the receptionist's small talk and went straight to his office. His bad news day was not over. A knock on the door. 'Come,' he snapped.

'You didn't wait, sir. A telegram. And...' he said pointing, 'I put that letter on your desk earlier, sir.'

Passant snatched the telegram out of his hand, 'Go.'

Swiss banks are careful how they spend their money: it was a cryptic message:

```
PLEASE BE INFORMED THAT YOUR ACCOUNT
HAS BEEN BLOCKED UNTIL FURTHER NOTICE.
STOP
    HB ZURICH STOP
```

How dare they? I'll deal with this later, he thought, and folded the telegram into his wallet.

Passant carefully slit open the large envelope and stared in disbelief at the contents: a blown up print of Adian McClusky's original, undoctored autopsy report and a sheet with his and Ross's Swiss bank account details. They were both signed by Woodruff following a short message: I will not supply the Dragunov a second time.

'How can you, you're probably dead,' he muttered. The implication obvious, others knew now. Who were they?

Code entered, he slid open the drawer to his secure filing cabinet. McClusky's autopsy report was not there. He scrabbled through several other files. Not there either. Archie Abbot had left his office an hour before.

'Woodruff, Netley, Sherwood-Reeves, I'll beard him in his den.'

*

Passant made a single call.

'Heston, if you value your freedom, you'll bring your side-arm and meet me outside the office in half an hour. We must use your car. Get Scammel too. We may need his father's assistance.'

'You have a place on the Beaulieu River. Drive there.'

'What's up, Jack?' asked Heston.

'Our Swiss operation has been uncovered... I believe Sherwood-Reeves has the details of our accounts... it can only be him. We have to silence him.'

Heston looked worried. 'The Government won't touch me... can't afford to.'

'If the information Sherwood-Reeves has is made public, they will make a clean breast of it, there will be a clear out of unresolved issues. You, and all your assets, Heston, will be included.'

Scammel unscrewed his hip-flask and took a long swig. 'They've got nothing on me,' he said.

'Think again, Scammel. I hope your drinking hasn't affected your aim.'

'Are you sure this is a wise move, Jack? His reputation is of an ace shot... I can't say I fancy taking him on.'

*

Anne was with him, Sims flicked on the loudspeaker, 'Sir?'

'I've had word that Passant has left the building in

company with Heston and Scammel. My informant says he was armed. I'm issuing a request for his arrest. He's after someone... as you are aware, it's possibly you, Sims. Keep your eyes open. I'll let you know as soon as we have him.'

'Who gave you the word, sir?'

'Need to know, Commander.'

'Thank you, sir. What make of gun does he carry or is that need to know too?'

Stockley-Grantham sighed, 'No it's not, young man. Colt... large calibre... forty five.'

'He means business, then.'

'Looks like it. Go careful.'

*

Sims sat smiling. She beside him frowning.

'You're completely impossible. Will you please tell me what's so amusing, darling?'

'He called me *Sims*. He's on our side, babe... home team.'

Anne shook her head, 'I will never, ever understand you, never ever. I bet you've still an appetite too.'

'That's a very good point,' he said.

*

The following morning the newspapers briefly covered a double fatality in Dorset - details were minimal. The cause of the deaths unknown: police are carrying out initial investigations, the report said.

On the ten o'clock morning news, the public was warned that an armed and dangerous man was being sought by the authorities. His name and an accurate description was given. An unnecessary extra piece of advice issued; under no circumstances was this man to be approached.

*

'I'll get all four of the lads down here, watch and watch about, to keep an eye on Jean.'

'What are *we* going to do, Sims?'

'Take our mind off things... take *Alice* out for a while. Not a lot else we can do until the law has nabbed him.'

*

Early the following morning *Alice Alacrity* had barely cleared the harbour at Hell Head Harbour when the phone rang at the house. Jean answered. 'Captain Sherwood-Reeves and his wife are out sailing. I'm not sure when they will be back.'

'Look, I've been talking to an old friend of his, James Fox-Eastleigh. I'm thinking of buying a yacht and needed his opinion on a couple of matters. Do you know what type of boat he has? I forgot to ask Mr Fox-Eastleigh.'

'Oh yes,' Jean said, helpfully. 'It's a large and old ketch called *Alice Alacrity.* Lovely boat. Don't like sailing myself, can't stand water that comes above my knees. Sharks are known to have taken people even at that shallow depth.'

'I can understand your fears. Some people are better on dry land,' said Scammel. 'Tell me, any idea where they're headed today? I might take my launch out and meet them. That would surprise them wouldn't it?'

'Well, let me see. Sims said they'd head upwind and give themselves an easy run home... to tell you truth, young man, I have no idea where upwind is today.'

'Look, you've been so helpful... can't thank you enough.'

'Oh, it's nothing,' Jean said.

Walking back to the kitchen she muttered, 'Should have asked him his name... never mind.'

*

'She said they were out sailing... heading upwind. If that's relevant, Laurence?'

'Essential knowledge if you're in a yacht. Don't you know anything, Scammel?'

'I know I'm thirsty,' he said.

Heston laid out a map on the table. 'Wind's west by south west. They'll be headed down The Solent for Gurnard Bay or The Needles. What sort of boat is it?'

'An old ketch... *Alice Alacrity.*'

'It's time we left,' said Passant.

*

They tacked many times - each one on a short reach. Enjoying each other's company, they did not concern themselves with an exact destination. As long as they were together, and home in time for supper, that was enough.

The fresh breeze gave Sims plenty to do. He refused to let Anne help him raise the mainsail. 'Sit down and steer,' he said firmly. 'I won't be argued with on this point... *steer!*'

Anne watching him working, wolf-whistled and shouted, 'You look lovely in that 'T' shirt. Where did you get those muscles, handsome?'

422

'Nocturnal wrestling with an ex wren second officer. She's a bit of a handful.'

'You've got to keep fit some how,' she said, laughing.

'Good a way as any...'

Sims scanned the waters. To starboard, several miles away, a launch travelling at high speed looked as though it might cross their path.

A few minutes later he looked for the launch again.

There exists a rule of navigation, and it is this: if a crossing boat is observed and its angular position relative to your vessel does not alter with successive sightings, then, you must be on a collision course.

'Sit and steer from the bottom of the cockpit, love... and do it *now*.' Sims started *Alice's* engine, rapidly dropped the sails and went down into the cabin. He lifted the bunk and from the locker beneath withdrew the loaded Dragunov. From their harnesses swinging on a hook he took Anne's Beretta and his Browning. He double checked both magazines were full and made them ready. That done, he grabbed two spare magazines for both guns. He then radioed Sam Bradley.

'Sam, get *Sylvie* round to Hell Head Harbour as quick as Christ will let you. Pick up three men who'll be waiting. When you've done that, get as quick as possible to us in Thorness Bay. Don't hang around, Sam, we may be in a spot of bother.'

He next radioed Hell Head House,'David, we could be in trouble. Sam's on his way to Hell Head Harbour with *Big Sylvie*. Bring Dusty and Jimmy Potts. Leave

Foster to look after Jean and man the radio. Full Speed ahead, David. Fully armed, lad.'

'We're on our way, sir.'

Sims returned to the cockpit carrying the guns and magazines. He looked for the launch: the same angular positioning. Anne grabbed her Beretta, 'What's happening?'

'Launch bearing down on us fast. Been on the same bearing each time I've checked... no coincidence. I've radioed the lads. Something's up, babe. Head towards the coast at Great Thorness. We'll delay things as long as possible. Keep your head down, love.'

She took a rapid look at their heading. 'There are some nasty rocks ahead.'

'I know, try not to run into them.'

He focused and fixed his binoculars. 'Launch: *Heston's Heist,* five hundred yards and closing fast. Heston at the helm,' he shouted.

At forty yards Passant fired six rounds.

'Too quick off the mark, Passant,' he called. 'Colt forty five, a singing cowboy's pop-gun.'

Passant ducked down and reloaded.

Scammel looked drunk. He stood up and wildly let go two shots way off target.

One of those rounds could have taken someone's eye out, Sims thought. Seems almost indecent killing such a twat. He squeezed the Dragunov's trigger. Scammel contorted, took several paces backwards in surprise and toppled over the launch's gunwale.

Twenty five yards and well within Passant's Colt's range, Heston spun the wheel hard to port. With a free hand he pointed his gun at *Alice* and fired. The launch hit its own wash and rolled violently. For a brief second Heston hung on to the wheel for support. Sims took this opportunity to shoot him in the back of the head. He lurched forward jamming one throttle wide open ahead and the other astern. Passant unable to lift the body clear of the wheel ducked out of sight once more.

'Rocks close... only Passant left, honey,' he shouted to Anne. 'When I say go, put in a hard to starboard, babe.'

A flash-back of them together in the little field, the old gun emplacement, and to the day of his shooting. 'All flares fired, darling,' she said.

'Go, babe,' he said, smiling at her. He dumped the Dragunov and took up his Browning.

Alice's twenty five tons took longer to turn. Heston's launch turning out of control came within a few yards.

Not to be left out, Anne poked her Beretta over the gunwale and emptied its magazine into the launch. 'That will keep his head down for a second or two.'

Passant stood up and fired. Sims felt the bullet sear through his side. Clutching the wound he let loose three rounds into Passant's chest. 'That's for murdering my mate Billy Ruffian... and I've still got ten left. Want some more?' he said, firing off another two shots.

It was not an immediate death. Passant looked furious - as though his job description didn't allow for him to be killed. He staggered towards the stern and fell into the launch's wake.

Alice and Anne were out of danger now. 'You can stand up now, babe. But, keep your eyes out to sea... not a nice sight.' He closed *Alice's* throttle and brought her to a standstill.

The launch in a series of crazy circles crashed and heaved into its own wash and wake several times. Twice it ran down Passant's body: thrashing propellers stripping long twisted rashers from his torso and severing his flailing arms. Sims, not sure if he had made a clean kill, thought, *fuck him*.

In the thrashing maelstrom created by his own boat, Heston's body finally detached itself from the wheel, slid sideways and pushed the other throttle also fully rearwards. *Heston's Heist*, going astern at around sixteen knots, made speedy landfall and splintered catastrophically onto the short stretch of unforgiving rocks of Thorness Bay. She quickly took on water, her engines gave a diesel death rattle, gurgled, groaned and stopped. The stricken launch floated clear a few yards and then sank, only the upper part of her once luxurious cabin and Heston's bobbing body remaining above the blood tinted waves.

'Sims, what's happened to you?'

'Not much... stand off one hundred yards or so,' he said.

'Are you sure?'

'Yes, stand off.' Pressing his 'T' shirt to his side he went to the cabin and radioed Hell Head House, 'Jack, contact Admiral Stockley-Grantham and ask for the janitors to be sent by helicopter to the coast at Great Thorness on the Isle of Wight. Tell him we've had a clean sweep. Unable to rescue the crew of three from an unfortunate shipwreck and a watery end.'

Sam slewed *Sylvie* alongside the harbour steps. Four men waited, Rear-Admiral Sherwood had arrived just as the lads rushed out of Hell Head House.

A minute into their journey, Jimmy Potts picked up the second, and *all clear* message from Sims.

Anne snatched the mike, 'Jack get medical assistance... helicopter, Lee on Solent... Sims is wounded. Get Haslar notified.'

This also picked up by Jimmy, he poked his head out of the mid-ships cabin and shouted, 'Sims has taken damage. They're asking for medical assistance.'

'How long before we get there, Sam?' asked Dusty.

'Got to be twenty minutes to half an hour,' replied Sam.

'Can you get any more out of her, lad?' asked the Rear-Admiral.

'Only if someone else takes the wheel, sir. I need to get into the engine compartment and back off the throttle stops... could break the engine, sir.'

'Give the wheel to me, and go and screw every last ounce out of her... if we break her, I'll get you another... go to it, lad.'

Less than ten minutes later the first of two Wessex helicopters could be seen heading towards The Island.

*

'Best I get on deck,' he said.

427

'Careful, darling, you've lost blood.'

'It always looks more than's been really spilt.'

'No, Sims. You really have lost a lot. Let me help you up the steps.'

'I can manage,' he grunted.

Sat on the cockpit deck, Anne said, 'Let me look at it, Sims.' She gently lifted his arm and 'T' shirt out of the way. 'Oh, God, that looks nasty, darling. I'm going to cut your shirt off and press it onto the wound. We need to stop you bleeding,' she said, her concern for him masked by the need for action.

As she did so, he sucked his breath in and leaned on her. 'Another one for the collection,' he said.

'Collection of what, darling?'

'War wounds.'

She tried a comforting response, 'Sims, if they are to give you a ring for every bullet you've taken... this one will get you to commodore,' she said, holding the shirt against the wound.

Complexion ashen. 'Naturally, *naturally!* That's why I took it,' he said. 'You accountants *do* take so long to catch on.'

The throbbing thump of the helicopter's rotor came upon them suddenly as it appeared at low level from the north.

'I want to come with you.'

'You can't. You need to look after *Alice* until help comes. Don't argue, love. One of the lads can help you sail her back.'

Anne watched the chopper until it disappeared.

*

'Anne, are you alright.' Were the first words her father spoke. 'And, Sims, how bad?'

'A nasty wound to his left side... looked clean, I think the bullet passed right through, though. As you can see, he lost a lot of blood... I want to get to Haslar as soon as possible, Father.'

'We need to take care of this mess first.'

The Wessex returned and lowered one of the crew with a rescue harness. 'Your husband asked us to come and pick you up, ma'am. We'll come back and fetch the bodies straight after delivering ma'am, sir,' he said to the admiral.

'Away with you, Anne.'

Jimmy Potts roped Scammel's legs around the ankles and hitched him to the stern of *Sylvie*. Dusty hooked Heston's body floating free a few yards away and followed Jimmy's example. Passant was a mess, David looked queasy but got on with the job of dragging him to the launch's side.

'Three more to his name... and, it's not even fucking tot time,' said Dusty. 'If he ever puts in a full day, it's gonna look like the bleedin' Somme.'

*

'Well, Commander...'

'Sure to be a Captain soon,' said Anne.

'And deserved too,' said Surgeon Commander Monroe. 'Anything to do with the conversation we had?'

'Yep. And, that's the last admiral any of those buggers are going to kill.'

'I'm glad to hear it. You're going to have to stay in Haslar for at least a couple of days... then, it's rest for you. You will need to convalesce. Which reminds me, no doubt you will do a little sailing. Perhaps, I could come like you promised... you could give me the full story.

'I look forward to it. You may have to give me a nudge. I have a feeling I'm going to have to answer quite a lot of questions.'

Monroe smiled. 'That's why I shall recommend at least a month's light duties, Commander.'

*

The Janitors commandeered a buoy lifting bar-boat to raise *Heston's Heist* and transport it to Pompey dockyard. Evidence of the truth would need to be removed. Their chief, Tina Dally, would talk persuasively to the insurers.

BBC news reported a triple drowning tragedy off the Isle of Wight coast.

*

He had been made comfortable on the sofa. Harry paid great attention to him. He knew something was wrong and gently sniffed the dressings, then lay down on the rug beside.

Jean came in, 'While you were away, Sims, someone called wanting some advice about buying a yacht. I am sorry, I didn't think to get his name. He said he was a friend of James.'

'Don't worry, love. I met him the other day. He

430

decided the sea wasn't for him... a bit too dangerous... not really his thing.'

She had not forgiven Sims for being shot. 'You'll need feeding,' she said, frostily and starting to close the door behind her.

'So, I don't get a kiss, then. It's all over between us, is it?'

Slowly the door reopened.

***

Chapter Twenty Five

Reluctant Hero.

***Extraordinary Meeting of
SIS Governing Committee.***

Air Vice-Marshal Hanson, Admiral Stockley-Grantham, Major-General Lewis took coffee before the meeting. Stockley-Grantham, his elbow on the table and his other hand on his knee, smiled and said, 'He has a stroppy reputation. Perhaps we ought to see how far we can push him... see how he stands up for himself. Might be entertaining.'

'Could be fun, and by God we could do with a bit of light relief,' said Hanson, dropping two sugar lumps into his coffee.

Major-General Sir Richard Lewis coughed, 'I'll open proceedings... threaten him over the money, that should get him going. I'll throw in a softener first. Now this is the manoeuvre we must do: at the right moment and if necessary, both of you come at him from the each side... a pincer movement.'

'Perfect,' said Stockley-Grantham.

Sims faced the formidable and stoney faced group sat

on the opposite side of the table. I wonder if they have a pulse? he thought.

Lewis tapped for attention, 'We have studied the evidence before us and are of the opinion you have no charges to face. Well done, Commander, your exploits over the past few years are impressive.' He paused and, when he considered he had waited long enough to throw Sims off balance, said, 'However, it is also our unanimous opinion that the money you possess, formerly that of Gerald Radleigh deceased, is not rightfully yours and should be immediately handed to the Exchequer. The exact mechanism for the hand-over is to be finalised shortly. In the meantime all interest earned on this illegal deposit is also to be forfeited.'

Eye to eye Sims looked at each of them in turn. 'Quite finished are we? I thought it might come to this. The cash is *mine*, and I'm not about to give it up... I hope you're all taking notes... *it's mine*. There is a deal I will do... it's not negotiable. My captaincy, or I take no part in SIS.'

'You are not in a position to make deals, Commander Sherwood-Reeves. We can break you and your family.'

'*Break my family!* Can you all be so thoroughly stupid as to believe I haven't covered my tracks and that I haven't expected something like this to occur... give me a break, I've heard more persuasive arguments on a stokers' mess deck,' he said, half standing up.

'You had better keep your tongue in check.'

He sat down again. 'Why? I might not be able to defeat you, I'm pretty sure of that, but, I can, and will, run you ragged. Don't think for a moment I can't and won't. So, your move, I guess. My information about Commander Crabb and MI6's flagrant and unchecked use of tax payers' money, buys protection for my entire family and myself. I have it written, signed and distributed to several locations where, I might add, you have no authority. So, make sure we live out our natural lives fully. If any aspect of our deaths seems implausible then the shit will really hit the fan and you... all of you will be crucified. As you can see, it's in your own interest to make sure we live long and healthy. After 2057 I guess the truth will be out about Buster, and as Anne's and my one hundredth birthdays will be well behind us, I don't think we'll worry too much what you do... looking at you lot, you'll all be long gone, anyhow. And, just so it really sank in, I'll repeat what I just said: *my captaincy, or I take no part in SIS.* Award it or we part company. Sort that lot out if you can.'

Admiral Stockley-Grantham could no longer stifle his smile. The others started table thumping.

Bastards! They're taking the piss, thought Sims, standing up and preparing to leave. 'I'm off,' he said.

The table thumping stopped.

'Stay where you are, Commander, things are not what you think,' said Air Vice-Marshal Hanson. 'In the murky world we inhabit, we find we are always in need of fighters. There is no doubt in my mind you are Admiral Billy Ruffian incarnate, you pass scrutiny well.'

Still furious, he asked, 'Scrutiny for what?'

'Your new role.'

'You haven't said what it is, and what if I don't want it? What if I tell you all to get stuffed?'

'Sims, I think it's time to calm down. When you've heard what's on offer, you may think differently. I need to see you tomorrow... here, 10:00 hours on the dot,' said,

Stockley-Grantham. 'Please attend.'

General Lewis took over, 'Young man, some think you are a danger to all that we stand for. However, the important thing is, all of *us*, Commander, think you are a danger worth bearing... ...Admiral Jessop said you possessed an old head on young shoulders and that you were loyal. I would have added, a head that is sometimes a little hot. However, we need that freshness and loyalty... and, I suppose, with those benefits we have to accept your tendency to overheat. Welcome! Welcome officially to the senior ranks of the new British Intelligence Service.'

*

Anne and her father were waiting for news at Hell Head House when he called, 'How did it go, darling?' She sounded worried.

Her father listening in, 'Come on, we want to know.'

Sims scratched his head. 'How did it go? That's a difficult one. The buggers tried to wind me up... they succeeded. I might have come across a bit bolshie... let my mouth off... could have been a big error.'

'Sims, what happened. What did you say?' He could tell Anne was frowning a special.

'Don't panic, I left them with plenty to think about.'

'Yes, I can imagine, and that's all very well, but what happened?'

'Bit of a mystery really... looks like I'm into something special... not sure exactly what at the moment. A kind of SIS freemasons without the bare legs. I hope Stockley-Grantham will tell me what later. The cash is ours, though, babe... I made sure they understood that.'

'Are they trustworthy?' she asked. 'Can you trust them?'

'Well, funny enough, I think so. Anyhow, we've got the cash and I've a meeting with the boss first thing... gonna have to stay overnight.'

'Don't pick up any more war wounds, Sims. It won't only be Jean who'll be angry if you do.'

'Yes dear.'

*

'Come in Captain.' Admiral Stockley-Grantham smiled and pointed to the chair opposite his. 'Coffee?'

'Coffee, please, yes... Captain? Since when?'

'Since yesterday. We had a few things to tidy up... couldn't tell you then. I thought I'd tell you face to face today.'

Sims wary, 'No conditions attached like, "we want the dosh"?'

'No. No conditions. There's mixed feelings in Admiralty House and SIS, though. Let's say, the doctors were of different opinions. Many gave the verdict it's legally and rightfully yours, others have no legal argument against, they are simply outraged at your good fortune. Fortunately, those in favour were in the large majority and, importantly, that included the Minister of Defence.'

'Hmm, well, I'm not going home until I've got that fourth ring sewn on. Perhaps you'll be good enough to give me the name of a good naval tailor?'

'Business, Sims, business, Le Fanu, Creasy and Greave, they're still alive... innocent?'

'Le Fanu, yes, good man. The other two, not sure, nothing positive though. Billy put them on the list, he must have had suspicions. I think a close watch is needed on Rede-Elliot and then there's Blunt of course. Surely we can't let him off?'

'We watch him very closely... for the public's benefit he'll be unmasked one day, but not by us at the moment. He thinks he's safe where he is. We keep tabs on him. It needs to be left that way for the moment. Enjoy your convalescence, Captain.'

'Thanks. And they definitely don't want the dosh?'

'Definitely.'

'Hmm. Wouldn't make any difference if they did.'

*

At eight o'clock that evening, the staff car drove away from Hell Head House. His jacket slung over his shoulder, and as casually as he was able with a bandaged midriff, Sims strolled into the hall. Harry sniffed his coat to see where and with whom he'd been, he then checked the dressings. Roles reversed with their dog, Anne bit him. 'You're late. How are you feeling? Weary?'

'Yeah, busy day.'

'Beer?'

'Unless there's any champers, it'll have to do,' he said, throwing his jacket over the back of a chair.

Anne was half-way to the kitchen before the obvious registered.

'*Oh God, oh God! Jean, Jean!* Come and see.'

'Took you long enough,' he said, smiling. 'Told you I'd get it, didn't I?'

'*Oh God,* I don't know what to do.'

'Try putting something appropriate in the freezer.'

Frostiness long over, 'Put it on, Sims. I want to see

437

what my boy looks like,' said Jean.

The two women fussed around him - made him parade up and down and around the hall. Then, Anne photographed him.

'I'm going to phone Joss. And, Dad ought to be told.'

'I'll see to the drink... nobody's gonna get any sense out of you two.'

*

Hell Head House.

He looked at the small group around him. Captain Miles Stinton and Admiral Sherwood sat slightly apart. Earlier, Miles confessed he was wrong about the motives for Billy's killing. Sims had said it was plausible reasoning, and that he too had thought along the same lines and at first couldn't accept anything other than it stemmed from an order from the highest authority.

He addressed the small meeting, 'Do you want to know a hard truth? A truth almost sadder than his death. It was about nothing high level. Not about Buster Crabb's defection. Not the result of some great opposing ideological entities fighting it out to the end. And, no battle of the gods. Billy's death was a simple low level murder committed by three cornered rats. And, through these vermin, I lost a friend and Britain a top admiral. Suffer no regrets for your roles in their comeuppance.'

He turned and addressed his squad, 'Sub-Lieutenant David Mountford, Leading Seaman Dusty Miller, Leading Seaman Jack Foster and Leading Stoker Jimmy Potts, you were all fresh out of training... you all performed so well. In the future much may be written about what happened and why: read avidly; believe sparingly... warily... carefully... cautiously. I wish I could paint you the bigger picture. My new role in SIS does not permit me to do so. Believe me, I regret being unable to, lads.' He shook each of their hands in turn.

'Now, before we drink a toast to Billy Ruffian and then start eating and drinking in earnest, there is one other thing you should know; there isn't one of you I wouldn't work with again. So, wherever you go and whatever you do, keep in touch. And, above all, please take care.'

David stood and gave an emotional vote of thanks. Anne in tears managed the toast, 'To Billy Ruffian, chance meetings...'

'... and *Alice Alacrity*,' added Sims.

*

Slow to heal, his wound frustrated him. They could not sail *Alice* on their own - for different reasons neither capable of raising the mainsail. As happy as they were sailing with Anne's father, Miles Stinton or Surgeon Commander Monroe, *on their own* was how they liked it best: silly chat and the laughing moments it evoked. Private times, intimacies, confidences and *Alice* whispering to them.

They enjoyed their walks together. On one, Anne confessed she always felt close to her mother when they sailed *Alice*. Sims told her he felt the same way. 'I feel her near,' he said, one day. 'I talk to her and she answers. Not with words: with breezes, ripples and rustles... I have to let my mind go and listen.'

*

Sat with Anne in the kitchen, Jean declared he had stopped laughing. 'I haven't heard him say anything rude for ages... and where has his smile gone.'

'I can't get to the bottom of him at the moment. I thought if I said nothing he'd come round.'

'You'd best have a long talk with him, Anne love. Don't let him off the hook until he does.'

'I'll do that. Where is he?'

'He's gone upstairs this last hour... and when you're there, don't forget what you went for, my girl,' she said, smiling.

She found him lying on their bed.

'Sims, you're going to have to talk to me, darling. What's on your mind?'

'Nothing much... I've been thinking and getting nowhere.'

'Keep going.'

'I suppose getting nowhere just about sums it up. In the scope of things, Anne, I don't feel as though I have really achieved anything. Get rid of Les Grands Amis, Passant and his gang, and another will take its place.'

'Maybe you're right: only partially though. How would it be if we did nothing? How could you guarantee they wouldn't take over completely. What we, you, are doing is helping to keep the balance. I think you know this. There's something else isn't there? Come on, Sims, out with it.'

'Hmm. You know as well as I do, we got quite close to the lads. I worry about them. They're still green and there will be times when it seems to them that madness and chaos lie at the heart of all. What are they going to get themselves into? David and Dusty have been drafted to the far east. There's big trouble brewing there. Are they really ready to face what they may be up against?'

She took his hand. 'You weren't, Sims. You came through, though. You only had your wits and accuracy: they, on the other hand, were trained by the very best: *you.*'

'That's all very well, but every time I give a lecture I feel as I'm conning these new recruits into an early death. You said they look up to me. I don't want to be someone's hero, Anne. I don't want people to get killed trying to emulate me. I've been lucky that's all. Millimetres lucky. Minute fractions of an inch lucky; seconds and milliseconds from being topped. I've been lucky finding you... If you hadn't been with me I'd be dead. I'm not brilliant, Anne: just fucking lucky.'

'Sims, it isn't simply down to luck. You are brilliant at what you do: thinking, shooting and displaying so much resolution and courage. And, you cannot say you haven't achieved anything... that is absurd. You revealed and closed down a Soviet spy cell almost single handedly. You exposed and neutralised les Grands Amis and their drug running. You brought back Radleigh from behind the iron curtain and got him to sign a confession about Buster, and then MI6's cavalier and criminal use of British Government funds. You found Billy's killers and effectively put an end to them too. You are one of the reasons the Royal Navy is to be so strongly represented in SIS. You have forged strong bonds between The Forest Brothers and Great Britain, and..' she laughed, '... and, you became a millionaire whilst doing all that. Darling, how can you even begin to think you haven't achieved much. Look closely at others around you, measure their performance. Sims, it doesn't bear comparison.'

'I didn't do it on my own... you were always there. And, don't forget, Billy said espionage never ceases. Do I carry on until one or both of us are killed and we leave our children orphans... we know what that feels like.'

'That's not quite true. I still had father.'

'Yes, well... maybe. Anyway, it's not a nice feeling, love. And, how long will it be before I feel I have to keep showing my worth... I've seen this happen to other people... it's destructive.'

'You do not have to prove yourself to me or anyone at Hell Head House: nor to Maggie, Derek, Mo, Chief, Pearl and all the others. And, Sims, your new role is in recognition of the work you've done... see it as retirement from the front line. They said you will never get a medal, this is their reward. Don't you see that? If you were to do nothing for the rest of your life, you will still have done far, far more than most. I am so very, very proud of you.'

'Billy's list isn't wiped clean yet. There's Blunt; Creasy and Greave. And, what about Blunt? Billy went to great lengths telling us about him, and he's still swanning around in Buckingham Palace. There's also Rede-Elliot: just how clean is he? Think about Greave again: SIS liaison with CIA... Billy must have suspected something going on there. I didn't get any of those, did I?'

*

She spoke to Monroe, 'Is he fit enough to put load onto his wound?' she asked. 'To do work: he needs to do work.'

'What manner of work had you in mind?'

'Sailing *Alice*...' she took a breath, '...on his own.'

'If I may ask, why alone?'

'He needs to straighten certain things in his mind. *Alice* does this for him. In a way, she talks to him, and the sooner he has time alone with her, the better he'll be.'

'Tell him to come and see me tomorrow.'

*

For three weeks he sailed nearly every day: occasionally with Anne, though mostly solo. He took on colour again, his tan darkened, his face brightened. Jean noticed and said he was smiling again and that he'd said something quite disgusting at breakfast. Anne decided the time was right. He was ready.

*

She sat waiting for him on the front steps at Hell Head House.

With little trace of stiffness he strolled up the drive. 'What's Alistair doing here?' he asked. 'Not after Jean, is he?'

She smiled, 'No of course not. He's not here.'

'So, what's with the Jag?' Sims asked, sauntering over to it.

'Read the note on the steering wheel.'

For my darling, you deserve it.

'Bugger, I told him never to call me darling.'

A giggle replaced her smile; this was her Sims; Sims the sod; her sod... he was back.

He knelt before her. 'Anne, you have to believe me: it was a crazy moment... we were both lonely... it won't happen again. Anyway, he's got flabby buttocks and far too many wrinkles on his joy-stick... it's like he's got a naked mole rat in his pants.'

She laughed and clutched herself. 'Stop it, Sims, or I'll pee myself.'

*

As so often their habit, the settee was drawn up to the French windows. With his arm around her shoulders they sat looking down the long lawn towards the glittering Solent. Anne looked up at him, 'In just a few years you've come so far. It's been such a long haul, Sims. Where do we go from here?'

'Upstairs?'

'You know I didn't mean that, you sod.'

'How about Butlin's... Clacton?'

'I shall bash you in a minute.'

'Will I whimper?'

'*Sims*, I'm warning you: where do we go from here?'

'God knows... together.'

Though the notion pleased her, she said, 'I don't think together's strictly a destination, darling.'

As it rippled and rustled the curtains, a light breeze whispered to him.

'Yes it is, he said.'

The End.

Essential
Ranks of the Royal Navy

Stokers:
> *Junior Stoker   JM(e)*
> *Ordinary Stoker   M(e)1*
> *Leading Stoker   LM(e)*
> *Petty Officer Stoker   POM(e)*
> *Chief Petty Officer Stoker   CPOM(e)*

Officers:
> *Midshipman*
> *Sub-Lieutenant*
> *Lieutenant*
> *Lieutenant-Commander*
> *Commander*
> *Captain*
> *Commodore*
> *Rear-Admiral*
> *Vice-Admiral*
> *Admiral*
> *Admiral of the Fleet*

45th Commandos — Royal Marine Commandos - The author advises not to play rugby against them - dismemberment being a strong possibility.

Admiralty House — Administrative home of the Royal Navy - based in London.

Admiralty Regulations — Regulations covering every aspect of Royal Naval life.

Admiralty Standing Order — A single Admiralty Regulation.

Aide — An officer appointed to assist high ranking officers - personal secretary.

Albion — One of many types of service pistol. It was a variant of the Enfield Mk1 revolver with a spurless hammer and therefore requiring a full pull through to fire. It was manufactured by Albion Motors, Glasgow hence its name.

Annie Oakley — Semi-fictional American gun-toting cowgirl.

A priori — Knowledge independent of experience. According to one American philosopher, independent of fact.

Arethusa — A training ship moored in the Thames. It primarily trained orphans for future service in the merchant and Royal Navies. It was a terribly hard life for those lads. It is not to be confused with HMS Arethusa.

AWOL — Absent without leave.

Big Sylvie — Notorious Portsmouth prostitute.

Boat — Submarines are always called boats in the Royal Navy.

Boiler maker — The universal tipple for matelots in Portsmouth at the time of Billy Ruffian's Courier. A half pint of bottled brown ale mixed with half a pint of mild ale from the barrel.

Boom — A spar running along the lower part of a fore and aft sail.

Bosham Castle — Does exist. Though, it is in fact, a cottage.

Bow — The front, or sharp end, of a boat.

Bowsprit — A spar extending forward from the bow to

	which the forestays and, therefore, the foresails are attached.
Brigantine	A sailing vessel with two masts. The foremost being square rigged, and the main-mast rigged fore and aft.
Bulgogi	A delicious Korean beef and vegetable dish. The author first made this in the UK and later had the pleasure of eating it in Korea. The UK version was a good match.
Bulkhead	Wall.
Bull	Centre of a target.
Bunting tosser	Signalman.
Buster Crabb's grave.	The omissions of the sentiments on Buster's grave were rectified much later and done at a time when his grave was given a complete make-over. This probably coincided with the extension of the 50 year rule covering the episode of his supposed demise.
Button (The)	Small wooden cap on the very top of the 143 ft mast at HMS *Ganges*.
Butts	Originally a safe area at the target end of a shooting range from where the targets could be raised and lowered, and the scores recorded.
Celadon	Denotes a type of ceramic as well as its greyish green colour - also known as jade green.
Chandlery	A shop or company dealing in ship's supplies - ropes, sailcloth, rigging equipment etc. Originally the room in a house where candles were stored.
CIA	Central Intelligence Agency - USA.
CO	Commanding officer.
Coxswain. (1.)	Senior seaman rating on board ship responsible for discipline.
Coxswain (2.)	Helmsman of a motor boat or small sailing vessel. A coxswain's certificate proved one's ability to pilot such vessels.
Cryptanalyst	Essentially, a code breaker.
Cutter	In the Royal Navy a cutter was a two sailed sloop rigged unpowered sailing boat of between 30 and 35 feet in length.

Glossary for both Rites of Passage and Hawkshaw.

Dabtoe	Stokers' slang for a seaman.
Deck	Floor.
Deckhead	Ceiling.
Dockyard maties	Dockyard workers.
Ensauté	Neither myself or my French friends think there is any such word - it's another word Sims made up. Sauter does exist and means to jump!
Fanny boats	Tourist boats taking holiday makers around the dockyard waters.
Fathom	Six feet - approx two meters.
Fenders	Protection pads suspended over a vessels side to protect against chafing and impact and damage when berthing. In the Royal Navy they were hauled inboard as soon as the vessel was underway. To not do so was considered sloppy behaviour.
Firing squad	Execution squad.
Flag Officer	Term applied to those holding the rank of admiral.
Flag Papa	Blue Peter. A square blue background with a white square at its centre. The white square is approximately one third of the flag's height and width.
Flotsam	Floating debris as opposed to Jetsam which is rubbish thrown overboard.
Fore and aft Springs	Mooring lines running from the bows running rearward and from the stern, running forward to the shore. Their purpose is to restrict fore and aft movement of the boat. They are used in addition to normal bow to shore and stern to shore mooring lines.
Frigate	There's little point in looking at a Royal Naval ship and trying to distinguish some particular feature that determines it as a Frigate. They may come in different sizes and carry different armament. The term describes the ships role rather than its shape - anti-submarine; convoy escort etc.
Gaff	A spar to which the head/top of a fore and aft sail is attached. It is tensioned upwards by a 'topping lift' or 'Gaff

Halyard.

Golden Bell (The)   No. 60 Charlotte Street, a public house in Portsmouth loved and frequented by Sims and also, coincidentally, by the author. It, and the quaint street it sat in were bulldozed down and now lie under a car park! Happy memories buried in the name of progress - may the Portsmouth town planners responsible, rot in hell.

Grog   Rum 95.5 proof - 54.5% Vol diluted 2 parts water to 1 of rum. Named after Admiral Vernon who introduced the dilution in 1740 - Vernon's nickname was 'Old Grogram' after the grogram boat cloak he habitually wore.

GRU   Russia's largest intelligence agency.

Gunwale   The upper edge or planking of the side of a boat.

Haslar   The Royal Naval hospital in Gosport.

Heaving line   Exactly as the name implies. A lightish rope with a turks head at one end for heaving to shore or to another ship. Once received, a larger rope was attached and that hauled across.

Hell Head   The original name for what is now called Hill Head.

Helm   Whoever's at the helm is steering the vessel whether it be by tiller or wheel.

HMS *Alacrity*   A fictional frigate based on HMS *Alert*.

HMS *Arethusa*   Leander class frigate.

HMS *Bellerophon* (1)   An Arrogant class, 74 gun, ship of the line. This *Bellerophon* is the ship on which Napoleon surrendered to the British. The French still believe that Napoleon actually won the battle of Waterloo and that the British cheated!

HMS *Bellerophon* (2)   Admiral *Billy Ruffian's* first ship. This ship fought at the battle of Jutland.

HMS *Bellerophon* (3)   Also the name of the gunnery school at Whale Island Portsmouth. To avoid confusing matters too much, the author decided to use only its common name: Whale Island.

Glossary for both Rites of Passage and Hawkshaw.

HMS *Dolphin*	Home base of the Royal Navy submarine service.
HMS *Dreadnought*	Britain's first nuclear submarine.
HMS *Ganges*	A shore based training ship situated on a spit of land at the confluence of rivers Stour and Orwell opposite the mouth of Harwich Harbour. HMS *Ganges* was conveniently situated there, enabling it to take full benefit of the freezing winter time winds coming straight off the North Sea. Boys from the age of fifteen and three months were subjected to a year of brutal training there. During the Author's time at *Ganges*, it was not unknown for deaths to occur when under punishment. It was so cold there.
HMS *Pembroke*	Royal Naval barracks in Chatham.
HMS *Salisbury*	A *Salisbury* class type 61 aircraft detection frigate.
HMS *Scarborough*	Type 12 Anti submarine, *Whitby* class Frigate.
HMS *Start Point*	A fictional submarine depot ship based on HMS *Rame Head* and HMS *Hartland Point*.
HMS *Sultan*	Engineering and nuclear engineering training establishment in Gosport.
HMS *Vernon*	Torpedo and Anti-submarine depot in Portsmouth close to Spice Island.
HMS *Victory* (1)	Nelson's famous ship. Too many honours to mention.
HMS *Victory* (2)	Shore base barracks in Portsmouth.
Home on the Range	A truly awful 'saddle song' of the West.
Hulk	The hull of a ship - sometimes derelict.
Hydroplane	A submarine is fitted with both front and rear hydroplanes. They maintain the trim of the vessel when underway. Think aircraft elevators - operating in reverse though.
Inner	The second circle from the centre of a target.
Jack	Civilian term for a Royal Naval sailor. Especially Portsmouth and other naval bases.

Jarama	A famous battle in the Spanish Civil War. It took place in February 1937 to the east and close by Madrid. Estimates vary between 6000 and 25000 dead.
Jetsam	Rubbish thrown overboard as opposed to Flotsam which is either wreckage, lost cargo or naturally occurring floating debris.
Jib	A sail forward of the main mast - usually triangular.
Jibing	Changing on which side of the sails the wind is acting. There is an important difference between jibing and tacking. Because the wind passes around the stern, jibing requires extreme care as it is possible for the mainsail to violently slam over from one side of the boat to the other and in doing so break the mast and rigging. (See also tacking and wearing).
Keel haul	An old naval punishment whereby a rope is tied the wrists of the offender, then passed under the keel of the ship and then tied to his ankles. He is then hauled under the barnacle encrusted ships bottom. Depending on the severity of his crime, this may have been carried out more than once.
Ketch	A sailing boat with two masts - the main mast being larger than the rear or mizzen mast.
KGB	One of a number of Russian Intelligence agencies. The KGB operated mainly from Russian embassies and consulates. Therefore, its members were afforded diplomatic immunity.
Killick	Leading hand.
Lanchester	A submachine gun used by the Royal Navy. Dangerous, in that it was prone to accidental discharge if dropped.
Lee Enfield .303	Service rifle.
Lee on solent	During the period the books are set in, the Royal Naval air station, HMS Arial was located there.

Life story	Service record.
LM(e)	Leading stoker.
Magpie	The third circle from the centre of a target.
Marking time	Marching on the spot.
Marline Spike	A pointed rod especially used for parting the strands of rope when splicing.
Martini Mk3	A .22 target rifle - lever action as opposed to bolt action. the lever fitted snugly to the front and extending below the grip, and was operated by being pushed forward which opened the breech.
Master at Arms	Senior Regulator. Think naval policeman.
Matelot	Sailor - from the French, matelot meaning sailor!
Mess deck	Living quarters for ordinary matelots.
MI5	Military Intelligence responsible for internal security in the United Kingdom.
MI6	Military Intelligence responsible for intelligence matters outside the United Kingdom.
Mizzen	The lowest or sole sail on the mizzenmast.
Mizzenmast	The rearmost mast on a sailing vessel.
NAAFI	Naval, Army and Airforce Institute. This acronym rather impolitely referred to as meaning: No Ambition And Fuck-all Interest.
Neaters	Pusser's rum without water added.
NID	Naval Intelligence Division.
NKVD	Soviet law enforcement agency. Its duties included: espionage and political assassinations abroad.
Nozzer	The first six weeks at HMS Ganges were spent by new recruits in the Annexe - they were known as Nozzers.
Onslaughted	A word fabricated by Sims.
Orwell	A river flowing from Ipswich to its confluence with the river Stour inside Harwich harbour and then flowing immediately into the North Sea.
Outer	The fourth circle from the centre of a target.
Pompey	Portsmouth.
Pontoon	A floating platform often used as a dock.

Port	Left hand side. See also Starboard.
Postie	Postman.
Pusser	Admiralty approved.
Pusser's rum	A potent spirit made in heaven.
Ratings	Sailors of the lower deck.
Ratlin (ratline)	Rope ladder rungs to help climb rigging.
RDF	Radio Direction Finding - pre-GPS stuff.
Réglement des comptes	Settling of scores.
Rosyth	Royal Naval dockyard Scotland.
Roy Rogers	One of those excruciatingly awful Hollywood singing cowboy heroes. The line, 'before I get those dirty rats who shot your little girl and labrador, let me sing you a little song', may not have ever been spoken. It does however, sum up the entire genre of the Singing Cowboy.
RPO	Regulating Petty Officer - not generally liked. Pathologically hated by Sims.
Sally Port	The defensive door in Old Portsmouth through which crews left for their ships anchored in the Solent.
SBS	Royal Naval version of SAS.
Sheets	Confusingly, these are not the sails but the ropes that control their fore and aft tension.
Ship	Surface vessel. Submarines are not ships, they're boats.
Shotley Point	The spit of land at the confluence of rivers Stour and Orwell opposite the mouth of Harwich Harbour. HMS Ganges was conveniently situated there enabling it to take full benefit of the freezing winter time winds coming straight off the North Sea.
Slack water	Tide neither ebbing nor flowing - still.
Sloop	When used to describe a sailing vessel, it means a vessel with one mast, one mainsail, and one jib, both rigged fore and aft.
Snort	Taking on fresh air in a submarine.
Spice Island	An area of Old Portsmouth. Its name carried from the old days and so called by sailors because the 'spice of life' was to be found there - namely, whores and booze.

	It had nothing to do with spices.
Spithead Mutiny	16th April to 15th May 1797. Sailors mutinied for better food, pay and treatment.
Starboard	Right hand side - a corruption of the word Steerboard from the time when a ship was steered with a rudder device fixed to the side of the vessel. Naturally, to place a vessel steerboard side to the dock wall would have been to invite damage. Hence the Port side went to the dock wall. As most people are right handed, the steerboard was placed on the right hand side of the vessel thus allowing the helmsman to be on the inboard side of the rudder.
Stern	Rear end.
Stour	A river flowing from Manningtree to its confluence with the river Orwell inside Harwich harbour and then flowing immediately into the North Sea.
Tacking	Changing the direction of a sailing vessel with the wind passing around the bows. (See also jibing.)
Tannoy	As Hoover is to vacuum cleaners, Tannoy is to ships' loudspeaker and broadcast systems.
Tiffy	Artificer.
Tiger Tops	Tiger beer topped off with a drop of lemonade.
Topping lift	This term is usually applied to the device that raises and lowers a crane's derrick. Rightly or wrongly, the term was often used for the gaff halyard.
Tot	Daily rum issue of 'grog' for all ratings over the age of twenty - 3/8ths of a pint.
Turk's head knot.	A large round knot resembling a Turk's head gear. Often used to provide weight at the end of a heaving line.
Twelve Bore	A shot gun.
Wearing	Royal Naval term for jibing. (See Jibing)
Whaler	In the Royal Navy this describes a three sailed, two masted sailing vessel of

	between 25 and 27 feet long.
Woods metal	Also known as Lipowitz's alloy - melts at 70°C.
Wren	Member of the Women's Royal Naval Service. Also known as Jenny Wrens.

27060588R00262

Printed in Great Britain
by Amazon